MODERN

Paul Magrs

MODERN
LOVE

First published in 2000 by
Allison & Busby Limited
114 New Cavendish Street
London W1M 7FD
http://www.allisonandbusby.ltd.uk

A catalogue record for this book is available
from the British Library

ISBN 0 7490 0484 3

Printed and bound in Spain by Líberduplex S.L., Barcelona

For Joy Foster

1
The Relevant Lizard

When she was nineteen Christine's parents gave up on her. It was for her own good. Eventually she'd come round to their way of seeing things and everything would get back to normal.

That was the plan, according to Dan. Margaret wasn't quite so sure.

'All we've got to do,' Dan said, 'is let her go her own way for a while.'

'Her own way!'

He nodded slowly at Margaret and she started to clear the kitchen table. She bustled him out of the way so she could wipe it down. She bit her lip, slopping too much water on. Dan held his ground.

'If you ask me,' she said at last. 'Christine will go her own way whatever we do.'

Dan gripped the back of the chair. 'She'll soon get sick. A little bit of freedom goes a long way.'

She darted him a look. 'What's that supposed to mean?' Then she looked at the lino. 'You've tracked mud in from the garden. I've mopped that this morning.'

'You'll see,' he said, 'Christine's all right.'

'She's easily led.'

Dan headed for the back door, scuffing dirt into the lino. 'I don't reckon so.'

Margaret was raising her voice after him. 'You don't know what it's like for girls! That age, she . . .'

Dan was gone, banging the kitchen door shut. He was stumping off to his outhouse at the bottom of the garden.

That bloody outhouse, Margaret thought. She didn't even know what he did down there. If anything serious was going on, he'd shut himself up and wait till it all blew over.

She watched him from the kitchen window and she knew he was wrong about Christine. Dan thought things went away of their own accord but it wasn't true. It was like he thought the mud on the lino cleaned itself up, or the washing up got itself miraculously clean and put away. As Margaret let the washing up bowl fill with hot water she was working herself up. By the time she made a start on the dishes she was seething. He was too passive. He used that shed as a hideout. She racked up a couple of plates and then she stopped, yanked off the rubber gloves, and went after Dan down the garden.

It was a muggy day. The air felt like warm bath water. Dan had cut half the lawn this morning and left the mower lying in the middle. The stripes of lighter green against the darker, longer grass irritated her too. Bits of new trellis were propped by the fence, waiting for his attention. Now she thought of it, it seemed like Dan could never finish anything. He never had.

She rapped on the sun-blistered door. She set her mouth determinedly, ready for him. I won't get shrill, she thought. He always says I get shrill and over the top. He talks back quietly, reasonably and he says I'm mental. Well, I'll be reasonable too.

After a second he opened the door. His slowness got her back up. He was holding a terracotta pot with what looked like a few twigs stuck in it. He had a cigarette hanging unlit from his lower lip. Margaret opened her mouth to start.

'You're fretting, aren't you?' he said.

'No, Dan, I just think . . .'

He held up that pot like it was a prize specimen. 'Hm?'

'I think it's an awful idea.'

'Oh, come on, Margaret . . .'

'What about when she realises? She'll feel like we don't care anymore.'

Dan set his plant pot down. 'I didn't say stop caring. I just said we should try not to interfere, for a while.'

'Interfere!'

'You know what I mean. We shouldn't try to put her off her boyfriends. We shouldn't go on about going to college. Those kinds of things.'

Margaret pulled her cardigan tighter. Her hands trembled. She didn't know where to put them.

Go on, he thought. You just try saying you've never nagged at Christine. Deny you've ever badgered her about exams.

Margaret fiddled with her buttons instead, which made him sad. Her face looked pouchy; the rouge on her cheeks was too garish in the outdoor light.

Why does everything have to be a big deal? he wondered. Margaret pushed things too far. Christine wouldn't be so bad if her mother didn't get hysterical. There was no nice way to tell her that.

'I don't want her to feel neglected, Dan. You know what they say about neglecting kids.'

He shook his head. 'She's hardly neglected. And she's not a kid anymore.'

They stood looking at each other for a second. She started to play with her wedding ring and, finding it not on her finger, remembered she'd put it on the window sill. There was washing up to be done.

'She might go even further off the rails,' Margaret said, moving back towards the house, picking her way over the flagstones Dan had laid on the lawn. She thought, he hadn't set them right. Someone could trip.

'She'll see sense,' he said, and went back into his outhouse to light his cigarette.

*

Christine cottoned on fairly soon to what her parents were doing. She was no fool. That year she had given up the idea of improving her qualifications for good, deciding that her intelligence wasn't the sort that was made for passing exams. She wasn't sure exactly what sort it was, but she was quick enough to realise that hanging about with the smarter set at school hadn't made her happy. In the early part of the year she was nineteen she was letting her hair grow long and wearing clothes that her mother said were tatty; peasant shirts and crotcheted tank tops. Her hair was a mousier blonde now, where it had been golden before, and she put dark rings of make-up round her eyes.

'You're supposed to put make up on to draw attention to your best features,' her mother said. 'Not black them out.'

This was before her mother had stopped interfering.

'It's just the look,' Christine said. So were her cork-soled sandals, and the ridiculous purple platform shoes that made her legs look so skinny and unsure when her mother watched her leave the house and totter on the front path, on the arm of the boy who had called for her.

The boys who called for her were the worst thing. This series of scruffy-looking lads (rough diamonds, Margaret found herself calling them) were what finally made Margaret get Dan to think of a way to take action. It was as if their daughter was bringing home the most alarming-looking specimens she could find. They came slouching into the porch in denim jackets that never looked clean. They wore tight-fitting t-shirts and skinny little jeans.

Margaret remembered that older one, Brian, who had knocked the barometer off the wall as he stood about waiting for Christine. He'd apologised and everything, but the thing was spoiled. And it was an heirloom! The glass of the bulb was cracked and useless now. 'It doesn't matter a bit,' Margaret found herself saying, clearing up the shards on her hands and knees. 'It was a silly place to hang it anyway. Right in everyone's way.'

This Brian wasn't someone she wanted to rub up the wrong way. He had those old, dirty jeans on, too, like they all did; the crotch faded away so revealingly, faded away in a kind of sexy relief map. As she lifted the wrecked barometer Margaret couldn't help noticing his jeans and she blushed.

It's not that I want to keep her a little girl forever, Margaret thought. That would be mad. But she has to know about all the dangers she could get herself into. The worst thing about Brian was that he hadn't helped her clear up the mess he'd caused. Maybe he was even laughing at her.

Christine had found it quite funny, for a while, to see these boys in her parents' house.

'You're too careful,' she told her mam. 'Everything has to be dusted and straightened up all the time. You can't breathe in here.'

'I keep a nice house!'

'And there's too much furniture in it.'

'Too much!'

'All these ornaments. It looks like a shop. You've got to expect that things are going to get broken.'

Margaret thought it was a strange kind of argument, where everything Christine accused her of sounded like a compliment.

Christine liked to see Terry, or Brian, or Simon, coming in with the smell of lager on their breath, clumping their boots on the fawn carpet of the hallway; their voices too loud and big for that house. Her father always whispered. It was the first thing anyone noticed about him. Christine had learned only recently that men didn't have to be quiet. My mother, she thought, is living in a bubble.

Nowadays, in these days of not interfering, of her mother deliberately not clucking her tongue and looking the visiting boys up and down in quiet despair, her father was quieter than ever. Whenever Christine was around, he'd scuttle off to his outhouse and poke about in his primulas and primroses. The most you would hear out of him was the sharp tapping of his hammer as he set about his endless task of trellising. He wouldn't rest till their back garden was entirely wrapped around in trellis as high as he could make it. Christine started to miss her dad. They hadn't sat together in his shed for ages. He hadn't given her a secret Woodbine and he hadn't poured her a cupful of brandy from his flask in weeks.

'Dad,' she asked him one day while her mam was out of the way. 'Are you not talking to me, or what?'

'Not talking to you?'

'It's like you're avoiding me.'

He chuckled. 'How could I ever avoid you, Christine?'

She was still coming in late, with bleary eyes and fingers of mascara smeared down her cheeks; her hair matted and limp with nightclub sweat. Her parents made no comment whatsoever. She took up smoking in the house; wandering room to room hardly taking the cigarette out of her mouth, but still nothing was said. She wondered how far she could push them.

Her mother acted nervous around her. Christine had never seen her as bad as that. Margaret was talking as quietly as Dan did now. The new way Christine was getting treated started to make her feel guilty. Her parents seemed much older, suddenly. They were distant from her. It felt like she had moved out already and now she was living with polite strangers.

All the same, she knew what they were up to. They were giving her enough rope to hang herself. That's what it felt like. Christine, tempted to test them out further, was unsure of her footing; she waited for the moment the floorboards suddenly vanished and she was yanked into the inevitable retribution. But what could she do? She couldn't just start towing the line. She had to keep the effort up. Keep knocking about with these fellas that she met at work; the ones who laboured on building sites and roadworks; the ones who came into the bakery for their sandwiches and pasties; who couldn't help chatting her up and offering to take her out. She couldn't start saying no to this parade of fellas. Who knew when it all stopped? They were giving her attention now, but how long did that last for? Her mam and dad didn't understand. The clock was ticking the whole time and she had to make the best of it. They'd forgotten what the urgency felt like.

Mind, she thought, if truth be known, all the fellas she met seemed a little bit the same in the end. There wasn't a lot of variation.

Christine started to miss her parents badgering her. It was incredible, but it felt like something was missing when she stood with a new beau on the doormat and said, 'We're off down the fair now,' or, 'We're going out to that new all-nite place!' Her mother would just give a wave on her way through to the kitchen, calling: 'Have fun then, sweetheart!' She sounded strained, though, as if fairs or clubs were terrifying places.

As the weeks went by she was amazed to find her parents' tactics working on her. She went out less. The boys who asked her out seemed less and less appealing. They would be hanging over the shop counter and all she would see were their blackheads, their greasy hair. When they turned up at her door she'd notice how this one had jug ears or couldn't put a whole sentence together. And she'd groan inside at the thought of having to spend a whole night – a whole night! – with someone as dull as that.

They've reined me in, Christine thought. Somehow they've put a control on me. I've stopped having fun.

Anyway, the bakery hours were long and she had to be up early to start hefting the trays full of hot bread. She loved her work; even the being on her feet all day, the burns on her hands off the metal trays. She loved popping pastries and dainty cakes into clean white bags and scrunching up the tops just so. After a while she realised she was going whole weeks without a night out.

There was one night though, in early March, when the full force of her parents' sly success hit her like a slap in the face.

The three of them were sitting in front of the telly, watching the early evening news with their supper on trays. An item started up about a woman who had murdered some children and that was when her mother broke their silence – and the new house rules.

'Christine,' she said suddenly, flicking her eyes worriedly at her husband. 'There's a boy who I'd like you to meet.'

Her daughter stared at her. Dan, who she'd hoped was asleep, sat up and glared.

'What?' said Christine.

'A nice boy,' said Margaret. 'Here, give me your trays, you two.'

As she watched her mother struggle to her feet Christine felt a reassuring spark of disgust flare inside her.

She's started interfering again. I knew it wouldn't last long. She's got me right where she wants me.

Her mother did a mincing walk to the kitchen, holding the trays. There was something triumphant about her, even from the back. Christine felt like spitting.

*

I'm breaking the rules that Dan laid down, Margaret thought. There could be ructions. She hated the tense silences Dan kept her in sometimes. It was worse than shouting.

This is worth it, though. Michael is worth it. They'll all see what I mean.

She had first seen Michael in her bank. She'd been waiting in the queue, staring at nothing, tapping her bank book against her fingernails in a kind of tune. The bank was musty and panelled in fake wood and something in the atmosphere of the place always made her fall into a trance. She often daydreamed about the shelves and shelves of banknotes behind the walls. She could almost see them. Then she imagined that the man in front was going to pull a shotgun from his sports bag and there would be a robbery. They'd all have to lie on the floor and be hostages and she would have to wear the same clothes for days.

When her neighbour Lily Woods spoke to her Margaret jumped. She hadn't even known the woman was there. Her first thought was, well, at least I won't be a hostage with strangers.

Lily was saying, 'That's our Michael working there. Look, he's going to serve us.' She had a croaky voice that made her seem old. Margaret had known her, to say hello to, for years, but had no idea how old the woman was. She'd always had frizzy old-woman's hair.

'Michael?'

'My nephew,' Lily Woods glowed and clasped her own bank book. Margaret hadn't known that Lily had any relatives at all. She was one of those people who seemed to exist independently of the usual ties. There was a sister, Margaret remembered, who'd been ill. The only time Lily had left their street was to go and nurse her. She'd left Margaret a house key, in case anything happened. Margaret popped round to check one day and there wasn't a single framed photo in the place. It hadn't been that clean round there, either.

Margaret looked at the boy her neighbour was nodding and smiling at. She hadn't seen him before. He was a little red in the face; slightly plump, but not unattractively so. His hair had thinned already. He looked perhaps twenty five. It was his fair, babyish hair that made Margaret's heart turn. Michael looked as if he didn't need to shave yet.

She liked the way, when it was her turn to step up to his counter, he smiled so nicely; as if he really meant it. And he opened her bank book very carefully, reading its columns with respect, as if her safest secrets were written inside.

'Is he courting, your Michael?' she asked Lily Woods, when the old lady at last followed her out of the bank into the sunshine.

Lily seemed startled to find Margaret waiting for her. 'He's waiting for the right girl, our Michael,' she smiled. 'He knows that some of these girls can turn a boy's head. They can spoil a man. I've warned him.'

Margaret watched her neighbour trot away down the main street. Just the way she held her head gave away how pleased she was with herself.

But how pleased Margaret would have been if Christine

had gone for a job in a bank! Back when Christine was going to go for her A levels, banking was one of the things Margaret tried to steer her towards.

'Have you seen what they have to do?' Christine had laughed. 'Who wants to sit all day with stiff bits of paper in all different colours? Filling in numbers and ticking tiny little boxes? It would be just like being at school. And the smell of the money on your hands all the time! It was you, mam, who said that money spreads germs, remember. Oh, no thanks.'

Margaret had given in. She was imagining that man with the gun in his sports bag again. You wouldn't get that in a bakery.

Michael must enjoy his bank work, Margaret thought. He was grinning away, sat at his counter. I'll get Christine to come and have a look at him.

She wondered how she could do it in a subtle way. She'd have to do it without any help from Dan.

*

'You're always complaining about this bank. You said they were hopeless.'

They were standing in the queue. Margaret wouldn't listen to her daughter. She was peering through the crush of bodies on a Wednesday lunch time to see if Michael was serving. There he was. In a different suit, even. A dark blue one. He was smiling even more than last time. He must really love his work.

'You've got a proper job now, Christine,' her mother whispered. 'And you need a bank account. A proper one.'

'That's the first time you've said it was a proper job.'

'Well,' said her mother. She glanced her daughter up and down, wishing they hadn't had to come in the middle of her lunch break from the bakery. Christine's hair was up in a sloppy pony-tail with wisps standing out. She was even in her white pressed smock with – god help them – flakes of pastry down the front.

16

As their turn came round Christine narrowed her eyes at her mam. 'What are you up to?'

Margaret led her up to Michael. She put her palms on the counter. 'This is my daughter Christine, Michael, and she would like you to open up a savings account for her.'

'Ah, right,' said Michael. He stared at the range of coloured stationery on his desk. 'That's . . .'

'She's decided she's got to start saving up,' Margaret went on. 'And planning for the future. You can't leave that too late, can you, Michael?'

'No,' he said, still looking for the right forms. 'That's quite true, Mrs . . .'

'Mrs Fletcher,' Margaret held her hand out. 'And my daughter, Christine, who works in the bakery almost directly opposite you.'

Michael looked up at Christine. 'Oh? I go there sometimes. You do lovely egg and cress baps.'

Christine stared at him. His eyes were watery. Yes, she recognised him. 'Do we?'

'Yes . . . you've served me a few times.'

Christine rolled her eyes as her mother beamed.

*

By then there was nothing any of them could do to stop Margaret. The rules had changed again. Maybe, if Christine got herself in with Michael, she'd think again about her job. She might even put her brains to good use and go in for the exams. Maybe it wasn't much different to shopwork. Serving people at a till like Christine already did; but it just looked better. Margaret liked the look of the few women who worked at the bank. Their grey suits and skirts, their hair pulled up neatly, their smart name badges in their lapels. They had alarm buttons under their desks, Lily had told her. So maybe it wasn't as dangerous as all that.

And even if Christine didn't get the same kind of job, she'd still have a better life with Michael than with those other lads. She'd have security for life. He seemed so mature, compared.

Margaret just hoped Lily wouldn't get wind of what was going on. She thought the old woman would have a few things to tell her nephew about Christine.

'Couldn't you see our Christine working in that bank?' she asked her.

'Christine?' Lily had said, surprised.

'I can see her sitting there, next to Michael.'

'Can you?' Lily was giving her an odd look.

Keep it subtle, Margaret reminded herself. Don't give too much away.

In Margaret's mind it was a fait accompli. Her husband tried to complain. He said, 'I thought we were . . .' and 'This is worse than . . .' but he didn't get much further than that. Keeping her nose out of it in an effort to not cause bother was one thing. This business with Michael was quite another matter. As Christine's mother, she could see exactly what was best for her. Michael had come along at the right time.

'On your own head be it,' Dan said.

Margaret felt like he'd given her back some control.

She leapt in with both feet. The next time she was in the bank alone (with a jar of ha'pennies she suddenly needed to change for notes) she made him an impulsive offer.

'Your Aunty says you haven't been in the area for long.'

He blinked. He wasn't used to personal questions at his counter. 'That's right.'

'So you can't have many friends here yet. You can't have much time, with your work and everything.' She was holding up the queue, but she didn't care.

'It's all been hectic, yes,' he said.

'Why don't you come out with us?' she said quickly. 'My husband and my daughter will be there. You've met my daughter. Christine. Every Sunday we drive out some-where. It's our traditional run-out in the car. Why don't you come along?'

He looked embarrassed. 'Oh, well, I'm not sure I . . .'

'You wouldn't be imposing.'

'It's kind of you, Mrs Fletcher.'

'Rubbish. What were you going to do on Sunday?'

He opened his mouth and she jumped in before he could speak.

'There. Nothing. This weekend you're coming out with us to the safari park. How about that?'

Michael accepted, if only to make Margaret leave and get the queue moving again.

At home, later, he told Lily he was going out on Sunday with the Fletchers.

'Oh?' his aunt said, twisting in her chair. Just the way she said it made Michael feel shifty all of a sudden.

'It's only to look at the animals,' he said.

'Hm,' Lily Woods said, scrunching her toes in her moccasin slippers. 'I was the one saying you should get out more.'

*

They were going to the safari park because Margaret had a thing about animals and she preferred to see them in the wild. One of the best things about their new colour telly was the documentaries. She would sit glued to images of the savannas and plains of Africa; gaping as cheetahs bounded through the grass and ludicrous, exotic birds boomed out their mating calls. Margaret would blush if the documentary started to show the animals doing anything rude – and they usually would, of course. But she loved to see them running through the wilderness. She could watch, quite impassively, as big cats mauled and tore at the bowels and haunches of a fallen zebra. Christine and her father would put down their knives and forks in disgust but Margaret would carry on eating her supper and say, 'Well, that's just nature, isn't it?'

She found she was looking forward to their run-out to the safari park with particular pleasure.

She made sure Dan asked Christine to come.

'What do I want to see some scraggy old animals for?'

They were sitting in the outhouse again. Her father wiped out his single, chipped mug with a filthy rag, and poured her a shot of brandy as a bribe. 'You know what she's like. And how long is it since we had a proper family outing to somewhere like a zoo?'

Christine swallowed the tart warm booze and grimaced. 'There's something else, isn't there?'

He sighed and laughed. 'You were never backward at coming forward, were you?' He shook his head and gave her another splash from his hipflask. 'It's this lad she's suddenly got keen on you meeting. This Michael.'

'Oh, god . . .'

'Just give her a chance. It'll soon fizzle out if you play along for a bit.'

Christine eyed her father. 'That's how you were both treating me, dad! Is that how you think you get women to behave themselves?'

He chuckled. 'I know for a fact it is, lass.'

*

Dan talked to him like he was already one of the family; sitting him down in the front room as soon as he arrived and watching him sip his tea. Michael was flattered by this, flustered and hot in his work suit, his belt fastened too tight. He liked the way the older man asked him quietly, easily, about his work at the bank, and he could give easy answers to questions about the interest rates and the different kinds of accounts. He thought it was good of Dan, to size him up as gently as this, and to treat him like a prospective son. Dan would talk to anyone like this, though. He had a way of making people feel confident.

Michael was looking round at their house. There were pictures of Christine at all different ages on the walls. It was a proper family house.

'The girls are still upstairs,' Dan said. 'Doing whatever they do to get themselves ready. Squirting on scent, I suppose. Checking that their hair is right.' He blinked and realised that Michael had less hair than he did.

'My mother was like that,' Michael smiled, and took a huge mouthful of tea.

'Where's she?'

'She died last year.'

'Oh, that's terrible, son.'

Michael shook his head so Dan wouldn't feel bad about it. 'She was quite old. She had me very late . . .'

'Still,' said Dan. 'It's a terrible thing to be without a mam.'

The Sunday lunch dishes were cleared and drying. That was Dan's Sunday chore. He scalded them clean; the water evaporated off the clean white plates almost the instant he put them on the rack. Even the roasting dish had been scrubbed squeaky clean, and the chicken carcass was wrapped in foil and stowed in the fridge. The last shreds of meat would do for sandwiches when they got back from the zoo that night.

Now Dan was having a quick rest in his swivel armchair before running the family into the countryside. The car was ready on the drive and tuned up to go. He and Michael talked a little about cars and what sort Michael might like to buy when he had saved up enough money.

'A family sized car?' Dan raised an eyebrow.

'I might as well. I don't want anything sporty. And . . . and you never know, do you?'

They both looked at the tea things on the table, embarrassed.

Dan said, 'What you want is something comfortable and practical. Something you can use for a run-out on a Sunday. That's all ours gets used for, really. But it's a smashing runner.'

Their runs-out were sacrosanct. It had been a while since they had all been out together and just the fact that Christine had consented – however reluctantly – to come along today had made the day into something special. Even Dan felt that. It was a relief to him. In recent weeks he and Margaret had been reduced to running out to places by themselves – a stately home, a park, a ride into the Dales – but it wasn't the same. Even an irritable teenager kicking along behind was better than just two of them. Walking through that park had been the worst. Afterwards Margaret had told him he'd hardly said two words to her. 'I was relaxing!' he said. 'That's what you do on a Sunday.'

'There's relaxing,' she said, 'and there's ignorance.' She had looked at him evenly. 'You've not got much to say to me these days, have you?'

This had been on the ride home, last Sunday. And Dan had been glad of the traffic lights that came up on red just then, suddenly, preventing him from having to think of a reply.

'Just what I thought,' Margaret had said. After a moment she let out a sigh and that had been the end of the conversation.

For years Dan had wondered what he could do to make Margaret happy. He had even asked her, holding her arms down tight during rows, trying to make her calm down. She could never give him an answer. There was never a straight reply. He had given up trying to guess. In his opinion some people made themselves unhappy on purpose.

Dan plucked the silver cigarette case from the coffee table and flipped it open for Michael. Luckily there were still a couple of cigarettes in there. They'd been put there especially for guests. They looked dried out.

'No thanks . . . I don't . . .' Michael's stomach was turning over with hunger. Why hadn't they asked him for Sunday lunch as well? It felt like his insides were folding in on themselves and the sight of those few old fags made him feel queasy.

'You're very wise not to smoke. You'll see out longer than we will. We've smoked for years, Margaret and I . . . but not in the house now, of course. But your generation is much more sensible. We didn't know what it could do to you. I was a working man . . . I've worked with my hands. There's no shame in that.'

'No, no shame at all, Dan.'

He was surprised Michael had called him by name. 'But you've . . . got it up here. That's what counts. But don't get me wrong. I'm happy with the life I've managed to give Margaret and Christine.'

Michael was looking at the dregs of his tea. It was hard water round here and there was limescale scum in his mug. He thought: I'm being offered this bloke's daughter. He's as good as giving me her on a plate.

Michael knew the likes of the fellas Christine had been knocking about with. His aunt had tried to tell him, but he was too flattered to really listen. He knew their types from school – stroppy show-offs; fella's fellas and hard lads who played sports and stuff . . . the kinds he never could compete with. But maybe now he was getting the edge.

He was getting to see Christine – the kind of girl who hung about with the hard lads; who jeered and chimed in with their coarse flattery, their bravado. She was a girl who had lived fast, in a way that Michael – if he was honest – never had.

As they waited for the women, titivating themselves upstairs, Michael started to feel like a kid. Sitting there with her dad, looking down at his own shoes; new-buffed, shining. He'd cleaned them this morning, like he did them every morning, ready for the bank. Then he saw how his trousers rode up too high, over his socks. They were halfway up his legs. And they were wrong. They weren't even fashionably halfway up his legs.

Christine would come down those stairs and she would look at him, up and down as he stood for her, and she would decide that he was wrong altogether.

But . . . her dad likes me, he thought. Her mam likes me – if the way she went on in the bank was anything to go by, and if the way she fussed over him when he came in today counted for anything. So maybe that was enough to get him through a day at the safari park. Perhaps it would end with Christine seeing sense. She would see what kind of man he was. And maybe her parents could put some pressure on her . . .

*

It was the wrong sort of weather for looking at animals. There weren't many cars queueing up at the gates to get into the park. It was as if everyone else knew better; that it wasn't even worth going out in the rain to see wild creatures. The animals themselves would have more sense, and they would stay indoors too.

Here they were though, and they might as well pay to get in and to see what they could see. As the column of cars shunted up to the netting fence and the tollbooth, Margaret could feel herself getting quite excited at the prospect. Somewhere beyond that fence, in amongst all those very English-looking trees and fields, in all of that grey English drizzle . . . were lions and tigers and bears. The brochure in her hands was cool and laminated and she flicked through hurriedly for the map.

She passed it to Michael and Christine who were sitting in the back. They had exchanged barely a word, either on meeting, or in the hour and a half it took to drive out here. She could see Michael was scared stiff of her daughter – who had made no effort, in the end, at dressing herself up (the scruffiest sweatshirt from her bedroom floor, the usual patched and hemless jeans). There was a yard of space between them, and a bag, filled with sandwiches and fruit that Margaret had put together at the last minute. Michael took the brochure and map with fake enthusiasm.

'Baboons!' he said. 'They've got baboons!'

Margaret was glad Michael was joining in. She glanced sideways at Dan as he nudged the car forward to the toll-booth. She saw him wince at Michael's exclamation.

*

All the monkeys were subdued by the rain. Their hair hung down, stringy and wet as they huddled in close to the tree trunks. Their pelts were the same colour as the bark.

'You can hardly see them,' Margaret said, peering past the raindrops on her window.

Michael said, 'They look like they're waiting for the bus to come.'

He's wanting to be funny, Margaret thought.

The Fletchers' car moved at a stately, funereal pace around the looping roads of the park.

'Keep your speed down,' Margaret urged her husband. 'It looks like you can't go back round once you've passed through.'

'I'm only doing fifteen miles an hour!'

'Yes, well,' she said. 'It's a waste of money otherwise. I wonder if the fences are electric?'

One hardy monkey had left his fellows and was sitting right by the roadside showing off a pale pink erection. Margaret looked away from him as they slid by in the car.

Other cars were zipping by much faster, and overtaking them, as if they had decided there was nothing worth looking at.

Michael said, 'The funny thing is, it's the faster cars that get the baboons jumping on them.'

'It's true,' said Margaret, glad that at least one other person was talking. 'We haven't had a single monkey land on us. Look at everyone else's – they're . . . cavorting all over them!'

Dan gave a humourless laugh. Margaret sounded almost put out by the monkeys' lack of interest.

Christine turned listlessly to look at the car behind with its freight of dripping baboons. She smiled at the people inside, who looked a bit scared and shocked at their new passengers.

'He's panicking, look,' said Michael.

The driver of the car behind was batting his hands at them. Next thing, he put his foot down and yanked the steering wheel. His engine roared into life and without waiting for the Fletchers to get out of the way, he swung onto the grass and overtook them. His car shot down the road and swerved tightly, repeatedly, on the gravel.

'He's trying to shake them off!' cried Margaret. 'That's cruel!'

The car took the corner ahead so quickly that the six baboons assaulting it plopped off the bonnet one by one, and fell into the grassy verge either side.

'He's left them for dead,' said Dan quietly.

'I can't believe I just saw that,' Margaret said, as the car disappeared from sight, glad to be out of the monkey enclosure.

She looked at Dan.

'He's right in a way,' said her husband. 'Those monkeys can be vicious. You've got to watch out. They'll have your windscreen wipers off – or your wing mirrors. If they landed on my car, I'd shake them off as well.'

'Oh, you wouldn't!'

'If it came to it,' he said, nodding. 'I would.'

'But that man could have killed them! The poor little brutes.' Margaret was craning anxiously now, as their car rolled past the wet grass where the monkeys had been thrown. She wanted to sound like the kind of woman who hated to see anything being hurt.

She started unclipping her seat belt. 'Stop here, Dan. I want to get out and check they're still breathing . . .'

As her hand reached to open the door, she felt Michael's meaty fingers crushing her own.

'Don't go out there!' he shouted, right up close to her ear. 'They'll rip your face off!'

'Michael!' She couldn't believe he was being so rude. She felt tears spring up.

'He's right, mam,' Christine put in. 'You can't go running around in a safari park.'

'But . . .' she began, and looked at Dan. Dan's face was tight and he was lighting a cigarette – even though he wasn't supposed to in the car.

'Are you mad, woman?' he said. 'Who do you think you are? Jungle bloody Jane?'

With that, Dan put on his own burst of speed and took them straight to the next set of electrified fences.

Margaret watched the stunned monkeys for as long as she could, wanting to see them stir.

*

When they had driven round the whole circuit of enclosures it was time to park the car and walk round to see the things in cages.

All four of them were relieved to get back on their feet. For the last half hour or so – after the baboons – the car had become quite stuffy and oppressive.

Michael and Dan went looking for the Reptile House, which Christine said she wouldn't mind looking at. They were so pleased that she sounded keen on something, finding the reptiles had become their task for the remainder of the afternoon.

Margaret was happy looking at the flamingoes by the lake. She leaned over the fence and tried to talk with her daughter.

'I thought they were meant to have very long legs,' she said.

'They're sitting on them.'

'Don't they look like big pink chickens!'

Every single flamingo was asleep, with its bill and neck curled round underneath itself. Their heads were knuckled away and, ranged at even intervals on the muddy bank, they looked almost oven ready.

'Well . . .' said Margaret licking her lips. 'What do you think?'

'About?'

'About Michael. What about the way he tried to save my life! I could have been outside with those monkeys, not even thinking about my own safety! And he stopped me!'

Christine turned to her. 'Did you do that on purpose, then?'

'Don't be silly. But what about the way he shouted, eh? What a booming voice he's got! You'd never expect that! Didn't he sound so . . . manly!'

Christine shook her head. 'Jesus.'

There was a shout again, as her father and Michael came up the path towards them.

'Well, we've found the Reptile House!' said Michael loudly.

*

The heat in the Reptile House greeted them like the heat of the swimming baths. It reminded Christine of the moment of plodging in the yellow disinfectant bath, and then going round the corner and coming face to face with the pool and feeling the standing heat battering at her chest, drawing her in. As she followed the others into the dark, muggy corridors of the Reptile House, she felt exposed; as if she was going in wearing her swimming costume. But the place didn't smell like the baths; it was a musty, old smell, not the clean smell of chlorine.

It wasn't very busy. While they were looking at the pythons there were a few other sightseers peering into the illuminated compartments, but they soon passed on and the Fletchers had the eerie place to themselves. All around them, as they bent to stare through glass, there was a dank sound of dripping and hissing and, though it could have been Margaret's imagination, a terrible slithering noise that accompanied them through the corridors.

She pointed out the Golden Python to Michael. 'Doesn't it look fake! They've just painted that bright yellow.'

Like most of the reptiles they saw that afternoon, the pythons were sleeping. They rested coiled about each other. Dan came to peer over Margaret's shoulder and suddenly she was conscious of watching the creatures sleeping; as if it was improper. She backed away from the

28

two men and left them to stare at that promiscuous jumble of coils.

'Looks like old inner tubes,' she heard Dan say.

Their party was drifting apart from each other. Margaret had an urge to call them together, to look for lizards together, as a family, but she supressed it. They'll get sick of me going on at them, she thought.

'Look at this blue one!' she said, realising that she'd got into the hall filled with lizards with legs. But everyone was looking at other things. Even Christine seemed interested now, so that was something.

It took some looking, some searching out, to find some of the creatures in their cells. Christine found herself staring through pane after pane at heaps of rubble and sand, at branches and nibbled leaves, and sometimes she still couldn't find the relevant lizard. One cell she looked into contained only two paint pots and a dried, encrusted brush. She felt cheated at that.

Before she could move on, a small door opened in that cell and a man reached into it for the tins of paint. Christine jumped in alarm and he grinned at her.

She stared. She hoped she hadn't looked frightened. He was hoisting himself right into that tiny space and putting himself on show for her. A lithe, skinny young man, with dark cropped hair and a quick, jeering smile. He was in overalls. He was only there to refurbish the small room, but his sudden slithering appearance had scared her. He winked and waved the brush at her. She could see he was laughing at her.

Christine moved on.

In the next window she saw a reptile that looked like a toy; a podgy blue bean bag, with its toes splayed and rounded, its body lumpy and badly stuffed. You could just about see the stitching, she thought, and its wide, brown eyes looked just like those stapled on her old teddy. Then it moved its head jerkily, in one beady, nervous gesture and flicked her a glance, and then its tongue . . .

I've seen enough reptiles, she thought. She didn't like the way they were kept on their own. That was cruel.

She turned to look for the others. But the chamber was empty, and so was the next one, and the next. How long had she been staring at these couple of cells? And how could they just bugger off and leave her to it?

*

It was in one of the very last corridors that he caught up with her.

By then the constant hissing and dripping noises were unnerving her and she still hadn't found the others and she had given up looking at any of the lizards, even though they were starting to wake, hungry, expecting to be fed.

It was just as she was deciding she'd find the exit that the man in the painting overalls came round the corner and she bumped into him. He flashed that grin again.

'You looked really fucking bored before,' he said.

'I was.'

'Most girls would scream when they see me coming through that hole, like a giant human-size snake. Most of them do scream. I test them out. But you didn't.'

Christine shrugged and pretended to be interested in the snakes again. The brilliant lights exposed every blemish of their gilded hides. She stared at the crispy sheaths of their used skins. They were draped on ragged branches like pairs of old tights.

'You must be a girl who doesn't get scared.'

'I'm hard enough,' she said.

Was it true though, she wondered. Am I hard?

He was standing behind her. She could see his thin face reflected in the glass. He pressed against her back and she could feel him. 'Are you?'

*

In the office there wasn't much of anything. He'd made no effort to make it homely. On the desk there was a heap of papers, a pair of shears and a scabby pair of lizard-handling gloves. Christine looked around and saw a calendar with a woman showing off her full, brown-nippled breasts. On top of a filing cabinet there were three wire cages with mice inside. One of them was running on a little wheel thing.

Jake took her shoulders and made her face him. His breath smelled of oil. When he spoke it was in quite a refined way, she thought, like he came from a posh family. She liked the combination of that with the dirt under his fingernails – she stared at them as he started to unzip his overalls – and the smuts of white paint on his skin.

He pushed his mouth to hers and his lips were salty and warm. Their softness came as a shock to her; when everything about him she had seen so far, everything that had made her follow him here, had seemed so hard.

I can give as good as I get, Christine thought. She made sure her tongue went into his mouth first.

His teeth caught on her lips, snagged her tongue, and then nipped down her neck. She found she loved their jaggedness. He was taking her hand and guiding it right under him, and she felt the surprising weight of his cock and its slick length. She took hold of its warmth and realised she hadn't even known he'd pulled it out.

It was funny, but the office had nothing to do with reptiles, really. You'd never know where it was. It could be an office anywhere.

'Lie down,' he said.

'I'm not lying on the floor . . .'

'Go on. Go on . . . for me.'

He lay her down on the gritty lino, and urged her to slough layer after layer.

The glass of the door was pebbled, and Christine found herself thinking, as Jake hauled himself, skinny and naked, on top of her, that anyone outside could see right in. They'll see me with him. They'll be crowding in to watch. The thought was exciting and she cried out as he wedged himself inside her.

She'd expected him to be rough, but he wasn't. There was a watchful tension in his face as he lifted himself on his elbows and he slid into her. She nudged her knees on his slim, smooth sides. She wanted him fucking her harder, to make her cry out, to bring people running and she imagined that all the lizard, snake and reptile eyes were upon her; glaring through the door at their keeper and his girl as they writhed.

He was almost tender with her; filling her up completely. It was the first time she'd felt that. He knows what he's doing, she thought.

When he came inside her she could feel him shoot straight into the heart of her. And on her skin she could feel scores of tiny, leathery, padded feet.

*

'We've been waiting for you so long!'

Margaret was yelling across the forecourt outside the Reptile House. She and Dan and Michael were sitting on a park bench. It was chilly but the rain had eased.

Christine walked steadily, smiling stiffly, across the paving stones towards them. She could feel a slow dribble inside her. She ignored it. She put on a tight smile.

The three of them on the bench were eating Ritzy cheese crackers from the box. Margaret always kept a packet of them in her bag when they went on runs-out. Michael was eating biscuits too, with crumbs down his jacket, and he was looking up at Christine as she walked carefully towards them. He was anxious to see if she'd perked up at all.

2
Immaculate Batchelors

Michael was surprised when she said it.

He looked up from the table with a mouthful of Corn Flakes and a dribble of milk on his chin and he seemed hurt. His aunt almost took back what she had said, but decided she couldn't. The needs of others are greater this morning, she thought.

It was a bright Saturday morning. The perfect kind of day and last night Lily had lain awake in the quiet house and resolved that the whole day would work out fine. She could make it come out right; so that there were no arguments, no tensions, no feeling that something wasn't right: the whole thing would not turn out to be a sad compromise. When she'd heard that the reception do was to be upstairs at the Anchor and that the bride's mother wouldn't be there at all, Lily Woods had started to think this was one of those events that could have a sickly, wasted feeling about it. A sense of not doing things right. I'm not having that, she thought. It's going to be proper. It's going to be lovely.

She was ironing Michael's shirt, drenching its neat folds in steam as he sat having breakfast. He looked red and flushed already, in anticipation of being fussed over and congratulated all day. After she told him she was going over the road to the Fletchers' house to help out there, he stared at the anemones set out on the oil cloth. He gazed at their violet frills, their dense black hearts and he was frowning heavily, like things had already started to go wrong.

'But maybe I need help too,' he said. 'It's my big day as well.'

Lily was folding his shirt so that it came out in that square, boxy shape, with the arms tucked back, like they did in shops. 'Men need less help than women do. And that poor girl hasn't got a mother's help today. How do you think she feels?'

Michael scowled and his aunt was surprised at him. 'I've got no mam or dad today,' he said.

Lily pursed her lips. You've got me, she felt like reminding him. That's more than Christine's got. All she's got – that poor girl – is that old father of hers. What use will he be on her wedding day? He was like an old, shambling, useless thing at the best of times. But since his wife walked out he'd been like a ghost. It had become obvious who held that marriage together; who had kept the house and given him the incentive to keep up a decent-looking life. Lily shuddered to think what the scene was like at the Fletchers' this morning. No flowers ordered, none of the right laundry done. No proper bridal breakfast. A last minute grab-and-dash for the right outfits, the things they would need. Lily wouldn't trust Dan to do things properly in his wife's absence.

Lily had been up since five this morning, once her resolution was made. She'd need all the time she could get if she was going to carry both sides of the new family through the day. Lily had sprung out of bed and busied about, still in her nightie – making sure Michael would have everything he would need. Laying out his new peacock silk waistcoat on the banister right outside his bedroom door. She wrote out laborious instructions for how to tie the silver-grey cravat. And she thanked her lucky stars that he wouldn't be ill and hungover from a Stag Night. There hadn't been a night of revels with a host of his male friends. He hadn't been alcohol-poisoned and stripped and dumped in a phone box hundreds of miles from home. So this morning there was no groaning and thick-headedness, no holding down of raw egg and milk concoctions and no vomiting. That was a mercy. She thought, at least he won't need me to cajole him and bully him all the way to the altar, or whatever they had instead of an altar at a registry office. A counter, that's what they probably had.

She told him, ravelling up the iron's cord and sliding it away, 'It's worse for Christine. Do you know what it's like for a girl to be without her mother on her big day?'

The way Michael was staring and frowning, you'd think he had a headache after all. 'Christine's not like that,' he said. 'She's not that sort of girl.'

'When she's getting married,' said Lily firmly, pulling on her padded, tapestried jacket, 'every girl is that sort of girl. They all want fussing over and all the proper traditions. Christine's no different.'

He stood up. 'I'll come over with you . . .'

Lily almost laughed. 'Well, you know that's not allowed, don't you?'

'Oh. Yeah.' He looked careworn and paunchy in his vest thing and his boxer shorts. Now she was starting to feel bad for him. She had to go right now. She couldn't be in two places at once.

'You get yourself a shower and get dressed. Slowly, mind, Michael. I want you looking immaculate. Like a credit to me.'

As she left the house Michael sat down again and looked at the anemones his aunt had put in the bowl. He knew she'd done it to mark the day as special. Flowers for him. The thing was, anemones weren't that festive to look at, really. To him, they looked sort of ominous.

Crossing the road outside, Lily was checking the wedding kit-bag she had packed at six that morning. Curling tongs, blue garter, confetti, glitter, a variety of blushers and eyeshadows. She knew Christine wasn't exactly expert with make-up. The bag was an old leather one with fraying straps; an old-fashioned doctor's bag.

It was just before nine when Lily arrived at the Fletchers' place to make her house call.

*

The hallway was crammed with flowers. There was no one to let her in, so Lily eased open the door and was left to stare at the bouquets and arrangements – some of them were laid out on the stairs. The air thick with summer pollen; the clean scent of sap. On the telephone table she counted thirteen buttonholes: fat, frilled ivory carnation heads, their stems neatly pinched with tin-foil.

Most of the flowers gathered here were yellow and white, and cream seemed to be the colour for the day. Lily nodded at this. No one would be fooled – not least her – if the Fletcher girl came tripping out of the house adorned in brilliant white.

Lily touched a number of vellum petals, peered into the thick trumpets of her namesake blooms and felt the rich leaves for dew: all fresh and ready. Then she looked at a basket of irises put to one side on the hallway windowsill. The card, printed out by some flowershop girl, said simply: 'All my love, mam.' Lily tutted. You'd think some people could forget their problems for one day at least, wouldn't you? It was this kind of self-centredness that was splitting up families everywhere.

There was a rustling from the staircase.

'Mrs Woods?'

In the gloom of the top landing Christine was standing in a (black!) lace bra and pants and she was holding a veil. Yards and yards of netting. She'd be creasing it.

'Christine,' Lily smiled and grasped the banister. 'I've come to –'

'What's the matter? Michael's all right, isn't he?'

Lily was satisfied by the sudden tightness in the girl's face. So she thinks something of Michael, after all.

'He's just fine,' Lily said. 'I thought I'd come over and see what needs doing here. This is the nerve centre, isn't it? I thought you'd appreciate some . . .'

'That's very kind of you,' said Christine. 'Dad's supposed to be helping me with the frock and all . . . but he's useless, really. Look . . . make yourself a cup of tea and introduce yourself to everyone. I'll finish my hair.'

The girl's learned some manners, Lily thought. That must be Michael's influence rubbing off.

Christine was smiling again, gathering up the length of veil and Lily thought how odd it was, looking up and talking to this girl she hardly knew, and the girl was in her bra and pants. But that's what weddings are like, isn't it? Suddenly getting thrown into someone else's family, feeling intimate and caught up with them. Everyone mucking in.

Christine was long-limbed and her skin was very pale. Almost ivory herself, in fact. She'd had her hair cut sensibly, like a page-boy style, with the colour sorted out at last so it was a clean blonde. Of course Michael would think she was lovely – him who'd hardly had a girlfriend before. A slim girl like this was bound to turn his head. Not so slim as all that, Lily thought, as Christine dragged her veil back into her room. She's got a little pot belly coming – a small, rather attractive one – but just enough to show . . .

Lily let go of the banister as if it was hot.

She wanted to shout the girl back down the stairs.

Is that it? Is that the reason for all the hurry, all the fuss?

Lily backed away. Why hasn't Michael told me? How could he not tell me?

With her face burning she tiptoed through the fresh arrangements of flowers, lugging her doctor's bag.

I'm a fool. Curling tongs; what have I brought those for? Christine's hair is straight as anything. And the make-up . . . probably Christine would laugh . . . she certainly wouldn't want to use any of Lily's old-lady's make-up.

I'm making a fool of myself, getting mixed up in this lot, Lily thought. They don't want me anyway. I'd be better off going back home. I've got my own outfit to see to, my own hair to tong . . . and I should be talking to Michael. And maybe I was just seeing things. Maybe Christine simply has a little tummy that she tucks away in her tight jeans. Quite attractive, really. Better than those Twiggy girls, looking just like boys. Anyway, looking straight up the staircase at someone isn't going to give you the most flattering view, is it? Even the skinniest person would look distorted like that . . .

At the end of the hall Lily pushed open the door to the kitchen.

The noise burst out at her and she was cowed suddenly, and shy, at the sight of a room full of men.

Dan, in a morning suit of perfect, felty grey like all the rest of them, turned round to look at her. He was holding a tumbler of what looked like whisky up to his mouth. 'Mrs Woods!' he smiled warmly and all the other men were looking too.

She felt ashamed, standing there in her old coat and housewifely work-clothes. This was like walking into some secret male ceremony. There must be fifteen of them, she thought, all with their drinks and cigarettes, sitting on stools and ranging about, the air trembling and raucous at this time in the morning.

'I came to help out,' said Lily. 'I thought you might need me.'

All the other men beside Dan she didn't recognise. He pushed his face in close to hers, putting a friendly arm over her shoulders, ushering her further into the room. She could smell the drink on his breath and held her own as he started to introduce everyone; a whirl of men's names. His brother, Peter, his grown-up nephew, John, and other, younger men, who were described, and laughed at being described, as old flames of the bride.

Lily stared about at them, baffled. All the old boyfriends are here, too? What's Michael supposed to make of that? It's like a whole football team, here in poor Margaret's spotless kitchen. But the boys – who Lily had observed going in and out of the Fletchers' place over the last couple of years – looked nothing like themselves. They were clean-shaven and their hair was washed and cut. Their borrowed suits fitted them perfectly and they talked and laughed quite differently to how she would have expected. Even their cigarettes and glasses of drink didn't make them seem like rough types.

Dan was pouring her a drink and she balked.

'Oh, a cup of tea, please.'

Out came one of Margaret's best cups and saucers from the cabinet. White china with golden trim. Lily wasn't sure Margaret would want these out in this company. Dan winked at her roguishly as he topped up her tea with a splash of whisky. 'We'll all have a snifter to help us through our nerves, eh?' he said and added, 'Why don't you wait for Christine in the living room? The dress is in there. We thought she could put it on in there, so she wouldn't have to manage the stairs . . .'

Lily took her tea and found herself propelled into the living room, the hearty voices starting up again behind her.

Well. They've thought of everything, it seems like.

She sat down in Dan's swivel chair and stared at the wedding dress, which lay full-length on the settee.

It was cream, after all. Puffed sleeves. She couldn't make out the cut of it, exactly, as it lay there on the cushions. She'd have to wait till Christine came down.

Lily sipped her scalding, heady tea and gazed warily at the serving hatch between living room and kitchen. What if, while I'm helping to haul the dress on, over the bride's head, or while I'm fastening the hundreds of hooks and eyes . . . What if the serving hatch flew open . . . and we're exposed to the hungry view of those immaculate batchelors?

*

Why the haste? Why the speed? That's what Lily Woods had wanted to know in the first place.

She'd had her suspicions already and over these couple of months that led up to the big day, she found herself wanting to have it out with her nephew. But his whole manner had changed and he had become bluff and hearty; almost sure of himself. That mood of his deflected any hard questions. I haven't the heart, Lily realised, to sit him down and ask him the things that his mother would have asked him, had she been here. In the end I'm just pleased to see Michael happy.

And he was happy. He seemed to be swelling up with pleasure. That's why she'd thought it funny, the way he was frowning this morning. It's a lot to take in, though. A big change in life.

But why the haste? Why the speed? She'd never really believed in whirlwind romances. If she let herself dwell on the problem long enough, the answer seemed all too obvious. She knew the type of girl Christine was.

I might be an innocent in many ways, but I'm not as daft as all that.

Michael's a good boy, though. He won't have done anything bad.

Lily had taken to watching him when he didn't realise, as he ate the dinner she'd made him; forking up beans, letting the sauce dribble through the tines as he watched telly. His gaze abstracted, as if he was spending those months always thinking about something else. Lily decided that she just couldn't know. You could never know what went on inside a man's head.

Usually Lily Woods prided herself on knowing what was coming next. Her sister Ruth, Michael's mam who had died last year, used to say that their Lily had no common sense but she could see round a few corners. She had that gift of insight that came up every other generation in their family.

At the age of fifty two Lily still hadn't done anything with that supposed gift. 'But what do you do with the gift of insight?' she'd asked her sister.

This was while Ruth was lying, piqued, in what was to be her death bed. Lily was there to do things round the house in those final weeks, and Ruth hadn't been best pleased that Lily was turning over her own problems. 'You should put it to good use,' said the older sister. 'Get it trained. You could help people see into the future, or contact their loved ones, like Great Aunt Sally used to.

That's what you should do. Not just fritter it away.' She coughed – racking, thick – and Lily had to help her sit up straighter, arranging the pillows. 'I wish for God's sake you'd warned me this was coming.'

Lily's eyes widened. 'I didn't know! How could I know?'

Then the son, Michael, had come in and Lily had watched him stare solemnly at his mother's ashen face and he was listening to what she had to say to him. And, in that moment, Lily had one of her genuine flashes forward into the future. She could see Michael sitting at his counter in the bank, her local branch of the bank, with the toffee-coloured fake wooden walls and the drowsy rubber plants. She could also see herself waiting proudly to be served by him, and then him coming home every night to her house in Brunswick Avenue. She knew she could tell her sister that Michael would be all right.

He is, too. I've seen him all right.

*

He hadn't wasted any time, that was for sure. Lily had imagined Michael would be one of those slow boys, who didn't go running after the girls much at all. Who waited and let the good ones come running after him. Yet here he was with Christine Fletcher at his beck and call. Sometimes Lily thought she didn't understand how these things worked at all.

She had pictured Michael always being there as she grew older. Perhaps selfishly, she'd seen him as her ideal companion as she slipped into her dotage. A strong, reliable man about the house. Still and all, if Christine was what he really wanted, then she wouldn't stand in his way.

Has Christine tried to trap him? Is that behind this? Lily knew that this kind of thing went on. Unscrupulous girls, preying on hapless men like Michael.

Lily wished – not for the first time – that Christine's mam, Margaret, was there. They weren't exactly best friends, but they could talk and, between them, they could have had the whole thing out in the open. Sorting it out like only two mature women could.

But there's another funny thing, she thought. Margaret waltzing off like she did, to who knows where, a month or two ago. Wasn't it her who had been so keen on Michael in the first place? By all accounts, Margaret had just about thrown Michael and Christine together. She'd set herself on fixing them up, come hell or high water; that was the way Michael told the tale, laughing and going over the whole, marvellous story of their zoo trip together. The day he and Christine had fallen in love, that's what the story had become.

So why isn't Margaret here? Even if she and old Dan in the kitchen have fallen out once too often, you'd still think Margaret would be here to glory in what she'd certainly see as her triumph. Lily realised she had gulped down the rest of her whisky and tea and her breath was sour with alcohol. She felt like banging on the serving hatch for more, but stopped herself.

I need more insight, she thought. I need to harness all my disparate, random flashes of the future and what-people-are-truly-thinking and I need to put them to better use. As it was, she found herself adrift as anyone else. Going along with the ritual of the day, with all the stages and scripts and costumes laid out ready.

Then Christine came in with her hair neatly combed and a Chinese dressing gown wrapped tight about her. It was a beautiful, rich orange silk.

She smiled at Lily and then at the dress.

Lily thought: I wonder if I'll get a look at her tummy again.

'I hardly ever wear dresses,' Christine said.

'You could hardly wear jeans going down the aisle.' Lily heaved herself out of the swivel chair. I sound too stiff and old-fashioned. She won't want my help.

'Oh, I want it all proper,' said Christine, picking up the dress with both arms and holding it out before her. 'I really want to go the whole hog.'

*

For all his brandy in the outhouse and whisky in the kitchen on the morning of his daughter's wedding, Dan was no kind of drinking man. He had the taste for it, and in moments of stress it could come in handy, but as a rule, he could take it or leave it. When Margaret had packed up a couple of suitcases and called a cab to the station, all of a sudden on that Wednesday morning, he had run out down the front path after her, he had shouted with most of the neighbours watching, he'd yelled after the taxi after it was long gone – but he hadn't turned straight to the bottle. He had been baffled and hurt, but he hadn't spent the past few weeks drunk all the time.

The drink we're getting through this morning, he decided, me and all the lads, that's just celebratory; that's just Dutch Courage.

He'd need a clear head, he'd need to be sensible, to get all of this wedding stuff off the ground. It had fallen to him. As had the upkeep of the house. When Margaret first went, neglecting to tell him when or even if she'd be back home, he hadn't known where she'd kept silly but essential things like the clean tea towels. Where were the bills and receipts put away? Why hadn't she left all the phone numbers he'd need?

The way he'd started to look at it, it was as if they'd been on a run-out somewhere, and halfway down the motorway he had taken his hands off the steering wheel, his feet off the pedals and said: 'I'm tired of driving now. Would you just take over for a bit?' Margaret: who'd never sat in a driving seat all her life. She wouldn't have a clue.

The last weeks there hadn't been a peep out of her. No phone calls, no letter, not even a stinking postcard. Of course, in the past they'd had their fights and odd, fraught silences. In a way, he could understand her shooting off for some time alone – if only it hadn't been now. The fact it was right before Christine's wedding – a wedding, as far as he could see, she had bloody well engineered – the fact she was going to miss said wedding was really worrying. The few times he had let himself dwell on this thought it had really disturbed him. He thought he'd never see her again and that pained Dan more than he'd ever thought. When he woke he'd look at the small dish on her bedside table, the one where she put her earrings before sleeping. He loved the tinkle noise they made when she dropped them in. He looked each morning, as if the earrings would have reappeared overnight and she'd be lying there beside him; mouth open, staring at the ceiling as usual. But the pillow beside him was flat and unruffled, and the earring dish was empty. Last night, a late night, he'd realised how used to Margaret's absence he must really be. He'd sat up in bed smoking, fretful over today's arrangements, and he'd even used the earring dish to tap his ash into. Margaret would have a fit, seeing that, he thought.

Isn't there something nice, though, about being completely in control? I've got all my own way. Margaret would have had twenty fits by now and god knows what state she'd be in this morning.

He loved getting all the groceries in; deciding to try out cooking new things. Maybe it took something like this to rock your old self slightly out of its orbit, and to make healthy alterations. So when Margaret eventually returns, we'll be refreshed and I'll be ready to take up more responsibility and even enjoy it. He could share the load better with her. She would see what a lesson he had learned while she was away!

He had even taught himself how to cook Chilli Con Carne from a magazine he had found under the settee while hoovering. (Hoovering, me! Reading magazines, me! And cooking!) He decided that Chilli Con Carne would be the first meal they would have, the day she came back.

He grinned to himself, pouring another finger of whisky, and the lads in the kitchen noted his pleasure and pride and wondered what he'd be like if it was them – or one of them – that his daughter was about to marry.

His brother took his glass from him and said the cars would be coming soon. 'You've got to stand up and give your girl away. We can't have you smashed, Dan.'

'I'm not getting smashed. I'm just chuffed.'

'You can lay off the drink, anyway. Bad example to the lads here. Plenty of time for that after.'

There was a honking of car horns on the drive outside.

'That'll be the limos,' someone said.

Dan was feeling very distant from it all. His brother Peter was taking charge. 'You lot – you get in first and we'll see you at the registry office. Make sure they know we're on our way.'

Dan's nephew John said, 'We haven't seen Christine in all her gear yet. We can't miss that before we go.'

Dan's brother was looking harrassed.

'Sorry,' Dan said. 'I was miles away.'

His brother's face clouded. What bushy eyebrows he's got, Dan thought. I'm glad I never got those. 'Well,' Peter said, 'I suppose if Margaret's not here now, she'll never be. And now you know. If she's not coming back today, she'll never come back. At least you know.' Peter sounded so philosophical, all the other men in the kitchen had turned to listen.

The horns in the drive started up again.

Like we're all going off to war, Dan thought. A cavalcade.

The kitchen door opened and Lily Woods came in once more, dusting her hands, looking pleased with herself. She was looking a lot less bashful than last time.

'Well,' she said. 'Here she is.'

And in came Christine with her dress on. She held herself tall; her veil up and grinning at them all. Her fists were clenched to hold up her layers of skirts and she was stepping onto the lino to twirl and give them all a view.

Mam would burst into tears just now, Christine thought. She'd be proud and upset and it would be the end of her having to worry about me. Typical mam. There's only dad who can see things right through to the end.

*

It was a cold day, but it was bright and when the photos eventually came back it looked as if it had been a perfect summer's day. Dan stood in the park outside the registry while the photos were being taken. It took so long that the shadows of the trees kept moving and the clouds were whizzing by overhead. He kept getting chilly and had to move from patch to patch of sunlight. More and more people were pulling cameras out of handbags and wanting to take extra pictures. Dan himself was in great demand, almost as much as the happy couple; showing off his tail coat, beaming, and putting on a good front. He was shivering, though.

Christine doesn't look chilled at all, he thought, even with her arms bare. That Michael's hardly taken his arm from around her waist, as if he's scared the breeze is going to catch under the billowing cream of her frock and lift her away from him. To Dan he looked like a fella who could hardly believe his luck. He'd turned up in his taxi alone and he stepped up to the small crowd's applause looking bewildered. Looking like: who are all these people? But they all knew who he was and the role he was stepping into. He seemed stunned and Dan recognised that look from his own wedding day photos.

What a turn-out we've got. Dan found he knew only about half of them. He was turning a blind eye to those who hadn't made the effort of dressing up – the ones who looked like Christine's biker pals. When they all filed into the small, square, searing white registry office, there had barely been room. The girl who presided over it all didn't look anything like a vicar, and she'd stammered her way through the service. Not a service, really. More like lots of instructions and then there was some form filling. Dan sat proudly on the front row and made sure he followed every detail of those forms getting filled in. He could feel the attention of everyone in that room craning forward to see as Christine and Michael put their names down on paper.

Lily Woods came in late. Halfway through the service the heavy door inched open and she came tripping in, her face scarlet. She was in a print frock from Marksies. She'd left herself no time after helping Christine with the dress, and she'd had to rush home to get herself sorted out. She squeezed herself through the crush to find a spare seat. As the registrar continued, haltingly, through her lines, Dan could hear Lily breathlessly apologise to everyone she passed.

Silly bitch, he thought. Fancy offering to help like she did, unasked for, and then almost spoiling it all. He had a throbbing in his temples as the service was winding up. All the tension, he thought – and that last drink. He'd be glad to get out in the sunshine again. Glad to have a drink at the lunch afterwards.

One thing Lily Woods did do right, and that was when they came out of the registry office, into the wide street of Georgian buildings. While everyone else was chucking confetti over Michael and Christine as they emerged into the sun, Lily was opening plastic vials of gold and silver glitter. She whooped and threw the contents up in the air. All the cameras snapped. The glitter, tinselling down, came out on everyone's photos and the bridal couple turned out dusted with this fine, shining powder. It put a particular glamour on the day; a slowed-down quality, that invested it, in retrospect, with a potency and a properness. A day that, in actuality, had rushed by so quickly.

For Dan it went quickly because he found himself fussing. It was his responsibility. He was in the role of both father and mother. Outside in the park, it was him checking the drop of Christine's hemline and arguing with her when she wanted pictures where she held up her dress to show off her white stack-heeled boots. He was the one clutching the bouquet when Christine and Michael had photos taken of them holding flutes of champagne and toasting each other. He was the one who wanted everyone to enjoy themselves at the reception, and he worried that the Anchor – to his mind ideal – wouldn't be high-class enough for some of the guests. Not the bikers and the old boyfriends and the younger lot; they'd have fun anywhere. But for the likes of Lily Woods who, he was sure, would look down their noses at the choices he had made.

The day slowed down as he gave his speech in the restaurant where they had lunch. He was nervous and sure he couldn't be loud enough. They'd talk over the top of him. He said a few faltering words about what kind of daughter she was and they all started applauding to cover his awkwardness. But they're listening, he thought. They want to hear what I've got to say about her.

Afterwards, he toyed with melon balls and slivers of transparent ham and looked shyly at his daughter and her new husband. Michael was turning round backwards in his seat to talk with his aunt, who was at the next table, amongst people she didn't know. Apparently she was complaining about this to Michael.

Dan overheard his new son-in-law saying, 'But this is the family table, Aunt Lily. Dan's had it all organised for weeks.'

Lily was turning back to her own place setting with scalding cheeks. Dan sipped his wine and allowed himself a moment of satisfaction. Well, that's the old busy-body put in her place, anyway.

He wanted a word with his daughter. He wondered when there would be a quiet part of the day, when he could say what was on his mind. Nothing in particular; just something more private, more special than standing up in a restaurant and making that toast – blushing and making a Charlie of himself in front of all these people. He wished they could have ten minutes sitting in his garden outhouse, having a fag and a cupful of brandy between them; her sitting in that voluminous, incredible frock and him in his monkey suit. He could say something like, I'm handing you on to another man, and I know he'll care for you, but I'll always be your dad and I'm not going anywhere . . .

Maybe tonight, at the dance, when they put music on at the Anchor . . .

Wasn't it traditional that father and bride dance together?

He called the waiter down to the family table and insisted that everyone should be given more wine. He wanted the afternoon to ring with the popping of corks.

It's this that I've worked for. It's one of the days – the day – that everything in my world is staked on.

*

It wasn't the kind of dancing she'd expected, of course, not the sort you'd really want to be doing, with your nephew holding you and everyone looking on. Lily expected something more graceful, more like a tea dance. Something a touch more Cary Grant and Katherine Hepburn. But this was a young people's wedding. It was a different age and she had to give in to that. If she had organised this, it wouldn't have been the Anchor and everyone wouldn't be in ordinary pub gloom, carrying trays with pints of lager over to tables littered with ashtrays, cigarette packets and handbags.

Maybe, in the end, Dan had judged it right. The young people here seemed to think the set-up proper. It was their kind of affair; they didn't like to stand on ceremony. Even Michael – so stiff and self-conscious all day – seemed relaxed and expansive late on that night when he at last took his old Aunt in his arms and danced her round the sticky floor.

The song was 'Those were the days, my friend', which Lily recognised off the radio. Michael jogged his elbows and it felt like his huge arms could go round her twice over. He had to bend awkwardly to hold her and when he talked his breath was beery.

'It all came out right in the end,' he said. She looked up to catch his eye, but his glance was flicking about everywhere. It was still like he couldn't believe that all these people had come out to see him getting wed. He was nodding at a group by the bar. Lily recognised them as his friends from the bank. She was pleased they were there; they seemed very fond of him. She didn't think he was the type that made friends easily.

'Yes, it was all very good,' she said and realised she still sounded rather prim. It was important to her that they knew they had her blessing.

'I am sorry about the family table business, Aunt Lily. Of course you should have been sitting with us. But you know Dan's had to do everything on his tod. He couldn't remember everything . . .'

She patted his back lightly to stop him going on. She was embarrassed at the fuss she had made, back in the restaurant. 'Don't start that again. It's forgotten, sunshine. Anyway, I got to talk to those nice pals of yours from the bank. They were very nice to me. One of them was telling me about this savings plan I might . . .'

The Rolling Stones came on then and it became too noisy and frantic for her to carry on with her story. She excused herself and let him dance with the younger ones.

*

Dan was in the thick of it. He was dancing right in the middle when 'Honky Tonk Woman' came on. Sweat streamed down his face and he lurched a little as he danced with his daughter, but he couldn't sit down yet. How often do I get to dance at my daughter's wedding? He was grinning at everyone.

For a second Christine was worried about how red he looked. A slower song came on and she took hold of her dad in an attempt to slow him down. Even then he kept jogging on the spot.

'My little girl,' he said quietly. She felt it rather than heard it, his voice mumbling into her layers of silk and tulle. 'I wanted to tell you – I'm always your dad -'

'I know, dad.'

'And I won't be running off. Whatever.'

She tightened her grip on him. 'I know.'

He's drunker than I thought, she realised. He isn't holding it so well these days.

He went on, 'Whatever you've been up to – you're still my princess, you know. And we can work it all out . . .'

*

Michael came to sit with his aunt at a table beside the dance floor. He brought her a Campari and lemon. Make the old girl feel like someone special. He'd not really thought yet, about how she would feel, when it came to him moving out of her house and across the road. She must feel dreadful, really. Losing his company already.

She sipped her drink and smiled at him.

His eyes were gleaming and he suddenly felt brave. He started talking loudly, so that people around them could hear.

'I've done it all properly, haven't I, Aunt Lily?'

She nodded. 'You have, Michael.'

'Wouldn't Mam be proud, if she was here to watch? I reckon this is just what she would have wanted for me. I've got the perfect girl.'

Lily wished he would shush up a bit. It sounded like he was crowing. Mercifully he bent his head in closer over their table and hissed at her, 'And it's come together so fast.'

'It has indeed, Michael.'

'Will you be shocked if I tell you why?'

Lily felt the blood drain from her face. Michael was drunk, showing off. Like a big soft child. He was leering at her.

'What?' she said.

'You mean why, Aunt Lily.'

'Tell me why, Michael.'

'It's all right, now! It's all above board! We're safe and wed! Home and dry!'

'Tell me, Michael,' she said.

'Christine's having my baby, Aunt Lily,' he said. 'I've given Christine – that girl over there that everyone loves – I've gone and given her my baby.'

Lily put down her glass very carefully. She picked up her handbag.

'Where are you going?'

'I'm going to have a word with the father of the bride,' she said, inching past Michael's stool.

'He's over there, dancing,' Michael grinned. 'Dancing with my wife.'

Lily left Michael on his stool and she waded onto the dance floor again. Dusty Springfield was playing and the whole lot of them were swaying, swinging their arms about, gazing moonily at each other. In the very centre she found Christine, dancing alone, taking up more space than anyone else in the great bell of her dress.

Christine could see Lily nudging towards her. Keep away, she thought. I'm dancing by myself in the middle of the floor, under lights in my wedding dress. This is my moment. I want to be stuck here forever; the most important one in the room. It's the dress that marks me out as unique. I want to keep feeling like this.

Then Lily was in front of her. 'Where's your father?'

'He came over queasy,' Christine shouted over Dusty. 'He's gone out for some air. On the fire escape.'

*

Lily made for the source of the draft at the back of the room. Under the exit sign, the quietest part of the pub, the emergency door was swung open, wedged by a fire extinguisher. She could see the purple night sky; the rooftops of the town centre. And a lumpen silhouette bent over on the railings.

'Dan?' she said, coming up behind him, hating how familiar his name sounded on her lips.

She stepped gingerly onto the fire escape platform. It was three storeys above the car park. She looked down and saw dark cars, a skip, treetops and then she came over dizzy. She touched his shoulder. 'Are you all right, Mr Fletcher?'

'To be honest,' he said, looking round at her, his face all drawn and his tie undone. 'I've never felt worse in all my life.' He hiccoughed and then groaned. He sounded to Lily like he'd been swallowing hot coals.

'There's something we need to discuss,' said Lily.

He tried to straighten himself on the railings. 'I don't think I'm in any shape to discuss.'

'It's important, Dan.'

'I actually think I'm going to throw up.'

'I mean it, Dan. I want to know if you know about this. All this.'

'All what?' he said, as if he couldn't care less.

*

'Christine?'

Michael was by her side suddenly.

'Where the fuck have you been?' she burst. 'I've been left dancing by myself and then your bloody Aunty came up and . . .'

Michael's face was shining. 'There's someone you've got to see.'

'Who?'

'Someone.' He grabbed her hand. His was slick with sweat. 'Come on.' He pulled her eagerly through the knot of dancers. She was treading on her hem. She didn't want to spoil it. Michael was pulling her along too eagerly.

Then someone else was saying, 'Christine!' above all the music and the stamping of feet and she was being pulled into an embrace at once familiar and odd. She knew instantly that everyone in the room was watching her hug this woman. A woman in a scratchy tweed suit that smelled like it had been hanging up for years. A mothbally smell.

Christine drew back and looked at her mother.

'I couldn't help it,' Margaret said. 'I had to come in the end.'

Christine found she was crying and clutching her mam's hands. She couldn't speak. It's the dress, she thought. It's stopping me saying what I want to.

What made her cry was her mother's hair. It hadn't been set properly. It looked lopsided and just wrong, like she hadn't made the effort. And her clothes are wrong, too, she thought. Her mother had come back as a bad impersonation of herself.

Christine was shaking her head, trying to take it all in. Oblivious to Michael and the other guests standing grinning nearby.

'But what's the matter, mam? Where did you go? Why are you . . . ?'

Margaret smiled. It wasn't the nervous, flinching smile of recent years. It was warm and it reminded Christine of being little. A different, earlier mam.

'Hey Jude' was coming over the speakers.

'No questions now,' Margaret said, putting her finger to Christine's lips. 'Later. I'll tell you everything later on. I just had to see you. Go and dance with your husband. He's here, look. Waiting for you.'

Margaret took Michael's elbow and shoved him gently at Christine. 'Go on. Now – where's your dad?'

Christine showed her, wordlessly, and watched her mother set off calmly towards the emergency exit. As Michael started to draw her into his steps, she was shocked to see that the back of her mother's stockings were tattered and ripped.

What was she thinking of?

*

Lily noted with grim satisfaction that he'd managed to be sick right into the skip, three storeys down.

Dan heaved and heaved again and it sounded like everything he'd eaten for weeks was coming out of him. He stooped, breath juddering, on the rails and she rubbed his back, bent close to him. She had turned all practical and was coaxing him: 'You'll be all right now. This is the best thing. This is the best way. Better than keeping it all in. You know it is.'

He shuddered under her hand and she was starting to worry for him. *He doesn't sound well at all. I wonder if I should call someone.*

'You've got yourself all worked up,' she said. 'That's what it is. Your nerves are all to pot. I'm not surprised. You've put a lot of work into today, and all by yourself. That's too much for any man. But you've done us all proud, Dan. You can let go, now. Let it all out.'

He was quieter, stiller. Lily nodded and drew back her hand.

Then she looked around.

'Margaret!'

Margaret was out on the platform too. There was barely space for all three of them.

'What's the matter with him?' Margaret asked.

'He's got himself a bit tipsy. Worrying over everything.'

'Dan?'

He started to lift himself up. It was like, Lily thought, watching someone haul themselves out of a well. She was aware of Margaret drawing herself up, preparing herself as Dan turned to look at her.

'What,' he said, and swiped his chin with the back of his hand. 'What are you doing here? Why are you back here now?'

Lily had to step aside, back to the doorway, as Margaret lurched forward. 'Dan . . . I don't know . . . We have to talk about this. I've mucked it up, I know . . .'

She wanted holding, even Lily could see that. Dan's face

was dark, perplexed – but his arms went up, automatically, to take hold of his wife.

Three's a crowd, Lily thought and began to draw away.

'Dan,' Margaret was saying, 'I shouldn't . . .'

'No,' he said thickly. 'But you're back and we can . . .'

His knees seemed to buckle then and his body jolted. Margaret gave a little scream.

'Dan?'

More sick was coming out of him, vile-smelling, watery. Margaret fell backwards as the vomit splashed down them both, and through the metal grating of the platform. Lily pushed in to help, just as Dan lost his grip on his wife for the last time and tumbled over backwards, headfirst across the railings.

Lily banged her own head, so that the iron bars rang, but she held on tight – watching stars whirl – diverting her from the stench, the shock, the crunching sound as Dan hit the skip below. And she lay like that, clasping hold of Margaret, until the wedding guests came running out at last to see.

3
A Thing of the Future

There was a photo of the newly-weds in which they were standing either side of Dan's hospital bed. His bedclothes were very smooth as if, for the fortnight he'd been lying there, he'd barely stirred. Dan's eyes were glassy and staring because he'd only just come round and those of his daughter and her husband were similar because of how little they had slept during what was meant to be their honeymoon.

Michael had hold of one of Dan's hands and Christine had the other. She could remember the feel of that hand, years after; how limp it was and cold. It felt like a lump of corned beef, held in one piece only by its yellow fat.

Each of the three in the picture were staring straight at the camera. Later, whenever Christine came across this photo, she was always surprised that their expressions didn't show, didn't shine with, the immense relief she remembered feeling the night that her father woke up. All three faces looked startled, as if they hadn't known anyone in the room even had a camera. As if someone had pulled it out of their handbag and snapped this moment without asking.

Which was true enough. Lily Woods still had her insta-matic in her bag, two weeks after the wedding. Two weeks of hospital visiting and trying to coax the newly-weds to come home and eat and sleep properly and not spend all of their time right by Dan's side. For two weeks she had carried her camera back and forth on the bus to the hospital and not even realised it. It lay there, powdered with glitter, a shred of confetti caught in its shutter, in the bottom of her bag, with a few snaps left to take.

The night that Dan returned to life, Lily Woods – who everyone later claimed was responsible for the miracle –

recalled her instamatic and preserved, in one swift and excitable swoop and click, his first new-born, tentative moments, forever.

*

Christine had clutched her father's hand day after day and stared into his face. It was strange how, as the days passed, his face was becoming less lined and less creased. There was a definite visible change in him. She mentioned this to everyone who came to see – Michael, Lily, his brother, her ex-boyfriends. It was as if the tension was easing out of him and he was relaxing at last. He was rejuvenating before her very eyes; each wrinkle ironing itself out, and Christine wondered where it would all end.

For a fortnight she could hardly be budged from the orange plastic chair at her father's side. It looked, Lily Woods thought, for all the world as if she had married her father instead of Michael. Christine was devoted to him.

'What was I supposed to do?' Christine said whenever she was asked. 'I thought my dad was dying. I couldn't go off on honeymoon, could I? And leave him there . . . lying in the lurch.'

Lily knew this was true and indeed, she'd have thought much less of her niece-in-law if she had wanted to go swanning off on honeymoon. But it seemed like she had no interest in Michael at all. Lily tried not to think of Dan's fall off the fire escape as a blight already on their marriage, but it was hard not to take these things as omens.

The wedding night itself had taken on a lurid, nightmarish quality in Lily's memory. Christine in that huge frock, insisting on being helped into the ambulance so she could ride with her father. The ambulance-men stuffing huge quantities of silk through the doors after her. The shocking blue lights shining on her face as she kissed Michael a hurried goodbye and the blood on the front of her dress and caked on her father's face as he lay strapped to his stretcher.

Lily remembered Michael calling taxis and the party descending into chaos and her trying to tell people they couldn't all follow the ambulance to Casualty; not the whole wedding party and not drunk as they were. She tried to think calmly and found that she couldn't. Michael was the coolest one; getting them a cab as she stood there in the downstairs foyer of the Anchor, her head still ringing with pain where she'd banged it and all she could think about was the smell of Dan's sick on her. The vomit of a dead man, she'd thought, rather wildly and then she'd realised that Margaret had gone. Margaret was nowhere to be seen in the milling crowd that came down from the wedding party and were standing, stunned, in the foyer and car park, some of them going, ghoulishly, to look into the skip.

When she pointed out Margaret's absence to Michael he didn't seem surprised or very interested. He's in shock, too, Lily thought.

Then they were all sitting in Casualty together; Michael with his silk waistcoat unbuttoned and Christine wringing her veil in her hands, furious that they weren't being told anything.

The staff nurse had been good. She came to suggest that Christine and Michael shouldn't go too far that night. She looked them up and down and said that her father was in a dicey situation and they should stick nearby. Lily took this as bad news, but Christine seemed relieved someone was telling her what to do. The nurse offered them a slim, tidy bed in the small room next door to the private room where her father was. They took it.

Lily Woods wasn't catered for. She didn't feel much like going home that night and she found herself, at the very end of a day that had begun with such meticulous planning, sleeping in the waiting room.

Christine hadn't thought once to ask what had happened, in all the chaos, to her mother. Lily shook her head and drifted off, wondering at all the problems their

59

family seemed to have. My family now, she thought; they're my problems too.

*

'I thought hospitals were short of beds,' Michael said, clicking the door shut behind them. He stared gloomily at the cramped space and hung his suit jacket on the oxygen cylinders stored against one wall. They looked to him like massive soda siphons.

Christine tossed down her veil and clutch bag. She plucked at the bloodstains on her silk. They had faded already to a sickly maroon. I'll never use this dress again anyway. She sat on the truckle bed, testing its springs.

'Mam ran off again. Did you see?'

Michael came to sit by her and the bed moved slightly on its castors, as if it wasn't used to the weight of two. 'No.'

'She pelted down the stairs. I thought she was coming with us, to get dad sorted. But I saw her, running off to the main road. Not even a backward glance.' Christine's tone was lifeless, as if she had no particular opinion of her mother.

'Let's not go over it now.'

'Do you know why they've asked us to stay tonight?'

'Well,' said Michael. 'Obviously they can see we've just got married. They're being . . .'

'Oh, don't be so thick. They've asked us to stay because they think he'll die tonight.'

'No . . . They said he was stable! They said he would pull through . . .'

Christine shrugged. 'They do. They think tonight's the night.'

Michael put a hand on her bare shoulder. It was freezing. It felt small under his hand; bonier than he remembered. 'He won't die. I promise.'

She touched his hand.

Michael tried to divert her. 'Anyway . . . tonight is the night, isn't it? For us?' He smiled.

Christine tugged her hand away from him.

'I only meant . . .'

'You wanker.'

'It was . . .'

'My poor bloody dad's fighting for his life on the other side of that wall and all you're thinking about is . . .' She shook her head at him. 'You can sleep on the floor. There's only room on this for me.'

Once the lights were off and they were both lying in the places Christine had decided, she tried to stay awake all night, listening for the sound of her father resuscitating through the thin wall. All she could hear was Michael breathing.

Just before she found herself going off to sleep she leaned down and tugged on the sleeve of the shirt he was sleeping in and told him he could get up on the slim bed if he was careful. She wanted him to hold her; she wanted something to hold.

Next thing, early, she felt the first of her morning sickness coming on. She lurched off the bed to grab one of the cardboard chamber pots that were stacked twenty deep in the corner of their room. Michael woke up and watched her, amazed.

*

Michael wished he had his car already. All of this ferrying about and hospital visiting would have been a lot simpler if he'd been able to drive them. His dream of having a hatchback seemed like a dream from a hundred years ago. He remembered talking about it with Dan like it was a certainty. The last few months he'd been piling dream upon dream; it seemed profligate and ridiculous now, like tempting fate. Thinking he could have a car, a wife, a child, and even go to Rome on honeymoon. He'd been asking for too much. It was like begging someone to come and kick it all in.

Now Christine would hardly leave the ward where her

father lay and Michael was going back and forth in buses and taxis with his Aunt. Lily, it seemed to him, had developed a whole new language lately; she communicated through these swift tongue-clicks and shakes of her head. She isn't her usual self, he thought and she isn't taking command at all. She didn't have too much else to say for herself and this made Michael feel worse. She told him when he should phone them a taxi home, and she prodded him to cajole Christine to come home too, but that was about it.

'If Christine's not going to come home,' said Lily, daringly, in the back of a cab during the first week, 'then I don't see any reason for you sleeping over at the Fletchers' place alone. That's silly. You'll feel like a housebreaker.'

He knew she was right. The sensible thing was to stay put at Lily's. But that idea filled him with dread. 'So,' he said. 'It's not only my honeymoon put on hold, it's my whole marriage.' Even to himself he sounded bitter.

'That's not the way to look at it, Michael, love.'

'Aunt Lily, when I go to the hospital, Christine looks at me like she doesn't even know who I am.'

'That's just concern.' Even so, Lily herself was concerned by Christine's dogged bed-watching and the bags under her eyes. And the last few times she and Michael had turned up at the private room, there had been other people there; ones that Lily recognised as other wedding guests. They would be standing with Christine, talking quietly, and when Lily and Michael came in they would look at the new arrivals like they were complete strangers. Maybe that's fair enough, Lily thought; maybe these were friends of Dan's from years back. Still, she felt for Michael having his nose pushed out.

Lily knew there were things Michael was bursting to talk to someone about, but she wasn't the woman for that job. In a taxi one night, coming home, he'd been complaining and said something like 'conjugal rights'. Lily threw up her hands and told him she didn't want to hear; he had no right trying to tell her such things. Michael fell quiet, hurt.

Just after this he started on about going back to work.

'Someone's got to bring home the bacon,' he said.

Normally Lily would have applauded this, and felt a glow of pride. Now she thought, that sounds heartless. And, who'll come with me to the hospital?

'But you've got two weeks off work,' she pointed out. 'You're supposed to be in Rome.' The bank had been very good to them.

'Well, I'm not in Rome, am I? And here . . . I'm less than useless. I might as well go back to work.'

That day, they had turned up at the hospital room and three of Christine's ex-boyfriends – in their greasy jeans and their tight t-shirts – had been sitting looking at her dad. Lily was frightened Michael might say something. She could imagine a fight breaking out over the tidy bed; tubes dislodged, popping out of Dan's nose, the heart monitor crashing to the floor . . .

But Michael had been quiet. She could feel him bristling, though, at the way Christine and the ex-boyfriends talked among themselves about her dad, and once again, for the duration of their visit, Michael and Lily were left staring into the old man's face.

'I don't suppose she'd notice if I never went to visit again,' Michael said.

'Oh, sure she would, Michael,' said Lily. 'I'm surprised at you. She's distracted, that's all. And remember how you were, when your mother was sick, hm?' Actually, thinking about it, Michael had been rather sanguine during that whole time. Thinking about his exams, thinking about moving towns. But wasn't that the way of it? The young lot had to be selfish, Lily thought, in order to be able to move on. It was how they survived. Still, Christine had gone up hugely in her estimation for the steadfastness of sitting by her father's bed.

Lily asked Michael not to go back to work just yet.

'When Christine looks at me, it's like she wants to throw up.'

Lily tutted. 'It's morning sickness. When she looks at anybody she wants to throw up.' Michael looked embarrassed now. 'You don't know much, do you?'

'Less and less each day.'

'You should read up about it, about babies and everything while she's busy with her dad. And that's another reason why you just have to go along with Christine. And why you have to forget about what you want for a bit, Michael. That babby she's got growing inside her. That's all down to you.' Then Lily gave him a look which Michael took to mean: You've had your fun and now you have to tag along and pay the price. Then their cab arrived in the darkened Avenue and they climbed out.

*

Aunt Lily was someone who'd never married, so there was no way she was ever going to understand. To her, it was all too clear cut. Life had no raggy edges. Michael's life was nothing but raggy edges, he thought, and the more he thought about it, the more it seemed it had always been like that. All this making up of an orderly life, of at last getting in with the bank and doing things properly, that had just been a pretence. As if he could change his whole life by cutting his hair and getting a decent job. Now he thought, that hadn't even been his own choice; he'd been reacting to what his mam had wanted for him. He was behaving well to appease her and she wasn't even here to see it. The only person he was appeasing now was Aunt Lily and she couldn't understand the things he might want. Christine had been one of those fast girls and look at her now. She looked middle-aged with worry.

Michael was ashamed of himself all over again.

At the end of the second week, though, Christine turned to him and said something directly. 'They reckon he's on the mend,' she said. To Michael and Lily, though,

64

there was no visible change. A slight fluting noise coming out of Dan's nose as the air hissed past the tube. 'It's the signs in his brains,' Christine said proudly. Michael thought about signs and portents; about dragging the entrails out of sacrificed animals. He wondered if the hospital was giving Christine false hope. But he was glad she wanted to tell him first.

'You look wrecked,' he told her, after she gave him a peck on the cheek and they sat down in the orange chairs.

'What Michael's trying to say,' Lily broke in, 'is that we've been talking and, if your dad is showing an improvement, you've got to start looking after yourself better.' She looked her niece-in-law up and down. Christine was back in her ratty clothes that her mother had hated so much. What had happened to the blushing bride?

'What if I miss him waking up?'

It sounded like a fair enough answer to Lily.

'He'd think everyone had abandoned him. He'd be scared.'

Michael said, 'It can't be good for the baby, you sitting around here, hunched over, drinking machine coffee.' And smoking outside in the rain, he thought. He'd seen her in the foyer once or twice, sucking greedily on cigarettes. They'd driven up to her in a taxi and found her like this, looking like someone who'd escaped.

'Don't tell me what to do,' she said quietly and sounded, Michael thought, very much like her dad. The quiet voice that seems like it isn't in control, that it doesn't get the last word.

Michael knew enough to leave well alone.

*

'What we should do,' Lily said in the cab, afterwards. 'is get some shopping in for her. We should stop somewhere now and buy a whole lot of stuff and fill the Fletchers' house with provisions.'

Michael couldn't see the point.

'I think she's cracking,' Lily said. 'I think she's coming home. Especially if her dad really is getting better. The nurses will bully her to come home. We could get their house all ready and welcoming. We can tell her that it's all ready for her and she hasn't got to worry about coming back to somewhere dark and bleak.'

Michael got their driver to stop at a large supermarket on their route back home.

'Will he wait for us?' asked Lily anxiously. She stared at the huge supermarket. She'd never been to one like this before. It was the kind of place where people with cars went and stocked up with food for a week.

'We can phone another taxi from here, when we've finished.'

'They've got phones and everything,' said Lily, marvelling at the size of the car park, and how busy it seemed.

*

These were her first set of automatic doors. As they walked up to them, Lily was amazed by the easy way other shoppers hardly even paused to let the glass doors swish open. They seemed used to them and were confident that they would work and not trap them inside or squash them flat. Or leave them standing on the outside and refuse to budge. She stepped onto the sensitive doormat and smiled with real pleasure when they parted. Her smile irritated Michael. He hid this by going to fetch a trolley.

'You've been here before,' she told him, looking at a stall of fresh cut flowers and a queue at a cigarette stand.

'We take turns to go out and fetch sandwiches for work,' he said.

'Sandwiches!' she said. But hadn't Michael talked about getting his lunch from Christine's bakery? He'd said the bakery's sandwiches were nice. But he preferred the ones the supermarket made, it seemed. He was shoving the trolley through another set of glass doors and Lily was surprised at how many aisles there were, and how many checkouts down one wall of the place.

The noise was surprising, too. She'd always had the idea that these big places were for younger people, for families starting out, and it seemed it was true. There were young couples going about with toddlers hanging off their trolleys. They were buying things in bulk. She liked to do her own shopping closer to home, bit by bit every day, making a trip out of going to different shops, but she could see the sense in this kind of arrangement. This place must have everything you could possibly need, all under one fluorescent roof. It was like a thing of the future.

Now she could imagine why Michael wanted a hatch-back. She could see him with Christine, loading up a trolley, a toddler strapped into the trolley's seat; and they'd be collecting up more stuff than two people could ever carry between them.

'When I get a car,' said Michael, as they came into the fresh fruit aisle, 'We could get your week's shopping as well, Aunt Lily.' He must have been thinking along the same lines she was.

'Christine might have her own ideas about what she wants to do on a Saturday. Why would she want to do an old lady's groceries?' Lily was glad Michael was talking about the future again. Pushing his trolley down the clean lino of these aisles – aisles wide as motorways, they seemed like – had made him brave and expansive.

'This is what it must be like in America,' his aunt said.

She spent some time examining the chickens and the pork joints in the fridge cabinets. She didn't like the way they came ready wrapped up in cellophane. It made it look less like meat. You couldn't touch them properly for quality. Also, the flickering light made things look sickly and unappetising. Nothing to do with food at all. It put her in mind of the hospital again.

'What would Margaret say,' she said, choosing a chicken for Sunday at last, 'if she knew we were filling up her fridge?'

'I don't suppose she'd care now,' said Michael. He's picking up daft things, Lily thought. The kind of things you'd never really eat. Paté. That white kind of cheese flecked with blue. She wondered if he was buying things just to impress the other people who went past, glancing into his trolley on the way.

'Oh, she would care,' said Lily.

'She's a strange woman,' he said. 'When I first saw her, I thought, well, she's a proper sort of mumsy mum. Like, she was all house proud and wanted to do everything right. When I first went round she talked like the Queen. And then did you see her, when she turned up at the reception? She looked like she'd been living rough.'

'She turned up, though,' said Lily. They were heading towards the tins aisle now, she saw. If there was a nuclear war, you could live off these tins for years.

'Yeah, but as soon as Dan had his accident, she soon buggered off again.' He was plucking tins of baked beans, butter beans and sweetcorn off the shelves without even looking at the labels or comparing prices. 'There's something really funny about that.'

Lily thought about Margaret that night and how she'd hardly been like the woman she knew. That strange tweed suit, her hair all wild. 'What's that supposed to mean?'

'I reckon she came back to do just what she did,' said Michael. 'She pushed him off that old fire escape, didn't she?'

'Michael!' Lily hissed. 'People will hear you talking like that! That's libellous.'

'Tell me that's not what happened.'

'It was not! I was there! You weren't!'

'If I know you, Aunt Lily, she could have gone running out there with a carving knife and killed him and you would still say she'd not meant any harm. You know what's wrong with you? You're too nice.'

They wheeled on towards the dairy products and Lily felt rather pleased with herself. 'Michael, I saw. It was an accident. He slipped . . . they were making it up at the time! I looked away for a second because they were kissing, and next thing I knew he had . . .' She lowered her voice again. ' . . . been sick a bit more and he slipped and . . . fell.'

'So you weren't looking then? At that precise moment?'

'Well . . . no . . .'

'See?' Michael hefted out a carton of what must have been six pints of milk. 'She pushed him. She wanted him dead.'

'That's a wicked thing to say.'

Michael's attention had slipped to something else. 'Look.' There was a papier mâché cow's head sticking out of the wall by the milk cartons. Life sized. Michael pushed a button and it gave a melancholic, pre-recorded moo.

He's a child, Lily thought. Talking like this, he'll get someone into trouble.

As their trolley filled up and Lily vaguely wondered how they were going to pay for all this stuff, she found her thoughts going back to Margaret. Her neighbour, at her own daughter's wedding in that peculiar disguise. Lily still felt guilty for not trying to find Margaret in this past fortnight, to tell her that Dan was still alive. But there had been things to do, bigger things to pay attention to. Lily could hardly bear to think of Margaret still running about the place in her ripped stockings. Out of her mind because she thought Dan had been killed. In her heart of hearts Lily thought that was why Margaret had fled. It was all panic.

And did she, like Michael clearly did, think herself to blame? The poor woman must be distraught. She could be lying in a ditch somewhere.

As they stocked up on toiletries – toilet rolls in boxes of twenty-four! – Lily let herself ponder what Michael had said. What if she had missed something in that second she had glanced away? She was only being polite and letting them have a moment alone. But what if Margaret had given him one quick, flat-handed shove over the edge? You weren't ever to know what went on in a marriage. There could have been any number of covered-up reasons for Margaret suddenly going insane. She'd looked a bit insane, that night. For the first time since then Lily was allowing herself to revolve the possibilities about Margaret, as she tried to concentrate on the things they would need.

The flickering lights were giving her a headache. A blinding one. They couldn't be good for you, lights like these. Lily hadn't had a migraine in three years, but it looked like she might have one coming now. It was down to the lights. When she tried to look at things on the shelves she was starting to see dark spots in front of her eyes. Michael had noticed she was distracted. He was impatient with her. He was picking up fancy shampoos for his wife. He didn't know what it was like, getting migraines. How Lily had been plagued by them all her life. She was waiting for the coloured spots – indigo, green, acid orange – to come crowding in, and then she'd be sure of what was happening to her.

The fact is, someone's going to have to find out about Margaret soon. If anything happens to Dan – if the worst happens – she'll need to be notified.

Lily let go of the trolley and gasped. Her hand went up to her forehead.

Michael was staring nonplussed at washing powders and he noticed their trolley sliding past without his aunt behind it.

'Aunt Lily?'

Her face was stuck in a wince. Her eyes were jammed shut.

'Those blessed lights have brought a migraine on,' she said. 'I'm not coming in here again.'

Through the flashing coloured lights she clung to one lucid thought: the future gives me a headache.

Michael sighed and retrieved their almost-complete shopping. 'Let's get you home,' he said. He only had a small amount of sympathy left, he found, even though Lily's face was white and she looked like she'd drop at any moment. He was sick of hanging around sick and older people.

He grasped her elbow, to help her along like a real old lady. She shrugged him off.

'No,' she said, frowning even more heavily.

Michael was embarrassed now. Other shoppers – one of the younger couples, with a kid tagging along, eating crisps – sailed by and gave him and his aunt a curious look. She was touching both temples now with her hands. She'd gone into a trance to fend off the pain. He felt ashamed of her standing there in her self-knitted cardy, brown with cream piping; her old-woman's skirt, probably home-made, too, her woolly ribbed stockings. I must look like a daft lad out with her. And now this little display!

'Someone,' said Aunt Lily in a shaky voice. 'Is trying to tell me something.'

Still holding her head in her hands, carrying it so carefully like a giant egg, she walked away from both him and the trolley. She was heading for the exit.

'Get me a taxi.'

She didn't even sound like his Aunt Lily. 'We have to pay first,' he said, and, even to himself he sounded whingy. 'We have to go through the checkouts.'

Michael started to bolt back for the trolley.

'Leave it,' she said. 'We haven't got time.' She let out another gasp.

'Look,' he began, fiercely. Then she grasped his arm and pinched it hard, as if it was him that was in a dream.

'We have to go back to the hospital. Right now.'

'What?'

'I can see it clear as day,' she said. 'He's . . . coming through.'

Michael gaped at her.

'Get us a taxi, Michael!'

'How can you possibly know what . . . ?'

Her eyes flew open. 'Get on that bloody phone, sunshine.'

Aunt Lily never swore. Michael found himself doing precisely as she directed. He was abandoning their shopping. He was hurrying to the phone cubicles. He was checking that Aunt Lily was following behind him, and she was, marching like a sleep walker. He was ringing them a cab that would take them straight to the place they had so recently escaped.

*

In the lift up to Dan's floor she almost fainted. There was a sickly smell in there, of oil and grease, and it couldn't have helped her migraine. She sagged against him and he was surprised at how little and frail she felt. He put his arms around her, just like he had when they were dancing. Even then she had felt more substantial. His aunt was wasting away in front of him.

'We're here now,' he whispered to her. 'We're almost there.' It was as if he was taking her in for treatment.

'I've never felt it like this before,' she said, leaning against him.

The lift doors pinged open.

The corridor seemed just the same as usual. For a moment or two in the taxi, Michael really wondered if his aunt was right. She was supposed to have something of the Second Sight. His mam had always said it was true. Just because he didn't understand it didn't mean she mightn't see things. So he'd gone along with it and arrived half expecting the corridors to be hectic with doctors running to Dan's room, their white coat tails flapping. Christine to be standing waiting at the lift, announcing that everything had come right.

But it was quiet. An old woman in a nightie shuffling towards them wearing a shower hat and holding a rolled up Woman's Weekly like a baton in a relay race.

In Dan's small room they found no change either.

Christine looked up as they burst in, clearly expecting someone else.

'What are you back for?'

Then she saw the state Aunt Lily was in.

'She's had a turn,' Michael said.

Lily tottered forward and looked for a moment as if she was going to collapse on the bed beside Dan. She put both palms down on the pink candlewick bedspread and took a couple of ragged breaths. Conserving strength, Michael thought. What's she playing at?

'It was a turn, all right,' said Lily, 'the likes of which I've never known.'

Then she reached out and put her hands to Dan's forehead.

Christine jumped. 'What are you doing?'

Michael held her. 'Leave her be . . . for a second.' He found himself restraining his wife.

You could see the tips of Lily's fingers turning white with the pressure she was pushing onto Dan's temples.

'I'm getting a nurse,' Christine said. 'Get off him!'

Lily had lowered her head and they stared at the white curls of her nape, her creased old-lady's neck.

Then she dropped her hands, stepped back and sank into a plastic chair.

'She's fallen asleep,' Michael said.

'Dad?' Christine was saying. Her voice was very high.

Michael looked up to see Dan staring furiously back at him.

*

In the end, after all the excitement and relief and, once she'd regathered her wits, Aunt Lily standing there snapping photos of them in the hospital room, Christine found herself getting disgusted with the lot of them. Dad was back to life and the nurses came dashing and, later on, the doctors came strolling in, all declaring him almost back to normal, a miracle recovery, a chance in however many thousand. Once they'd all said this and the official news was out, it seemed like everyone could go back to normal. But Christine couldn't join in with the collective sigh of relief. You'd think it was everyone else who'd sat with him day and night, willing him back to life. It was like they all owned him and shared a part of his – baffled, hesitant – triumph.

And as for all the attention that old Lily Woods got! That was the most embarrassing thing of all. They clapped her dowager's hump and they pumped her tiny hand. Every visitor who popped their head round the door wanted to hear the tale of Lily laying on the hands. And everyone had an ailing relation that Lily might be good enough to go and visit. Dan lay there as Christine told the story again and again. He listened with a frown (since waking his wrinkles and creases had started to reappear) and all he could recall was blinking open his eyes the moment Lily sank, exhausted, into the chair. Of the kerfuffle on the fire escape and his fall, he could remember nothing at all. His life ran in one seamless cut from dancing with his daughter at her wedding, to waking up here and these faces looking at him. He had nothing more to add. Maybe that's just as well, Christine thought.

The visitors and wedding guests that turned up seemed rather disappointed that there was no more dramatic side to Dan's near death experience. No revolving tunnel of light, no angels, no heavenly voice telling him his time hadn't come yet. He was such a disappointment to them! They were relieved to see him, but they also wanted telling about the other side. The attention moved over to Lily; who, as the layer-on-of-hands, would be bound to have an answer or two. At least Lily Woods had had the good sense to take herself home and keep a low profile for a week or so. She had told Michael that the experience had, not surprisingly, sapped her and she needed to rest.

Christine thought it was all bullshit coincidence and superstition. She wouldn't listen when Michael started on about his aunt's fit of prescience in the supermarket. All Christine cared about was how soon her dad could come home.

He didn't talk much.

Not that that was much to worry about. Dan Fletcher had never talked a whole lot anyway; and when he did it was quietly, modestly. The last time she had seen him talk was her wedding day and it had been surprising at the time, how forthcoming he'd been. Suddenly telling her, all emotional, things like what it meant to be her dad. The accident had happened, sent him into a sleep, deep inside himself, and he'd come back as the quiet dad she knew. Nothing to be worried about there. But it was odd, to sit by his bedside in visiting hours, and for not much to be said. For the room to be as quiet as it had been before.

For the last few days he was kept under observation, they put him in a ward with lots of other men. The others, still in the thick of their worries and illnesses, tried to get him chatting in that way they did to keep their spirits up. Like they were all in the army. Christine watched him rebuff them. He had no interest in them. He stared blankly at their wives when they came to visit, bringing fruit and books about warships and fighter planes. He smiled when his daughter turned up, but most of the time Dan's smile was distant. He looked like he was trying to snag some memory.

'You don't have to be there so often now,' Michael said to her one night.

She was looking in the fridge. It was still empty.

Since Dan had woken they had both been sleeping where they were supposed to, at the Fletchers' house, though they hadn't yet coincided in the same bed. Michael was back at work and sleeping regular, night-time hours, and Christine was tumbling into bed whenever she could. They hadn't actually lain side by side at home yet and Michael thought that odd.

It was as if they were warming up the house for Dan's homecoming. But they were spreading the heat very thinly.

Since Michael had moved in they had been living off take-aways and fish-finger sandwiches. For all of Lily's good intentions, the house on Christine's return was as bleak and foodless as she'd feared. Michael watched Christine staring into the fridge and thought about their filled trolley abandoned in the supermarket aisle. But he knew he couldn't go into that story with Christine again.

'I said, you won't have to go up to the hospital so much now. He'll be out soon.'

She slammed the fridge shut. 'I have to go more now, if anything. He needs someone to talk to. What kind of logic is that? Once he's awake, leave him lying by himself to get lonely?'

Michael opened his bag of crisps. He wondered if he should say something about the bakery. They'd phoned three times to find out when Christine was coming back. She was meant to be back from her honeymoon by now.

'Yeah, maybe you're right,' he said. Then he thought, this is how it's always going to be. She makes herself sound fierce and right, and then I just give in.

She put the kettle on. 'I'm going to bed soon.'

It was going to be their first proper night together. He wondered if she realised the oddness of that. Truth be told, they hadn't slept together much at all. When they'd had sex, three times in total, it had been on the couch in the Fletchers' front room, late at night. He'd been amazed that neither Dan nor Margaret came down to disturb them. Christine had been guiltless and brazen, turning up the gas fire and shucking her jeans in the dim light and this had excited him so that he was hard and sticky before she'd even touched him. That seems like years ago, he thought.

When he'd visited in daylight hours and had to make small talk with her parents, he'd blushed whenever he sat on the settee, sitting in the same place where he'd been jammed with Christine in a mound of cushions, the anti-macassars slipping all over and making them laugh.

They'd never slept together, though. He hadn't even seen her completely naked. She had only seen him with his suit trousers down to his knees, his white shirt yanked up to his throat. It felt like they had never really been vulnerable to each other.

Now she was saying, 'Are you ready for bed?' and he could hardly believe it. Any thought of Dan or the hospital, or his Aunt Lily fretting at home across the street, went out of his mind. Christine was asking him to come to bed – however dull-voiced and ordinary she sounded doing it – and it seemed like proper life was going to start again.

4
The Loudest Shouters

How long was it since she'd seen Brian? He'd been standing round her dad's bed with the other lads. Just after her dad recovered. He'd smuggled drink in for them all, to toast her dad like he was a baby. She hadn't seen him since.

It was months now. She had spent a full sweltering summer growing larger and larger. She'd seen hardly anyone. And now here Brian was, unexpected, standing in the rain. Christine had to let him in. What could she do? It was pitch dark. He had rainwater streaming off his nose. She let him follow her quietly down the hallway to the kitchen and gave him a clean tea towel to dry his hair. They both laughed then, because he'd lost all of his long blond hair. He'd had the whole lot shaved off. It was the new style.

She had hardly recognised him at first, standing in the dark at their front door. She opened it without a thought that it might be dangerous. She hadn't thought once about using the little chain that Michael had fitted on the door.

Brian was still in his ripped jeans and the denim jacket he had painted himself. On the back, Jesus at the Last Supper, holding a spliff up to his lips. Lips very much like Brian's own. He came stomping into the kitchen in his same old bovver boots and Christine was reminded of those times when he was just another loud, obnoxious boyfriend invited round to upset her mother.

Now he was gentle; not letting her do anything for him. Making her sit down at the kitchen table and letting her settle. She sank gratefully back on the wooden chair, her spine uncricking gradually against the hard slats. She pressed her hands down on her stomach and felt exposed, suddenly, sitting there in her nightie.

'I'm huge, aren't I?'

He was emptying tea leaves straight into the sink. He shook out the pot and watched the dark clots drop. Michael would have a fit. He hated that. He always said, it would be him, later, who'd have to unblock the U-bend.

How nice, she thought. How nice to have this fella come round and make his own cup of tea.

'I wouldn't say huge, exactly.' He grinned, showing tiny, pointed teeth. Christine felt sticky and uncomfortable as he started to get mugs out and spoons from the drawer. She could also feel the fingers tapping at her again. Rap-tap-tapping from the inside, right down on her fanny. The wrong way round to feel sexy. Rap-tap-tapping like the little goats wanting permission to cross the bridge. Tiny hands – and four of them – keen to get out.

'It's twins I'm having,' she explained. 'Isn't that just my luck?'

He was spooning new tea leaves. 'Michael must have more balls than I thought.'

She grimaced, and then felt bad for laughing behind Michael's back.

'He won't mind me being round, will he? I only came to see you were all right. Old mates, and all.'

'It's fine. Honest.'

'That's what kept me away before, really. I mean, I'd go spare if my lass had her exes coming round to check on her . . .'

'Honest, Brian. He's not even here. He's out with his Aunt Lily somewhere.'

'Oh, yeah?'

'Some kind of meeting. Church.'

As the kettle whistled on the hob, Brian got up to finish making the tea. Christine watched his tight little bum in his jeans. Michael had let himself turn a bit flabbier these past few months, as if he was keeping pace and growing along with her. The two of them even laughed about it sometimes. Now, though, she couldn't remember what a tight little bum looked like in the flesh. Or what anyone else besides Michael looked like in the nude.

She didn't like to look at herself in the nude these days: her belly hard and huge, her titties like melons, the nipples out like saucers. It was like somebody else's body. When she was a small person, really. She had always been a small person . . .

Now she couldn't even remember if, when she and Brian had been going out (When she'd been sixteen, wasn't it? That long ago?) they'd ever had sex. She'd been so free and easy then. Memorable things had been easy come and easy go. But she had let the memory of whatever happened with Brian go and there was no getting it back now. She would no more ask Brian straight out – Brian, did we ever do it with each other? – than she'd ask him to make love to her tonight, here on the kitchen table. Make love to this vast new her.

The idea of even lying down on a hard table made her flinch. It put her in mind of a doctor. A shiny, busy, bald pate bobbing between her knees. Some professional anti-septic-smelling man, shining a pen torch up her and giving his considered opinion.

There was a thump and a gruff muffled curse from above as Brian put their steaming mugs down on the oilcloth.

'Is that your dad upstairs?'

She nodded. 'He's doing the spare room up as a nursery. He hasn't stopped for days. He works through the night sometimes, painting and that. He's scared the twins will be born before he gets it done.'

'He's a star, that man.'

Christine sipped her tea. Blew on it, sipped it again.

'I mean, how many fellas come round after . . . like, an accident like he had? How many live to tell the tale? And to still be up and about on his feet . . . doing things round the house . . . I think he's a star.'

Now that Christine thought about it, Brian was one of the few boyfriends that her parents didn't mind so much.

He *was* interested in things they were interested in. He asked Dan about his gardening and about his little building jobs. So even if he looked as rough as the rest (even rougher than some; broader, more muscular; he let his hair grow longer and he wore that denim jacket boasting that he took drugs), even so, they still gave Brian a tacit measure of approval. At least, in comparison to the other boys that braved the Fletchers' porch. Christine remembered now: part of the reason she'd chucked him and moved on – No hard feelings, right, mate? – was her parents' relative enthusiasm for him.

'Dad's been making these little animals out of balsa wood and painting them. He's going to stick them on the walls of the nursery. They're really good! Except – the monkeys give me the creeps a bit.'

Brian shook his head. 'Dan can turn his hand to anything.'

'He always could.'

'So he's just the same as ever?'

It felt like Brian was probing her. His questions were like, and moved with the same blind, insistent rhythm of, those twenty fingers inside of her. Playing 'twenty questions' with her. She breathed out and tried not to grow irritated.

'Michael says he's moody,' she said.

'Ah, well.'

'That's what I say. He's got a right to be moody!' Christine lowered her voice. 'He's lucky to be alive, I say, but Michael reckons he's changed.'

'How?' There he was again with his how and why.

'I can't get out shopping now, right? I can't even leave the bloody house. And Michael's got this new hatchback thing. He goes driving out to the Superstore for all the shopping and he takes dad to help him. Off they go, happy as Larry . . . except two hours go by and then they're back at last . . . both of them in a foul mood, slamming the car doors, the front door, slinging the carrier bags on the kitchen table. Then both of them go storming out. Dad down to his outhouse and Michael off to God knows where. And Muggins here has to unpack all the shopping.'

She warmed her hands on the sides of the mug. 'Afterwards neither of them would say what it was all about. I keep imagining them. Yelling up and down the supermarket aisles. Everyone looking at them.'

'Well,' said Brian. 'Two fellas out like that. They're bound to argue.'

'Are they?' Christine had cornered Michael about it that night when they both lay under their Continental quilt and the house was quiet about them. Christine hated that silence. She'd keep hearing growls underneath the windows and banging on pipes that sounded like hammers. She often spoke in the night, just to make some noise.

Michael said, 'I'll tell you, Christine. I've never seen anything like it. That temper of his. It came out of nowhere . . .'

'But that's not what my dad is like.'

'It is now.'

'What did you say to get him angry?'

'I never said anything! One minute he's picking up bread, the next he's screaming blue murder at me for moving the trolley away . . .'

Christine thought Michael was just having a go. He was trying to pick fault and really, he had no right.

Brian shrugged. 'That Michael. He's a bit stiff though, isn't he? I can see that getting on Dan's nerves.'

He made it sound so straightforward. Christine could see the sense of what he said. She'd been so long finding the best of Michael, not picking fault with him, she'd missed out the blindingly obvious. Sooner or later – bang on the head or no bang on the head – her father was going to decide that Michael was a prat.

Sometimes she would watch Michael glaring at Dan, when he thought no one was paying attention. Dan in his velour swivel chair, like the Captain of their ship. Dan would be rocking in it, laughing at the Benny Hill Show. Michael, glaring at him, disgusted.

Christine would think then: Michael is coveting my dad's chair. He's jealous of dad still being man of the house. He wants dad out.

But to Christine, her dad was still Captain of their collective ship. During this sodden autumn, as Christine drifted through the house in muggy, oversized night-dresses and slopped about in slippers, she felt as if she was full-bellied in the wind. She was a ship about to set sail and she was taking the whole house with her. In the billowing nights, timbers were groaning and tethers were aching to snap. And the Captain was still her dad. He sat in his plush swivel chair and Michael was on the settee, mutinous.

'Is Michael still at the bank, then?' Brian asked.

Christine nodded. She was getting properly suspicious of him now. Not even before, when he'd been for some reason anxious to grease in with her parents, had he been such a careful question master. Still she found herself opening out to him; hands on her swollen belly; holding forth.

'He's been taking all these exams. Says it will mean more money in the end. They take him off on courses. Put him in hotels and the bank pays for it.'

'They must think a lot of him.'

'He's the brains in this house.'

'You made the right choice, I think, Christy. You're better off with the likes of him. Not a waster like me, eh?'

She looked down at her hands and didn't know what to say. Tonight she felt heavier than ever. The rain on the kitchen windows was making her hypersensitive.

I never used to be like this. It's funny. Brian's talking to me like I've made a success of myself. But what have I done, really?

'Here.' Brian had a bottle of whisky stashed inside his jacket. A handsized bottle from which he splashed some into their mugs, just like her dad always did. How big his fingers looked round the bottle. 'Drink up. I didn't come here to make you all miserable, you know.'

'Was I looking miserable?'

'A second ago you were.' He held out his mug for her to clunk with her own. 'There. You're brighter now.' He narrowed his eyes at her. 'You are happy with Michael, now, aren't you?'

'You're taking the piss.'

'Would I?'

'Yes, you would.'

'I'm asking harmless questions.'

'Harmless!'

'There's no harm in questions, now.'

The question was: how happy could Christine be, given the circumstances? Relieved, of course, that her dad was safe and well; back to normal. Relieved that the twins were (touch formica) okay so far, and everything was on course. Relieved that . . . relieved that she was married to Michael. Yes he was a prat, in many ways, with his natty suits and his talking about bank stuff. With his estate car and his plans for moving up in the world . . . and yes, he wasn't sexy like Brian was. He would never have the effect on her that Brian could, just by breathing his tea and whisky breath at her . . .

But she was thinking, at the same time, of Michael falling asleep as she lay there each night. Her feeling stupefied and heavy, but liking the comfort of his surprisingly hairy legs against her. (Not a scrap of hair on his chest, though.) She even liked his paunch. She touched it for comfort almost as often as he felt her belly. So Christine was quite confident about how she felt just recently. If Brian asked anything more, there were answers she could give him.

'But I want to know,' she said, after he'd slopped whisky into their mugs a second time. 'I want to know who you're asking this for.'

His grin subsided a little. He clucked his tongue. 'There was never any shitting you, was there, Christine Fletcher?'

'No fucking chance. Tell me what you're up to.'

Brian sucked a slow breath through his jagged teeth. 'It's your mam, Christine. Your mam's been getting me to ask about you.'

*

Lily had to tell him not to look around.

'There's nothing to see. It looks like any other church.'

'I want to see the kind of people that come here.'

The two of them had arrived early and Lily parked them near the front, right under the pulpit. Michael was craning around to look at the other visitors, mostly pensioners, in dribs and drabs, dressed up against the weather. The small church was starting to smell of damp wool.

'And when the service and everything starts,' Lily added quietly, 'You certainly can't go looking round at everybody. You're supposed to face front and not look, if someone's getting a message. It's rude and it might break the contact.'

'Not even if it's really interesting?'

She smiled at that. 'Not even then.'

'You've become quite the expert, Aunt Lily.'

She'd been coming to the church for a few months now. The couple who ran it and a number of the regulars would nod at her when she arrived. Tonight they had all been taking a good look at her guest. She wondered if they thought Michael was her young man.

The pastor and his wife were shuffling onto their podium. Seeing the two of them together always made Lily want to laugh. He was tiny and she was gargantuan, with the biggest beehive Lily had ever seen. Both of them dyed their hair jet black. She wondered if they did it together, standing over the bath. Or maybe they both pretended to each other that this was natural and they dyed themselves secretly. The two of them were chatting with another couple on the stage. The out-of-towners. The medium and her husband. He was in a neat grey suit and his hair was silver. She was in midnight blue silk and her hair was frosted gold. Her eye make-up was bruise coloured and she looked altogether too dramatic, Lily thought. She was taking notes on how these things were run.

'They're about to start,' she hissed to Michael.

'I hope this is going to be good,' he said, sitting up straighter on the pew. He was starting to wonder why he'd ever agreed to accompany her. It looked just like ordinary church, like religious church. There was even an old woman on an organ; one hand pressing out ominous chords and the other diddling out a tune that wouldn't keep still.

'Oh, I hope it's worth it. But you never can tell with peripatetic mediums. They go up and down in quality.'

Boys in white shirts and black trousers were going along the rows with golden plates. Lily nudged Michael and produced her own ten pence piece. This was another thing that was like normal church. He wondered what they could want money for.

The young man pushed the plate under his nose discreetly. There was already a fair bit of money there. Aunt Lily tossed her coin in and Michael dug into his trouser pockets. When he looked up the boy was smiling at him. His hair was trimmed short; wetted and combed into a flick. Michael had an impulse to flatten it where it had sprang free. He looked in his hand to see what change he had. He was taking too long. The organist had finished and the woman with the large beehive was starting to talk. Still that boy stood there, until Michael emptied his whole handful of change onto the plate with a clatter. Then the boy smiled again. It wasn't a happy-clappy smile. It turned up at the ends. It was an odd smile and Michael didn't return it. The boy winked at him and turned smartly on his heel and went to the back of the church as the announcements were read.

'Healing the Sick Night has moved again,' the woman with the black hair read from her sheaf of notes. 'Now it's Wednesday. It will still be held in the crypt. Old Time dancing is on Tuesdays now.'

Lily was nudging Michael again. He glanced at her and she was mouthing, 'Healing the Sick,' as if it was a secret they shared.

Then the woman in charge gave a long speech about two young women in America who had invented Spiritualism a hundred years ago, and look what a boon they had brought the world. Michael was surprised it was such a recent thing. The woman moved onto a quick discussion about the Two Worlds and how they were connected by a group of terribly important, sensitive people and she finished up by introducing one of them to the congregation.

The woman in the blue silk with the golden hair stood up promptly. She was introduced only as Sheila. Michael had been watching her throughout the speech. Her eyes had been like a hawk's; raking the occupied pews. She looked as if she was already muttering under her breath.

Sheila stood in the pulpit and said that, as she had to have a little longer to power up, they might all like to stand and sing her favourite song, 'The More I See You'. The pastor hurried around to the front, put his leg up on one step, rested his guitar on it and started to strum as the congregation stood.

Sheila continued to gaze at the singers and her finger-tips were touching her temples. Lily was nudging Michael again and again now, as if she had lost all control over her elbow.

*

'You've got to believe it was an accident,' Brian was saying. 'A complete coincidence. I walked into a pub and there she was. I'd have recognised her anywhere and she could tell it was me, straight off. She did a little double-take, but I'd seen through her disguise. She was in a pinny and her hair was grey and she wore marigolds and she was smoking a fag as she emptied the ashtrays, but there was no mistaking Margaret.'

'But where was this?' burst Christine. 'Where is she?'

'I got her to talk to me. I knew you'd want to know. I made her take a break and sit down with me in a cubicle. She had a bitter lemon.'

'Where?'

'She won't let me tell you exactly. She says if I do, she'll move again and there'll be no finding her this time. All I can say is that it's a village not too far from town. She didn't go that far at all.'

'But why? Why did she go there, Brian?'

'She wouldn't tell me much. I should have said that at the start. I reckon she'd had a breakdown or something. She was different. All she wanted to hear about was you lot. About your father. And how you and Michael . . . and the baby was getting on.'

'And you told her?'

'Of course. But I promised I'd find out more for her and tell her . . . give her a message from you.'

Christine put her face in her hands. 'You shouldn't have told her anything. You could have forced her to come and see for herself.'

She waited for him to say something, but it never came. She took her hands away from her eyes and looked at him. Brian's face was slack. He nodded.

"Evening, Dan.'

Christine turned awkwardly in her chair – a stab then, an odd twinge – to see her father in the kitchen doorway. In his painting clothes, streaked with pink. He was still holding a wet brush and an open tin of pink. His face was black with fury.

'You'll TELL her NOTHING. You had NO fucking business INTERFERING anyway!'

'Dad . . . !'

'Keep OUT of this, you fucking SLUT. If it weren't for YOU anyway there'd never BE any of this.'

Brian was on his feet. He moved towards Dan. 'Look, there's no need to get, like . . .'

'Don't TALK to ME in my HOUSE!' Dan screamed and hurled the pot across the room.

The paint disgorged itself across the table and the floor and the tin itself crashed through the kitchen window. There was an explosion of glass and pink. The wind and the rain came into the room and everyone started shouting.

'I DON'T want that fucking whore's NAME mentioned in this house AGAIN! Do you HEAR me? She's a fucking WHORE!'

'Okay, all right, Dan, just . . .'

'Dad! Calm down . . . you'll . . .'

Dan was pacing the room, kicking at the chairs. He gave the oilcloth a yank and cleared everything off the table. Tea pot, mugs, the lot went crashing to the floor.

'Dad . . . !' Christine's arms went over her belly.

Dan grabbed at Brian's jacket and slung it at him. 'GET your filthy ARSE out of my house. Sniffing round my WIFE and my fucking DAUGHTER! Are they both WHORES that you can have, eh? IS that what you want, you cunt?'

Brian faced up to the onslaught. Dan was throwing his fists around now and Brian gave a shrug, as if to say he'd crack him back, if that's what he was looking for.

'Brian, just go.' Christine said. 'He won't calm down till you've gone. It'll be all right.'

'I can't leave you with this..!'

She grew shrill. 'Just go, Brian! Fuck off!'

He looked stung for a second. Dan stopped slapping at him and leered. 'See?' His voice returned to its usual pitch. 'Even that bitch doesn't want you round.'

Brian looked at her. 'Christine?'

She was biting her lip. 'Fuck off, Brian.'

'Right.'

Dan listened for the front door slamming behind him. 'Good riddance,' he said, and threw open the back door. Then he marched smartly out into the dark.

Christine sat in the gale from the smashed window and put her face down on the cool, bare formica of the table. She felt stinging drops of rain on her face. Then the pains began in earnest.

*

'You've got to promise me, lover, that first thing in the morning you'll get yourself to the doctor. I know you don't like going and your husband knows as well. He's telling me that. But we can see inside you and you have got to go.'

The medium gave a nod and pointed again at the woman in the back row. 'Do you promise us, now?'

Michael was itching to turn round and look. He guessed that everyone else was too. In fact, Aunt Lily had half-turned her head and was casting a sly glance back along the pews.

'Yes,' promised a faint voice from the back of the church.

Sheila beamed and dismissed the woman with a wave of her hand. She moved on to a woman in Michael's row.

'I've got your husband now. He's telling me . . . what? Speak up, sweetheart. He's telling me that he's glad you never buried him in that red jumper. Did he tell you? He hated that jumper you knitted him. The one with the round neck.'

'That's right, I did . . .'

'Don't tell me, lover. He's saying the round neck used to irritate him. He used to tell you, he liked V-necks better. But he's glad you never buried the jumper with him . . .'

'It's still in the wardrobe at home . . .'

But the medium had moved on.

'I'm looking for Margie, Margaret, Mandy . . . No, some-one beginning with L . . . an older lady. With a gentleman called Derek who's gone over. I've got Derek now . . . no, I've got someone talking about a Derek who's still on our side . . .

'Can anyone on this side of the room . . .' She swept her arm to encompass Michael's half of the church. 'Can any of you lot claim a Derek still in this world?'

Michael was impressed at the pace of the whole performance. He wondered if the people Sheila had shouted at so far could have been planted. She was getting lots of details right. But most of the stuff she was saying so far was about things like jumpers and standard lamps, as if the whole thing was a process of verification: matching up the living with the correct dead. And then she would move on, as if that was as much as people needed to know.

He was veering between dread and hope that he would be picked. There seemed no hard and fast rule to who would come through. The way Sheila cupped her ear and scrunched her face made it seem that only the loudest shouters on the other side stood a chance of being heard. Wasn't that just like life on this side? It made even the afterlife seem like the playground.

Lily gave him a supportive look and touched his knee. Whatever she'd said at the start about church protocol, she'd forgotten it all now. Whenever someone was getting a message she didn't care about having a look at them.

Then the medium was staring straight at Lily.

'You've got a Derek on this side. I've got an older lady talking about a Derek.'

Lily blushed and shook her head. 'I don't know any Dereks.'

'Daniel,' said Sheila.

'Dan!' Lily said. 'We know a Dan.'

'I've got an older lady who's passed over telling me about Dan.' Sheila was listening hard. 'And she says she doesn't know why she's speaking through me, because she reckons you've got the gift more than anyone.' Sheila looked put out. 'Is that right, lover?'

Lily came over modest. 'I'm not sure . . .'

'Well, it's your sister I'm talking to. She says you've got quite a strong gift. Well, she is being cheeky! Saying you're better than I am. She's having to shout at the top of her lungs to make me hear!' Sheila gave a bellowing laugh then, but it was clear she wasn't happy. 'Now, your sister was called . . . Rita?'

'Ruth!' Lily cried out.

'Now, don't tell me!' said Sheila tetchily. 'I said, don't lead me on. That's how people think I fake it. Just say yes or no. Now, your Ruth has come on to give a message to you and her son . . .'

Michael felt himself flushing as well. His guts were turning over. He looked at Lily and she was pale.

'Ruth's getting faint now. Perhaps you can tune in better than me, lover . . . ?'

Lily shrugged helplessly. She had no idea how to go about such a thing. The medium gave a wry smile.

'Ah, here she is. Shouting up. She says you're having problems with a fella called Dan. He had an accident.'

Lily couldn't contain herself. 'That's right! He fell!'

'Don't tell me. Now. He's gone a bit funny and he'll never be right again.'

'What..?'

'Ruth's saying that Dan isn't – or he won't be – the reliable man he always was. He's going the same way his wife did. Does that make sense to you?'

'Oh, yes,' Michael found himself saying aloud.

'So you have to watch out. Especially with the kiddies on the way. The girls.'

Lily clutched Michael's knee.

'He's a bad bugger. Excuse my language, but that's what Ruth is saying to me. Dan isn't the same anymore. He's been somewhere bad and brought some of the bad back with him. She's fading now. She's hurrying up. All she says is, watch the girls with him. There's some question about the girls. It's no good. She's gone now.'

Michael and Lily stared. They didn't dare look at each other.

Sheila grinned at them. 'Will that do for you, lovers? That's all I could get.'

*

There was tea in the crypt for the congregation afterwards. Lily led the way downstairs, quite at home, and Michael was left to follow in her wake, staring gloomily at the green nylon curtains beside the hospital beds. He didn't fancy drinking where they healed the sick, but he queued for his tea from the urn with the rest. The boys in white shirts were serving on. He looked for the one who winked at him and got winked at again for his pains.

Aunt Lily moved through the milling congregation and Michael was surprised that she wasn't talking to anyone. The rest of them were in clusters, talking animatedly about the messages, picking them apart. He'd have thought Lily would be in great demand – she got the most complete and consequential communication – but no one wanted to talk to her. She was making towards a small shrine in the corner. A crisp white table cloth covered with nicknacks and beside it stood the pastor, his guitar leaning on the shrine. He was sucking on a biscuit and smiling as Lily approached.

Some question about the girls. The whole message had given Michael the creeps. He hated the idea that Sheila had talked about his daughters before they were even born. It made everything seem mapped out and already horrible. He wished he hadn't come tonight at all. He wondered where to go and stand.

Sheila the medium came in with the pastor's wife and a reverential gap opened up for her to pass through. She headed for the tea urn and Michael nipped discreetly away. He headed towards Aunt Lily.

The pastor was wagging his finger at Lily and she was crimson again, but this time with pleasure.

'She can always spot another talent, you know. She spotted my wife.'

Michael hated his straggly bow tie and his dyed hair. He hated the way Lily was being taken in by his chat. She'd gone all coy.

'Oh, I'm sure I'm not very talented . . .'

'You will be. But you have to watch out, dear, because people like Sheila are prone to getting jealous of greater talents.'

'Oh . . .'

'Yes, and I'm not saying that it'll be a pack of lies she's told you on that stage tonight, but she might just have twisted it slightly, just to get her own back.' His voice was quite low and he kept flicking a glance at his wife's huge beehive and the medium, across the room. He took in Michael and nodded, drawing him into the conspiracy. 'I'm really stepping out of line to tell you this. But I think a pinch of salt is in order. She was trying to scare you off.'

With that, the pastor moved away, taking his empty cup and saucer and his guitar.

'Well!' said Aunt Lily. 'I never knew it was so cut-throat.'

Michael set his own cup down on the shrine table. 'It's all crap.'

'Don't put your cup on the cloth! You'll mark it.'

He tutted and went off to find the vestry toilets.

They were filthy. The white tiles were cracked and the floor was sticky and wet. He felt queasy and just wanted to splash some cold water on his face. Fancy letting the toilets in a church get this dirty.

He looked up into the mirror and let the water stream down, feeling it cool his cheeks. He stared at himself until the door opened and someone else came to stand at the urinal. He looked. It was the collection boy, looking back at him.

'So that was all true, what Sheila was saying?'

'If you believe in that stuff. I don't know.' Michael fumbled with paper towels and scraped his face dry. Why's he talking to me? I could do without this now.

The boy went on. 'So you've got a wife? And you're having bairns?'

Everyone gets to know your business in places like this. 'Yes,' he said. 'We've got twins on the way.'

He turned round and the boy had his cock in both hands. It was thin and hardened and he was cradling it. 'That's what I'd call a waste,' he said and Michael didn't know what he meant at first.

He leaned on the wash basins and found he couldn't move his feet. The collecting boy smiled again and nodded and looked down at himself. He closed his fist around his cock and drew back the skin a little. It looked like he was holding a nectarine in his clenched fist. Michael wondered how to break the moment. He didn't know how he'd got here.

He jumped at the sound of the door as the pastor came in, still lugging his guitar.

'What a night!' he said heartily. Michael turned quickly back to the basin. The boy hadn't moved at all.

'Oh, you naughty boys,' the pastor said, shaking his head, and put his guitar down on the slick tiles.

'You naughty things.' Then he walked up to the boy and Michael bolted out.

*

Lily loved being driven home in Michael's hatchback. She felt so far off the ground and the engine hardly made any noise. And if anything ever happened en route, say, a blizzard, then if they had to camp out overnight, there'd be no problem! They could curl up in the hatchback under the blanket he kept there. It all felt very secure.

They were quiet for much of the drive back to the Avenue.

She wanted to talk about the service, though. Michael didn't seem in a talkative mood. He was oddly silent for much of the time. But she wanted to talk it through before they got home. She couldn't talk about it with anyone else there.

'What a nice bunch of people!' she said, as they got onto the ring road. 'There was such a sense of warmth. They all care for each other. Did you hear them murmering and muttering, about that woman who's going to be ill?'

Michael grunted.

Lily stared at the lemony street lights. 'They all say I should really get my gift trained up.'

He wanted to ask her, *who said that to you, Aunt Lily? You didn't talk to hardly anyone all night.* But he didn't say anything.

'I could have told them all about Healing the Sick. I never said anything about my experiences in that line. Aren't you proud of me?'

'Healing the sick . . .' Michael sighed and shook his head.

'Well, I did, didn't I?'

'You don't know what you did.'

'If I told that lot in there what happened, they'd have no doubts.'

'Yeah, well.'

'Dan says . . .'

'Maybe, if you did heal him, you should have just let him be.'

'Michael! What a thing to say!'

'I don't know if I believe in all that stuff they were saying back there . . . but it was right, wasn't it? He is different to what he was. He's a pain in the bloody arse.'

'Ah, now, Michael. I know you and Dan don't see eye to eye. It's often the way. You took his little girl away from him. A father is allowed to be cross about that. You and him have never got on.'

'We did at the start. Then he had the accident and . . .'

'Don't go believing that Sheila. She was just laying it on thick for the punters.' Lily clasped her bag primly. She was talking like a professional medium already. She was talking like it was showbusiness.

'The pastor explained it to me,' Lily went on. 'Sheila was just trying to unnerve me. She's jealous of the power she can see shining out of me.'

'Jesus,' said Michael. 'And that's another thing. Whoever heard of a church where they never mention God? Or Jesus?'

Lily bunched her lips. 'It's just different . That's all.'

Michael shook his head and steered them into the Avenue. Jesus to that church was like chopsticks in a

Chinese restaurant. There if you want them, if you can handle them. But if you want to use a fork instead you can leave them in the packet.

*

They found Christine sitting in the cold. The kitchen was dark and the pink paint had started to dry on the table, the floor tiles and on the sink. Lily dashed about, crunching the glass underfoot and screeching. Michael was shouting into Christine's face and holding her frozen hands.

Christine's face was puffed out as she did the breathing exercises she'd been taught. She hadn't moved from the spot since the pains began. She had stared at the livid splashes as they formed their tougher skin of pink and concentrated on breathing, riding it out.

'Can we get her into the hatchback?'

Michael could picture them, loading her in like groceries. He saw himself holding onto her tiny ankles, pulling her into the car. All the neighbours watching in the night.

'Where's Dan? Where's your dad, Christine?'

She puffed and blew and groaned and counted.

'I'm phoning an ambulance,' Aunt Lily said and ran to the hall.

*

'Michael has been with her all night. She was fantastic. They're all fantastic. All of them.'

Somehow the wreckage of the kitchen didn't look so bad this morning.

At nine o'clock Lily was round in her marigolds, scrubbing at the surfaces with bleach, scraping the paint off.

Dan was pacing the room and grinning like a madman. He was spruced up and itching to get to the hospital. 'When can we go?' he kept asking. 'I want to see them! I want to see them!'

Lily straightened up and smiled. 'Not until they open up shop. They're all exhausted. They've been working hard.'

'I can't believe I missed it all!'

'You've been working hard too, Dan. Falling asleep in the nursery. And all this going on.'

'I slept like a baby. The most important night in this house for years and I'm sleeping like a baby!'

'There's not much you could have done. It was all Christine's show, bless her.'

'My little girl! All my little girls!' Dan sat down at the table. In a way he felt bad that he wasn't at the hospital, remembering how Christine had sat by him those weeks when he was there. He hadn't even been there for the biggest night of her life. Would she forgive him?

'Isn't she a marvel?'

'She can make a scene when she wants,' Lily said ruefully. She glanced at the wooden boards Dan had already nailed on the broken window.

'She's not a quiet soul,' he chuckled. 'She must have been furious!'

'Well, it's over now.'

Dan was still chuckling and nodding. Yes, Christine must have been livid about the pain to do what she'd done to the kitchen. And wasting his paint, too! But now she was delivered, safe, and there were two little girls lying in a glass case beside her bed in the hospital across town. Two girls named already. Named by the exhausted mam and the amazed, wide-eyed dad who sat beside them all night. Judith and Jessica. Named already in a fit of early-hour inspiration. Judith and Jessica.

Lily snapped off her rubber gloves and said she was phoning for a taxi. If they stopped on the way for all the flowers and chocolates and furry toys that Dan said he wanted to buy, if they stopped for all the flowers and chocolates, furry toys in the world, they would still arrive in time to see the new family.

Great Aunt Lily and Grandad Fletcher were on their way.

5
Little Girls

They were both called 'the babies'. They were both called 'the girls'. Grandad Fletcher called them both his 'little darlings'. Great Aunt Lily called them 'my little lambs'. Daddy called them 'sweethearts' and to mammy they were just their names. They were called Judith and Jessica. Woe betide anyone who called them Judy or Jess within mammy's hearing.

Judith was also called the noisy one. The rebellious one, the naughty one. She was the one who had a proper little personality all of her own from the first moment that anyone saw them in the glass box in the hospital, Judith awake, yelling, kicking, irritated at the plastic tag on her ankle; Jessica soundly asleep beside her. Judith always stood out. She was the noisy one. The one with the huge lungs. The bawler, the mawler, the tomboy.

Jessica was called the quiet one. She was the one that people noticed second. She was the one who went along in her sister's shadow. She was 'the second born', the 'fifteen-minutes-after'. Judith would hold those fifteen minutes over her like they were the most exciting fifteen minutes that the world had ever seen. Jessica was the belated one. The one that missed the boat.

Mammy and daddy loved them equally. And grandad and Aunt Lily loved them equally too. But Judith would have it that everyone loved her most because she was the one with the most go about her. She was the one who wanted to know everything about the world. Who stood up in the cot and demanded to be taught to crawl, walk, talk, feed herself, before the ideas even occurred to Jessica.

To Jessica it always seemed natural that they would all love Judith most. Judith was entitled to it. Judith was even welcome to it. Jessica could see the sense. She loved Judith more than anyone else in the world, too. So she could see the sense in it. Judith always had the best ideas.

Ideas like when that little lad with all the frizzy ginger hair came round to play. He came round to play with his mammy because she was a friend of the real mammy's. Except mammy didn't like her much, because she had frizzy ginger hair as well. In the garden, playing with the little boy, Judith gets the idea of making his hair nicer. Grandad Fletcher's tin of white paint lying there from doing the fence. He'd let his little darlings watch as he painted his fence white. They had stood there watching as he stood on his ladder, climbing up carefully, dabbing the white on the tall fence that boxed in their garden to keep them safe. Judith got into the paint and the two of them held the ginger boy by his arms and he squealed. Judith had the idea of painting his hair white. And it worked! It was really good. He moved about a bit much but they got it all in his hair and you couldn't see that much of the ginger. But he moved around too much and then some got into his eyes and he started screaming so much out came the mammies from the kitchen door and there was hell on.

There'll be hell on, was what mammy always said when there'd been trouble and she warned them that daddy would be furious with them when he got home. Sometimes he didn't get home that same night. When he was on a course it could be nights and nights later. But mammy would be saving the hell on up and she'd tell him. But daddy would never really tell them off. It was the hell on with mammy that was the worst. Because she could really yell. Hell on with daddy was easy.

'Him's got pretty hair now,' Judith told the mammy as she grabbed up her little boy. He was dripping white on her arms and her dress. Jessica looked at her sister like she was talking a different language. Him's got pretty hair now. Judith said it was Jessica's idea to play with the paint. Jessica couldn't even say the word 'idea'. She got the biggest smack, but she was proud.

Judith always knew how to talk to people. And she did it so loudly. 'I'm not a very good talker yet,' she yelled at the postman one morning. 'Well, to me you sound very good,' he said, and mammy laughed. 'For a little girl your age you sound very good indeed.' Judith hadn't been so sure. 'I'm not a very good talker,' she repeated. 'Yet.'

What was Jessica like as a talker? Did they get much chance to find out? Was it always Judith speaking up, so much readier with her tongue than her sister? If someone was asking them something, like, Do you want juice? Do you want to go to see Aunt Lily? was it always Judith who did their talking for them? Was it Jessica who deferred to Judith because Judith could say things much better than she could anyway? And did this make Jessica lazy, like Christine feared and worried to Michael about? Did Judith do all the asking and answering? Did Judith do all their questions for them?

There were a lot of questions Judith wanted to ask. She watched everyone that came into their world and there was a lot she wanted to know about them.

Grandad Fletcher made fences all around their garden. But why did he spend all his life making fences? Didn't he ever go to work like daddy did? Did Grandad have a job and was it really just making the fences higher and higher?

Grandad Fletcher liked to sit with one twin each on his knees. He liked to help mammy bathing them. He liked to rub dry their wispy fair hair with the softest towels. They both liked the smell of his breath when he did this. Judith wanted to ask why his breath smelled strange and different to mammy's and different to everyone else's. But mammy didn't want to answer.

Great Aunt Lily was another one that Judith wanted to know things about. Like, how come she lived in a separate house from the rest of them? How come she was over the big road that you weren't to cross by yourselves, in fact, you weren't to go out the front of the house at all, else there'd be hell on, the cars come round that corner like mad. How come Aunt Lily had to be sent home across the road and couldn't she live with the rest of them?

And where was Aunt Lily going when they waved her off on a National Express coach? She went away again and again and again on the coaches and came back, all shining and beaming, and she brought her little lambs presents from Blackpool and Edinburgh and Brighton and everywhere. She brought them cuddly animals and once she brought them sticks of rock but mammy had said she was stupid for bringing the bairns rock and put the pink sticks away in the kitchen drawer and Judith had to pinch Jessica hard to make her cry and to make her complain.

What did church meeting mean? What happened there? Where did Aunt Lily go to make her come back so happy and pleased with herself?

Maybe it was the same kind of thing daddy went to, except he never went on the National Express coach. He went in the hatchback, stowing his bulging bags in the back and going off for a week or two weeks in his best suit, the one that smelled sour, and coming back eventually when his little girls were on the point of forgetting who he was, what he looked like. Was he doing the kind of things Aunt Lily did? Aunt Lily didn't go off wearing a sour smelling suit. She never wore a grey suit like daddy. She had on one of her cardies that she'd knitted for herself, a big version of the bedjackets and cardies she would make for the twins and unveil out of tissue paper in the living room for mammy and mammy would go on all pleased and look at them and then, when Aunt Lily had gone home across the big road, mammy would put the cardies in the kitchen drawer.

Did Grandad Fletcher like Aunt Lily or not? When everyone was together they would get on fine, like when Aunt Lily comes across the big road carrying a fat pink cake in both hands, fizzing birthday candles on top. Grandad Fletcher even slaps her back then and kisses her on the white puffy cheek as the grownups have little drinks of sherry and it's the twins' birthday. Doesn't it seem like he's fond of her then?

Like it seems he's fond of daddy when he's opening a can of beer for him, in the kitchen, on nights when daddy comes back from a faraway course and the girls are allowed to stay up, swinging their legs at the kitchen table, staying up late to welcome daddy and all the grownups are drinking these cans of beer and the girls can have juice. And everyone is smiling then.

But other times they're shouting at each other. They've seen Grandad Fletcher all upset. Really yelling and screaming like something's gone wrong, he's hurt himself, he can't make anyone understand. That was frightening.

Other times daddy's yelling back at him. They've seen daddy hitting Grandad Fletcher in the garden and Grandad hitting him back. Proper hits that make noises. Covering themselves in mud. The grey suit covered in mud and green and Grandad Fletcher's forehead bleeding. Jessica and Judith watching through the kitchen window as mammy locks the back door. Lock the silly, stupid bastards out, she says.

Other times Grandad Fletcher is saying Lily is a witch. He doesn't want Christine taking the girls round her house. But they like going. When mammy waits for the traffic to go and she holds their hands so there's a girl either side of her and she walks with them up Aunt Lily's front path. They like going into her quiet house and the smell of the flowers and her sideboard with all its pictures on. They like all the pictures of babies she's got there in golden frames, babies they've never seen before, they remind the girls of the babies they've been told they once were, not so long ago, and like they are in the baby photos that mammy pulls out in albums to show them. Those baby pictures are under cellophane though, the kind that you pull up with your fingernail, not in golden frames and glass like the babies Aunt Lily keeps on her sideboard. It is Judith, of course, who asks her who are these babies and it is with just a touch of envy, like, why hasn't Aunty Lily been displaying framed pictures of babies closer to home? Babies she ought to love rather more than all these strangers?

'These are my Spirit Babies,' Aunt Lily explains in a tender voice. 'They have all passed over and I am the one to look after them. They're my babies, you see. All forty-seven of them. And I look after them like your mammy looks after you.'

Except mammy doesn't look impressed with this. Next time Grandad Fletcher starts on about not wanting the girls to visit that old witches' den and how the whole business gives him the bloody creeps, mammy starts to agree with him. And she tells him all about the forty-seven dead babies on her sideboard.

Daddy always says there's nothing wrong with it. You won't have a word said against her, says mammy. She's a lonely old soul daddy says. She's out of her tree says mammy. She does a lot of good daddy says. It's a load of old shite says mammy.

Shite is a fantastic word. Judith gets it down to perfection.

That's shite, this is shite, you're shite, she's shite, nursery school is shite, the teacher is shite, this house is shite, daddy's shite, Grandad's shite, the fences are shite, the big road is shite, the spirit babies are shite, Jessica, Jessica, Jessica is shite.

Mammy can't help it. She laughs at first. Judith says it more to make her laugh more. Mammy is shite, mammy is shite, mammy and daddy are shite. Mammy hits her then on the legs and Judith cries and mammy cries and Grandad comes in to see.

Jessica has picked it up. She's learning fast. Shite shite shite shite shite bugger. She gets hit as well and this starts Judith laughing.

Judith makes Jessica say shite at nursery school. In the sand pit flicking sand everywhere. The teacher has it in her hair. Everyone's got it in their hair. Everyone is laughing. Then Jessica says that the sand pit is shite. School is shite.

Jessica is sent home, and though the teacher knows that Judith isn't bad like her sister is, she can't separate the sisters. One might be nice and one might be horrible with a mouth that needs washing out immediately with water and soap, but you can't separate the sisters.

Why are you always in trouble? mammy asks. *From the first day you were there it was trouble. Why do you always get into trouble at school?* It was the doll down the toilet, the little girl's doll and I ended up having to buy a new one. It was the splashing everyone with water. It was the thumping little boys. *And now it's this. Judith I'd have expected it off. Using language like that. Now you, Jessica. What am I to do with you?*

They both hang their heads as mammy crouches in front of them in the kitchen. But the sun is coming through, lighting up their straight fair hair, which is held back neatly by clips with fake daisies on. They are in pink candy-striped pinafore dresses. And they look adorable to Christine in the afternoon sun. She takes their hands and laughs and the trouble is forgotten and she dances them round the kitchen to whatever is on Radio One.

'You're bringing up two monsters, there, lass,' Grandad says as he smokes at the table. But he's laughing as well as they dance.

6
A Choice of Two Desserts

It was useless trying to escape round Aunt Lily's house when she was having a sitting. She didn't like the interruption, the breaking of her spell. The first time Michael felt unwelcome at his aunt's house came as a shock to him. This was Aunt Lily who had practically begged him to come and live with her when his mother died. The same aunt who had gritted her teeth and watched him move across the road with his wife and new family. Now though, she had new interests and a new social circle – she even had a whole new career! – and Michael found he had to make an appointment to go round and see her.

He went over the road one night and there was an unfamiliar couple perched on the edge of Aunt Lily's green velveteen couch and they were staring at Aunt Lily, who was in a trance. They hardly noticed Michael, standing in the doorway in his coat. Their faces were flushed and puffy and the young woman looked as if she was about to burst into tears. To Michael, they both looked poor. Her coat was white and dirty-looking and her hair was stringy and unwashed. He'd tried to warn Aunt Lily against the types of people she was letting into her home. But since his aunt had gone professional it was open house round here. There was a constant procession of strangers to her door.

'I hope you're charging them the going rate,' he'd told her.

She fluttered her hand at him and made a dismissive noise. This had been on one of the now-rare occasions when he popped round to find his aunt on her own. 'Not everyone can afford that. I ask them what they think they can pay me, and that's quite enough.'

Michael had been appalled. 'But they'll be ripping you off! You've got skills! You've gone professional! You're not a charity.'

Lily shook her head at him. The way she did that these days got on his wick. Like she was suddenly all knowing and stuffed full of compassion. 'I'm here to help these people. They've been through traumatic times.'

He tutted. 'We've all been through traumatic times.'

His Aunt narrowed her eyes at him and it was as if she could see all the way into him. Michael coughed and mumbled something about the kettle boiling and let the conversation drop.

Today though, he found it infuriating to see this couple – her in the dirty white mac – sitting there and staring as his aunt's eyelids fluttered and her eyes rolled back in her head. While she was in one of her so-called trances, this pair could be looting the place. Had she even thought of that? By the time she came out of the influence she could look around and find her whole house gutted. She was far too trusting. She was kidding herself.

He hovered at the doorway and started to wish he hadn't come over now. But it was almost ten o'clock at night. He hadn't expected her to have clients this late.

The couple turned to look at him, looking put out. Aunt Lily was frowning now. Her eyes flew open and glared accusingly. Then she rolled them and slapped both arms of her chair.

'Michael, you've snapped the link.'

'I'm sorry . . .'

'It's taken me almost half an hour to get into this state . . . Oh, never mind.' She smiled at the couple on the couch. Her voice went softer. 'I'll not get it back tonight. What about tomorrow?' She pulled a diary out from underneath the chair cushion and flipped through it. 'Michael, wait for me in the kitchen, will you?'

It was like being in an office. As the couple started to mumble at her he did as he was told.

He listened to their murmering through the serving hatch as he got tea things ready. The sound of their voices reminded him of people going to see the manager in the bank. The same respect, the same muted hopefulness of people banking on things.

The front door slammed and then Aunt Lily came bustling into the kitchen like her old self.

'Bless them. They've lost a daughter. They were hoping I'd find out more about what happened to her.'

'What?'

'A little girl. The police have given up the investigation, of course.'

'Aunt Lily, what are you getting into?'

'It's important work, Michael. No one else will help them.'

He let his breath out in a hiss as she rinsed some cups. He was surprised to see her sink full of dirty dishes. It wasn't her style at all. When she brought the tea over to him at the breakfast bar she pulled out a polaroid photo from her cardigan pocket and held it in front of his nose. It showed a pink-faced baby lying in blankets. 'That's Hazel. I think I've got a frame somewhere.'

'Another one for the sideboard?'

'And my prayers.'

'Aunt Lily . . . I don't like you getting into this.'

She stowed the picture away. 'Don't you, indeed.' She settled heavily onto her chrome stool. 'Now, that's very interesting. Since when did I let you know that I didn't like you getting involved in the things you do?'

'What?' He was on his guard suddenly.

'I've let you go along, getting in with the Fletchers, doing what you wanted with your life. I've taken a back seat, even when I didn't approve . . .'

'Well, yes . . .'

'Well, keep your nose out, Michael. I'm doing a good job here. I'm offering hope.'

'But it's people's real lives that you're getting involved in! They'll be believing every word you say.'

'What else is there besides people's real lives? What else is there to get involved in? Tell me that.'

They both sipped their tea for a moment.

Let it drop, Michael told himself. Just say what you came to say. Don't interfere.

'Anyway, I've come over to invite you to Sunday dinner. Christine asked me to tell you.'

'Well! There's a turn-up!'

'She's making an effort.'

'Good! I would be delighted to come. And will Dan be there, too?'

'It's a family Sunday. That's the idea.'

Aunt Lily looked pleased. 'Mind, you don't sound too over-the-moon about it, Michael.'

'Don't I?'

'You look tired.'

He shrugged. He was still in his bank suit, she thought. Rumpled, sweaty-looking. Time was, he'd have changed into his after-work clothes and been all scrubbed up and dashing about. Taking the girls out somewhere, looking pleased with his life.

'Is that Dan behaving himself?'

'He's okay.'

'I think he should get himself looked at.'

'He won't go near hospitals again.'

Aunt Lily drew in her breath. 'It's better to know if something's gone wrong.'

'You've always got to know, haven't you? You've always got to look inside and find out the truth.'

She raised an eyebrow at the bitterness in his voice. 'Michael . . .'

'Well, maybe Dan would rather not know. If there's something wrong inside his head and that's why he has his funny turns, maybe he's better off not knowing.'

'It's since he fell off that whatchamacallit.'

'We know it's since then, but we don't talk about it.'

'You know what happens if you don't talk about things, Michael?'

He drummed his meaty fingers on the breakfast bar.

She went on, 'They fester up inside you.'

He jumped up from his stool. 'Good! I'm glad! I'd rather be full of fester than having the truth dragged out every day!'

'Oh, Michael . . .'

'I would! I think it's sick, to tell you the truth, Aunt Lil. All this truth.'

'You don't know what you mean.'

'Yes I do. You just want to be in on everyone else's secrets. That's why you do what you do. You just want to be part of something.'

He whirled out of the kitchen then and was gone.

Lily narrowed her eyes and finished her tea. There was something that boy wasn't telling her.

*

He turned right at the end of the road and kept on walking in the dark. He couldn't face home yet. Christine would have bathed the girls by now and put them to bed. He'd have missed the big dressing up, the palaver of them trying out their school uniforms. There was still a month before they started at the Infants, but the dress rehearsal had been tonight and he'd missed it all. He'd get hell for that but he wasn't in the mood. He could imagine Christine and Dan sat there, cooing as the girls twirled round in their grey skirts and white shirts. The striped ties on elastic, their hair up in pony tails. Truth was, he couldn't stand the idea of them dressed up like that. In little adult clothes. They were still babies, really. Even if they did talk like they did. And swore. Words they'd picked up from Grandad Fletcher. Making Christine laugh. She said it was harmless. She laughed every time.

Michael kept on walking towards the ring road. His feet carried him on, further and further away from home, his soles rasping on the dry pavement. Pushed out of my own house. But it has never felt like my own house in the first place. It's always been the Fletchers' house. They made that plain enough. When he came back from his courses or just from a day at work it was like he was a visitor. One that they didn't have to make much effort with. And when he arrived Dan would be helping out with the girls. Sat on the landing, blow-drying their hair. Yards and yards of golden hair and Judith would be chatting away in that croaky voice of hers and Jessica would be listening, wide-eyed. Christine reckoned her dad was a wonder with them. But he was unstable. He wasn't to be trusted. Michael didn't know what to do.

He crossed the ring road at a run. The traffic was slack. It was late. The whole place had shut down for the night. So different from the places he went on his courses. When they put him in hotels in city centres; Manchester, Birmingham. He'd be in the thick of things there. Looking out the window at the city streets and they would never be empty or quiet. At any time in the night he could put his shoes back on, take his room key and pop down to reception. Ask the concierge to call him a taxi. Go off to any part of the city, find somewhere still open. It was his other, different life, where he didn't work by someone else's time-table. Except, in the daytime, when he sat in conference rooms with other people getting trained up. Staring at blackboards, listening. Hearing all about the computers and the difference they would make. But that was great as well. He was learning stuff that people didn't know yet. About the things he'd be able to do, just by pressing keys on a board. That was opening up a new world, too. Everyone would have to know this stuff eventually, he could see that. And he was being one of the first.

Yet when he came home they treated him like a soft lad. The one who was keeping the house running, but who wasn't really welcome. And there was Dan, seeing to his little girls. Dan was changing them into little monsters with his language. They were getting bigger and taller and they talked more every day, even Jess. But they were growing up different to what Michael expected. He had no input, it seemed like.

At the hotel training sessions even the most mundane questions were taken seriously. You only learn by asking questions, the woman had said. Michael muddled along and never could quite ask the easiest questions, the niggly things he didn't understand and assumed he ought to know. He let others ask those simple things and as the woman explained, patiently, he nodded as if he had known the whole time. The people asking the daft questions amazed him. It was as if they assumed they had every right to be listened to, even in their ignorance. Everyone had a right to chirp up, he thought, and say what they wanted.

It was a mild night. Not a breath of wind as he hurried himself on and stepped onto the Common. He was just out for a walk. Clear his head. A couple of years ago he'd have thought this whole area – the trees and their rustling blue shadows, the long grass around the scrubby hills – was dangerous. Muggers, murderers, all sorts. He'd never have come out for a quiet walk at night, not here. Now it seemed safer than home. Here he wouldn't say something and get his head bitten off. He wouldn't put his foot in it and end up criticising Christine or her dad. At home, it seemed like everything he said could be construed like that. Even when he didn't mean it to be.

'What do you know anyway?' Christine jeered. 'You're never here. You haven't got a clue what goes on here.'

He left the path and stamped through the long grass. He loved the dry shushing sound of it. In the moonlight the grass was bleached and dry, as if the sun had sucked all life out of it. It was a warm summer, this one. A parching one. Maybe it was the heat that made him feel like this. He was listless. He wanted to run but he couldn't muster the energy. It was only at night, with the dark making things cooler, that he found he could re-energise himself. He was like a lizard, soaking up the daytime heat, lying stunned, and then expending it at night.

He loved the cracking of dry twigs under his feet as he walked under the trees. Gun shots, breaking fingers. He was losing his bearings and he didn't care. Announcing his presence. Stopping to stare up at the interlaced branches, black against the prussian blue of the sky. Black against the smokey orange from the lights of town. A tight mesh of black holding him down to the dry earth. He stopped for a rest, leaning against a tree. He should have changed. He was in his bank suit. He'd been in it since seven this morning. He could feel the dry sweat on him and it was like he was caked in sand.

*

The only thing Michael had done right in recent months, as far as everyone at home could see, was get them a video. Videos were new and not many people had one. There was one weekend, when he returned from a London course, that he unpacked a large cardboard box from the hatchback. Under layers of silvery packaging Christine had found the video and she stared at it without knowing what it was. Her dad did, and he explained to them all what it could do, while Michael sat there proudly. They must be the first in the Avenue with such a machine.

They could tape things to watch again and again. They could watch things twice the speed – and how they all laughed, trying the machine out, to see football players zipping about on the astroturf, or newsreaders gabbling silently away. Or they could freeze-frame things into perfect pictures, or watch them one frame at a time. And you could use the tapes forever. It was strange. If you didn't like what you had recorded you could wipe it over with something new. These things weren't meant to last forever. But you couldn't record over something with blank. Something else had to go over the top; over and over in layers. Once you'd recorded the first thing, it seemed, the tape couldn't go back to blank.

The girls had their own tape and they liked so much what their grandad recorded on it, the first time he'd tried it for them, they wouldn't hear of it being taped over. Rather, Judith wouldn't hear of it. She kept the tape by her bed and only she was allowed to hold it. She could even feed it into the machine herself, letting the mouth of the video take it into the back of its throat and making its snorting whirring sound as it swallowed the whole thing down, lights blinking. Grandad Fletcher had taped them Disneytime on a Bank Holiday Monday and the girls were keeping it forever. They actually owned real bits of Disney films and they could watch them to their hearts' content. They even had that favourite scene: the monkeys singing in the jungle, about being the king of the swingers and a jungle VIP. Michael worried that, with all their winding and pausing and repeated viewings (till they knew every line and every gesture by heart), they would end up stretching and snapping their tape or worse; rubbing the video's innards, its heads and buttons down to nothing.

But, 'Leave them be,' said Christine, glad to have the two of them out of her hair as she saw to Sunday lunch. Judith and Jessica sitting on the settee; the remote control snaking out on its lead from the video and clutched in Judith's hand. The two of them reciting and intoning the words of the 'King of the Swingers' quietly, all Sunday morning. 'You better let them do what they want now,' Christine would say. 'They'll be at school soon and they'll have to do what they're told then.' She tossed her head and he noticed how she'd been letting her hair grow again. 'They'll have to do as they're told forever after that. School's the beginning of the end, isn't it?'

Michael wasn't sure. For him it had been like torture, but it was also the way he'd got himself away from the place he'd grown up. But it wasn't like that for Christine.

'So we should let them do what they want for now.'

Still Michael wasn't sure. He thought the girls would run wild.

'What harm are they doing?' Christine said. 'Sitting and watching the telly. They're angels.'

One thing about Christine, he thought, and that was she always had the girls immaculate. She loved to go down Mothercare and buy them the bright, trendy clothes they had there now. It wasn't like it used to be. Michael looked at his own baby pictures, and Christine's, and they would both be in the old-fashioned things. Home-made bonnets and booties and bedjackets. Tiny versions of the things old women wear. Christine wasn't having that. She would see him looking at the old albums and laugh. She was building up her own books of polaroids of the girls.

'They'll fade away to nothing after a few years,' he said. 'I bet you anything those instant photos won't last.'

He liked the small, square photos from his own childhood. Thick, curling prints. He looked again and again at the one of his mam holding him as a baby in their garden. Her legs looked skinny and knock-kneed. She had no stockings on and her skin was mottled. He looked at that photo and it made him want to cry. He looked at it as Christine stuck her own pictures in the new book. She held up her new camera and used the last shot up on him. Whirr, hiss, shunt. Instant pictures. Not the same somehow. They stared as the image of him came up out of the grey, blue, yellow bruise colours of the polaroid. He looked glum and red-eyed, with the old photo album on his lap. 'Oh, that's lovely,' Christine said. 'Happy bloody Larry on the settee.' She slipped the picture into the back of the book. Banished. Mostly the book was pictures of the girls in identical, fashionable Mothercare outfits, standing side by side. You could hardly tell them apart at birthdays, Christmas, outings to the zoo. The latest pictures Christine was putting onto the self-adhesive pages and sticking down with cellophane; the girls in their red and grey school uniforms. The night he had missed them dressing up in rehearsal. Grandad Fletcher was there, proud with his white hair up in tufts, his retinas glaring red at the camera flash.

'That will be Aunt Lily,' he said as the door bell rang. Christine groaned and went back to the kitchen.

'Would you see to her? I've got to baste this bird.'

He opened the door to his aunt and she was in a new chenille jumper with an enamel badge on the front. A fairy with gossamer wings.

'Do you like it? One of my regulars made it for me.'

'What?'

'She makes fairies.' Aunt Lily pushed an apple pie into his hands. Its crust crumbled at the lip of the plate as he took it and she stepped inside. 'I threw this together this morning. Now, where are my pet lambs?'

He nodded at the living-room door. He could hear them singing along with the monkeys. From the kitchen he heard Christine slamming and banging the roasting dish onto the oven shelf.

'Smells nice,' said Aunt Lily. 'Proper Sunday.' She peered into her nephew's face. 'What's that look for? Like you've lost a pound and found a shilling.'

'I'll give the pie to Christine.'

'Hm.' Aunt Lily took herself off to the living room.

In the kitchen Christine flicked back her hair. 'Doesn't she think I can make my own dessert? I've done a bloody trifle.'

'It's just a gesture.'

She flung open the fridge and put the pie right at the back.

It struck Michael then that the way she was tossing her hair was a princessy kind of thing. And it was lightened and cut into a page-boy style. It had taken him this long to realise that Christine had given herself Lady Diana hair. That's who she was modelling herself on. She'd bought a blank tape ready for the wedding, he knew. 'It's something we'll keep and the girls can have for posterity,' she had said. 'Just think! They can own that wedding forever!'

'I can smell lemons,' he said.

'I've shoved a lemon inside the chicken. It's lemon gravy, too.'

'Very posh. Don't we normally have just ordinary gravy?'

'I was thinking. Why do a chicken and have beef gravy with it? It's ridiculous.'

Michael took a can of lager out of the fridge. 'I suppose so.' He was surprised she had even bought any tins in. She had threatened to stop all that. 'I suppose it is ridiculous.'

'Mam used to do beef gravy with everything. Even when we had chips and beans.' He was surprised to hear her mention her mam. Then she added, 'So I'm ringing the changes.'

'Good idea.' Now he was trying to chime in.

'I hate those things that you go along with for the sake of it.' Christine turned to scrape the carrots. He watched as the peel came off in expert, orange strips. 'Never questioning or looking at what you might have had. So I looked at one of the old Elizabeth David books mam had had for years and never used. So we're having lemon gravy.'

Christ, Michael thought. She's been reading again.

'I dread to think what you eat when you're away on your courses.'

'I manage on my own.'

She turned to look at him. 'Yes, I suppose you do.'

Then there were squeals in the living room.

'Grandad! Grandad! Grandad!'

The old man lay in for hours on a Sunday morning. When he came down the girls greeted him as if he'd been away for weeks. And then, over the top of the Jungle Book noise, came the sound of ho-ho-hoing and Michael knew that Dan would have one girl sat on either knee and his Aunt Lily would be sitting across the room smiling at them.

*

There was a bit of fuss over who was carving the chicken and Michael found that he and Dan were glaring at each other for a moment. Michael didn't really care, but their tussle seemed as much a part of family gatherings as the napkins out and the candles lit. Before either of them could do anything Christine took up the ragged-toothed knife and the specially pronged fork and she reduced the lemon-scented chicken to steaming rubble on the plate. No messing about. Aunt Lily made approving noises and Michael felt like cheering. Go on, you old bastard. Make a fuss about that. He thought Dan's outbursts were futile, self-indulgent things. The old man showing that he could still have an impact. It was pathetic.

The girls were sitting with their hands in their laps. They looked like they were about to say grace. Christine had put them in what looked like party frocks, with lace collars and sashes. Was it all because Aunt Lily was there? Only last weekend, Michael could remember Sunday lunch being bedlam. Christine flinging things down on the table, the girls squealing and twisting. Grandad Fletcher sat there with a face like thunder. Then the gravy spilling everywhere on the bare wood of the table.

Judith asked Christine if she might put Disneytime on in the background, because it was all mostly songs and it might be nice. Grandad would want to hear it. Of course she could, but quietly mind, and she jumped up to fiddle with the remote control and returned to her place. Aunt Lily beamed at her and Grandad Fletcher said how tuneful it was, the king of the swingers, as he ladelled out greens for himself, the lenses of his glasses steaming up. He held the dish right up to his face, as if he was sniffing the sprouts. He said, 'You're not like your silly mother. All the rubbishy things she liked when she was a little girl. Who was it you made us listen to, Christine? That fat-faced boy with girl's hair?'

Christine laughed.

'And then she wanted to go all punky. She needed a talking to. All that eye make-up. Going out with these rough-looking lads. I had to put a stop to all that!' He chuckled and spooned up bread sauce.

Lily put in, 'I remember seeing Christine dressed in, like a bin bag type thing. That's when she was a punk.'

'For all of two weeks,' said Christine, shooting a glance.

'She was coming out the front door with her hair sticking up. Wearing bin bags! Imagine!'

'She went wild,' Dan said.

Jessica's eyes were wide. Judith asked, 'Were you a punk, daddy?'

The old man grunted. 'He wasn't anything.'

*

Dan sat with the girls on the settee after lunch and they were intoning the dialogue from the Disney clips to him. He was smiling and nodding with a girl either side of him as Lily cleared the table.

Michael was gulping down another can of lager in the kitchen and hoping it would clear his indigestion. Christine stooped by the sink. 'Give him some credit,' she said. 'He couldn't have behaved any better.'

Michael shrugged.

'He's so good with the girls.'

'They behave really well for him.'

'They know they won't get away with nonsense with him.'

'You mean they're scared of him.'

Christine shook her head wearily. 'No. But it's no accident that they only misbehave with people who'll put up with it.'

'Like me?'

'You're not going to make this into a competition.'

Michael took the yellow gloves off her and made a start on washing up. Christine always made a right mess of the kitchen when she cooked. He remembered how his mam and Aunt Lily both cleaned up as they went along. They did that out of consideration. Out of being house proud. He reckoned that Margaret would have been like that as well. Everything in the kitchen that Sunday was filmed in grease. She'd even left bits of brussels and peelings littered on the sides.

'Dad doesn't think the girls ever really misbehave,' Christine said. 'He says it's only when you come back. It unsettles them, he says, you going backwards and forwards. It confuses them.'

The water in the tank, coming out of the taps, was red hot. Burning up money all the time, leaving the tank switched on.

'Is that what he says?'

'He sees them more than you do. He knows what they're like.'

Lily must have been waiting outside the kitchen with her tray of dirty china. In the pause that followed she came in and dumped it beside Michael. 'Here you go! Here's where the workers are hiding!'

Christine decided to be kind and retrieved the apple pie from the fridge. 'We can have cream with this. Now we've got a choice of desserts.'

'A choice of desserts!' said Lily. 'What more could you ask for?'

'Michael was telling me you've been contacting murder victims,' Christine said, getting the bowls out.

Lily looked cross for a second. 'Well . . .'

'That must be awful work. It's very good of you to do it.'

'Someone needs to,' said Lily stiffly.

'You must put people's minds at rest.'

'I do, I think. That's what I'm there for.' She took up the trifle spoon. 'Some of these people don't even know if their loved ones are alive or dead. Or where their bodies have been put to rest. If I can help to take some of the anxiety out of their minds, then I'm doing a good job.' Digging the spoon into the trifle, she made a little sucking noise each time as she dolloped it into bowls.

Michael was quiet.

'It must be frightening though,' said Christine. 'You don't know what you're going to call up.'

'I do it for the sake of others,' said Lily. 'I have to do it for them.'

'But what if . . .'

'What?'

'Like, one day, you call up the wrong person?'

'What do you mean?'

'What if, one day, you called up the devil?'

'Oh, Christine, I . . .'

'But what if you did? Called him up by accident? And what if you couldn't get rid of him?'

Michael took the trifle bowls into the living room.

*

Later that afternoon they drove out to a family fun pub on the ring road for a pint. It was the pub that Dan used to take Margaret to after their Sunday runs-out. This what what the Sunday runs-out had dwindled to; just the last, tired part of the ritual.

The girls were excited at the thought of the fun pub's playroom, which was new. Especially the room full of coloured balls and the slide that bombed down into it. Christine showed them to it and joined the others in the bar.

Lily looked strained and tight-lipped with her sweet sherry. She stared at horse brasses and Michael was wondering if she was thinking about the devil. Did she even believe in the devil? Christine had just been making trouble. Surely no one believed in stuff like that these days. But it was true, Lily had turned very quiet.

Michael pointed to a sign above the bar. 'We could have come here for our lunch and saved Christine the effort.'

Dan snorted. 'That's for people on their own and lazy buggers. It's shameful. I pity them for having to go out for Sunday lunch.'

Christine had a bitter lemon and she barely touched it. Her dad took sips of his Guinness and smacked his lips every time, looking round to see who else was in the bar. Michael was starting to feel the benefit from his lager.

'Sunday pubs are different now,' Dan said. Michael wished he would pull those hairs out of his nose. Thick grey bunches of them. He even had Guinness froth on them. 'It always used to be the fellas in the pubs on a Sunday, while the women cooked the lunch. These used to be a place for men.' He smiled. 'Remember that, Lily?'

Lily didn't remind him that she'd never been married. She gave him a wan smile. Christine said, 'Not any more, dad.'

There were kiddies running to and from the games room. They were given ice-cream cones upside down on plates and stuck with smarties to look like clowns. They were playing on fruit machines with their mams. It was more like a café than anything. A waitress stood behind a counter shouting out numbers. There were fluorescent signs that read: Pork dinner! Lamb dinner! Beef dinner! and kiddies portions of everything.

'It's better like this,' Dan decided. 'You see more of life.'

'It's more sociable,' Lily said.

'A man gets a chance to show his family off,' Dan said. 'Before, down the pub, it was just old fellas with their papers and pipes and dogs, not saying anything. And they say that the family is breaking down. That the old traditions have gone. Well, it's the other way around, isn't it?'

Lily was looking intently at him.

'This kind of place is showing that the family is anything but dead. Family is still the most important thing.'

Christine had her sickly smile back on.

Dan took a longer swig of his Guinness and Michael found himself thinking choke, choke you old bastard. Then the old man put his glass down, gave them a bleak stare and said, 'I want to know what you two are playing at.'

Christine looked shocked.

'Don't give me that. I've known you long enough, Christine. Something is up. I know a mile off when you're covering something up.'

Christine flicked her hair and blushed. 'Nothing's up! I don't know what you mean.'

Then Dan turned on Michael. 'I want to KNOW.'

'Dad . . .' Christine began.

'NOT you, Christine,' he snapped. 'I want soft lad HERE to TELL me. In his OWN words. His own FINE, educated WORDS.'

Lily was sitting with her mouth open. Christine sagged back in her chair. And suddenly Michael thought: I know what I'm going to say to him. This is the moment I say it.

'I'm moving out.'

Christine made a noise in her throat. 'What?'

'I have to get out for a while. This isn't working.'

Dan blinked. 'Did I just hear what I thought I heard?'

'A trial separation,' Michael said. He touched Christine's sleeve. 'I'm sorry, I . . .'

'You're going to WALK OUT on my DAUGHTER? On the GIRLS?' Dan was hunching up now and starting to rise.

'Dad,' Christine began. 'We haven't talked about any of this. I don't know . . .'

'What about the GIRLS, eh, sunshine? WHAT about THEM?'

'Mr Fletcher,' said Aunt Lily, who was also standing up by now. But they never found out what Lily was about to say. The manageress was standing beside their table. She was panting and stammering something about the room full of coloured balls. Her hair was like a tall, frosted meringue. 'Something awful has happened,' she told them.

'The girls..?' Christine snatched her handbag and set off at a run across the monogrammed carpet. As the others followed with the manageress heads were turning at every table, looking up from their pints and menus.

Lily was holding onto Michael's arm; her nails digging through the soft cloth of his shirt. He dragged her all the way to the play area.

In the room of coloured balls a toddler, a little boy, was howling and his mother was shushing him, grasping him to her breast. An older boy was standing there with a white face, gulping back tears. Judith and Jessica were being held by their shoulders by two of the bar staff, both young girls themselves.

There were coloured balls all over the floor.

The look on the twins' faces was peculiar. They both seemed disinterested; as if all the shouting and moaning had nothing to do with them. As if it were the adults acting up, as usual.

The manageress strode over to them. 'Here they are. Little vixens.'

'What's going on?' Christine asked, looking wild herself by now.

Everyone was talking at once and Dan decided he was taking charge. 'Now, now. One at a time. There'll be a simple explanation. A misunderstanding. Has there been a fight of some sort?'

Of course there's been a fight, Michael thought. You can tell it from the air. It had a static cling about it; like the action was all over but the hatred was still there, bristling; like static off the girls' nylon dresses.

The mother of the two boys was yelling again. 'They held Darren underneath the balls! They were suffocating him!'

Her toddler howled again when he saw everyone looking at him.

'Kevin tried to help and they attacked him, too! They ripped his hair out! And look at them! Not a bit of remorse. They're animals!'

Dan looked placid suddenly. 'No, I can't believe that. They're just little girls. Just playing.'

'Playing, he says! They're wicked.'

Lily put in, coming to stand beside Dan, 'Sometimes bairns play rough. And I'm sure they didn't start it . . .'

The manageress gave the nod and the barmaids let go of Judith and Jessica. 'Now, look,' said the manageress.

'We need to get to the bottom of this. This kiddies room is closed right now and there'll be no more playing for anyone.'

Christine asked the mother of the boys, 'Are they all right now?'

'They're distraught! How would you feel if someone had tried to drown you?'

The manageress swung round. 'No child can drown in a room full of balls. It's been proven safe.'

'Darren nearly did! He was blue! I saw an advert saying you could sue for things like that . . .'

'Now, now,' Lily broke in. 'What if the girls apologise nicely? Would that help?'

The boys' mother glared. 'That would be a start.'

'Judith?' Aunt Lily coaxed. 'Jessica?'

Christine darted a mute glance at Michael. He knew she wanted him to step in and do something, say something. But he was rooted to the spot.

Grandad Fletcher was saying, 'Come on, sweethearts. Grandad's little darlings. You've gotten a bit out of hand. Why don't you say you're sorry, hm? To the nice lady and her little boys?'

Judith smoothed down the front of her frock. She seemed to consider her grandad's words. She glanced at Jessica and back at the boy she had pushed under the plastic coloured balls and held there.

'I'm not apologising to that fat little cunt.'

The adults stared at her.

'Or his brother. Or his fucking mother. They can all fuck off. They're all cunts.'

*

Michael didn't stick around. He decided that this was the beauty of his new life. The new life he had decided on when they first sat down that afternoon in the fun pub and Dan had goaded it out of him. This was his new life and he was walking out. He walked straight out of the pub into the ring road. He could leave them to it. He didn't have to put up with it.

He was out on the ring road and he was miles from anywhere. The traffic was fierce and it was doing a fine job of drowning out the ringing in his ears from the yelling and the things that Christine said and her father said when he turned and started walking out. He didn't even take the hatchback. He left it in the car park of the fun pub.

He jumped over the fence of the car park and jogged away down soft verges. It was spitting onto rain and the sky was lowering down. He was alone for the first time all day and it felt good.

He found himself jogging all the way to the Common. Jogging, unshaven on Sunday lunch time in his scruffy sweatshirt and his jeans. Under the trees the raindrops plopped heavier, filling the cavernous, gloomy green spaces with noise. But a peaceful noise. His head cleared a little and he still felt drunk, rocking in the orbit of his new life. Alone for the first time all day. Leaning against the clean, damp green bark of a tree. And then he wasn't alone anymore, suddenly. He wasn't the only one out on the Common on Sunday afternoon.

7
Owned by Strangers

One of the first new things was the three-bar electric heater. His flat was freezing. The heater was a present brought two nights after he moved in; unveiled from its box, plugged in with aplomb. Warming the two rooms up nicely; the elements juddering slightly with disuse, giving off the acrid smell of old dust burning. But it was a nice gesture; a generous one from someone who was, after all, just about a stranger.

Christine had said he couldn't have the girls over to his new place to visit until he had made it habitable. Her girls weren't going to stay in a pigsty. The walls were scabbed and peeling and the corners of some were dark with mould. He was ashamed when Aunt Lily came round to help him arrange his few, pitiful belongings. He couldn't believe how little stuff he had. She pitched in with her spare kitchen utensils; a few old pots and pans, and two sets of cutlery and plates and cups, in case he got visitors.

Aunt Lily came round with a basket of dusters, polish and bleach. She rolled up her sleeves and tried to make the place decent for him. She knew as well as he did that he wouldn't get the girls at all if he lived in this state.

He couldn't live with her. He had spared Aunt Lily the embarrassment of having to say no, by telling her first that he needed more space. So he came to this flat, closer to the centre of town, three storeys up from the kebab shops and bookies. She couldn't have had him living with her again. It would be as if they had never moved on. She had her full life now; moving about the country on the buses, meeting new people and giving them their messages. Hers was a quite different life and, if her nephew was back at home, five years older, she might just be tempted to slide back herself, and be there just for him;

making his tea and watching telly together in the evenings. Back to being a plain old aunt. She had more to do nowadays so she was glad when Michael made this move first and found himself somewhere else.

About the actual split with Christine, Aunt Lily kept tight-lipped. She hated the idea of them breaking up like this. Curiously enough, the image that kept repeating on her was of the flowers that Margaret had sent them. The battered arrangement she had seen, pushed aside in the hallway, on the day of the wedding. That seemed to be the saddest thing; flowers from Margaret, who didn't even know the troubles that the young couple had faced.

Lily knew that it hadn't been working for Christine and Michael. She knew it was doing them no good with him living there. You could see at one glance that there was nothing between them. The way they sniped and bickered at each other didn't have any sexiness in it; it wasn't a fond kind of sparring. It was just irritation with each other. Exhaustion with each other. From the very first they had been pushed up against each other and pretty soon they'd got sick of the effort of holding themselves there. And why shouldn't they? Although she believed in marriage and the vows they took and everything, Lily couldn't see the sense in keeping arrangements that made everyone unhappy.

Usually people stayed together for the sake of the bairns. But Lily could see – it was only too plain – that the girls were happier, more settled, with things as they were now. With their daddy out of the way and seeing them even less than ever. It broke Lily's heart when she realised that. Something will have to be done about it, she thought.

They need time. They need a little spell of peace. Christine claimed that the girls misbehaved and said the things they said because they never knew if they were coming or going. She was sure, with the new way of things, they would calm down. There would be no more scenes like the one in the fun pub. No more terrible scenes like that.

Lily had gone home that Sunday afternoon and she lay down on her bed with a headache. That filthy language coming out of the girls' mouths. It was the most shocking thing she had ever heard. And she couldn't help linking it to what Christine had said, in the kitchen, about calling up the devil by accident.

In the gloom of her bedroom, with the curtains pulled and billowing slightly in the rainy breeze, Lily had dozed and dreamed about the devil. Could he speak through small children? If he did, would he say things like cunt, cunt, cunt, fucking? Words that would scald on Lily's lips. Words she didn't believe she had ever said.

But I invite spirits in, don't I? I ask them to let me be their medium. They speak through my lips and there's no one to say they won't speak filth.

And she, in her trance, might never know the things she was saying.

Could it be the girls have a gift of the same sort?

What sort of thing is speaking through them?

Lily shivered in her light doze. She woke and had a little cry at the thought of Michael walking out on his wife and bairns.

*

The Fletchers pulled out of the street party at the last minute and demanded their money back. By then it was too late and the two women from the far end of the Avenue who had done all of the organisation, trooping from door to door each Friday evening collecting the money, said no, flatly, they couldn't give a penny back. It was all accounted for.

Dan shouted at them from his doorstep and told them that their street party was a rip off.

'It isn't even going to be like a PROPER street party! No TABLES out, no BUNTING! All you women are planning is a kind of PICNIC on blankets!' It was to be on the patch of wasteground at the back of the Avenues. Dan couldn't see what they needed all that money for, in that case.

'For the picnic food,' said one woman.

'For the entertainments and games,' said the other.

'We can make our own entertainment,' said Dan. 'ANYWAY, I wouldn't want to eat YOUR rotten FOOD.' The two women began backing away with their collecting tin. 'You both look DIRTY. So we're pulling OUT of your BLOODY party! Piss OFF!' And he banged the front door shut.

'Anyway,' said Christine, sitting at the kitchen table and explaining to the girls. 'What's the point of running around in a field on the day of the wedding? We want to watch it on the telly, don't we? And video record it? And see what her dress looks like. That's what we all want to do.'

Please say yes, she thought. Agree with Grandad. She didn't want to be caught in the middle.

The girls nodded and got on with their breakfast. Good as gold.

'It doesn't seem five minutes since it was your wedding dress, laid out on that settee through there,' Dan told her.

The girls looked up at this, interested.

'Yeah, well,' said Christine. 'That was a waste of time, wasn't it?'

'Don't say that, love.' Her father studied her face. 'You don't half look like her, you know. It's incredible. And to think, those two old bitches coming round, asking US to pay to go to their bloody party! They should be paying YOU! You could be, like, a lookalike for them!'

Christine flicked her hair. 'Do you reckon, dad?'

'Oh, yeah. You could rake it in, you know. You could be a star turn.'

She had already noticed it herself. It was great to hear it from her dad, though. These days, Christine was holding herself with dignity. Her whole look was fashionable now. Maybe her time had come.

Dan went into town on the little local bus. He chose tins of wedding biscuits with the faces of Charles and Diana on. Parker pens inscribed with the date, mugs with crests on like they gave away at school for the Coronation, and commemorative coins in boxes inlaid with velvety stuff. He could present them to the girls as momentoes as they sat and watched the wedding. He hoped it would make it up for them, for not going to the party. But the party would be a washout, he was sure.

They were playing patriotic music in Woolworths. He went up and down the aisles with his basket, a spring in his step. He was picturing the girls in their red, white and blue frocks bought especially for tomorrow. For a second it made him sad that they wouldn't have anywhere but their front room to wave their little union jacks. But he was buoyed by the thought that, had Michael still been there, he wouldn't have had the chance to make this decision on behalf of the family. With that useless lump out of the house, Dan was master in his own house again. He was playing daddy once more and it made him feel twenty years younger.

He caught up with Lily Woods in the queue. He looked into her basket before she noticed him and she was buying the same coins and mugs.

'Are they for the girls?'

Lily gave a little jump and turned round, blushing. 'Oh, Dan . . .'

'Are you buying those for the girls? Because I already have.'

She looked down at his basket. 'Oh, look, great minds . . .'

'We can't all give them the same stuff on the wedding day.'

'I suppose not,' she said. He frowned at her. The woman was wearing more blusher than usual. Blue eyeshadow. He wondered if she'd done it on purpose. Red, white and blue. She's trying to make herself more glamorous, he thought. She had one of those frilly-necked blouses on. He wondered why she was making more of an effort these days.

'Why don't you put yours back on the shelves?' he suggested and wiped his forehead, which, he realised, was damp with sweat.

'I don't see why,' Lily smiled. 'I'm ahead of you in the queue.'

She was trying to flirt with him. He was outraged. 'Lily, I mean it. This is what I'm buying them to commemorate the Royal Wedding and I'm the girls' grandad. That gives me first dibs. Now get your fat ARSE back in those AISLES and put them BACK!'

She stiffened and coloured. She hadn't reckoned on him having one of his turns in Woollies. She looked around to see if people were noticing but no, he'd been talking quietly, if nastily.

'No, Dan. I got here first, I'm afraid. And, besides, I'm buying these pens and coins and things for Michael to give the girls. These are a father's gifts. And, believe it or not, he's got first dibs over you in that department.' Her mouth did a prim sort of twitch as she finished and she squared her shoulders at him. Try and argue with that, she thought.

'You fucking HUNCHBACK,' he hissed at her.

Lily turned away from him and prayed that the queue would hurry up.

'You're determined to mess up our family. You ALWAYS have been.'

'What does that mean?'

'You're a fucking WITCH. You put the EVIL EYE on our Christine's wedding in the FIRST place. Coming round, shoving your BEAKY nose in.'

Lily had tears pricking up.

'Don't give me that. Everything BAD that's happened to this family and you've been THERE. Even at the reception with me on the fire escape. YOU were there.'

'Dan, I want you to leave me alone.'

The girl at the till was ready for her now and she was emptying Lily's basket, looking confused. Lily had tears running down her face.

'Don't you SERVE her!' Dan shouted. 'I'm warning you!'
He made a grab for the mug that the girl was holding. She
yanked her hand back.

'Dan!' Lily shouted.

'Buying STUFF for the girls. How dare you!'

The checkout girl started shouting for the manager.
The queue behind them was twittering with interest.

'They're from Michael!' Lily cried. 'For their poor dad to
give them!'

Dan laughed harshly. 'He isn't their dad! Didn't you
even figure that out, you STUPID cow? How could HE be
their dad?'

'He is! Of course he is.'

'That Michael hasn't even got it in him to be their dad.
Did you never work THAT out?'

The manager arrived then and he stammered at Dan,
asking him to leave. Dan threw down his basket of
souvenirs.

'I don't even WANT any of your Royal Wedding SHITE.'

He stomped out of the shop, and, shaking, Lily reached
for her purse.

*

The days leading up to the wedding were hot but the
nights came in freezing, especially in Michael's flat, with
its bare walls and its worn-down carpet. In the evenings
he didn't know what to do with himself. There was no telly
there yet. He could really do with one, and a video. Just
before he'd left home, they had joined a new thing, a video
club. They sent you a catalogue of everything you could
hire, one at a time, a week at a time, and if you paid thirty
pounds you could choose ten films from their list. All up-
to-the-minute stuff. Just before he left, Grease had
arrived in the post. He hadn't even got a chance to see it.
He hoped Christine had remembered to send it back.
Maybe she would think about how they had gone to the
pictures to see it together. Queued up outside with all the

teenagers. He wondered if it would make her sad. It seemed wrong that you could watch Grease at home. It wasn't a night out anymore.

Of an evening, then, Michael found himself wandering the streets. Whenever he got back from work he was still bristling with energy, with wanting to talk and do things and back at the flat there was no one. He hadn't realised how busy home had made him. Christine said he did nothing at home, but he must have done, to make his time feel so empty now. And with the Royal Wedding day coming up, and the street party and all, he was going to feel really alone.

I should be making more of an effort to get the girls over to mine, he thought. It was tidy now, if bare, and it was warmer, because of the heater that he'd been given. Christine will have to let me have the girls over to stay. I'm giving her all my money. I've got rights. That's what Aunt Lily always says. I should make more of a fuss about seeing them, or they'll think I don't want them at all.

He had bought a second-hand bed settee for them and put it in the living room. He was all ready for his girls to come and stay.

I'll phone Christine. I'll tell her I want them this weekend. We'll have fun. I'll tell them it's just like camping out, living somewhere like this. They'll enjoy it. I'll tell Christine.

But first he needed a walk. He needed time to clear his head.

Clearing his head was a euphemism now, even to himself, and it involved walking out of the town centre, purposefully, in the light evenings of June, out past the ring road, and up onto the Common. That's where Michael went to clear his head. Oddly, also, to give him courage to talk to Christine or even think about getting back into his life. He had a lot to think about. He had a lot to clear out of his head.

You met interesting people here, too, despite every-thing. Here he had met the man who had given him, freely, that electric bar heater, on the very afternoon he had walked out on his family. That wasn't the first man Michael had met on the Common, but he'd been the one who wanted to talk most and the one who had seen him again afterwards. An older man, balding, in a lambswool Marksies jumper and old jeans. He was the first man that Michael had gone back home with.

'Have you got somewhere to go?' the balding man had said and Michael, surprised to be talked to, said, 'No,' and without any fuss the man had led him quietly back to his own place. A small terraced house right by the Common. A cold house too, it seemed like, or at least, Michael was cold. He stood in the man's bathroom, shivering, and the man had warmed him with his towels, hissing through his teeth, rubbing some life back into him. Michael had been soaked with rain and worried he'd catch a chill. The man had taken his clothes off him and made him stand under his shower while he watched and Michael didn't say anything. He hardly said anything to the first man he had gone home with, just stared in interest at what the inside of someone else's house looked like.

The man had switched on the lamps in his bedroom and lay the warm, dry Michael down under his heavy continental quilt. He told him his name, Andrew, and he slid under the quilt and took Michael's cock into his mouth. That was warm too and Michael felt like he was coming back to life.

Michael found his flat after that, in the shabbier part of town, and he'd seen Andrew again, in a pub, and went back to his house again. This time the place was familiar and Michael was more bold, if still baffled, in what he was doing. He told Andrew how cold his flat was and Andrew turned up at his door with the electric heater. And Michael went out to the Common almost every night.

Would I be doing this if I hadn't walked out? He wasn't sure. He leaned against his usual tree as dusk came down, softening the light and the noises of the woods. In the hotels where he'd stayed on courses he had done a thing

135

or two. He had taken a man into his room once, someone else on his computer course, and they had both had a drink too many and neither really knew what to do with each other. They hadn't kissed, they'd hardly touched. They had just pulled on each others cocks and it had all been a disaster, really. They'd left each other, ashamed. It wasn't really being unfaithful. Other nights Michael had taken taxis to gay pubs in those cities he stayed in, and went to see what people were like. Steeling himself before he went in, expecting to see . . . what? Men in dresses and make-up and men in leather looking frightening, wanting to beat him up and do terrifying things to him. He was never sure what to expect at all. Never sure if he'd see someone there just like him.

But this was the place for him. These woods. There were educated people here; you could tell just by a few muttered words. They were professional men and he was sure some of them must be married, like him, with kids. It was no different, really, to going off for a game of squash.

They brought their dogs and you could hear them coming in the twilight down the cinder paths, smoking and coughing and the figures waiting patiently under the trees would stiffen in readiness; waiting for heads to turn.

The night before the wedding there was a younger man who approached Michael and kissed him, full on the mouth. It was the first time he had been kissed like that and he stood, stunned, relishing the burn of the man's stubble on his face and closing his eyes as the younger man touched his cock. He wanted to ease Michael's jeans all the way down to his ankles, and Michael was nervous of being that exposed. He tried to murmer a complaint, but the boy shushed him and pushed Michael's hand to his own cock. As they went on, with the younger man crushing and pushing himself against Michael – and Michael could smell the peppermints and cigarettes on his breath – he was wondering about phoning Christine on the way home tonight. He could call from a phone box and (full of bravado from coming into this young fella's gob;

sucked and licked and brave again) he could demand to see his girls on the night after the party in the street.

They were joined then by a burlier man, pushing his way into their company. The prickle of the wool of his jumper, the fleshy bulb of his cock nudging into their hands. The boy looked up and happily kneaded at the man's balls and Michael's heart jumped: how many more would come out of the shadows, wanting to join in? He wasn't used to this kind of thing. It was darker now and he couldn't see an awful lot. He jumped again when the bigger man, gasping, asked, 'Michael?' and it turned out to be Andrew, standing there, panting out his breath as the younger man sucked him off.

We're both being unfaithful now, Michael thought, and came in a rush up the younger man's neck and shirt. He apologised and tried to look for a hanky.

'Am I still coming round yours tomorrow night?'

Had they planned that? They had.

Michael reached down to pull up his pants and his jeans. Cold again. The hairs on his legs stiff and erect. Why do I want to knock around with an old guy like that? But it's the same old story, isn't it? Michael – flattered that anyone was interested in him in the slightest – saying yes, yes, anything, to the first one who came his way.

He started to back away, onto the gravelly path, and could see quite clearly, the younger boy stooped over Andrew, his head nodding back and forth. 'Come the next day,' said Michael. 'Come the morning after. I'm doing something.'

Andrew was nodding as well and Michael turned and ran out of the copse, his flies still open, and the Common humming with life behind him.

*

On the afternoon of the wedding they had to keep the curtains drawn in the living room so they could see the telly. Christine sat on the couch with the girls in their patriotic dresses and she tried to ignore the sounds from the field at the back. Out there, the whole street was shouting and cheering at the egg and spoon races, the sack races, the dads' twenty yard dash. She went into the kitchen to take a tray of sausage rolls out of the cooker and she watched the street party for a few minutes and could swear blind she saw Lily Woods out there, getting involved.

We're never involved, she thought. What's wrong with us lot, that we can never be the same as everyone else? Are we better than them? Is that what we think?

'All that out there's got nothing to do with the Royal Wedding,' said her dad. 'It's just running around being daft. They aren't watching the actual wedding, are they? Not like us.'

This was the first thing he had said to her all day. Ever since she told him that Michael was coming to fetch the girls that tea time so they could stay over with him.

'What does he want them today for? We're having a family day.'

'Michael's their dad,' she sighed.

'Christine, Christine,' he shook his head. 'Everyone else might believe your lies, but don't think you can kid your old dad. Give him that much credit, lass. Them girls could have any number of fathers, and don't you pretend other-wise. All right?'

In the quiet that came down after that exchange, they watched the Royal Wedding for four hours non-stop, from the glittering procession up to the Cathedral, right to the leaving for the honeymoon. Christine and her dad said hardly anything to each other and the girls cheered and cheered.

*

Their dad's hair was longer than they were used to. When he opened up the back door of the car for them to climb in, Jessica wasn't sure at first. What if he wasn't the real daddy? He didn't seem like the real one, somehow. His clothes weren't familiar, either. He had been away from them and he'd bought new clothes. They were newer, somehow. Maybe he had cleaned himself up specially for seeing them again. Their mammy made a comment about his hair having grown over his shirt collar. The two of them talked funny to each other. Very politely. Daddy opened the car door and told them to climb in and Judith was doing it, sliding along the hot leather of the back seat like she could see nothing wrong. She recognised her daddy all right. He was familiar to her. Jessica just followed, full of doubts.

The two girls were hot and tired after a day in the living room watching the television. The curtains drawn all day and the sunlight coming through in two orange oblongs. They were still in their patriotic dresses, though Judith hated hers, hated its frills. Mammy had told them to keep on those dresses for going to daddy's, and there was a suitcase he was stowing in the hatchback, which was filled with pressed clothes to wear for tomorrow. Katy the white cat, who Jessica couldn't be without, was also pressed down inside that case. They were only going for one night, mammy had told them. It would be just one night without her. Their first night apart, but it would be over in a flash. Daddy would soon bring them back. They had to spend some time with him, too. That was only right and fair. They needed a daddy as well.

Grandad Fletcher didn't come out to see them off. He didn't think they should be going at all. After the wedding had finished on the telly he went stumping upstairs for a lie down. He hadn't even said goodbye to them.

Mammy was crying now, and trying not to.

'For God's sake, Christine . . .'

'I know.'

'It's only one night!'

'I know!' she said, with one knuckle pressed up to her mouth. 'Let me have a blub if I want, all right?' She looked daddy up and down, and, watching from the back seat of the car, Judith knew she was taking in his new, tidy clothes. 'They've never been away from me before. That's all it is.' She hugged herself and shivered in her loose cotton dress.

'You can't resent me having them for one night!' daddy hissed. 'I've not seen them at all! You have them all day, every day . . .'

'I know, I know, Michael . . .'

'Well, don't go . . .'

She nodded and touched his arm. 'I'm not.' She tried a smile and Michael was confused now. 'Brave heart,' she said, biting her lip, letting go of his arm. He shook his head and moved away.

He turned and said, 'Christine, I meant to ask . . .'

She looked at him sharply. 'What?'

'Did you send Grease back to the video club?'

She breathed out hard. 'Of course I did.'

He nodded and climbed into the driver's seat and told the girls to wave at mammy as he pulled out of the driveway, turned the corner, and took them out of the Avenue.

*

Judith watched town slide by with interest. They were going into the middle of town and some of it she recognised; the centre and the shops. It was all very quiet and she knew that was because of the wedding. People were still at parties, like the one on the wasteground out the back.

As daddy drove them quietly through the streets, and the streets became less familiar, she imagined they were on that procession they had watched on the telly. On the pink tarmac and following behind the golden coach with the princess in. When the princess had been let out of the coach, at the foot of the scarlet staircase, her helpers had to pull out the train of her dress first. She had sat patiently as they unfolded and stretched out the creamy skin of her train. When eventually she had walked up the steps into the giant church, the tail of the dress had followed her, for yards and yards behind. Judith had liked the way her blue eyes glittered as she walked amongst the people and the flowers.

She kept glancing at mammy to see if she liked it too and mammy was staring hard as well at the princess as the music began.

Daddy put on the radio and they were still playing the music from the wedding. He listened for a second and then turned the channel to one playing pop. Blondie. The radio crackled and hissed.

He parked in a street that Aunt Lily would say was dirty. The girls stood and waited by a heap of stuffed bin bags in the alley as he locked up the hatchback and hefted their suitcase. 'All this stuff!' he grinned at them. 'I think your mam's packed a bag for a month!'

Judith turned round to see Jessica's eyes go wide at this, and they did. A month! she was saying, and Judith shook her head quickly to reassure her.

Daddy's place was up stone staircases. It was dark and smelled of wee. Someone had dropped their fish and chips on the way up. His flat was right at the top, under a skylight that punched hot air down onto the small landing. Jessica was looking at the potted geraniums, smelling them, pulling a face, as daddy unlocked the door of his flat.

He busied himself in his kitchen (which was the same room as his front room, only behind a counter) as the girls took in their new surroundings. He had a Star Wars poster – The Empire Strikes Back – on the wall above his cooker. On another wall there was a framed photo of the two girls when they were much, much smaller. They looked like different girls. Judith thought it odd that there were pictures of them here, a place they'd never been. It was like being owned by strangers. Jessica was squeezing her hand hard.

'Did you enjoy the wedding then?' Daddy made them tea in grown-up mugs. He patted the settee and got them to come and sit down. They both nodded. 'Look, I got you these.'

On the coffee table there were presents wrapped up in red tissue paper. One pile each. Jessica sat forward quickly, but wouldn't move to open them until Judith gave the nod.

'Can you read your own names? And tell whose is who?'

'Of course,' said Judith, and slid Jessica's parcels over to her.

Daddy sat back to watch them shred the red paper. 'They're just souvenirs. For today.'

Just for today? Judith wondered. What was the use of presents given just for today? She opened the padded box with the shining coin inside. The princess's head was on it, facing upwards. 'Can you spend this in shops?'

'No!' he laughed. 'That kind of coin you keep. You keep it and give it to your own little girls, later.'

Our own little girls? Judith stared at the coin, and saw that Jessica had opened hers, too.

'That's your own little piece of history,' daddy said.

They knew that daddy worked in a bank. He knew all about money. Mammy said he came home from work stinking of it. Money smelled sour, Judith always thought; like the smell of daddy's grey suit.

'I'll give you pocket money, as well, for spending at the shops,' he said. 'That's good, isn't it? You'll be getting two lots of pocket money from now on, when you come to see me. One from mammy and one from me.'

Jessica spoke up. 'Mammy puts our money in a post office account. For new shoes at Easter and for when we go to the school.'

Michael smiled at her. He was enchanted at her saying so much to him. He suddenly wanted to gather Jessica up in his arms for saying so much to him. Judith did all the talking and there was something about her canniness, her carefulness, that meant he would never grab her up for a hug like he wanted to his quieter daughter. But he resisted the urge to cuddle Jessica now, in case he put Judith out. Instead he grinned at her and didn't say anything and watched her unwrap the souvenir pen, the tin of Royal Wedding biscuits. The silver pens were a big hit. He found some paper for them and they drew pictures of the wedding at the coffee table as he set about making the tea.

He let the beans warm up in the pan and stared out of his kitchen window, past the spider plants (which he'd let grow dusty; each leaf with a baby of its own, parched and suspended) and watching over the rooftops of town. Down behind the terrace of shops there was another street party finishing with the last of its sticky buns, and bunting strung out, as the sun began its slow slide out.

*

'Are you cold girls?'

There was a definite chill in the flat as he decided it was time, almost, to turn the sofa into a bed for them. They had to have their baths first and he lugged the electric three-bar heater into the tiny bathroom to warm it up for them. Soon it was quite toasty in there.

'Are you warm enough, girls?'

As they grew over-tired and testy, they bonded themselves against him by repeating the things he said to them.

'Are you cold, girls?' Judith said.

'Are you warm, girls?' Jessica laughed.

It became a game then and Michael just had to give in to it, with a laugh of his own. 'Do you want bubble bath? I think I've got some.'

'I think I've got some,' Judith repeated in a prissy tone. 'I think I've . . .'

'That's enough now,' Michael said. 'It's time you had your bath.'

There was no telly in his flat, so the night was finishing early. He was worn out with them, with the effort of having to find things to say all the time, to keep their minds occupied. He hated the dull silences that had slotted in from time to time. He had pinned their drawings of the wedding up in his kitchen and the three of them had stared for some time at the princess, twice over, trailing her massive dress on a staircase.

'She just copied mine,' Judith said. 'She copies everything I do.' It was true Michael thought. Jess's princess was an unkempt version of her sister's.

Michael whipped up the foam in the bath and prayed that the immersion would cough up enough hot water. There would be hell on if the girls went home and told Christine that daddy had made them sit in a cold bath. For a second he was tempted to test the water with the tough skin of his elbow, like when they were babies. But they weren't babies now and the danger back then had been water coming out too hot.

And it isn't with your elbow you test it, is it? It should be with softer skin. Christine had told him that.

They wouldn't undress in front of him at first. They stood stubbornly on the bath mat in their union jack frocks. Judith was dumbly shaking her head.

'But I'm your dad!' he said.

They compromised, eventually, so that Judith would undress herself and then she would help Jessica, who still found it fiddly to do. Then he would come in with his hand over his eyes and help them into the bath and then he could open his eyes, once they were both sitting in the bubble froth. He thought it was a bit of a palaver, but he went along with it.

When they were safely sitting, one at each end of the tub, he sat on the toilet lid and talked to them, like he knew Christine did. Their small arms were shining with water.

Look at them, he thought. Perfect clean limbs, suds sliding off them.

'Do you want me to wash your hair?' he asked.

'Do you want me to wash your hair?' Judith mimicked.

He didn't ask again, knowing it to be a hassle. They used to scream when Christine combed their tats out under the hairdryer. Best keep it all easy tonight.

'Is the water hot enough?'

'Is the water hot enough?'

'Is the water hot?'

He had put the immersion back on while they were undressing. He turned the tap on now to see if he could warm it a little. It turned with a tinny shriek. The girls giggled as the water poured in and he made sure Jessica, who was nearest the taps, wasn't close enough to get scalded.

'Warm things up for you, girls!'

They laughed. 'Warm things up!'

'Warm things up for you, girls.'

It was going all right, really. He put on another bar of the heater. Pretty soon it was cosy in there, for the first time ever, he thought.

*

When they were put to bed under the clean sheets of the bed settee he went in for his own bath. He used their bath water, because there wasn't much chance of getting any more out of the tank tonight. But he liked the idea of using their water. Making him closer to them. It felt like a proper home, tonight.

It feels like that because I've got someone else's needs to see to. It isn't just me, putting myself first. I've got to have a proper bedtime and everything and I can't sit up through the night staring out the window and I can't go walking the streets. I've got those two to think of and it makes me better, somehow. More organised.

The flat was so cosy, warmed right through. He slid under the still foamy water, looking down at himself and lying right back in the bath.

145

Tomorrow might be tricky. What if Andrew comes round before I've taken the girls back? Tricky questions. I should have said don't bother coming round at all. What do I want with a fat old bloke like that?

He started to scrub himself with the sponge.

Nothing. There can be nothing I want with a fat old bloke, surely.

I'm the girls' dad. I'm a dad. Dads don't do the things I do. I'll push Andrew away from the door. I'll tell him I don't know who he is.

Christine cried when I took the girls today. She didn't want to, but she cried. She's missing me. She hates our family falling apart. She's seeing what it's like, left alone with her father. She's seeing what her mother had to put up with. And she needs me, Michael, still. I could still be a husband to her. I could still be there, being daddy.

His ears pricked up. Was that the girls moving? Had one of them got up? They were asleep, though. When he'd left for his bath they'd both been asleep; breathing deeply, flat out, no complaints, no wanting to stay up late. He had left the bathroom door ajar, to listen for them.

There it was again. One of them, or both, had woken. They'd be scared, in the dark, in a stranger's flat.

It's still amazing. They can make noises, do things, completely independent of me.

Quiet again. Perhaps they've gone back to bed. Perhaps I didn't hear anything. Noise from outside. We're in the noisy part of town; the middle of town.

He hoped the street noise wouldn't frighten them.

He was lying back in the suds with his eyes closed and when he opened them again he saw that the door was further open. One of the girls was standing there in her nightie. She was looking down at him with her hair mussed up.

'Judith?' he asked, starting to sit up, cover himself, slipping on the old enamel of the bath.

'Warm things up,' she said. 'Warm you up, daddy.'

He chuckled. 'The water's a bit cool now, yes.' He wanted to tell her to go back to bed, back in with her sister. He hated the thought of her looking down at him in the bath. 'Go back to . . .'

She bent to touch the electric heater. 'Shall I put this on hotter? And warm you up more, daddy?'

Bless her heart. It must be Jess, not Jude after all, being thoughtful like that. His quieter, fonder girl.

'Don't touch the heater, sweetheart,' he started to get up. 'Watch your fingers. It's . . .'

But she was picking it up. He could see the burning orange elements as she lifted it in both hands. She squealed. The noise ran through him. She held it out in front of her.

He shouted, 'Jess! Put it down! I said not to touch it!'

She howled and held it over the bath. Her skin was blistering on her fingers. They were both shouting now.

Michael was scrambling out of the bath, splashing dirty water over the side. His daughter screeched as he stumbled and slid.

Then the strength was giving out in her arms and it was with relief that she dropped the hot, heavy metal of the thing.

She covered her ears and her eyes with her burned hands and sank to the floor, shrieking, as the bath sent plumes of steam up to the ceiling.

The noise was tremendous. Daddy was quiet. All the lights went out.

*

Lily had her own key. Often, when Michael was at work, she would pop into his flat to clear round for him. She knew what it was like for men on their own. It was no bother for her to help out. And, besides, this morning the girls were with him. All her favourite people together in one place.

She hauled herself up the stone stairs. She tried not to take the squalor of it all to heart.

Maybe soon he'll find somewhere nicer. Maybe soon there will be a house. On one of the new estates they're putting up.

She let herself into the dark flat.

Well, they're not even up yet, at ten in the morning. It must be all the excitement from yesterday. It must have worn them out.

The girls were sitting side by side on the bed settee. They were sitting in the dark with a duvet, a sheet and wet towels wrapped around them.

They were clutching each other like two little monkeys and shivering. They were both soaking wet.

8
Nasty Trick

For the rest of that summer Jessica's hands were band-aged.

Christine had to unwrap them carefully, clean out the burns and bandage them again every morning and every night. Jessica squirmed and cried each time. She had to be held still while her mother put on the special balm.

'This will cool them. It'll cool them down and make them better, love.'

Christine hated the blisters on her daughter's hands and the fat purple welts that the blisters turned to. The skin looked too tight, too red and sore to belong to such a young girl. The skin was damaged already. Jessica would cry whenever anyone paid attention to her hands.

She'd have scars. Thick bands across each of her fingers and her small palms. Christine had to tell her that they wouldn't always hurt; they wouldn't always be like this. The skin was young. It could heal itself. She would be able to forget all of this.

All summer Jess couldn't put her hands in her pockets. She couldn't play with her toys. She couldn't bite her nails, though she longed to.

'She's growing up to be a nervous child,' Grandad Fletcher said. 'She'll grow up with nerves just like – Well, you know who.'

Christine found herself standing between her dad and her bandaged daughter. 'Is it any wonder she's nervous? Is it any wonder at all? After that?'

At last there was a difference between the twins. To differentiate them, people had more to go on now, than, how much one talked while the other was quiet. Now they could see plainly which one it was with the wrapped-up hands. The one who had been involved in the father's misadventure. The one who, as Christine put it, had tried to save his life. Trying to grab the hot fire as it fell into the bath. A little girl like that, put at such a risk. She could have been killed herself, had the metal welded itself to her flesh and she hadn't been able to drop the heater. What presence of mind her daughter had; trying to save her father.

Christine was angry at someone. She wanted to be furious with someone; tear a strip off them, scream blue murder in their face for what her daughters had been exposed to. Michael, of course, was who she really wanted to yell at.

She was superstitious enough not to go shouting at the dead.

When they stood at the graveside and she looked at Jess with her clumsy, bandaged hands Christine felt her heart split and drop inside her chest. She couldn't even hold her daughter's hand. Instead she put her arm along her shoulders, lightly, over the stiff new fabric of her black coat. The girls' new black coats, bought in a rush for daddy, would have to do for winter and for school.

Christine had put the pair of them into mourning for their whole first year at the Infants.

Then, as autumn came in, and the girls stood in the corner of the yard, they needed special care from the teachers and assistants. 'Their daddy's dead,' is what the headmistress told the staff before the school reopened.

When that whole generation of five-year-olds arrived in September, the mothers at the school gates and the other five-year-olds themselves all knew, 'Their daddy's dead.' And the girls had been there when it had happened. He had died in a flat and the girls had been left alone with the body all through the night.

The other kids would scare each other telling the tale, and they'd race across the playground, to the step where Jess and Jude were waiting for playtime to end, and they would badger them with questions: What's it like to have no dad? What's it like to see a dead body? Did their daddy have a ghost?

Jess and Jude would bide time, tight-lipped, until they could go back into the classroom.

Jess's bandages were off by then, her hands were meant to be healed. She kept her mitts on all of the time, even when she was indoors and to her, the skin felt too tight and tender. She could never go running around in the whipped-up breeze and kerfuffle of the playground, never dash about and collide like the other kids.

All the others bounced around heedlessly. If they fell, all it took was a dinner nanny to help them up, brush them down, flick away their few tears and they would be off again. They never hurt themselves really. To Jess, it seemed that most of the other kids were made out of rubber. They were more like Jude than her.

Out of solidarity, Jude stayed on the sidelines with her sister. She was furious with her; in the simple, clean way that Christine wanted to be furious with someone. Jess had been somewhere and seen something that Jude never had. Jess was one up on her, now. And she had somehow, in some way that they never talked about in their house, taken their daddy from them. But, 'It was an accident, an accident,' their mam had told them a thousand times, hugging them both close.

'Daddy was careless and he had an accident. He'd have died whether you were there or not.'

Jude had walked into the bathroom in the dark and she had seen the dark shape lying there in the water. Black burnt bits floating on the surface. The smell of it pushed itself right into your head and it stayed there for months. Ages afterwards Jess and Jude would be able to remind themselves of that burnt smell.

She had found Jess staring at the bathtub, afraid to touch her dad. But Jude had wanted to see the moment before. The actual moment it had happened. It was something her sister had robbed her of.

They were supposed to do things together. To the outside world, however, the sisters were bonded in mutual protection and, for a while, silence.

*

'It's no good if they're going to clam up,' Dan said. 'They can't go through life saying nothing.'

'It's the shock,' Christine told him. 'They'll come out of it.'

Dan shook his head. He hated the stories he had already heard, of how the girls were being picked on at school. It was natural, because kids were curious and wicked, but he wasn't prepared to see his granddaughters suffer so early and grow up soft. 'They have to snap out of it. If the other bairns see them weak like that, they'll go under. It starts that soon. They could be ruined for life.'

Maybe they already are, Christine thought. Maybe their father's death has spoiled them forever.

What was he playing at? Did he do it on purpose? What kind of sick stunt would that be? To murder himself when he was alone with the girls, when he knew they would be the first to see his body lying under the shallow water and suds. She couldn't believe such a thing of him. It had to be an accident.

Then she would look at Jessica's bandaged hands, especially early on, when the burns would matter and bleed yellow dirty stains on the cotton. She would wonder if Jess could have done something bad. But she pushed the thought out of her mind. And the thought that, had anything bad gone on, it would have been the other one, the naughtier girl, Judith, who did it. But they were just girls. She was a bad mother herself, to let herself think such things.

It's not worth going over it, Christine. Just get on with life. You can't let yourself dwell.

Lily Woods might know more. Lily had been the first one there and she had seen Michael lying naked in the

152

bath. What had his expression been? A rictus of agony and shock? His hair standing on end like in a cartoon? A comic expression of mild surprise and dismay? Or a smug, pleased grin in death, revenged upon them all with his suicide?

Christine had to know, but there never seemed to be any way of asking Lily exactly what he had looked like. Did the skin boil and burn and turn scarlet like a lobster's? Had he been scorched black in the water? Christine kept imagining him in different, tortured poses.

She hadn't gone into the chapel of rest. She hadn't gone for a last look at him. 'He wasn't even my husband when he died,' she said at the time. 'We were already split up. I'd changed my name back to Fletcher and everything.'

She felt so hard and determined, saying that. The words were coming out of her but she didn't believe them.

'Nothing was signed, Christine,' said her dad. 'He's still yours. You should go and look at him.'

She pulled herself out of his grasp, thinking of her mother. No papers had been signed there either; her mam and dad were still bound together and he'd made no effort to go and look for her. Dan must have realised this too, because he went quiet and wouldn't push the point.

Lily Woods was inconsolable. She didn't say much at the funeral, or in the weeks afterwards. The girls started school and still Lily didn't come round, and didn't make any acknowledgement of this big step for them.

What right has she got, Christine thought; to take it all to heart worse than anyone else? Who does she think she is?

Christine gritted her teeth one day and decided to go over and see her. She expected Lily to hate her. She could see how she might. Her nephew had died as a direct result of getting involved with Christine. If he'd married any other girl, he'd still be alive now. He'd have been a happier man. Christine braced herself and, without telling Dan where she was going, crossed the big road.

Lily had kept her curtains drawn for weeks. When she opened the door, saw Christine there and softly exclaimed, there was a musty, unaired smell drifting out from behind her. She was in her housepants and a fairy sweatshirt and she seemed not at all surprised or angry at Christine turning up at her door. 'Come in, love,' she said, and Christine stepped into the gloom of her hallway.

'I'm sorry you have to come over and see the house in this state,' Lily began, and led her into the living room. She had candles lit, dripping wax onto every surface. The air itself felt waxy and thick. There was a sickliness to it that Christine could taste as she sat on the settee. Lily's tiny china ornaments on their doilies looked pathetic and dull.

'No . . . You don't have to make an effort for me.' Christine murmured.

'I'm sorry I haven't been over. Those little sweethearts. I've hardly seen them at all since . . . since before. I saw you all leaving for school though, the first day you took them. I was watching from upstairs. I waved. Did you see me?'

'No . . .'

'Oh . . . How are they getting on? Are they settling in?'

'They're fine,' said Christine. 'They're settled.'

'Are they making friends?'

'They've got each other, haven't they?'

'I suppose so.'

Lily sat down. She sagged into the chair as if it had no springs in it. The two women looked at each other. Christine was starting to wonder what she'd come over to say.

'I've hardly slept,' Lily said at last. 'Ever since. My hair's falling out. I get these headaches.'

Christine blinked. Why do I want to hear about Lily's complaints? What's wrong with the woman?

'I can't sleep,' Lily went on. 'I won't let myself until . . . Well. I've cancelled all of my appointments and my visits. I'm using up all of my time and energy on him . . .'

Christine didn't understand at all.

'I don't follow you.'

Lily plucked at the arm of her chair. 'I'm trying to get him. I'm trying to find him. For you. For us.'

'Who?' Christine sat forward suddenly. 'Michael?'

'Of course, Michael. I can be of some use. I can . . .'

'Lily, no.'

'I can, Christine. Sometimes I feel so close. He seems so close. I can hear his breathing at night. I can smell him. I've heard him call out . . .'

'Lily, you'll drive yourself crackers, doing this.'

'It's my job. I'm the only one who can . . .'

'He's dead,' Christine snapped. 'Michael's dead. None of us want him to be dead, but he is. No one will ever talk to him again, or see him again. You can sit up awake for weeks on end, but there's no getting him back. He's gone, Lily.'

Lily put her face in her hands. 'You don't understand. You don't believe. Michael did . . .'

'I don't want to hear about this.'

'He heard his own mam talk to him. He believed in it. And I'm good, Christine. I can make him come back for you . . .'

Lily stood too, and she was clinging onto Christine's arm. Christine shook her off roughly. 'Leave him be, Lily!'

The old woman fell back, onto her chair.

'Leave him alone. And leave us alone, too.'

Lily watched Christine leave and, as the door banged, she started to pray.

*

Everything Christine had wondered about his death, Lily had wondered too. There were questions that she needed Michael to answer. She wanted him to come back and say yes, it was an accident and random things do happen. And that he was at peace, at peace, at peace. She would be content then. She would act as his medium and link him back with his family, let him talk to his girls.

They would need him to say things, everything he had wanted to tell them as they grew up. She could, in effect, become their father for them and it began to seem to Lily that this was what her gift was meant for. Things weren't, then, as random as all that. She had a role. If only she could fetch Michael back.

She sat listening all night and all day, falling asleep only now and then, when sleep was sometimes indinstinguishable from her hardworking trances, and from the noises she picked up, the thrum of many voices, she would try to tease out the strand of words that she knew must be Michael's. She knew he would be talking, knowing that she was there.

This certainty had seen her through the shock of seeing him lying there, dead. That morning when she'd turned up with cakes and other street party leftovers when she had found the girls shivering in cold and shock. When Lily looked at him slumped in the water, naked as the day he was born, his unfamiliar, grown man's body, her first thought had been; I can still talk to him. He will come back, surely, for his Aunt Lily.

For a week or two she held onto his flat keys. She even kept the rent up on his batchelor flat, only so she could go back to the last place he had been happy – she was sure he had been happy at the end – and try to pick him up. She sat in his flat alone, trying to catch the sound of his voice as, across town, his closer family made the arrangements to dispose of his body. They were angry at her for not being involved, she knew, but she was thinking longer term. She was seeing the bigger picture. In the bare flat, Lily was trying to snare his eternal soul.

A man came calling on him one morning. A middle-aged man who said his name was Andrew and who looked surprised to see Lily there. She thought he looked harmless and she made him a coffee and he could tell by her tone that something was wrong. He sat as she carefully told him the story. She asked if he was one of his colleagues from the bank. Andrew was crying. Great heaving sobs came out of his thick body. She was surprised at the man, crying like that. She even touched his shoulder to calm him.

'The bank?' he gasped. 'I hardly knew him. He was just a friend.'

Lily wanted to know. 'But where did you meet him? How did you know him?'

'Were you his mother?'

'I'm his aunt. His mother is dead. He's with her now.'

The man nodded and wiped his nose and moustache with the handkerchief she'd given him and he said, 'I suppose I was his lover. Not his boyfriend really, not yet. No, we wouldn't call it that. We were just getting to know each other. Did he tell you about me?' His wet eyes were open wide, almost pleading with her. Lily's mouth was dry and her throat quite tight. She found she could say nothing in reply, though the man, Andrew, clearly wanted her to.

He nodded and stood up. 'I'll be going. I'm sorry. Is there nothing I can do?' He was composing himself and passing back her hanky.

Lily thought over his words again and again after he had gone, looking for some chink in them, looking for evidence that someone, some cruel-hearted person, was pulling a nasty trick.

*

Dan put his foot down. The girls were never to go back to Lily Woods' house. She was no real relation to them. Not now. With all her ways, she would do them harm. The dead should lie in peace. The girls had to go on and grow up properly.

He put his foot down with Christine. She had to pull herself together, too.

'Nerves and depression were behind all your mother's problems and she had to sort herself out. Margaret only went off her head after you were grown, and that's something to be grateful for, at least. She saved her madness up until then.'

Christine was shocked at the way her dad was talking. He went on, 'You've got to be strong. Your girls are still tiny and they need you.'

She was finding that she couldn't grieve Michael at all. I'm in a limbo worse than his. He never belonged to me ever. There's no one there for me to grieve.

Meanwhile Dan played with his granddaughters the games he used to play with Christine. He was the bogeyman again. He scared them and made them squeal. He chased them around the house. When they lay in bed at night he would come round the door and jump out: boo! And they would laugh and laugh. Grandad would reassure them then. He wasn't really an ogre because he thought the world of them. He would tuck them in (mammy was having a drink downstairs) and tell them that no one would ever scare them again, not really. He would be the only ogre they would ever see and he was only pretend. The girls would sleep, smiling, secure, knowing this. They would talk and laugh together in the dark about Grandad who, one day, licked Jessica's fingers. He licked away the bits of scar she was so self-conscious about. He nipped at her fingers with his old teeth. 'I'll eat you all up!' he cried and both girls laughed.

But he added, 'You know, your Aunt Lily is a witch and she really does eat up little girls. She had a little girl of her own once. And she ripped her into pieces and baked her in a pie. I don't want you – either of you – to go round Aunt Lily's dirty house any more.'

9
In the Sixties Cafe

It was the back of beyond, back of beyond, back of beyond and, when Christine felt herself drowsing off to sleep, that was exactly what the noise of the rails was saying to her.

She wished she had a cushion to rest her head on and go to sleep properly. Across the table, both girls were napping, propped against each other. Beside her, Lily Woods had her nose shoved inside a gardening magazine. She had brought a whole bagful of comics and books and drinks for the girls, but as soon as the train had left they had both dropped off to sleep. It was the best behaved they'd been in ages.

I still don't know what I'm doing, going off like this on a whim of Lily's, she thought. They were nudging through shallow forested valleys on a smelly train and she hadn't told her dad where they were going. Just, 'away, for a few days, out in the Dales somewhere'. The old man hadn't been pleased. Why wasn't he coming as well? If it was a family trip, a weekend away in the countryside, why wasn't he indispensable? But he hadn't pushed the point. Christine still wasn't back to what he called normal, even after almost a year. It was spring, for God's sake, and she hadn't shook the doldrums off.

Dad would go barmy if he found out I was with Lily Woods.

As if on cue, Lily turned her head and smiled at her. 'The girls are missing all the good views.' She nodded at the window. They were shunting through the thickest part of the forest and the light was a delicate, shifting green. They emerged onto a viaduct, a crumbling Victorian monstrosity that gave them a stunning view of the hills. Christine gasped and smiled.

'They aren't really countryside kids. I've never taken them much. This is the first time they've been on a train.'

Lily nodded and turned back to her magazine.

The old woman didn't appear to hold a grudge for the way she'd been cut out of their lives. Christmas and the end of the old year had come and gone and they hadn't seen anything of her. She made no reference to the period of her exile and Christine was glad. There were other things to think about today.

Jessica woke with a small cry and sat forward. 'Are we nearly bloody there yet?' She looked pale at the way the carriage was rocking as it entered another valley.

'I've no idea,' Christine smiled. 'Drink your juice.'

'It shouldn't be too long,' Aunt Lily said. She rolled up her magazine and stowed it in her bag, pleased with herself.

I've got the twins with me again. Christine is on my side again. She must believe what I told her. She must do, to come all this way, to make the arrangements and to bring the girls. She must have decided to set store by what I said.

And so she should. Lily knew that she was right. She knew her information was sound. There were some people prepared to pay a great deal of money for the kind of information that Lily could fetch.

*

There were baskets of flowers out on the station. No one else was getting off at the town and it seemed the display was just for them. Primulas reminded Christine of her dad and how he used to garden, all of the energy he put into it. She remembered him rigging up lights from the kitchen so he could dig and transplant through the night. All that had stopped now though and the garden had withered to nothing. The grass had faded and scuffed away where the girls had played. Dan had even given up repairing fences and trellises. Only recently Christine had started to notice how he was turning into a proper old man, short of breath, loath to leave the house.

Lily was taking both girls' hands and marching them up the platform.

'Do you know where we're going?'

'It's only a small town. We can easily find the place.'

They had brought two small cases with them. Christine found it odd, being in a new place and not knowing where they'd be sleeping tonight.

'Do you mind if we don't go straight there?' she asked Lily. 'I don't want to go running straight in . . .'

'Sweetheart,' Lily shook her head. 'This is your show. It's up to you. You've got the hardest job.'

*

That was true enough. Christine had tried to block it out of her mind so far. She would know, when the moment came, what she should say. It would come to her naturally.

They walked out of the station, through an empty car park, into a small town. There wasn't much here. A few shops along a high street, a café or two, a church at the end of the deserted market place. The girls looked disappointed.

The words would come to Christine easily. She had nothing to be ashamed of. It shouldn't be too hard, her side of the conversation.

When Lily came to see her last week, checking first that the coast was clear and that Dan was out on one of his rare forays into town, collecting his pension, Christine wasn't sure. But if there was the slimmest chance that Lily was right, then she was taking it. If she didn't she would only wonder. Christine hated anything preying on her mind, keeping her awake at night.

Lily had said: 'He came, Christine.' Her eyes were bright and her cheeks were flushed.

Christine looked up the street and down, in case her dad was on his way back. She let Lily in.

'Michael came, Christine,' Lily gabbled. 'At last.'

Her shoulders were all hunched up. Her body was full of tension. Something had certainly happened to her, whether it was Michael or not. Christine decided to let her talk.

'He said it had been so hard to get through. He never realised the effort it took, the danger, to make yourself heard. He said you have to shout really loud, and that it's like looking over the most horrible precipice and, at any moment, you could slip. It's like shouting down over the lip of a deep, deep tunnel. But he knew his Aunt Lily would be listening for him. And I have been, haven't I? Ever since the first moment he was . . . taken.'

'What did he say?'

'You have to believe me, Christine. I wanted to fetch you, so you could listen too. I asked him. He said there was no time. He said I'd have to relay it all to you . . . The message was all for you.'

Lily was full of zeal. Christine had to hand it to her. She'd not shown a moment's doubt. Here they were now, in a town where none of them had ever been, and Lily was leading them up the high street as if she'd been born here. She'd had a vision of the place, she said.

Christine wondered what it would be like, being certain. But I used to be. I used to know where I was. Until I was nineteen and everything went to pot after that. I met Michael, or I was shoved under Michael's nose and things got out of my control. No wonder she couldn't be certain of anything after that. Everything that was hers became someone else's property. That was when the choices she made stopped being just hers.

These days she dithered and she hated that about herself. Brian had called round a month ago and he asked her out. A decent interval of widowhood had passed. Her dad, nice as pie to Brian in his shiny suit, had said as much. Christine had never even thought of the word 'widow', but that's what she was. And now, 'You're being courted again,' her father said approvingly of Brian. All these old-fashioned words, applied to her. As if the things that had happened to her had pushed her into a different generation.

With Brian she dithered the worst. When he took her out – in his Top Man suit with the narrow narrow collars and his thin striped tie – she couldn't even decide what to drink. It was so long since she'd been out she'd forgotten what her usual was. He ordered her a pint of lager, just like he had when she was sixteen. It was the same pub; the Dog and Duck. But they'd modernised it inside; the walls were red and pink. There were brass fittings everywhere. Brian had Duran Duran hair, up in a quiff. He'd had golden streaks put in. He worked in an electronics factory and had a car.

He'd always seemed so much older than her. Back then, there were so many things she wanted him to tell her about. He'd had that bike and he saw more of the world she wanted to know about. Now he was talking like a kid. About films he'd seen, about nights out with the lads. He hardly asked anything about her, or her kids, or Michael. He was embarrassed, she thought.

In his car she couldn't decide whether to let him kiss her or not. He drove them out to a lay-by on the ring road and she was still trying to figure it out. He wanted to know if she wanted to see him. He must really have wanted to, she thought, since he knew she had kids. Someone in Brian's position, with his looks, could have his pick. I must really be wanted, she thought. In the end she kissed him. It seemed like twenty years since anyone had done that to her. He grasped her up close, as if it had been that long for him, too, though she knew that couldn't be true. He'd talked about some of the girls he'd been knocking around with. He did without nothing. But he pressed her to him and she felt gathered up for the first time in ages. He tried to get her to touch him, to take it further, but she was happy sitting slumped across him, twisted awkwardly in the passenger seat. She wanted to sit there and just not move. Brian had pulled and petted at her and in the end she'd asked him to take her home.

*

'What these two tired girls need – and I know I need too, is refreshments!' said Lily brightly.

'We'll go to a caff,' said Christine.

Lily's eyes sparkled. 'What about the café?'

'Not yet.'

'Oh, Christine, we might as well. We have to go there anyway. What's the point in running up two bills in an afternoon, hm? Let's go straight there.'

She's enjoying this, Christine thought.

'Do we get to have a fucking milkshake?' Judith asked, perking up. Her socks were hanging down. Both girls looked dishevelled from the train. We look like a bunch of waifs and strays, Christine thought. They didn't look like she'd imagined them, when she'd pictured this afternoon in her head.

'All right,' she said, swallowing.

They picked up their cases again and Lily led them smartly, unerringly, up a side alley, towards a cafe hidden away. A sign swung above the door. The Sixties Cafe, it was called.

*

Inside they were playing Mary Hopkin. 'Those were the Days, my Friend'. The tables had white plastic cloths and tomato-shaped sauce dispensers. There were about five women sat at one table, squashed into anoraks, three of them wearing headscarves indoors. They must have come straight from the hairdressers, Lily thought.

The walls were painted in swirling psychedelic patterns, sun-faded. Old LP covers were framed and set out proudly on display. The twins made straight for the juke box, lit up purple and gold in the corner, Judith digging into her small purse.

There was a hatchway into the kitchen. There was no sign of a waitress yet.

'Don't look so worried,' said Lily as they slid into a booth. Christine, scowling, picked up the laminated menu. 'It's not Sixties prices,' she said, flicking through. Then she looked at Lily. 'What do I say to her?'

'You'll know what to say. I feel sure she wants to see you.'

There was a yell from the juke box. Judith had kicked Jessica in the shins and now she was having a go at the machine. She rocked it back and forth, sending the needle skidding. The ladies at the other table cried out in dismay at the noise and started to grumble and tut.

'Shit,' said Christine. 'Now they're off.'

'It's all fucking old records on this!' Judith was yelling. 'Mam! It's all fucking old shite!'

Beside her Jessica was sobbing loudly.

'I'll go and see to them,' said Lily.

'Cheers.' Christine buried her head in the menu. She slid her elbow into a pool of grease and cursed. One thing about Lily; she would take no nonsense from the girls. She made it plain that their language never shocked her.

Lily set her mouth in a prim line of disapproval and headed for the juke box. The waitress was already there. In a smutty pinny and a black dress, her grey hair piled up in rollers, she had nudged the twins aside with her hips and was seeing to the juke box. She gave it a hefty thump. 'That's sorted it,' she said as 'Wild Thing' started up. 'Right, you two.' She grabbed both girls by the arms of their school cardigans.

'Fuck off – you're stretching it!'

'Get off me –'

Lily scuttled over.

'Girls!' she shouted. The twins looked up in astonishment at the steel in her voice. 'Now, shut up!'

The other customers were looking over with interest.

'Do you know who you're talking to?'

Judith was wriggling out of the waitress's grasp, her face scarlet. 'This bloody old bitch . . .'

'Judith!' Lily shouted and made the girl jump. 'You haven't been brought up to talk like that. Now listen. This is your grandma who's got hold of you.'

Judith's eyes boggled.

The waitress let go of them suddenly. 'Lily? Lily Woods?'

'And these are Judith and Jessica.' She flapped her hands at the girls. 'They're yours.'

Margaret took a step backwards. 'What are you doing here? How did you know . . . ?'

Christine had swallowed hard and stood up. She walked over to face her mother. 'Mam?'

'Oh, god,' said Margaret. Her hand flew up to pat her hair. 'You've come after me? These are your girls?'

Christine took a hestitant step towards her.

Judith looked up at her grandmother. 'Where the fuck have you been?'

*

'Dancing in the Street', 'Dizzy', 'My Guy', 'She's Not There', 'Happy Together'. It wasn't till 'Sweet Talking Guy' came on that Margaret came out of the staff toilet to sit with them in their booth.

The twins hunched opposite her, glaring at her every move. She looked lined and worried and she smelled of fresh hair lacquer. She lit a cigarette with trembling fingers.

Lily was sitting back with a satisfied expression. Her job was over now and she had succeeded in reuniting them all. Christine glanced in her direction, suddenly envious. My job's just beginning, she thought.

'I want to know, first of all,' said Margaret, 'how you found me.'

'That's quite complicated . . .' said Christine.

Lily broke in. 'It's simple, actually. Michael told me from the other side. He even said what days you work here.'

Margaret tapped her ash impatiently on the floor. 'What other side?'

'He's dead, mam,' Christine said. 'He died last year.'

'Michael Michael?'

'Yes, mam.'

Margaret bit her lip. 'Don't call me mam yet, love. I'm not ready for it yet.'

'Not ready!' Lily exclaimed, and then held herself back.

'It was an accident.' Christine said in a dull voice. 'A tragic . . .'

'And you reckon you've talked to him from the . . . ?'

'Other side,' nodded Lily.

Margaret shook her head. 'I don't know what's going on, but I don't like it. I don't believe a word of anything you're saying.'

'Mam,' Christine burst. 'We've come miles to see you.'

'And what do you want?'

She's making herself deliberately hard, Lily thought. She's trying hard not to look at, nor acknowledge, the two girls who are looking with such interest at her.

'It's not Dan, is it? Nothing's happened to him?'

So she does care. 'No, dad's fine.'

Margaret put her hand over her eyes and tapped her cigarette again. 'I haven't been back in years, have I?' She wouldn't look her daughter in the eye.

'There's been nothing from you.'

'We thought you were dead,' Judith said.

'I'm not dead.'

'But where were you?' Christine burst out. 'So much has happened. You've missed everything . . .'

'I went away and I meant to come back. You must believe that.'

'I don't think I do, mam.'

'With each year it became more impossible. I'd walked out of my life and . . . people pretend you can do that, for a month or two, or a year. And they think they can just go back into it. That their family will just close back around them, like nothing's changed.'

They waited for her to go on.

'It isn't true. Everything moved on so fast. There was no space to go back. You'd figured everything out without me. I honestly only meant to be away a little while. But then you were married with kiddies on the way.' She looked for a second at the glaring twins. 'Everyone had got older. You were different people. I was scared, Christine. I was scared there was no room left for me.'

She's weakening, Christine thought. We're getting through to her. 'You came back for the wedding.'

'That was so hard to do. I wasn't having an easy time of it then. No money, no proper job. And look at what happened! That was all down to me . . .

'I cause disasters wherever I go . . .'

'That's not true, mam . . .'

Margaret's mascara was running in thick lines. 'Yes, it is. I've accepted that.'

'Mam, dad was pissed out of his head that night . . .'

The girls giggled at this.

'He was pissed. He fell off the thing because he was out of his mind. And you ran away . . . ! You never even stayed to see if he was alive . . .'

'I know. I ran. I was too scared to stay. And that was why I couldn't ever go back, as well. Two big failures of nerve. I'm too scared to have a family, Christine. I always was.'

'You brought me up! You were the strongest one!'

'Christine . . . every night you were out, alone or with one of your lads . . . I sat up alone, fretting. Your dad said you'd be all right. He knew you could look after yourself. But I couldn't stop worrying. The worrying ate me away. I was too scared and weak the whole time. It turned me into a narky bitch . . . into the kind of person I never wanted to be. At home it was all fear . . .'

*

They walked with her through the town as the shops started to close. Christine wasn't sure where they were heading. She didn't know where her mam was living. The girls were lagging behind, dragging their good shoes on the pavement.

'You've managed, though,' Margaret said. 'You've brought them up. They're . . . what? Six?'

'Nearly seven. Horrors.'

'You don't take after me. That's the main thing. You aren't easily scared off by things.'

'I haven't had the choice, have I?' said Christine bitterly. 'I had to get on with it. Once the twins were on the way . . .' Inside she was fuming. What was the point coming out here for her mam? She was no help. There's no use trying to find someone to depend on. You've got to shut your mouth and look after your own. Margaret's got nothing to do with any of us.

Margaret touched her arm. 'It's a nice evening. Let's go and walk by the river. The girls can throw stones in the water.'

'I thought we were going back to your house.'

Margaret gave a tight little shake of her head. 'Let's walk.'

They carried their cases down to the path alongside the river.

'Here,' Lily said as they approached the rocks, and the girls decided they wanted to play in the shale and the plunge pools. 'I'll wait here with the girls and all the gear. You walk with your mam. You go and talk.'

The twins went running off to sit on rocks, stripping off their shoes and socks, tossing them behind. The water was gurgling and soothing; the colour of beer.

'Thanks, Lily,' Christine said, dumping her bags as her mother started strolling on ahead.

'Give her a little time. She'll come round.'

'You've been really good to us. To me.'

Lily sat down with a smile. As Christine hurried to catch up with her mam, she allowed herself a small glow of pleasure.

*

'When you were little, I don't know if you remember . . . but I used to do things, like smack you, and nip you if you were bad.'

'Yeah, I remember you doing that.'

'I used to make sure you always sat beside me at meal times, especially if we were out at a café, or something . . .'

Christine wanted to take hold of her mother's hand. She watched it, swinging along beside her as they walked. Margaret noticed and plunged her hands in her coat pockets. 'Every mother is like that,' Christine said. 'Worried in case their brats are going to show them up. God, I should know. The way those two go on.'

Margaret gave a quick smile and rummaged for her cigarettes. In the breeze, as the light started to fade, her hair was streaming out over the collar of her coat. It was kinky, mushroom-coloured hair. She'd stopped dyeing it and styling it. Christine could hardly believe that her mother wore curlers to work. At least they were out now.

'No, I was worse than most mothers.' Margaret blew out her smoke in one exhausted rush. 'I used to nip your leg under the table cloth, to warn you to be good. It became an automatic reaction. You'd behave if I took a good chunk of your skin between my fingers and dug my nails in. You had weals on your legs and arms and, remember? We'd hide them from your dad.'

'Mam . . ..'

Margaret nodded. 'That's not how a natural mother carries on.'

'I don't think there's any such thing.'

Yet Christine did remember what her mother did. She also remembered being shut up inside her mother's wardrobe, with the smell of mothballs in her nose and the fur and wool pressing her back into the dark. Whenever, as a child, she'd taken a screaming fit, her mother marched her to the huge, dark wardrobe, and it seemed to reach back miles inside. Christine was bolted inside to scream it all out. She remembered trampling on her mother's carefully laid out shoes and snapping heels off them and thinking that would get her into even more bother. She rubbed her snotty and teary face into her mother's winter coats and her saggy hung-up cardigans. She beat on the wooden walls and the hollow floor and Margaret ignored her for an hour or two.

'I did some awful things.'

Christine couldn't believe she was saying this now. These were huge things at the time which, when Christine was a teenager, she found herself wanting to bring up all the time, so she could rub her mother's face in her own cruelty. But she'd just about forgotten them now. Here her mother was, bringing it all up again, as if it was her only memory of her daughter as a child.

'It doesn't matter now, mam. I've got my own kids.'

'I've thought about it a lot.' Margaret walked on. She was in a world of her own. Christine couldn't distract her back to the present. That's what it is, she thought. I'm talking to a woman who's trapped herself in the past and her own misery. In that moment, Christine resolved that, whatever happened, she would never look back and get stuck there. She had to move on. Even if it meant forgetting things on purpose.

'I've thought myself back to then,' Margaret said, 'Over and over, to see what I was playing at. I wanted you to be perfectly behaved. I wanted you to be different and to be safe.'

'It was never going to happen, mam. I was like my two are. I had my own ideas.'

'I didn't want you going off the rails.'

'Well. I didn't, did I?'

Margaret let out a last, slow hiss of smoke. She ground out her cigarette on the tarmac like she was squashing a beetle. 'You did, though. You did.'

'What? Because I got pregnant early? That's just what you did, mam. You can't make out . . .'

'The way you did it, Christine. That's what counts.'

'I don't get you, mam.' Christine coloured. Her mam was looking her straight in the eye now, more than making up for her evasiveness in the Sixties Café.

'I know what you did. I knew the minute that it happened.'

'You knew nothing.'

'You reckon? You did the same as me, Christine. You got yourself knocked up, and you married the first fella that came along. The first dependable-looking fella that came along.'

'The same as you?'

They arrived at a park bench. As the air had grown dimmer a chill had crept up. Christine looked back to see if Lily had fished the twins out of the water. They'd be catching their deaths. But she couldn't see them at all. She sat down on the bench with Margaret.

'The same as you?'

'You aren't your dad's, Christine. Not naturally.'

Christine stared across the playing fields. The trees opposite had turned indigo and their shadows were sliding across the green towards her.

'But we . . . we go on the same! We look alike! We talk the same . . . we shout and . . .'

'People grow to be alike, Christine. You aren't his.' Margaret lit up another cigarette. 'He doesn't know. Or he never said that he did. Personally, I'm sure he must have worked it out at some time. But that's the kind of fella he is. Just going along with it. Going along with my story.'

'My dad . . .'

Margaret looked at her. 'He still is your dad, in a way. I can't take that away.'

Christine bridled and pulled away. 'You've taken every other fucking thing away. You went . . . and now dad . . . and dad the way he is . . .'

'We're two of the same, love. We're cut from the same cloth.'

Christine was shivering. Her jaw was shuddering. She couldn't stop it. 'Am I buggery the same as you.'

'No?' Margaret started to fasten her woollen coat. 'I tried to stop you turning out the same. That's why I punished you. That's why I was so hard on you. Stupid, now I look back. It was just cruelty, really. You can't get rid of what's bred into a child.'

Christine's voice was hard. 'I am not the same as you. There's no way I would ever leave my child, either of them. I would never . . .'

'Maybe you're right, love. I hope for them little lasses' sake that you are. They're going to need their mam if they're not to go off the rails.'

'I'll always be there for them. Whatever they do.' And I won't believe in what you believe. You don't get stuck in the past because of the things you do wrong. You can still have a future. She swallowed hard and said to her mother, 'There's such a thing as forgiveness. And I'd forgive them anything. Because they're mine.'

Margaret nodded and raised her eyebrows, suitably admonished. 'Well, good. You've got more guts than I have.'

'I will. They've got me for life, whatever happens.'

'I'm not asking for your forgiveness for walking out . . .'

'You know you wouldn't get it.'

Margaret caught her breath. 'Have I damaged your life so much?'

'Yes. It's been a fucking nightmare. Ever since you took me to look at Michael, the first time. Since then its . . .'

'You have to look at the good stuff. You have to weigh it up. Don't the girls make it all worth while? In the end?'

Christine wasn't going to be drawn. She'd had enough.

'Let's walk back to them. It's getting dark.'

They started to walk slowly, their soles dragging and scraping on the path.

'I can't put you up, you know,' said Margaret. 'You can't stay.'

'Mam . . .' Christine began. 'I don't want to. I want to get back on that train and I want to go home.'

Margaret nodded, tight-lipped. She'd not expected that.

'Christine . . . I knew the very day you were pregnant. It was the day at the zoo. Now, whether it was someone you had seen the night before, or what . . . I don't know, and I don't want to know . . .but I knew it wasn't poor Michael. I could see it in your face that day, that you were pregnant. Something about the way you held yourself. Something precious and careful about how you were. I can't put a name to it, but I knew . . .'

'You were right.'

'I knew Michael was just a dupe. I knew he'd be pleased as punch with marrying you, and having babies with you. I knew he was a fool like that. A good man like that. And I'd helped you get to him. I'd done it to another good man. Again.'

They were coming back to where Lily was sitting with the girls. She had pulled an old, threadbare towel from one of the cases to dry their feet for them. The girls were old enough to see to themselves. But they were letting Lily put their socks and shoes back on. They sat watching her like babies.

'Say goodbye to your grandma, girls,' Christine spoke up in the gloom. 'We're going back home now.'

10
Back on Top

'It's no good, lass,' he said. 'They wouldn't do it.'

Shopping in town wore Grandad Fletcher out. He liked to go to fetch messages, it made him feel he was still useful. Now because his eyes were bad and the doctor reckoned he shouldn't be driving, he went on the buses. There couldn't be much wrong with his head, he told his girls, because he could remember all the bus times and the routes. He was an expert on the buses.

He came back on Saturday morning with two bags of shopping, just a few extra things for the weekend, and he sat down heavily on the sofa. Mam was looking at him from her own chair. Her mouth had dropped open in surprise.

'It's like I say. They wouldn't do it. It's a new ruling, or something.'

'New ruling?' She didn't know what he was on about.

The girls were watching Saturday morning TV. They'd rather have been outside, but it was chucking it down. Their Grandad was taking off his cap, which was soaked black, and rubbing water out of his eyes. 'They reckon you have to go down on Monday. They don't do repeat prescriptions anymore. It's not the same.'

Their was a note of panic in mam's voice. 'On a Saturday? I can't even see the doctor till Monday. Why have they waited till a Saturday?'

Judith and Jessica both looked at their mother. It was more interesting than the telly. She was on her feet and walking to the door. She turned back again. She flicked at her hair.

'Sit down, will you, lass? You're getting all worked up.'

'Worked up?' She gave a hollow laugh. 'By Sunday night I'll be clawing the walls! Didn't you tell them? Didn't you say how much I needed them?'

Dan looked at her blankly. 'If they wouldn't give me a prescription, then there wasn't much I could do, was there? You'll have to do what they say. It's the law now. You have to see the doctor, on Monday.'

Mam swore and the twins blinked. She turned on her heel.

'I'm going for a lie down. I'm going upstairs.'

'You do that, love,' Grandad Fletcher said, with a sigh. He still had his carrier bags beside his feet. 'Now, which of you two lovely girls will make your Grandad a cup of tea?'

Judith made his tea while Jessica did his toast. He liked only one side toasting and the other left soft and white. He ripped his toast into shreds and dipped them into his tea. The butter melted and formed bubbles on the top of his cup. The girls liked watching him eat. He ate only soft and easy things. He was their great, grizzled baby.

'Why was mam so upset?' Jessica asked, pouring milk into his mug.

'It's them tablets she's always taking. They're not letting her have any more.'

'What are the tablets for?' Judith asked. 'So she won't have any more babies?'

'Not those kind. They're for . . . you know, like her nerves.'

Both girls nodded.

Grandad Fletcher went on. 'I think it's about time that pendulum swung back. Whatever your mam thinks. They were giving those things out like sweets. She was getting them by the bottleful. That's wrong. You shouldn't take anything unnatural, do you hear me, girls? Don't let anyone – doctors or anyone – give you anything unnatural to take.'

They nodded solemnly. 'Especially,' he said, 'with you two going up to the big school after summer. They do all sorts there, the bigger kids. They sniff glue, you know. And they have drugs and everything.'

'Like Zammo,' said Jess. 'On Grange Hill.'

'But that's down south,' Judith said. 'We don't have drugs in the north.'

'You'd be surprised,' Grandad Fletcher said. 'So, think on. You're getting to be big girls now.'

*

Mam stayed in bed, in her drowsy bedroom all that day and all the next. Her room smelled more and more sour each time the girls went up to see if she was still there. She lay under the duvet and there wasn't much she had to say to them. She just said she was all right and that they should go and play. Really, they were too old to be told to go and play now. Grandad brought her meals up on a tray and she couldn't touch anything.

He kept making what sounded like little threats at the door each time. 'I hope you're down in time for Dallas.' Or, 'The girls will want to see you up and about before they go to bed.' Or, 'You're going to miss Sunday lunch.'

He found himself having to do everything that weekend, even telling the girls to have their bath. There was something wrong in that, he thought; a grandad having to tell his granddaughters to go and have a bath. They were near enough teenagers.

He'd bought them pic-'n'-mix from Woolworths, and after tea they sat down to watch telly all night. Dallas wasn't the same without mam watching it with them. Grandad kept saying how ridiculous it was. He didn't believe a word of it. People didn't live like that. Bobby got shot by accident at the end of the episode and Jess wanted to go upstairs and tell her mam. 'Nuh-uh,' Grandad said, blocking her way between the armchairs with his hairy arm.

'Why not?'

'She's not well.'

'She'd want to hear what's happened to Bobby Ewing.'

'She fancies Bobby,' Judith said.

'That's as maybe, but you can tell her tomorrow.'

Jessica sat down beside her sister and they exchanged glances. Grandad wasn't supposed to tell them what to do.

*

Monday she made him phone a taxi to the doctor's surgery. The sun was out and she wore sunglasses but she hadn't washed her hair. The two girls waved them off.

'She looked like a film star.'

'Princess Diana.'

Mam was going off to have a stiff word with the doctor. As she'd waited for the cab, it was as if she was saving all her words up for him.

'Will she be all right?' Jessica asked Judith as they stood under the swagged curtains of the bay window.

'Oh, yeah.'

Grandad said they'd all get down the park that afternoon. Make up for the weekend. Start making the best of their summer holidays.

Mam came back three hours later with Grandad. She stepped out of the cab and snatched off her sunglasses. She was wearing a new blue coat. It had boxy, square shoulders. She'd had her hair set into a more swept-back style. It was tinted a darker gold. When she came into the porch she tried to give the girls a hug, both at the same time.

'I'm more like my old self,' she gasped and laughed. Under her sunglasses she was wearing a new eye make-up. Fuschia and blue. Like Pat off Eastenders. 'Now, are we going off down the park, or what?'

She was laughing quite a lot. In the kitchen Judith whispered to her Grandad, 'What did the doctor do?'

'I didn't go in the consulting room with her!' He shook his head. 'Whatever it was, it worked. She's back on top. That's what I like to see. My little girls, back on top.'

Judith hefted out the frying pan and set about making them all french toast, which was the latest thing she could do.

*

178

They took a tartan blanket for the girls to sit on, and the grownups sat on a mildewed bench. It was by a shallow lake. It was a special kind of lake, with a concrete bottom, Grandad explained. He pointed out the swans. The Council had put the lake in new, ready for the school holidays and Grandad had read about it in the paper. It was made specially so kids wouldn't drown in it.

Mam basked in the sun on the bench, her newly-painted eyelids closed and bright. Grandad went off to the kiosk to get them ice creams. He came back with orange lollies without sticks. They were in a kind of triangular packet with a chunk of ice inside. Fiddling with the wrappers kept them all quiet for a while.

They watched the kids splashing and running about in the water, which was the colour of old coins. Grandad Fletcher had once shown them his old money, kept in a metal box in his cupboard. The coins felt smooth and cold, with unfamiliar kings and queens almost rubbed away.

Jessica wondered why she and Judith didn't run around and yell as much as the other kids they saw. Other families sat out on their towels and, soon as they arrived, the kids were dashing about. She and Jude never ran about like it was second nature. Other kids did it without thinking.

The kids were almost naked, showing off their skinny white bodies. Jess felt buttoned up in the heat. Her jumper was a kind of red nylon stuff that was scratchy. She looked enviously at Jude's white cotton blouse. Ever since they'd been allowed to choose their own clothes each day, Jess had always made the wrong choices. Today was muggy and hot. Why had she put a jumper on? A polo neck, at that?

'Look at them daft bloody bairns over there,' said Grandad.

'Hm?' Mam was a million miles away.

'Those older ones. Up to no good.'

At the edge of the new lake, teenagers in cut-off jeans were playing around with what looked like milk bottles.

'Are they boozing?' asked mam, peering through the willows.

They watched one boy wading into the water, carrying bottles under both slender arms. He stooped to fill them, letting air out and the brownish water in. Then, in a graceful arc, he slung them as far as he could, to splash in the centre of the pond.

'That's a waste of time,' said mam. 'What does he think he's doing that for?'

'Showing off to the others,' Grandad said. 'All boys do at that age.'

They watched and listened to the deep thunk of each bottle as it hit the water. The boy's pals on the bank were laughing raucously.

'They've been on the cider,' said mam.

'Tell you what,' said Grandad. 'They shouldn't be doing that with glass. That lake is full of kiddies with bare feet.'

The boy waded back to the side to fetch more empties.

'Cut yourself to ribbons,' Grandad said. 'Going in there, now.'

Mam turned to Jessica and opened her purse. 'You'll go over to the kiosk thing, won't you, and get us more lollies? I've got a raging thirst on.' Mam looked at Grandad Fletcher. 'Same again, dad?'

He nodded absently and sat back on the bench, closing his eyes with a smile.

To get to the kiosk Jess had to walk right by the lake-side. She wished her mam had asked Jude instead. But she knew this was part of that whole thing, of deciding to make Jess do some things by herself. To not let her rely on her sister, like she did. Especially with them both going up to the big school. She couldn't stay in Jude's shadow.

She had two fifty-pence pieces clenched in her hand. They were sweaty and slippery. As she passed by the laughing teenaged boys she found herself pausing and then turning and marching over to them.

They were so tall. When she looked up they were just like silhouettes with ruffled up hair and the spangly light of the trees behind them. She put on her clearest voice and said, 'You boys shouldn't be doing that. There are kids in that water. They'll cut their feet to ribbons.'

One of the boys said, 'It's a little fucking dwarf.'

'Get the fuck away,' said another.

Jessica was transfixed by them. They were so huge and grown-up looking and yet they were doing childish things. And they talked just like Jess and her sister. 'You shouldn't be doing stuff like that.'

She was given a shove. 'Get back to your mam.' She stumbled. He'd pushed her right between the shoulder blades. They all laughed. A hoarse, frightening laugh. Jess whipped around. She wasn't going to cry. The one who shoved her was wearing bathing trunks, black ones. She could see his thing sticking out under the white string bow. Her hand was still clenched on the fifty pence pieces. She drew back her fist and punched him hard as she could right in the thing. Right in the balls. Mam had always told her, that was all you had to do to men and boys. That sorted the matter out every time.

He yodelled and fell forwards. As he folded up the others made surprised sounds, gasps and sniggers and they swore and started to shout. They gathered about him. And then they turned on Jess.

She ran. She ran like fucking hell.

Over the starry daisied grass, pelting hard between picknickers and bright pink flashes of sunbathers. She ran till she had stitches up both sides and she could hardly breathe because of her red nylon roll-neck.

She ran till she dared to look back and could see that they hadn't come after her. And anyway, what could they have done if they'd caught her?

She lay down on the grass and tried to breathe properly. Then she started to laugh. She held the fifty-pence pieces up to the sky at arm's length and placed them over the white disc of the sun. She turned them round, walking her fingers. She closed her eyes and looked at the red circle printed on her orange lids. It turned green and blue and red again.

When she opened her eyes and stopped laughing, everything looked black and white. It stayed like that for a few minutes.

She walked in the direction of the kiosk.

She was still remembering how soft and squashy, how tempting and fat his bundle of balls had felt in that tiny moment against her fist.

11
Included

Christine's dream was of getting back to work.

Sometimes she lay awake and thought herself back to the bakery. She was nineteen again. Laying things out on glass trays, setting them just so on paper doilies. Gassing with the girls again and flirting with the men who came in. She tried to remember the names of the girls at the bakery. Ange with the red hair, who'd been a laugh, who went off to college and never came back. Mrs Dalton who had those sticky out eyes like a fish. She had a problem with her thyroid, Ange said, and she wouldn't go in for the surgery. It was like one day her eyes would pop right out of her head. Perhaps they had. Perhaps that was why she wasn't there anymore.

Christine wondered if, when she got herself back to normal – got herself pulled back together, as her dad always put it – she could get her job back. They needed the money. Since Michael had died things had been pretty tight. Back then, she had worked hours in a row and the days went by in a flash. Busy and laughing. She couldn't imagine being on her feet that long now. Just the thought made her dizzy and threatened to bring a migraine on. She'd never had one in all her life and now it was two or three times a week. She had them more regularly than Lily Woods did. Lily claimed to get them when she'd been trying too hard to reach the other side. The multi-coloured lights dazzled her. Christine hoped her own problems didn't have anything to do with that.

Even going down town for a few bits of shopping wore her out. She came back on the bus each morning and had to lie down for an hour or two afterwards. They days had settled into easy routines, now that the girls were back at school, setting off early for the Comp. Christine went out every morning that she could and brought back a sausage roll and doughnut for her lunch, before her lie down. She went to her old bakery, checking out the place, and found being there comforting, if only for a few minutes. She still loved the smell of the pastries and bread. What she imagined was, being in a queue with customers who'd been going there for years, and one of those old women turning round and exclaiming at her: 'Ee, didn't you used to work here, pet? It was better service then, mind, when you were behind that counter.'

Nowadays they had microwaves. They never had those years before, when Christine was nineteen. She wondered if she'd be able to pick up the skill, to slam the hefty doors and jab the correct buttons in the way that these girls did. She asked them to heat a sausage roll for her one day, just to see close-up. She didn't like the way the grease soaked through the paper bag and the sausage roll inside was too hot and damp. Her dad told her that when things were microwaved, every particle of foodstuff vibrated madly, even when they were all down inside you. She hated the way her dad used words like 'foodstuff'. Like he said 'beverage' or 'collywobbles', or 'pull yourself together'. He was using the language of a different era with her.

All the girls working here were nineteen. She wasn't nineteen anymore. She still looked young for her age; she still looked like Princess Diana. But she wasn't nineteen anymore.

Outside in the precinct it was blustery and grey. It was a proper morning for the early days back at school in autumn. She hoped the twins were behaving themselves. The September morning was acting on her as a cue; as if she was expecting to return to school as well, and she was playing truant. How strange that she had her own girls at that age. She'd been shunted up the family tree.

*

Each time there would be something new to trigger the skiving. One of the twins would object to something and tell the other one, silently, with a roll of her eyes and a tiny nod. They had a pact. When that signal was given, they would both walk out together. There was a hole in the fence at the back of the playing fields. They would nip out and go to town.

More often, it was Jess who would be doing the eye-rolling and the head-nodding. Jude would give in and go off with her, even though Jude had new friends and found town boring. Jess couldn't skive off by herself. She wasn't big enough.

This morning it was the dinner-ticket queue and the bitches that gave them out. On Monday morning break the twins had to get themselves in the smaller queue in the dinner room. They had to wait their turn to have their names ticked off by the secretary. They were given five purple tickets, just like bus tickets. Their secretary never said a word to them. She looked furious the whole time, pressing on heavily with her ticks in the register and twisting off the tickets from the roll so that sometimes they tore with raggy edges. Jess supposed she'd rather be giving out the other tickets, the green ones, to the other, longer queue. That secretary got to take in money, from the kids who were paying for their meals. She had an old Royal Wedding biscuit tin that she would chuck all the coins in, and she would give out change as well. Perhaps the cross secretary with the purple tickets really liked handling money. Jess asked Jude and Jude just said, 'She's a mardy fucking cow.'

They had some of the smelly kids in their queue. The ones that smelled of piss.

When they had their tickets and were back outside in the wet, sheltering in the doorway of their House Block, Jess gave the signal. She couldn't face dinnertime again. Mondays meant first years got to be last in the queue. That meant standing for almost an hour by the lockers and getting let in two at a time. Last time Jude and Jess had been split up. Jess stood while the prefects and the teachers breezed past to get their own dinners. By the time she got in there were only a few things left. A bunch of pale chips and a couple of beetroot slices. They'd stood so long the chips had turned pink. Jess stared at what she was given and tossed the whole lot in the scrapings bin, which looked like a bucket of sick set next to the serving hatch. Your knives and forks went into another bucket of soapy water, and that made her want to throw up as well. The House Head, Mrs Goddard saw her throw her dinner out and told her off in front of everyone. She went on about Ethiopians and Live Aid and what that had meant. She breathed like a pig in Jess's face. She had one leg shorter than the other and the kids called her Peg. Her breath smelled of fish. Jess had burst into tears.

She wasn't going through that again.

'You can't skive off every bloody day,' Jude said, standing with one leg up against the wall and watching the older kids go by. 'They'll chuck you out.'

'I don't fucking care,' Jess said. 'I hate it. It's wank, here.'

'It's all right.'

'I can't do any of the work. It's all too hard. They don't give you enough time.'

Jude rolled her eyes at her, but it wasn't a signal. 'All they've had us doing so far is covering our exercise books in wallpaper and that.'

Even that had been a disaster. Jess had asked Grandad Fletcher to help. His eyes were bad. Her books came out terrible. They were almost the worst in the class. The worst had been the boy who'd covered his in pages of the Sun. The teacher had held them up to make everyone in the class laugh. 'Don't you have wallpaper in your house, Colin?' 'No, miss.'

'You have to skive off with me,' Jess said. 'Mam said we have to stick together.'

It was Library lesson and PE this afternoon. Both, as far as Jess could see, a waste of time. To her, this school seemed mostly to be about walking up and down dark corridors, hundreds of kids going from classroom to classroom for half-hour lessons. By the time you were sat down and unpacked your bag, it was time to be off again. It was shite.

'We'll be doing more about the Dewey decimal system,' she said. 'What do we want to know that for? Who cares?' And then it was Cross Country running. She didn't mention that. There was no way she was doing that again. They made you run miles in the mud and timed you. Jess had walked all the way and taken twenty-five minutes. Everyone laughed. Even, she remembered, Jude, who'd raced along and done it in fifteen. Why didn't they make Peg do it? She'd like to see her run up that hill.

'Come on, then,' Jude said, and they set off for the back of the Sports Hall, where the gap in the fence was.

Lads were smoking down there. Much older ones. It didn't seem right to Jess, that they should be put in a place with ones so much older. As the two of them got under the burst wire-netting fence the lads were watching.

'Come on,' said Jude. 'They're not interested in you.'

One of them is, Jess thought. He's looking straight over, a cigarette raised halfway to his mouth. He's recognised me. He's the one I punched in the cock.

Jude had told the story again and again, proudly; telling the other girls how brave her sister was. The other girls had given her an appraising look and Jess had felt brave, but not included in the way that Jude was included. Now she felt shit scared. She hadn't thought that he might be at this school as well.

*

In the Ladies' toilets by the Post Office, Christine ran into Lily Woods. She hadn't seen her in ages to talk to, and didn't much feel like it now. In the last couple of years Christine had let her go, feeling guilty about ever talking to her, since her dad hated her so much. If she saw her in the Avenue or in town, she gave a quick hello and hurried on. Lily always looked hurt, standing there with her mouth open. She looked a lot older now. Her hair was thinner and she was more bent over than ever. Today by the wash basins, Christine felt captured.

'The girls are almost all grown up now,' Lily said. 'You must be proud.'

'I am. They're going to school with no bother. Jude seems to love it.'

'And the other one?'

'She's more like me. I hated it at the start.'

'Well, they want to stick in. They want to get a proper start.'

Christine made a move to go. Lily reached out and lent on her arm. 'What about a cup of tea, hm? We haven't talked in so long.'

The old woman had stopped wearing make-up. She used to take such care with herself, Christine thought. Now she looked like anyone else from the precinct. She even had one of those tartan shopping bags on wheels.

They went to the café in the recreation centre. It was noisy and warm because it was right beside the swimming pool. All the pensioners seemed to come here and Lily was quite at home. She laid out their tea things and smiled at Christine.

'I'm not going to eat you.'

Christine fiddled with the tag of her teabag, hanging out of the pot.

'I know what your dad says about me. I know it's not you.'

'Are you still doing the . . . um, stuff you do?'

'I'm still a medium, yes. I'm getting known for it.'

Christine had seen a piece about her in the local paper. She had found a child who'd been missing. She'd found him, miraculously, alive in a block of flats, locked into a bare room. The police had given her a special medal and, in the paper, she was holding it up and smiling strangely. There was still that stream of people at her door.

'Dad says you're dabbling in things you don't understand.'

'Oh, he's always said that. Anything to spoil someone else's fun. Anyway,' Lily poured out their tea for them, even taking command of Christine's individual pot, 'if you don't dabble in things you don't understand, what's the point? What's the point of sticking to things you know?'

'It's safer,' Christine said. 'It makes you happier.'

Lily shook her head. 'No, it doesn't.'

Christine watched the choppy waters of the pool. There was a lesson going on for pensioners. She was surprised that they were in their bikinis; the size and shape of them. She was embarrassed.

'I hear you haven't been well,' Lily said.

'I'm all right.'

'That's not what I've heard.'

'Oh? And who's been telling you this?'

'You look all drawn and white. Not the Christine I know.'

'Well.'

'Well, nothing. You should look after yourself. Pull yourself together. Enjoy yourself more.'

Christine gulped down a mouthful of tea. 'The way I look at it, I've had my chance. Now everything is for the girls' sake. I've got to get them two brought up. As best I can. I just need to be together enough to do that, and then I've done my job.'

Lily smiled. 'You're still a young woman. You're lovely looking. You've got loads to offer.'

'Yeah, yeah.'

'You shouldn't write yourself off like that.'

'What do you know about it? You've never brung up kids.'

'No,' said Lily, reasonably. 'I haven't.'

'You've only ever had yourself to look after. Only yourself to think about. You don't know what it's like at all.'

'Maybe not. But I can see that you're not happy like you are.'

'You're just selfish,' Christine snapped. 'You've lived on your own all this time and you haven't got a clue what other people have to do. You reckon you're helping everyone else, going into your bloody trances and that, but you're not really doing it for them, are you? You're doing it for you.'

Lily looked stung.

'You're all self self self, Lily Woods and you always have been. The worst thing is, you pretend to care so much for everyone else. Going round like you're everyone's Nanna and it's all care-care-care. But that's crap. I think you just like poking your nose in. I reckon you just get a kick out of going into trances.'

'A kick!' cried Lily in a shrill voice, and burst out laughing. Christine was laughing too.

'A kick, she says! It's bloody horrible, going into trances! It's like being dragged down to hell!'

'Then why do it?'

Lily's laughter subsided. 'Because of what you said, really, Christine. You're right, I have always been on my own. Doing this, contacting people no one else can, draws me closer to something. To other people.'

'Oh, Lily,' Christine said. 'We've been really horrible to you, haven't we?'

'I think,' said the old woman cautiously, 'that sometimes you've been selfish and I've had the brunt of it. But we've all been like that at times, haven't we? You just chose between your dad and me. But he's blood, so I knew you would listen to him, not me.' She shrugged.

'He isn't blood,' Christine said. 'He's not my dad.'

'How do you mean?'

'Mam told me, when I saw her. She was as big a slut as I was.'

'Christine!' hissed Lily, scandalised. Others were looking. 'Is that what she said that day? Is that why you were so upset on the train coming back?'

'All sorts of reasons, Lily.'

'Michael never thought you were a slut.'

'No?'

'He still doesn't, pet.'

Christine narrowed her eyes. 'He's still there?'

'He still talks to me.'

'I don't know what to believe anymore. About all that.'

'He thinks you should be a bit more selfish. He thinks you should get yourself some life. What about that Brian?'

'Brian?' Christine looked blank. 'I've not seen him in ages. How do you know about him?'

Lily tapped her nose. 'Connections.'

*

'He's lovely, isn't he?'

'I can't stand babies.' Jude wanted to go in the arcade and play on the machines. Now they were skiving, she was quite into it. They might as well have a laugh. But Jess was crouching beside a push chair that had been left outside. The baby in it had been crying and he'd stopped as soon as Jess knelt by him and held his fat, squashy hand. To Jude he looked a bit dirty. What kind of mother left her kid outside the arcade?

'He stinks,' Jude said. 'Let's go in. How much money have you got, our Jess?'

Jess had fifty pence in her bag. She gave it to her sister absently and turned back to the baby. 'He must be scared, out here on his own.'

'He wants changing. Are you coming in or not?'

The baby was looking into Jess's face. She could swear he was about to smile at her, at any moment. The cuffs of his little suit were dark with grime. 'I'll stay out here with him. Wait for his mam coming back.'

'She'll be in here, an' all.'

'I like bairns,' Jess said. Jude tutted and went into the arcade. She was always lucky on the machines. If she won she could buy them dinner in the rec centre café. That

191

would cheer Jess up. Jess always thought about what she was eating. She ate twice what Jude did. She was getting fatter and now people could tell the difference easier. She took one look back at her sister and forgot about her.

'You're lovely, you are,' Jess told the baby. 'If I had you, you wouldn't be stuck out here.' The bairn was starting to cry again. Jess was talking too loud in his face. 'I'd be showing you off, I would. I'd be showing you off. You need changing, don't you?'

He kicked his legs and bounced in his push chair, as if he was saying yes. Then she thought she could buy him nappies and stuff in Fine Fare. She went round the back of the push chair and nudged the brake off. It was easy. It surprised her, how much heavier he was in the chair than a doll. It took more effort pushing. She took him to Fine Fare.

He seemed happy enough. He waved his arms about when she lifted him (and he really did smell of shite. She was doing him and his mother a good turn) and put him in the seat bit at the front of the trolley. They went through the turnstile and Jess pushed them off towards the baby aisle. It was quiet in the shop today. She usually came down on a Saturday with her Grandad, when it was really busy and they had to queue for ages. This was better. There were other girls with babies in the trolleys. They were going up and down. They had the whole place to themselves. Huey Lewis and the News were playing over the speakers. It was easy.

She hefted a bag of twenty nappies into her trolley. The blue ones for boys with the padding up the front. She'd seen the adverts. She was glad the baby she had was a boy.

Then she thought he should have a dummy. A blue one. And a jar of something – chicken, pulpy stuff – for his dinner, because he must be hungry. And a peachy dessert.

She didn't have any money, so that was a problem. But she headed for the wide aisle and thought, if I just walk through and keep my head down, they won't notice. At the other cash desks they're just getting on with their work.

At this end it's quieter. I'll just walk through. Maybe it's wrong to nick things. I don't know. Not when you're in need. But I'm the girl with scars on her fingers. I'm always the one who's in the wrong. If they want me they'll find me. It'll be easy for them. I'll walk through. I'll do it easy.

No one stopped her. She was through to the packing benches and the heaped up cardboard boxes. It was easy. She was on her way. The baby was jumping up and down in the seat between her hands. He was squashing his shite in his nappy even flatter. Great wafts of the shite smell were coming up at her. But no one had seen them. She'd made them invisible. Jess put her head down and picked up speed, making for the automatic doors at the side of the shop. Once she was there, they couldn't do anything to her. She'd be out and the baby was hers.

There was an old woman putting tins of cat food in a box. As Jess sailed past the old woman was looking at her funny.

'Hey, hinny,' the old woman started up. 'Aren't you . . . ?'

Jess was flying past. She ran over the old woman's foot. 'Fuck off!'

She laughed. The doors scraped open in time for her to shoot out, into the dark tunnel between Fine Fare and the cheap shop next door.

Jess pulled the trolley around and the bairn was squealing in her face as they trundled heavily through the dark. She didn't know if he was scared or pleased. The wheels made a lot of noise on the concrete, filling up the tunnel. She made for the light of the precinct ahead. When she got there she'd be out of it. And she'd nicked a trolley as well.

This was good going. Not bad, for the girl with scars on her hands.

12
Gone to the Goblins

Peg smoked in her office. There were three full ashtrays on her desk in the small, dark place. She'd put her desk right in front of the window so she could watch the world go by at break and dinnertime. If she saw anyone misbehaving she would rap on the window and they would look. She'd be sitting there with a fag in her mouth, by the light of her desk lamp, looking furious.

She caught Jess that way. Jess and Jude were doing what everyone else did at breaktime; walking right around the perimeter of the school buildings. There wasn't much else to do. In the Juniors there had been a yard and everyone had been there together. Here there was just a path that ran all the way round school. Jess and Jude had walked round twice that morning when they were stopped by Peg, banging on her window at them.

'She wants to see you,' Jude said.

'Me?' Jess mouthed at Peg, pointing to her chest. 'Her?' She pointed at Jude.

'You, you!' Peg was mouthing back. She looked like she was really shouting. She had one of her awful old blouses on, with the round, floppy collars that looked like it was twenty years old.

'Come with me,' Jess said to Jude as they walked round to the doorway of the House Block.

'The prefects won't let me in,' Jude said. 'I'll be out here.'

Some of Jude's friends, older girls, were knocking about outside the door. They looked Jess up and down. You could tell they were third years because they all had gel in their hair, making it stand up rock hard. Gel was forbidden to first and second years.

Jude was talking to the prefect on the door.

One of the girls, snapping gum, said, 'Is that your lass in trouble, then, Jude?'

'Yeah.' Jude looked up at the prefect. He was an older boy.

'She's fucking mad, your sister,' the girl said.

'No she's not.'

'She is. She's tapped. Everyone's on about the things she does.'

Jude turned on her. 'Shut up about it, Joanne.'

'They all reckon she's abnormal. You're all right, though, Jude.'

The prefect looked at Jess. 'Come in then. You can't bring your sister in.'

One of the other girls was backcombing her hair, wincing as she snagged at it. 'Twinnys always go everywhere together, don't they?'

'No they don't,' Jude glowered. She was sick of doing her sister's talking for her. She turned on Jess savagely. 'Get your arse in there and talk to Peg. I'm not going in for you.'

But the sisters couldn't stand in for each other anyway. Jess was so much bigger. She was in a different size skirt to her sister. They hadn't been able to be each other since Infants school.

*

There was a big boy sitting by the lockers, waiting to see Peg. He was in those tight drain-pipe trousers and a short-sleeved shirt. He looked up as Jess shuffled in and her heart started banging. He was that lad. The one she'd hit. Back in the summer when she'd been brave, when she'd still been one of the oldest and hardest girls in her old school. Now she was looking at him and his face was livid with spots. The pink on the white was like jam in semolina.

'You're not pushing in first,' he glowered. His voice was so deep.

'I don't want to,' she said. He had great thick eyebrows. He put his feet up on the bench opposite. Maybe he didn't remember her from the concrete lake after all.

'You think you're fucking fantastic,' he said. 'You and your sister. Don't you?'

'No.'

'You're only first years. But you think you're bloody great.'

She licked her lips. 'What are you seeing her about?'

'Never you mind. You're cracked, you are.'

'Mebbe.'

'You know what I'm going to do?'

'What?'

'I'm gunna give you a year or two. I'm not gunna get you back for a year or two yet. I'll wait till you get older.'

Jess couldn't breathe. She clamped her mouth shut.

'I'll wait till you've got tits and pubes and that and you're not a baby anymore. And then, guess what I'll do to you.' He was smirking and kicking at the bench with his trainers.

'What?'

'I'm gunna fuck you.'

The door to Peg's office came open. She stood there, hanging onto the frame, breathing heavily through her mouth. She reeked of smoke. She glared at Jess. 'Get in here, you.'

Jess stole a backwards look at the boy. He was nodding and nodding behind Peg's back.

*

'I have talked to your mother and she . . . wants me to talk to you as well. We have all decided that it is for the . . . best if I talk to you. Just having a small . . . talk. I want to see if there is anything . . . in particular, troubling you, Jessica. You can use this . . . opportunity to get anything . . . anything you like, off your chest.'

Jess looked down at her chest. She was wearing the grey woolly that she had to because of school rules. The one that stretched a bit further each time it went into the washer. Everyone's did. Kids with oversized jumpers were as much a part of school uniform as grey skirts, trousers, socks and red nylon ties. Jess used her extra long sleeves to cover up the chicken scratches on the backs of her hands. They were a fashion thing that she'd get killed for. Peg had gone mad about them in a recent House Assembly, ever since Lisa Glass's scratches had gone septic and yellow. The scratches were forbidden. It was a shame, because Jude, with her long fingernails, was one of the best at giving them. Jess had almost perfect chicken scratches on her hands.

Peg was talking nicely to her. Quite a difference to her usual tone. Jess was surprised because she'd sounded fierce when she'd called her into the office. Now she was talking nicely. She still did those wheezy pauses, which were all to do with getting her breath back. To Jess those pauses always sounded like invitations to jump in and guess what she was going to say next. Like she was testing you out. She'd heard Colin Jacobs do that once in an English lesson and he'd shouted what he thought came next and Peg had killed him. 'Don't you dare tell me what I want to say.'

Now Peg was saying: 'Do you want a . . . baby of your own? Is that what you . . . felt like?'

Jess merely stared.

'This is a strange time for a girl of your . . . age, Jessica. You are about to enter . . . puberty. Do you know what that is?'

'Yes, miss. We've done a bit about it with Mr London.'

'Well, very good, then you'll know . . . all about it. When it happens to you, however . . . you will find that it's . . . different for everyone. It can make you behave in . . . peculiar ways.'

It sounded as if Peg was going to say it was all right to misbehave.

'And it will affect certain . . . people quite drastically. Perhaps, especially those whose home . . . background isn't all that might be . . . desired, stability-wise. Those people might find the onslaught most . . . problematic. Do you follow me, Jessica?'

'Not really, miss.'

'I'm saying that you will find yourself worse . . . off. You will have a more difficult . . . time. This is because you come from what is called a single . . . parent family. The chances of you having . . . problems . . . are very much greater.'

'Do you mean because my dad is dead?'

'Yes, Jessica. I think your behaviour can be . . . attributed to that simple, sad . . . fact.'

'He's been dead for ages, miss. I was really small.'

'Yes, but you haven't grown up with the advantages that most other children have had. They have had . . . two parents. They have had a solid . . . supportive . . . family.'

Jessica felt like crying now. 'But there's my mam . . . and she's . . .'

'Don't take on, Jessica. All I'm saying is . . . sometimes, girls . . . like you . . . those who haven't grown up in a normal . . . family . . . they want to get themselves one as soon as . . . possible. Now, you know what I'm talking about, don't you?'

'You mean, having babies.'

Peg smacked her lips, pleased that Jessica had been listening. 'I worry about my girls getting themselves pregnant . . . too young. It still happens a great . . . deal. And, judging by your demeanour and your . . . behaviour, I would say that you are at risk from this sort of . . . outcome.'

'But . . .'

'But nothing. Do you know what men call girls who drop their knickers without a by-your-leave?'

Jess couldn't speak.

'They call them . . . cows. That's what they call girls who make themselves easy and go to bed with . . . anyone. We don't want you to turn out like . . . that.'

Jess's face was hot. 'I'm only twelve! I'm not going to do anything!'

Peg smiled and shook her head. 'You are on what we might call a downward . . . spiral. Already, Jessica, you are on a slippery . . . slope. You stole that child. You wanted that . . . child. Now, no fuss was made about it. The mother was reunited with her child after ten minutes and it was all right again. No harm was . . . done. The police didn't have to intervene.'

Jessica stared at the yellow lino. It was pitted with cigarette burns.

'What everyone . . . realised, Jessica, was that here was a . . . girl, who was crying out for . . . help. She was stealing a child . . . Yes, in order to draw attention to . . . herself. You might think that you look tough, not saying a . . . word, your mouth clammed shut. Now, what I see there is a little girl, inside of . . . you, crying out for . . . help. Aren't I right?'

Jess shook her head fiercely.

'Don't deny it. I'm glad we had this . . . talk. I think it has done a power of . . . good. There was all sorts of talk of child . . . psychologists for you. You don't want that, do you? You probably don't need them. I've been teaching girls for nigh on forty . . . years. There's nothing new to me. Everything you need to know, any help you can possibly need, can come straight from . . . me. Now, you'll do that, won't you, Jessica? You will come and talk to me?'

Jess scraped her shoe on the lino, rubbing out a scuff mark. 'If I do, will I not have to see a doctor?'

'That's right.'

'All right. All right, then.'

'Unless . . . you do something else wrong. After that, Jessica, I can't stand between you and them.'

'Thank you. Thank you, miss.'

*

She saw her again, later that day, in their English lesson. Jess kept her head down, over her book.

Peg had been teaching them an old poem. One that came in long columns down page after page. It made everyone giggle, this old, chuntering, rhyming Victorian poem. Dust fell out the books, puffed in sharp clouds, when Peg tossed them onto their desks. She read a bit of the poem to them each lesson and they had to say what it meant. She read, huffing and blowing; her cantankerous pauses punctuating lines. It was about goblin men coming after two girls. And about the fruit the girls crushed all over their bodies, so they were covered in pips and juices and rinds. Class 1G weren't sure what to make of that. There was some giggling. One sister asked the other to lick her. There was some laughing aloud at that.

To Peg it had a very simple message.

'It is all too . . . easy, boys and girls, but especially . . . girls, to find that you have let yourself go to the . . . bad. Most times you find out too . . . late. I never want to have to say about any of you, yes; I knew her when she was . . . twelve. But the poor, stupid thing has gone to the goblins.'

*

Sheila the medium was back in town. Her hair was silver now and she hadn't brought her husband with her. Some of the congregation muttered about that. From her place in the pulpit, as she waited to go into one, Sheila knew that they were gossiping about her. That came with the territory, though. When you moved around the country like she did, the world became a small place. It was like being famous. Not that she'd been on the telly, like Lily Woods had. Sheila's eyes flicked along the aisles and alighted on the more famous practitioner. There she was, looking smug, a younger, nervous, blonde woman sitting beside her. Both of them dressed up. She didn't know what Lily Woods was doing here, coming to see her. Come to catch her out, probably, the old witch. Patronising her. And I, thought Sheila, I was the one to discover her talent in the first place. Wasn't it me who told her she had the latent gift?

She bristled with irritation as the pastor got up with his guitar, encouraging the congregation to sing Sheila's favourite song, 'I Believe in Angels', by Abba. The congregation shuffled and wobbled and sang along under the cool breeze from the hole in the ceiling. Building work. The pastor's wife had said, 'The hole will bring us closer to the next world. There is no mediating ceiling tonight!' Sheila took it that the church was falling down. All in all, she felt gloomy about the whole business. But I should be going into my trance. I should be powering up . . .

Lily Woods was watching Sheila narrowly. 'She's not making contact yet,' she hissed at Christine as the song went on. Christine was singing in a quiet, croaky voice, glancing down at the typed sheet of words. 'I wonder why. I wonder if she's lost the knack.'

Christine muttered back, 'Why aren't you up there?'

'You can't do a turn for your local church,' Lily shook her head. 'Stands to reason. You know the people, know their business and their loved ones. It's easier to fake. That's why we all have to move around the country. It always has to be strangers.'

'Oh.'

It didn't work though, Lily thought. When she pictured the world of the mediums, it was a kind of third world, between this one and the afterlife. It was the twilight world of National Express coaches shunting along motorways, to and from major cities and minor towns in the middle of the night. All over the British isles the mediums were packing their overnight cases into the boots of coaches and taking out their knitting and ravelling up skeins of wool into booties and bedjackets through the night. And with each exchange of visiting medium, each cross and criss-cross of the spiritualist trail, the strands pulled tighter from church to church and, with each repetition to an out of the way town, Lily found herself recognising faces in crowds. How easy it would be, she sometimes thought, to not have a gift. It might even be possible to be a convincing fake.

Tonight she had to listen to a lesser medium. Lily didn't have a great deal of faith in Sheila Brown at all. She had heard horror stories from as far as King's Lynn about the things Sheila had mediated. Telling people they were going to die. Warning them that someone would be murdered in their beds. But tonight Lily was here for Christine's sake. She wouldn't stand in the way if Christine found herself intrigued by this life. In a way, Lily was flattered that Christine had come, secretively, with her tonight. She wasn't dismissing things out of hand, poor girl.

Sheila took some time warming up. She was flustered and flushed and the congregation murmured in support as she received a few messages, vague and unformed, that no one could claim. She stammered and looked close to losing her rag.

'Peter? Peter? There is a Peter who froze to death . . . Can anyone here take him? Can anyone here take Peter? He was little, only six . . . ?'

The audience members glanced at each other in concern.

'It's like bingo,' Christine hissed at Lily.

She looked back at Sheila to find the medium's eyes fixed right on her. She blushed, feeling caught out for talking.

Clear as a bell, Sheila intoned at her: 'Your husband. I can't get his name.'

Christine swallowed.

Lily nudged at her.

'But he's telling me that he wants you to understand that he loves you as the mother of his children.'

Lily stiffened. She shot a look at Christine.

'He never betrayed you, lover. It wasn't until you separated that he started to go with others. It wasn't until then that he understood that part of his nature.'

Christine had crushed the songwords sheet into her sweating palms.

'He hopes . . . your husband hopes . . . you can understand about his being . . . in the end . . . the other way
inclined. He never betrayed you. What's that, lover?'
Sheila scrunched up her face. 'Yes. He's telling you to
watch out for the girls. The two girls. It's the younger one
that he's especially bothered about . . .' She made her
listening face again, and then let out a long sigh. 'He's
gone now, lover. Did that make sense to you?'

Christine found herself nodding. 'I think so. Yes.'

'Good,' Sheila nodded smartly, and moved on. Nobody
came through quite as clearly after that, however, and the
session ended with the congregation going off to the crypt
for tea, quietly disappointed.

That was him, Christine thought. It was really him.

Lily bustled them back out of the church. 'I don't want
to go for tea, do you? I don't want dragging into the usual
tittle tattle. That Sheila will be crowing . . .'

Christine nodded and pulled on her coat. She followed
Lily outside. 'That was Michael, wasn't it? It was Michael!'

Lily rounded on her. 'Don't you believe it.'

'Why not? She . . .'

Lily flapped her arms. 'That woman doesn't know what
she's doing. She'd third rate, fourth rate. She's dabbling
where she doesn't even . . .'

'But it was Michael! He was giving me a message. But . . .
what she said about him being . . . the other way inclined
and . . .' Christine's head was whirling. She sounded very
young. Lily firmly grasped her arm.

'That wasn't the Michael you knew. It wasn't my
nephew. Look, she never even gave you a name! That's one
of the first things, to give proof. A name, and some details
to fix the person, to make sure the message is genuine and
it's getting to the right person. Otherwise it means
nothing, Christine. Otherwise it's dangerous.'

'It was Michael.'

Lily led them across the road and into the park for the
short-cut home. The dark box trees hemmed them in as
they walked quickly to the middle.

'How can you be so sure, Lily? Maybe it was a real message and Michael was telling me true stuff. Watch out for the girls, he said. And about betraying me and hoping I'd understand . . .'

'Your Michael,' said Lily, in a tight voice, 'was a loyal, proper husband. You both had your problems but you would have sorted them out. There's no question about that. I should never have taken you there tonight while that woman was on. She's filled your head with nonsense. Spiteful, dangerous nonsense . . .'

'But what if it's true, Lily?'

'Sheila Brown is a liar. The vibrations were all wrong tonight. I know , I just know when there is a spirit there, communicating with us. I can hear them too, usually. Much clearer than anyone else. That Sheila is known for giving out garbled messages.'

Christine strode on ahead, across the cobbles of the centre of the park. She leaned against one of the struts of the old bandstand and sank slowly to sit on the step, gathering her coat about her.

'Prove it to me, Lily.'

'What?' Lily stood before her, knowing what was going to come next.

'If you're so sure, I want you to talk to Michael now. Seeing as you're so good and that Sheila woman is so bad. I want you to tell me the true story.'

Lily sat down heavily on the wooden step. 'I can't just do it at will.'

'Why not? You do it for the police. For the telly. I've seen you. Do it for me. Now.'

Lily looked worried. 'All right, Christine.'

As she started to concentrate, fixing inwardly on herself, Christine produced her cigarettes. She flinched at the scrape of the match on the step. She inhaled and blew out a deep lungful of smoke. Then she cast a wary glance at Lily.

'I've got him,' Lily whispered.

'You have?'

'Don't talk to me.'

Christine nodded. Lily shuddered. Her voice went deeper. Her eyes flickered back.

'I will always be in love with you, Christine. It's like the moment I first saw you in the bank. Then I knew. You were the love of my short life and you still are now.'

'Michael?'

'And the girls will be just fine. You are doing a grand job with them. And your father . . . your old father is on the mend, Christine. You oughtn't listen to pretenders and people who don't know. Don't take any of it to heart. I loved you, Christine Fletcher, just as a man ought to love a woman. And no one can spoil that now.'

'Michael?'

Lily blinked and Christine watched her begin to emerge, startled-looking, from her brief trance.

13
Black Mud

There was one night when an ambulance arrived in the Avenue. Jess and Jude woke up when its lights were pulsing blue into their room. It was pulling up right on their drive.

It was the night when Lily Woods and Dan Fletcher were forced to speak again, after a number of years of pretending that they didn't even recognise each other. They sat in the ambulance with Christine and found themselves taking turns to grip her hands. Then they were sitting in the hospital waiting room together, having to work out who would go back to see to the girls. Who would get them up in the morning for school.

Dan and Lily decided together that they wouldn't tell the girls what had happened. They didn't need to know. Dan said it would just upset them and Lily had to agree. It could even lead to further trouble, if they found out what their mam had done.

It was decided that Lily would go back to Brunswick Avenue, and Dan gave her his key. She was pleased to see he was being sensible. All through this, even when he had banged on her door, demanding and pleading for help, he had hardly raised his voice. She got up to have one last look at Christine. But they were still pumping her stomach. There was a lot to get out.

'It seems,' Dan had said, quietly, 'that her doctor has been giving her the stuff in liquid form. In a bottle. She downed the whole lot tonight.'

Lily took a taxi cab back to the Avenue.

She wouldn't tell the girls a thing.

'You've got to fucking tell us!' Jude yelled. 'She's our mam!'

'Please,' Jess said. 'Is she dead?'

Lily thought the two of them looked like little girls again. She hadn't seen them in their nighties for years.

'No,' she said. 'She isn't dead.'

'That's something,' Jude said.

'Why can't you tell us, Aunt Lily?'

Lily's face was hot with shame. She was going to break down herself, any moment. She had to get these two back into their room. 'We don't know anything yet, sweetheart. They're keeping her in to look after her. She's in the best place now.'

She got them to go upstairs and lie under their quilts again. She sat downstairs in the dark of the living room and didn't hear anything else from them. Lily sat shivering, awake in her chair, till seven and there was no phone call.

*

The girls went to school the next morning, still wanting to know. Lily packed them off breezily. She said it was all something and nothing. She said it was all ladies' problems. She said, like as not, their mam would be home again by tea time.

'It's PE today,' Jude said. 'We need our kits. Towels and things.'

Flustered, Lily helped them to pack their school bags.

The girls dawdled to school. 'Do you believe her?'

'No, I fucking don't,' Jude snapped.

'She could be dead,' Jess said.

'I know.'

'She could be dead and they wouldn't tell us.'

'I know.'

On the school field just before nine, other latecomers were straggling through the grass.

'Shit,' said Jess. 'There's that lad and his cronies again.'

'Mackey?' Jude asked.

Jess nodded.

'He's all right. Thinks he's hard. Thinks he's lush, as well.'

'He's gunna get me,' Jess said. 'He's told me he's gunna get me.'

Mackey was kicking a ball about with his small gang. They were all smaller than he was. Arthur, the kid with no ears, just tubes coming out of holes in his head, who was known for beating littler kids up. Craigy who stank of piss like all his brothers. Tommo whose sister was the most beautiful girl in the school, she reckoned.

The whole lot of them were jeering at Jude and Jess as the two of them swished past, clutching their bags to their chests, heads down. They walked as fast as they could.

Jude had never been shouted at like this before. She turned on them. 'Why don't you all go and fuck off? You fucking spackers.'

Mackey pushed Arthur in the back. 'It's you she's calling a spacker.'

'You're all fucking spackers!'

Jude pushed Jess then, to make her run for the safety of the buildings.

*

There was a glass frosted door at the end of Christine's room. She saw the shapes of her two girls. They were just the right height, looking in through the frosted glass. She called for the nurse to let them in. No one came. No one came all day. The two dark shadows stood there for hours, their hands pressed against the glass so the flesh turned white, but they never came in.

Christine unclipped her tubes and yanked at them till her nose bled. She hauled back the stiff clean bedsheets. She lurched over the lino. She threw open the door.

She was in the corridor and it tumbled around her, the hot bright windows down one side revolving and the floor tossed against her bare feet like a rope bridge. And her girls were running down the corridor, away from her.

'It's Jess and Jude!' she shouted. 'It's Jess and Jude! Jess and Jude!'

*

That night Dan wouldn't say any more than Lily had.

'You can tell us, Grandad.'

'We need to know.'

He sighed. 'They call it keeping her in for observation. Your mammy hasn't been well for some time.'

They looked at him.

'Was it right,' he said, 'when she was up in her room all the time? That she slept so long? She's in the best place. They're seeing to her, at last.'

After it was dark, there was shouting in the Avenue outside. Jude looked out of the bathroom window and her heart jumped in shock. The shouting had followed the girls back from school. Mackey and his gang were in the street, shouting at their house. When they saw her they whistled and yelled. 'We're gunna get you! The two of you!'

Downstairs Grandad was doing his nut. 'Little bastards, I'm phoning the bizzies.'

First he was out in the porch in his pyjamas and no dressing gown, shouting back at the lads.

'WHY don't the LOT of YOU just FUCK OFF where you CAME from? You GOBSHITES don't even LIVE round HERE!'

Jess and Jude watched from the front window and Jude even laughed when the lads stopped shouting, surprised at the old man baying like that.

'GO ON! HADDAWAY you little BASTARDS!'

Grandad Fletcher slammed the front door and the bottom glass panel fell out on the path with a smash. 'FUCK!'

He stormed back into the living room.

'I want to know what you two are up to.'

'What? Grandad . . .'

'Filth like that doesn't come round decent girls' houses, acting like that.' He stepped towards them, where they were still kneeling backwards on the settee by the window. 'TELL me, you TWO. I need to KNOW!'

They were saved, for a second, by the thump of a brick through the shattered front door.

Jess looked at Jude as Grandad stumped off.

'It's you they're after,' Jude said. 'You started this.'

Dan came back with a rock and a piece of paper. He waved both in front of them.

'What are you DOING to this family?'

He rattled the paper and read it out to them. '"WE ARE ALL GOING TO FUCK YOU."' He ripped it to shreds. 'You fucking little WHORES. You're all the SAME. You're going just the SAME way.'

Jude started to yell back at him, but he slapped her down.

'Get the pair of you upstairs NOW before I tan your dirty little hides.'

The two of them hurried past him, and out of the room.

*

It was Cross Country again the next day. They both took the same shirts and shorts and towels, still wet and full of black mud from the day before.

'I can't do it,' Jess said. 'I can't do it again.'

'Course you fucking can. It's only running.'

'I'm fatter than you. I can't run like you.'

Jude looked her sister up and down as they changed into their dirty kits. They were further along the benches from the other girls. 'Look, I'll stay with you. I don't want to win this anyway.'

That day it was the trials for the county competition. Jude had thought she stood a real chance, or rather, her teacher, Miss Heath did. She wanted Jude to compete.

Miss Heath stood at the halfway mark, just before the track turned to quagmire, down by the Burn, and screamed at Jude, who was plodding along, last, with Jess.

'Pick up your feet! What are you doing, running with her? You're better than that, you stupid girl!'

'Piss off,' Jude hissed as they passed her, the mud splashing up their legs. She listened to Jess's breath coming in raggy bursts as they ran along by the stream.

'I can taste blood, Jude,' she panted. 'In the back of me throat.'

Miss Heath came jogging up. 'You two are last! The others are all nearly finished! The lads have started behind you. What are you doing, you stupid little bitches?'

'I'm running with her,' Jude shouted back. She was hardly in a sweat.

Miss Heath's face was twisted up red. 'You've blown it, Judith Fletcher. You stood a real chance in these trials. You had an opportunity to actually do something. You've flung the bloody thing back in my face.'

Jess had stopped now. She was bending over in the mud, clutching her knees and heaving. Jude stopped with her. She yelled at Miss Heath, 'I don't want to be in your race. I just don't.'

The teacher's face hardened. 'Right.' With that she jogged back up the hill to the school buildings.

'Fucking old lesbian,' Jude cursed. 'Are you okay, Jess?'

The boys were coming up the track behind them. They came jogging in a mass with their teacher in front of them, spraying up mud as they went. Jude pulled Jess over a bit so they wouldn't be in the way. The lads went sailing past, trembling the sodden ground of the bank as they went.

'I'm sorry, Jude,' Jess said. 'I can really taste blood . . .'

'I know.'

They watched the stragglers go by then. These were the last of the boys, who couldn't run very well. The fat ones, the skinny ones and the queers. Last of all came Arthur, with his wires sticking out of the holes in his head. He just walked along, pretending he couldn't hear anyone shouting at him.

He walked up to the girls, smiling at them. He stood there until there was no one else in sight.

'Oh, fuck,' Jess said. 'He's gunna go mental.'

'Piss off back to school, Lugsy,' Jude said. 'We're just having a rest.'

Jude hated the way he talked. He couldn't hear himself, so his words came out garbled, unformed.

'You're them two lasses,' he said. 'You're the two we're gunna get.'

Jude snorted. 'Yeah. So where's your hard mates now?'

'I don't need mates.'

'Yeah, you do. You spaz.'

He frowned as he read her lips. 'I'm not a spacker. You always call me spacker.'

'You're a fucking Joey. That's you.'

He took a couple of steps through the mud. Then he paused. 'I'm as good as anyone,' he said.

Jess looked up at him and then at Jude. She was shaking. Arthur was rubbing at the front of his shorts, plucking at his cock through the fabric.

'What are you gunna do with that, Lugsy?' Jude taunted.

'I've told you already,' he said. 'I'm gunna fuck you both. We're all gunna fuck you both.'

'Yeah,' Jude laughed, and launched herself upon him. Jess fell back as her sister flew at the boy. Jude smacked him hard in the face with the heel of her hand. He fell back into the mud immediately, landing heavily, winding himself. Jude dropped herself on his chest, balling her hands into fists and letting fly at his fat, contorted face. She was screaming. 'You come near me – or her – and I'll rip every fucking wire out of your fucking head! You fucking Joey! You fucking Davros!'

The wires had already come out under her blows. He was covered in mud and the holes in his head were bleeding.

'Kick him, Jess!' Jude howled. 'Kick him one when he's down!'

Jess hovered nervously beside them as Arthur squealed. 'I can't, Jude! I can't just . . . !'

'If you don't, he'll get you again! He'll wait till I'm not around! He'll come with his mates, all the other bastards, and they'll do what he said! He'll fuck you! You'll have his fucking sprog! Kick his balls off, Jess!'

Jess started kicking him, dancing round Jude and the prostrate boy. She kicked at his sides, right up between his legs. He made a solid, satisfying noise each time her sports shoe connected with him. It was easy. It was noisy and wet and black mud flew everywhere. It was easy, even though he twisted and tried to throw Jude off him, twisting round on his back so she was playing horsies with him. He bellowed and shrieked in the thick mud and Jess kicked at his arms to make him fall down again. He did and they cheered.

He fell face first in the mud. Jude pushed his face right into it. 'Kick him up the arse, Jess! That'll show the bastard what we're like!'

He coughed and spluttered and roared for a while. The mud came up in flurries. Jude pressed down hard with both hands on his curly hair and his face went down again.

She pressed down with all her might.

'Carry on kicking, Jess!' she screamed. But Jess needed no more telling. She was addicted to the meaty thumping noise of his body.

Jude took advantage of his not struggling so much. She lifted herself off his back and sat on his head. She let her whole weight onto his head and kept his face pressed deep into the black slime of the bank. She liked the hardness of his skull between her legs.

'Stop . . .' she gasped. 'Stop now . . .'

Jess couldn't.

'I said, fucking stop!' Jude yelled, and got herself up off Arthur's head. She stepped back. She looked down at him.

Jess's legs were trembling like she had run ten miles.

She backed away, the mud sucking at her shoes.

They were both still for a full minute, staring down at Arthur, who didn't move to get up. He didn't even lift his face out of the muck. His face was wedged deep into it.

One hand gave a quick twitch, making Jess jump. Then it stopped.

Jude looked at her. 'He asked for it. He made me defend you. I did it for you, Jess.'

Jess stared as her sister started backing away. It seemed like everything was getting further away. 'Jude?'

Jude was backing up the trail, up the hill.

'Look what you've done, Jess!' Jude shouted. 'Just look at what you've fucking well done!'

'Jude?'

Jude turned to pelt up the black hill. She was running back to school.

'Jude?'

Jess could still taste blood in the back of her throat. There was no way she could go running up that hill.

She would have to wait. She would have to wait, for others to come down, and find her here, with him.

14
Ways to have Fun

It was in the Home that Jess had a spurt of growth. As if, once she was separate from Jude and free to go her own way, she could grow to be different.

In her mid-teens she achieved the size she would always be.

In the Home Jess proved to be a fast grower and a fast learner.

She loved having breasts this size. So proud, upstanding and holding forth while the other girls were flat as pancakes. For a while her breasts gave her a measure of power in the Home. There were a few boys there over the years, outnumbered by all the girls, and Jess would sense the boys really looking at her. She could feel their dirty minds ticking over when they passed her in the corridors or out in the yard. Tick tick tick tick: their dirty Home boy minds went ratcheting over the problem of getting their paws on her breasts.

They wanted her – Jess knew – to be a mother to them. A dirty kind of mother they could come to and do the things they dreamed up sweatily in their minds.

In the showers she loved to show herself off to the other girls. She would stay longer under the jets to luxuriate in the fizzing water, soaping herself meticulously and staring the starers out.

By fourteen she was wearing her mother's bras and she wasn't ashamed of them being old and faded grey from the wash. One of the parcels her mother sent up to the Home was full of old bras. No letter. The bras had a lived-in look, as if she was already used to being a woman. If, when she was hooking up one of her mother's bras and jiggling herself into place, the girls were cruel and bitchy

– just like girls can be – she never heard them or knew about it. Jess was all confidence.

*

She was never pretty. At that age, it never mattered. Her lips were always thin and her smile was tight, making her cheeks bulge like she was eating something and couldn't be bothered to swallow. Pudding-face, she'd get called, sometimes out of affection. Her eyes were very deep set and so, on photos, all she had were these two black holes under her long, untamed hair, which she didn't cut after she was seventeen.

*

They made her look mysterious, those dark holes for eyes.
    That's what Cilla always said.
    Cilla from the Wirral, put away for suffocating her kid when she couldn't cope with it, like all the others in the Home, was fascinated by Jess's blowsy, mumsy body. For all that went on during their years together in the Home, for all Cilla's thoughts leading her elsewhere, it was to Jess that she always returned. She knew Jess inside out and so she should. When she lost Jess in the end she could have drawn a map from perfect memory that would cover every inch.
    No one ever satisfied Cilla from the Wirral like Jess did. And that was a big claim. She who tried so hard, in so many different ways, to satisfy herself. All her appetites ended up with Jess. Funny then – or not so funny at the time – that she could never quite do it for Jess. Oh, Jess loved her, she fancied her, she loved to have her try. But Cilla from the Wirral never quite pulled it off. Not entirely.

*

One morning in spring there was a parcel for Jess. She hadn't had one in years. She was coming up to twenty

216

now and there was talk that she might get out in a couple of years. Things were changing. Public opinion had shifted. The papers were no longer interested in stories like hers. There were worse things to look at and pry into. She'd been summoned up and told that, if she was on good behaviour, she might get out before too long. They'd give her a new name and everything, a new start.

It was a parcel from her sister. There was a green sticker on the back with the return address. Jude was sending her stuff; a padded jiffy bag, all selotaped up. You could tell no one had interfered with it. They hadn't had a look inside. Standing at the window where they gave the letters out, Jess rattled it close to her ear. It felt like some kind of book.

She read the return address. Jude was at university. This was the first Jess had known about it. She was behind on all the gossip. The last she'd heard from the family was when Lily Woods came up with cream buns for her sixteenth. She'd come all the way on the coach with a box of cakes tied with string. She'd told Jess all the news and started telling her messages from her father. Jess had found herself going mental, knocking the cakes and tea cups flying in the smokey lounge. Screaming at Lily to get out and never to come near her again. Well, none of the family had. They were as good as letting her rot.

Lily had no right telling me about them. They don't want me. And if they don't want me, my dad doesn't either. Lily had no right.

She walked back to her room to open the parcel in peace. It would take some careful unpicking. It needed a proper build up.

Jude should send me presents every day of my life, she thought. That's what she should do. Maybe this is the first of many. Maybe Jude is paying her dues.

She thought she'd have the bedroom to herself. The sun was slanting in, like a proper May morning. There were some freesias by the window Cilla had picked and the narrow room was scented with them. But Cilla herself was there too, sitting at the desk and swinging her legs, a pencil stuck in her mouth as she struggled to write to her dad.

*

Cilla from the Wirral, what a twat.

Jess shouldn't be awful about her, she knew, because Cilla had been her best pal these past few years. She'd been closest to her in the years when Jess learned to stand on her own two feet, like she had to at last in the Home, with no family, no twin, to stand beside.

But of all the people . . .

Cilla from the Wirral who wore blue flip-flops because she liked the noise of them on the lino in the corridors and couldn't be persuaded to wear something more sensible. Cilla who put her hair up in bunches like a little girl, though she was the same age as Jess. Cilla named, of course, for Cilla Black, because her father had fallen for her all that time ago, when she sang 'Step Inside, Love' on the telly. Gabbling out the higher notes, doing her bull-frog chorus. Cilla's father saying he wouldn't mind, even after all these years, giving Cilla one. The real, that is, the real Cilla Black.

When Jess looked at her friend from the outside she saw what everyone else did. Cilla the gawping, droopy-eyed twat; never above stealing girls' ciggies or make-up. Stirring up trouble with the House Mothers. Going behind everyone's backs and blithely making enemies. Telling new girls how the land lay in the Home and deliberately telling them lies. Jess could see Cilla wasn't the ideal kind of friend.

But Cilla clasped Jess at night like she was never going to let go, come hell or high water and Jess liked that. She liked the desperate feel of Cilla's fingers on her skin, even when she scratched her or rubbed her raw. She liked to touch Cilla's fanny and have Cilla say her fanny was all for fun now. She was having no more babies, being such a rotten mother first time around. Her fanny was all for fun these days and Jess could have all the fun she wanted with it

Jess would think: I'm having fun. Even in the Home I'm managing to get some fun. She wondered if it was the type she'd have chosen for herself, since this was all she was offered and she wasn't turning up her nose. Still and all, it made her feel lucky in life if she could nuzzle Cilla's fanny in their bunk beds. If she could guzzle on Cilla's brown-nippled breasts and they could plan together their fantastic escape; the great night out they would have when they got under the fence together and ran for one night's freedom knowing that, inevitably, they'd be caught up with again.

That still gave them one night of breathtaking adventure to plan and map out just for fun and they set to their plans with relish. There was nothing the Home could do to hurt them. They might as well sort out ways to have fun.

*

'She doesn't say much in the letter,' Jess said, passing it to Cilla. It was a single, peach-coloured sheet.

'She says "love" at the end,' said Cilla, looking straight at the bit where Jude had signed off. 'Your loving sister,' it said. Then she went back to read the rest of it.

Jess turned the book over in her hands. Jude had sent her a library book, hardcovered and battered from many lendings. It was six years old. There was a picture of a girl's face on the front, newsprint, blown up so the black dots showed against the white. It was called 'The Child Killers', by Katherine Marshall.

As soon as Jess had opened the parcel, she knew what it would be. Her heart jumped in her chest as she handled the book and she dreaded having to answer Cilla's questions. She flipped to the contents page and frowned. There it was. Chapter Four. 'Good Girl Bad Girl: The Case of Jessica Fletcher'. She slammed the book shut.

Cilla flapped the piece of paper. 'I don't understand this.'

In her brief note Jess's twin had written:

I got this out the university library on my OWN card and I don't WANT a FINE. But I thought you should see this. You never told US you were talking to this WOMAN about the family and everything and what YOU did. One of my friends who is doing first year SOCIOLOGY read it for a course and asked me if it was my SISTER she was reading about. I am HOPING that you don't know about this BOOK and it's as much of a SHOCK as it was to me. Read it and send it back to me so I don't get a fine. I am not saying anything about THIS to our MAM. She has been POORLY again.

Cilla made to take the book off Jess. 'Is it really about you?' she asked.

Jess snatched it away from her friend. 'No,' she said, and went off to find somewhere quiet.

*

Katherine Marshall's photo was on the back. Jess remembered her perm and her big glasses. It seemed a lifetime ago, when Jess was a kid. Katherine had been the first person Jess had talked to, properly, after all the attention, all the confusion going on.

Jess remembered most being led around the place, from room to room. In those first weeks, after Arthur died at school, she didn't have to make any decisions or do anything. Everyone made her mind up for her. It was easy. She just had to nod to say yes or shake her head. Yes, it was all her fault. No, she didn't want to see anyone. She didn't want to see her twin. No, Jude hadn't done anything wrong. Yes, she wanted her mam. No, her mam wouldn't see her.

I answered all their questions, she thought. *I took it all on myself. I deserved to be forgiven.*

I still do.

Katherine Marshall had come into the Home after a few months of Jess being there and she had talked to her just right. She had unlocked something with her careful, quiet words, and it had all come spilling out of Jess.

The biggest thing Katherine wanted to know about was Jude. She wanted to know what it was like being a twin. There wasn't much I could tell her at first. I had always been a twin. I didn't know any different. The person to ask, I said, was Jude herself. She had been born first and had fifteen minutes alone, in the first place. She had something to compare with.

Katherine had clicked her pen and said that it was me that she was interested in talking to and how I felt about my sister. She wanted to know if there had been a naughty one and if there had been a good one and if that was how people had thought of the twins. And if so, how did it feel to be perceived as the naughty one?

This got me talking. I had always been the quiet, better-behaved one. I had always lagged behind.

It said on the back of the book that Katherine Marshall taught in a university. Jess remembered her saying that and asking if she knew what a university was. Of course she did. Mam always said she wanted both her girls to go on and get their degrees and have the education she'd never had. Katherine Marshall taught at a different university to the one Jude had gone to. Katherine's was in the South.

*

She remembered telling Katherine that it was just like ripping daisies out of the ground. That instant when the stem stretches and gives a last protest. It bleeds a little sap on your tight fingers. The hollow sound as it gives. Girls picking daisies in the grass, knowing how it

221

sounded and felt. That was how Jess desribed it to Katherine.

Katherine came every day for two months to talk things over with her. They were given a special room to talk into the small tape recorder. Outside it was bright and everyone else was running rings around the Home, doing their exercise, wearing themselves out so they would be quieter in the night. But Jess was happy to talk to Katherine. A whole book about Jess and Jess only thirteen. She was kind and listened and her questions weren't stupid. She was especially interested in the daisy thing, which Jess had described. Pulling the wires out of the holes in Arthur's head, the wires that led straight into his brain and did the work of his missing ears; the second that she did that, it had felt just like pulling daisies.

Katherine wrote down a lot about that. She asked Jess just how it felt, to sit on a big boy's head in a dirty field and pull the wires out of his head. This was one of the last sessions they had together and Katherine didn't actually ask much about Arthur and how it had felt until she had asked a whole lot of other questions first. About her sister, her mam, her dead dad, her grandad and Aunt Lily. Katherine was very interested in all of them, as if she knew who they all were. It was only later that they got to the boy in the field and lying in black mud. Jess cried a lot at first and then she got over it and then she could tell Katherine exactly what it had felt like.

*

At the back of the Home were the generators and the place where the steam came out from the Central Heating. Gouts of steam rolled away across the gravel of the yard and frittered away over the fence. Jess came here to read, as she had with other books before, but never with one about herself. The only person who knew she came to sit here in her free hours was Cilla and she hoped Cilla would have the sense to leave her alone.

The book was hard. Katherine would keep interrupting it with little signs that led to notes with other bits of information, holding the whole thing up. Like she was stressing all the time how true this was, that people could go and check in the papers if they wanted, or in all the things that the Courts wrote down, and the police. There was a lot of stuff in Jess's chapter that wasn't really about her or her family at all; it was more about the place they came from and things like unemployment and divorce and the times they were living in. When it got to Jess she didn't recognise herself. Katherine said she was a sullen child, with eyes that came out dark on photos and did her no favours, making her look evil in the newspapers and that had gone against her; no one needing an excuse to say she was a devil child. She wrote that Jess hadn't got much schooling and her spoken English wasn't very good; her accent almost impenetrable and how difficult it had been to make sense of the recorded interviews. She said Jess had been a difficult subject; wrapping herself up in lies and obfuscations and veering away from direct questions. She contradicted herself and threw tantrums. Something traumatic must have happened to her. This was a very damaged child.

*

She lay the book under her pillow and kept it there as she mulled over what it said about her. In her spare time, when she wasn't doing duties or doing the things that everyone else did to pass the time, Jess would scour the chapter again and again, in case she had missed something. Katherine's book promised to explain everything about her. That's what it set out to do. People would understand all about Jessica Fletcher if they read these twenty-three pages but Jess felt none the wiser.

There was stuff about her dad dying and how she had seen him dead in the bath. There was even stuff about Grandad Fletcher falling off a fire escape in a pub. Her

Nanna was in there, too, although Jess had hardly ever seen her. And her mam's troubles were laid out for the world to see. Someone who'd borrowed the book before – maybe it was even Jude – had underlined some of the paragraphs in thick black pencil. They had drawn exclamation marks and question marks in the margins. They had written things like 'patriarchy' and 'decentred masculine role models'. Jess would puzzle over these notes as much as Katherine's bolder printed sentences. What did 'intersubjectivity' mean? Every time the words 'traumatised' and 'damaged' and 'responsibility' appeared they were heavily scored under in pencil.

She packed the book into a carrier bag with her toothbrush and a handful of tampons, a hair brush and two clean pairs of pants and, one night after their supper of chips and ham and pease pudding, she told Cilla that tonight was the night.

'The night we've been on about,' she said, sitting on the bunk and watching her friend start to panic. 'We've said for ages, we'd get out and have a proper night out. Do all the stuff we can't do here.'

'Where? Where will we go?'

'North,' said Jess. 'We'll go to nightclubs and pubs. Pick up some fellas and make them pay us in and buy us cocktails and we can keep them out all night. We'll get kebabs and a bottle of champagne to celebrate our freedom . . .'

'We can't do it now. You're meant to be on good behaviour.'

'Fuck that,' Jess snapped. 'There's something I have to do.'

*

Jude's university was in the middle of a city. In the small library in the Home there was a prospectus for the place, to encourage people to better themselves. Jess knew where all that stuff was, because they'd been trying to get her to study. She had the aptitude, they said, but she'd never put it to use. The fact that Jude was a scholar now proved it, she supposed. They must both have the same intelligence.

She looked at a map of the university and found where Jude was living. The exact hall of residence. She redrew the map on the back of Jude's letter. She imagined her sister in the centre of that huge place; free to wander out any night, into any street she wanted. It was much bigger than the town where they'd grown up. She wondered if Jude was ever frightened, with so much going on around her; to be in the thick of so many strangers.

*

Cilla didn't want to come at all. Her nerve had failed. The two of them sat in their room and stared at each other until the time Jess had decided on. Jess was waiting for Cilla to break down and beg to be let off their pact. Jess wouldn't budge and Cilla wasn't going to make herself look soft. She was heartened that they were going to her city.

Their plans had been made ages ago. They knew the chink in the system. It was right where Jess always sat, by the Central Heating pipes. It was the Home's blind spot; left unguarded during the hour or more when the House Mothers went round switching off lights and locking up doors. There were no cameras round there either. Jess had been meticulous.

All they had to do was make their beds look full. They stuffed all the clothes they wouldn't be taking under their duvets. The House Mothers were discreet with them, in a funny way, because everyone knew what they got up to. No one came barging into Jess and Cilla's room. They were like husband and wife, Cilla often said, and they were treated differently. They got married persons' privileges. Jess wasn't so sure. She didn't think the House Mothers looked that closely or paid that much attention to anyone.

It was getting dark already – a soft, lilac light – as Jess led the way to the back of the old buildings. Between them they carried only two plastic bags. Jess could kick herself for leaving her cigarettes. As they searched in the dark grass for the broken bit of fence, she looked down and saw that Cilla was still in her blue flip-flops.

'How the hell are you going to run in them?'

'They're all I've got, shoe-wise.'

Jess wrenched up the wire netting and the gash was big enough to get them through.

'It's so easy!' Cilla laughed, ducking through, feeling the netting wobble and shake as she snagged it on her anorak.

Jess shushed her. 'They could get us yet.'

But they didn't. There were trees and a little field to run through before they got to the main road and there was no one to stop them. No klaxons started blaring and no dogs came at them, howling and yapping. The branches of the black trees lashed at them and the thick mud sucked at their feet but behind them, the Home was silent; settling down for the night. Oblivious to their going.

*

'We can't hitch here,' Jess said when they got to the road. 'It's obvious where we've come from if we hitch here.'

They followed the road for about a mile, where it turned into a motorway. Cilla shambled along behind her down the soft verge in her flip-flops. Cilla was singing with happiness as cars slashed by. She was singing the monkey song from the Jungle Book. Jess laughed. She started to join in and they sang it again, right through together, until they reached the four lanes of the big road.

*

There was a hotel here; an old country house turned into a hotel on a lay-by. Jess had the sudden idea that they could walk straight into the foyer and pretend they were guests. No one would know. They could use the hand-basins in the toilets to wash the mud of their escape off their legs.

In they walked, up a disabled ramp into the orange foyer of the place. There was a baby grand piano and a display of novelty tea pots in a glass case. The receptionist narrowed her eyes at them as they came in, Cilla following Jess's lead and swinging her carrier-bag in a devil-may-care fashion. Jess led the way straight to the toilets and as they put their legs up on the basins and swabbed at them with damp paper towels, they laughed.

'We should have done this sooner!' Cilla gasped. 'We could have gone out every Saturday night! If only we'd known!'

Jess just smiled.

Out in the foyer again, Cilla got brave. 'Let's go to the bar for a drink. Look, they've got a big old fire going and everything.'

There were no other women in the bar. It was all youngish men in business suits sitting on leather settees. Some of the men looked at Jess and Cilla as they came up the steps into the bar area. They sipped at their pints and thoughtfully watched the only women in the hotel apart from the receptionist.

'Two Camparis and lemons,' Jess said.

'Oh, an eggnog,' Cilla shook her head. 'Have you got money, Jess?'

'A fiver.'

'I feel right shabby, coming into a bar with our carrier-bags. Who'd look at us?'

'They're all looking.'

'Shit.'

'No, in a good way.'

They sat at a small table with their drinks. Cilla produced a fresh packet of Marlboros and offered Jess one first.

'You've saved my life,' Jess smacked her lips on the filter. There was a version of 'Careless Whisper' playing on the speakers, without any words.

'No, Jess,' said Cilla, raising her glass to her lips. 'You've saved my life.'

'Get away with you.'

'It's true.' Cilla stared nervously at the business men on the settees. 'My life was rubbish before I got in with you.'

'And what's it like now?'

'It's fantastic! I never thought I could just walk out of there.'

Jess shrugged. 'My mam always used to say, you don't have to do anything you don't want. They can't make you. She said, just send them to me and I'll sort them out.'

'Why don't you go and see your mam?' Cilla asked suddenly. 'You're out now. You could!'

Jess shook her head brusquely. 'She'd have a frigging fit. Me showing up on her doorstep.'

'Oh, she wouldn't . . .'

'She would. She wants nothing to do with me.'

'I bet that's not true.'

Jess pulled a face.

Cilla went on. 'Well, if we're going to Liverpool, I'm going to see me dad. Will you come with me?'

She looked so hopeful. Jess couldn't believe Cilla thought they were always going to do stuff together. As Jess saw it, their reason for sticking together was what they'd left behind, on the other side of that fence. 'We'll see,' she said.

*

In a lay-by in the pitch dark, three miles down from the hotel, a lorry eventually stopped for them. The driver (he was so high up Jess had to crane her neck, shield her eyes and shout over the motorway noise to talk to him) wasn't keen on taking both of them. 'We go together!' Jess yelled, pulling her arm out of Cilla's anxious grip.

'If you want me, you get her as well. We're both going to Liverpool.'

The driver had grunted and they climbed aboard.

It started to rain and he didn't want them talking. He paid attention to the other lorries, giving them respect as they swerved from lane to lane.

'What are you carrying, then?' Jess asked.

He looked at her and scowled. He had a great black mole in the middle of his forehead, like an insect. Cilla sat on the other side of Jess and shivered, pleased that they weren't out in the rain. The driver put the fan heater on and the cab filled up with muggy steam off their damp clothes. Cilla was marvelling at how far they had come; totting up the mileage of their freedom with every passing roadsign.

The driver put a cassette on and sang along with Oasis to stop the girls talking to him.

*

Cilla fell asleep leaning against Jess, who felt she had to stay awake all night, just in case. She wanted to ask their lorry driver how close he could take them to Liverpool but, as the motorway lights stroked over them and the rain went on falling, there didn't seem to be much chance.

He hauled the wagon into a Little Chef car park. Jess peered around for signs. She had lost count of where they were.

As he parked he said tightly, 'End of the line for you two.'

'What?'

'This is as close as I can get to where you're going.'

'Where are we?'

He shrugged. 'Little Chef. I'm going in for some chips.'

'Chips!' said Cilla waking up.

'I've got fifteen minutes to spare,' he said. 'I need you two to get out and on your way.'

'Oh,' said Jess. 'Can't you take us the rest of the way? Go on, I'm sure you could . . .'

He was firm. 'I'm on a tight schedule.'

Cilla was bleary. 'Jess, what's happening?' She sounded scared.

'Sssh.' Jess pushed her face up to the driver's and hoped her breath wasn't too sour. 'If you bought us a burger and chips and that, and then if you drove us over to Liverpool, I'm sure we could come to an arrangement.'

He laughed gruffly. 'What, you'd make it worth my while?'

Jess smiled.

'Jess?' Cilla asked.

'We're sisters,' Jess said. 'And we do a sister-act. You know what I mean. You could have us in the back of your lorry. You'd never forget it.'

He laughed, hissing out his breath. 'Sorry, girls.'

'No, really,' Jess said. 'We could make your frigging eyes pop out.'

'I reckon you could,' he said. 'But, like I say, I'm on a tight schedule here. I'm five minutes behind as it is. I've got just enough time to run into Little Chef for my chips, and then get back on the road. So, some other time, eh, lasses?'

Minutes later Jess and Cilla were standing on the grass in the rain and the dark, watching the driver through the window of the Little Chef. He was gobbling down his chips and not looking at them.

'Did you think he was attractive?' Cilla asked.

'No, I fucking didn't.'

Their next lift came after half an hour, once the lorry driver had taken off again, without even a backward glance at his soaking hitchers.

They climbed into a younger fella's car. Jess got in the back so she could have a nap, which left Cilla bundling herself awkwardly in the front. It turned out the young fella – he worked in Insurance and had dark, spikey hair – was going right into Liverpool.

'Result,' Jess said. Then the car stereo started up again as they got onto the motorway. Some sort of hardcore dance music.

'What do you call this?' Cilla said.

He shrugged and smiled.

'Isn't it a bit . . . busy?'

'Oh, what would you prefer?'

Cilla said firmly, 'We both like Blondie.'

The Insurance man laughed. 'Where have you been? That's old-fashioned for young girls like you.' He was thrusting his chin in time to the music.

'We're old-fashioned girls.'

'Must have been in a time warp.'

'We're Doctor Who girls!' Cilla exclaimed suddenly. 'We're Doctor Who's girl assistants and we've been travelling in time and space for years! That's where we've been!'

The Insurance man looked at Cilla – she was waggling her bunched hair and grinning over her head-rest at Jess. 'Yeah . . .' he said. 'Right.'

'Yeah,' Jess said. 'We've been stuck on the planet of arseholes. Any chance of getting off?'

*

When they got to Liverpool, Cilla was full of herself. You'd think she owned the place. Their Insurance man dropped them off in the town and all the roads were full of kids going off to clubs. Boys with their shirts hanging untucked and girls back in mini skirts.

'What are they wearing sunglasses for at night?' Jess asked, feeling out of it.

'Oh, Jess,' Cilla was saying. 'I can take you everywhere, all over town. All the things you've ever wanted to see in Liverpool.'

Pushing down the street, Jess didn't have a clue where they were. She was holding her carrier close and scowling. She was planning to dump Cilla as soon as she could. 'I thought you were going to your dad's.'

'There's the Cavern where the Beatles used to sing. I could take you to the museum there. And we have to get the Ferry over to my dad's. You'll love that, Jess. We'll stand on the top and be like the Liver Birds. And I can show you the Albert Dock and we can stand by the window of the TV studio and get on the telly in the background, behind Richard and Judy.'

Cilla was away with all her ideas.

'What we said,' Jess broke in. 'Was that it was one night out. You're planning a frigging holiday, Cilla.'

'Well, we're free now, aren't we? We can plan all sorts.'

Jess shook her head. 'How long do you reckon we'll last? They'll have us picked up by the morning.'

'Oh, don't say that, Jess.'

'They're not daft, are they? They'll have the coppers onto us.'

Cilla took them into an old pub. It was full of older people, sitting in their smoke, drinking Guinness and bitter.

'I hate that frigging song,' Jess glowered as they stood by the bar. 'Those were the days, my friend.' She nudged Cilla. 'I've got no money left. You'll have to get that fella beside you to buy us a drink.'

As Cilla turned to the man in a tracksuit, Jess was thinking, what do we look like? Stood in a pub in our prison clothes. She could smell the petrol of the lorry on her, the dried up rain in her clothes. She reached up to pat her scraggy hair, looking at the mirror behind the optics, and felt twigs stuck in her hair. 'Christ. I look like I've come out of the jungle.'

*

She was surprised when Cilla succeeded in getting the bloke to buy them drinks. He was young with very pale skin and an earring in his bottom lip. He cleared two old dears off a table for them and they all sat down together. Cilla was winking at Jess, pleased with herself.

'What do you do then?' Jess asked.

He was talking to Cilla though, face up to her ear, shouting and making Cilla laugh. She's going to cack herself laughing, Jess thought, sipping her pint. Too excited. Cilla's not used to male attention.

The young man put his hand out across the table to Jess and she stared at how many rings he was wearing. 'Your sister's been telling me you do, like, an act.'

Shite. She stared at Cilla. Cilla looked back as if to say, That's what you said.

Jess got up and took a long swig of her drink. 'Stick with him if you want, Cilla. I've got stuff to do.'

She started to squeeze through the pub, not looking back.

Outside, Cilla came running up after her, her sandals flapping.

'What were you doing?' Jess shouted.

'I thought we could both shag him and get some money, quick, before . . .'

'Jesus, Cilla.' Jess carried on walking. 'He looked rough.'

Cilla pulled her round. 'What's rough? He didn't look rough to me. I'm fucking rough, aren't I?'

Jess looked her up and down. 'Yeah. You're dog fucking rough.'

They both laughed.

'Which way's the university?'

Jess felt in her carrier for her map on the back of Jude's letter.

*

Katherine Marshall had only said what Peg had said years ago. That was the disappointing thing. Katherine with her perm and big glasses and her tape recorder got to teach at a university and got her picture on the back of books. Yet she'd only said what Peg said, Peg sitting there smoking in her cardy back at the Comp. People did bad things because their home life was all wrong. A conclusion like that didn't take much getting to.

As Jess and Cilla took a rest in a shop doorway Jess looked at her hands. By the street light she could still see the pale bands of scars on her fingers. Peg and Katherine couldn't be right, really, though. Twins put paid to their idea. Jude and Jess had been brought up the same and they were different, weren't they? They were almost the same person, their mam had said once. A freak chance of cells dividing and making them two and here they were: twinnys.

All the same things had happened to the two of them, until the plug got pulled on Lugsy. Jess wanted to see Jude to talk about all of this. Jude would know more about it. She was studying now. She could explain it all to her.

It was easy getting into the university buildings. The porters looked them up and down and let them through. There were students about and they didn't look much better dressed than the two escapees.

'Fuck, we've been dragged through hedges and hitched cross the country,' said Jess. 'And we still look as good as this lot.'

They looked at students going through their pigeon-holes for post and going to and from the bar. There was a disco on in one of the big rooms. Jess waited for there to be a crush so they could slip through the doors without showing a ticket.

'Where can we leave our bags?' Cilla asked. 'I've not been to a dance in ages.'

They were playing older types of music. Things that Jess remembered from school discos. There were fluorescent pink signs saying 'Eighties Retro Night'. Jess dragged Cilla in the middle and they started to dance, at first feeling awkward and aching, clearing a space for themselves amongst the drunk students. No one looked at them like they shouldn't be there. They picked up speed and Cilla started lifting up her feet, stomping down on the sticky floor with her flip-flops.

'This is living!' Jess shouted. 'Eh, Cilla? This is proper dancing.'

She went running around the back of Cilla and did a kind of shimmy up and down her back and Cilla was almost crying laughing.

I can't believe we're dancing, Jess thought. She was laughing at Cilla, because Cilla looked so happy. Some people got to do this any night they liked.

There were cans of lager set out on a table. People were taking them for free. It was a cheap make and lukewarm, but as soon as they saw them, Jess and Cilla went over and drank quickly, thirstily.

'Jesus, Jess,' said Cilla. 'Students get it all, don't they?' She looked around the room, which looked like a school hall, with dingy blue patterned curtains high up. 'This must be what it's like if you're clever.'

'Yeah,' said Jess. 'I could have gone, you know.'

'What, to university?'

'I'm clever enough.'

Cilla laughed. 'Yeah.'

'I am. If our Jude is clever enough, then I must be as well.'

'Does it work like that?'

'Yeah. I could be here. I would have done Politics. I'd have sorted the world out.'

Cilla passed her another can. 'You shouldn't have got yourself put away then, should you?'

Jess was scanning the faces of the dancers, holding the can up to her mouth like a disguise. 'No, I shouldn't have.'

In the dark she could make out a bunch of girls against the radiator on the back wall. They hadn't danced all night. They were dressed in black with white panstick make-up on.

'Fuck me,' said Jess. 'There she is.'

'Who?' Cilla craned to see.

'My sister. And she's a fucking Goth.'

*

Later, in Jude's brick-walled study bedroom, while Jude was off making them cups of tea and taking it all in, Jess and Cilla were making themselves comfortable, sitting on her bed and looking round.

They were talking to a couple of Jude's friends. Sam, who wore a vegetable-dyed woolly jumper and had a shaved head, and another Goth, Alison, who had hair the colour of tomato soup.

There were candles lit and stuck in Chianti bottles, all around the small room. Postcards of Goya etchings were blue-tacked to the walls and Alison, feeling quite at home, was putting on records; the Pixies, the Cure. Jess recognised the flowery duvet she was sitting on from home. As she talked to her sister's friends she was looking along the walls and shelves of books, looking for any family pictures. It reminded her of going to her dad's flat when she was little. But there were no photos up here.

She was telling Alison and Sam, as Cilla drowsed off to sleep beside her:

'I wanted it to be like that bit at the end of Grease. When Olivia Newton-John turns up at the fairground and she's all dolled up with a bubble perm and hotpants and a space comes open in the crowd and John Travolta turns round and he's like, 'Sandy! You look fantastic, pet.' And she's like, 'Tell us about it, stud.' And then they go into that song. That's what I wanted it to be like. Jude seeing me suddenly at the party and going: Fuck me, there's our Jess.'

Cilla roused herself. 'That's what it was like, wasn't it?'

'Yeah,' said Jess.

Alison was licking a baggy looking joint. 'John Travolta was better in Pulp Fiction, wasn't he?'

'I don't know,' said Jess. 'I haven't been to the pictures, have I, since I was about ten.'

You could see Alison blush, even through her white make-up. 'Oh. Of course.' So Jess could tell she was the one who was doing Sociology; the one who'd been reading up about her life.

The door came open then and Jude was back from the kitchen, struggling to keep hold of five mugs and not spill any. Her eye make-up was all black and her lips were painted purple. She looked like a dead body coming in with the tea and asking who wanted toast and jam.

'That's our little ritual,' said Sam with the shaved head. He talked quite posh, and Jess stared at his white eyelashes. 'Everyone comes back to Jude's room every night and she makes toast. Her room is like our living room.'

Jude's hair had been sticking up with gel and hair-spray. Now it was flattened. She asked her sister, 'Do you want anything to eat?'

Jess shook her head.

Jude sat down on her desk chair. She wanted the others to go, but couldn't say anything. They were looking interested. Alison got up and slid a Throwing Muses CD into the machine.

'Who bought you a CD player?' Jess asked, smiling.

'Mam did,' said Jude. 'For my nineteenth.'

'Our nineteenth.' Jess said and coughed. I bet I've got fucking pneumonia. 'It looks nice. Loud.'

Alison turned the sound up and down again. 'This woman who's singing,' she explained. 'She's got fifteen separate personalities, she reckons. I think she's fantastic. Just listen to her lyrics. You can tell.'

'Have they let you out?' Jude asked suddenly.

Jess shook her head quickly.

Cilla hunched forward. 'We've done a bunk.'

'A bunk!'

'Jess found a way through the fence,' Cilla went on. 'We ran like bastards! We hitched lifts and everything. We came all this way to see you.'

Jess said, 'Cilla wanted to come here anyway, to see her dad.'

Sam turned the sound even further down. 'So you're on the run?' His eyes were wide as he gave Cilla the messy spliff. Jess thought he had lovely eyes. Cilla dragged deep and kept the rest of the spliff for herself.

'Fugitives from the law,' Cilla said.

'Fucking hell, Jess,' Jude said, standing up. 'What are you playing at? They'll be after you. You'll not be able to hide from them . . .'

'I know that.'

'So what's the point?'

Jess sat back against the brick wall. 'You wouldn't ask that if you'd been locked up somewhere like a prison.'

Jude laughed. 'I am locked up somewhere like a frigging prison. Look around you.'

'Yeah. It looks just like where we came from.'

'It's not as clean,' said Cilla.

'But it's different,' Jess said. 'You're getting an education. You're going to have a degree. What am I gunna get when I leave? Fuck all. I'll be a nowt.'

'You'll never get out if you keep running away.'

Jess pulled the library book out of her bag and tossed it at Jude, who sat down again. 'You said you wanted this back.'

'You could have posted it.' Jude held the book like it would burn her hands. 'Did you read it?'

'It was shite.'

'Why did you talk to her?'

'Because she was nice to me.'

'Did you know she'd put it in a book?'

'I can't remember.'

'Mam would do her nut if she knew.'

'Fuck her,' said Jess.

Jude glared at her.

Alison poked Sam and stood up. 'We should go. You've got family stuff to . . .'

'That Katherine should write another book,' Jess said. 'That's what I reckon. She should write a book with the real reasons in.'

'What real reasons?' Jude looked red, as if she was going to go into one of her tempers at any minute.

'For everything. There's a few things I could tell her now.'

'Like what, Jess?'

'Most of what I told her was lies. Wasn't it? You know, Jude. What I said when I was twelve and thirteen was just about all lies.'

Jude sighed. 'It's all history, Jess.'

'Wrong,' said Cilla woozily. 'It's Sociology.'

'It's Psychology!' said Sam, laughing. 'You should know, Judith. You're doing Psychology!'

'Fuck off, Sam,' Jude said.

'I could have told them what was what, back then,' Jess said. 'But I didn't.'

Jude looked down at her tea. 'I know you didn't.'

'Shall we go?' Alison asked awkwardly.

'It's all right,' said Jess. 'What I've found out is, it's best to have witnesses.'

She looked round and Cilla had passed out on the pillows. Jude spoke up, her voice hard and bright. 'You can stay here tonight. That's okay with me. Ali and Sam won't say anything, will you?'

The two of them shook their heads.

'You can have my bed, Jess. And Cilla can . . .'

'Cilla stays with me,' Jess said.

'All right. The two of you have my room and we'll talk about it in the morning. We'll have a proper talk then.'

Jess eyed her. 'Good.'

Jude drained her mug. 'Sam, can I sleep on your floor tonight?'

He grinned. 'Sure.'

'Is it bedtime now, then?' asked Jess.

'I reckon so, don't you? You must be shagged.'

Jess crumpled the plastic bag in her hands. She peered into it to see what else she had brought. 'Yeah. That's why I'm sounding so bolshy. Look, let me sleep and we can go over it tomorrow.'

There was a second, as Alison and Sam moved to the door, when the twins were both on their feet, waiting for the other to make the move, to go into a hug or kiss each other. But they hadn't kissed each other since they were six. They said goodnight and Jude left Jess and Cilla to her room.

The CD slid to a halt some time later and Jess got Cilla to bunk up. Cilla started looking around the room again. 'Look at all the stuff in here,' she said. 'Is she a bit gloomy, your sister? I don't know if I can sleep in here, with all these depressing pictures and that.'

'You'll sleep,' said Jess. She stripped down and climbed under the flowery duvet. They were used to sharing a single bunk. As Jess clicked off the desk lamp, Cilla was saying, 'Well, we got our night out on the razz, didn't we? We got a few drinks and we did some dancing. That's what we came for, after all.'

Jess squeezed her arm, telling her to shut up now.

*

Sam wanted cigarettes from the machine in the porters' lodge. Jude went with him and thought about a night lying on the cold floor in his room.

Behind his glass partition, the night porter stared at her balefully.

'He's a miserable old sod, isn't he?' she said to Sam.

Sam was about to tell her she needn't crash on his floor. Jude was staring back at the porter. 'Shall I tell him?'

'Hm?' Sam was struggling with the machine.

'Should I tell him who's turned up?'

'What? Jude . . . you can't . . .'

'I should do. I should do, really. You heard her. She's a danger to herself.'

'But he'll get the police in. They'll cart her off again. She'll . . .'

'Yeah,' said Jude. 'You're right.'

She stood there as Sam put in the right money and clicked the button for Marlboro Lights, but it was empty of them. He clicked for Camels, but they were gone, too. His third choice was Silk Cut and he was relieved to hear the thunk and the rattle as his fags dropped into the slot near the floor. Sam reached to pick them up, straightened and turned. He was unwrapping the cellophane and asking Jude if she wanted one, but Jude was over at the night porter's window, leaning in and explaining to him about her sister.

15
Quiet Life

Christine was proud.

She had a choice between being proud and being ashamed, was what her dad told her. 'Now you have to decide which it's going to be.'

Through the difficult nights he had held her like she was a little girl again and talked plain, common sense to her.

'Cut your losses, girl. You can't hold onto someone when they go too far. There are some things you can never forgive. Murder, for god's sake! Murdering a kid. She planned it. She set out to do it. She's wicked through and through, and we never saw it.'

But did we see it? Christine thought. We must have.

What kind of home did we make for them if this is what they do?

Not they. Just one. Just Jess.

'Evil's inside of some people,' Dan told her thickly, pouring them both a drink as they sat on the settee. They sat through the whole of one night like this and they had more conversations like it, every time Christine broke out and said she wanted to visit Jess in the home. Whenever she looked as if she wanted to forgive her daughter and go to her, Dan gave her a talking to.

'Evil's just inside some people. It has to come out. You did nothing wrong. None of it's your fault.'

Christine could believe it. She could feel all right about it. Except when she thought about the fact that a daughter of hers, a piece of her own flesh and blood, was in a room, a cell, in a faceless building in a place Christine had never been.

She remembered telling her mother, forcefully, tearfully, on that one time she saw her, that strange day out, that she hoped she'd forgive her daughters anything. She'd hoped she'd be able to forgive them anything they did. They would always be hers.

Her mother had nodded and winced. Knowing it was a tall order. Christine had bridled. Knew she would try to forgive, no matter what.

Then this. Then the hardest thing of all.

'Evil was inside her the whole time,' Dan said. 'You've got to think about your own life, and Jude's. You have to cut the evil out and move on. Be proud, Christine, be proud of the good things we've got here. Forget the rest.'

The years had gone on like that. With her father believing she had left the bad behind. That they were pushing on and making the best of it. No one knew how much Christine wanted to go to her daughter.

Every few weeks, every few months, she would pack a bag and prepare to take off, cross-country, to see Jess. The thought of setting out alone terrified her. She had never really been anywhere alone. She couldn't bear to think what Jess would say to her. If she went, she would have to face up to whatever she found. Each time, she would unpack her bag and sit on the end of her bed and try to invent the conversation they would have with each other.

Her Jess was an adult now. Just the same as Jude. It was difficult to remember that.

Christine still thought of Jess as the twelve-year-old she'd last seen, surrounded by people, official people in suits, clutching papers and files. They'd taken Jess out of her hands. They could deal with her and whatever was inside of her better than Christine could.

She hoped they had done a good job.

She rocked herself on the end of her bed and wondered what Jess had grown into.

And would she ever find out.

All these years later the same thoughts were still going round in her head. With no one to talk them out with, besides her dad, with nothing practical done, with no contact made, Christine hadn't moved on at all.

Like her mother, back in the Sixties Café, she'd stuck herself back in the past.

And she'd let her dad dictate her life to her.

There was something bad inside him, Lily Woods had said. He was the one with the bad inside. And Christine still listened to him.

Lily kept out of the way. She couldn't believe Christine wouldn't see her daughter. Lily was disgusted. That's what she looked like, every time she saw Christine.

What did Lily know about forgiveness? About daughters? Do-gooder. Spinster.

Michael would have gone to Jess. That's what Christine read in Lily's eyes. Michael would never have abandoned his daughter.

What did any of them know?

All of them telling her what was for the best.

But I did nothing. I held tight and ignored them all except dad.

She thought: I've been doing nothing for years.

Except now, perhaps, with this trip, she might be doing something positive. This might be a positive experience. She had dared herself to do this and come here and Jude, bless her, was helping out and being supportive.

It wasn't what she'd imagined. It wasn't visiting Jess.

I'm still not brave enough for that.

But it was something.

She sat in the hotel foyer having a fag and waiting for her daughter. She caught the bar man's eye and he brought her a vodka and tonic.

'It was all meant, you see,' her dad had said gently, cupping her face in his hands. His hands were almost closed up with the arthritis. 'You had two daughters and that gives you the choice. You can declare one a bad lot and cut her out of your life. The other will still be yours. You can be proud of Jude. Whatever else has gone on, she's still made a success of herself.'

*

Dan had come to Jude's Graduation ceremony. Christine had watched him all that day, keeping an eye open in case he had one of his flare-ups, but he was good as gold. He'd stood in the bar with his navy blazer on, the buttons shining silver, and he'd made small talk with the parents of Jude's university friends.

'They'll all be well-off types,' he'd worried on the coach to Liverpool. 'What will I have to say to them?'

'Get away,' Christine told him. 'You've as much right to be there as they have. It's your granddaughter who got a first class degree. In fact, she's better than all them. She got the top exams out of everyone.'

'They'll be talking all lah-de-dah.'

'Well, Jude's moved up a bracket, hasn't she? And we'll just have to move up with her.'

Secretly, Christine had been nervous, too. She couldn't believe it, standing by their seats in the big hall, when they had a fanfare of trumpets for the students coming in in their black caps and gowns and then there was a procession with the Royalty coming in.

'Look at her skin!' Dan leaned right across Christine to see the Princess's face as she went by. 'Who is it again? One of the one's you don't hear of much. But she does have lovely skin, doesn't she?'

'She's got the money for all the expensive treatments,' Christine said. Christine was in an olive dress suit from Marks and Spencer's. She had a friend, Bea, who said you could wear them once from Marksies, sponge out the arm pits, hang them up and take them back to the shop and get your cash refunded. Christine thought she'd like to keep the suit, though. She wished she had a hat to go with it.

She glowed with pleasure, seeing Jude march across the stage to take her scroll off the Princess. On the video they bought afterwards, it looked like Jude was stomping and in a bad mood. Christine knew it was just nervousness.

On the photos they took on the bit of grass that Jude called the quad, you could see the bump in Jude's dress already. She was showing earlier than Christine had. 'Not twins again,' Dan had laughed, touching Jude's belly as Christine snapped pictures. She wanted one with them all together.

'No, it's not twins,' said Jude. 'I've had the scan. It's just one big bloody baby.'

Dan was laughing about it then, in the sunny quad. Thinking it was a big joke now; Jude showing off that she was going to have a baby and her only just finished at the university. At first, when Jude had phoned, just before her exams started, he had been incensed by the news, shouting the odds at Christine, as if it was all her fault. 'Another one!' he yelled. 'Another one of you who CAN'T keep her fucking LEGS closed!'

'It's different this time,' Christine said. 'She's got her degree.'

'But she's got no money coming in. Where's the lad? Is he going to support her?'

Sam was going into computers. It seemed he was a bit of an expert and was set to make a lot of money. They weren't going to marry, but he'd buy a house for them, up by Newcastle. He was starting work there, the week after Graduation. When he was settled in and the house was sorted out, he would send for her. In the meantime Jude would have to go back home with Dan and Christine.

At the Graduation they'd met Sam for the first time. Jude had said how he'd got a shaved head and earrings, six of them all in one ear. But how smart he looked that day! He spoke very politely and nicely to them, shaking both Christine's and Dan's hands. Christine had stared at the tiny holes in his ear where he'd taken the rings out for meeting Royalty. Dan was very impressed with him. 'They always said computers were the thing of the future. That lad's got their whole lives mapped out for them.'

'Do you think they'll be all right, dad?'

'I do, lass. This family is on the up at last.'

*

But who were they forgetting?

Christine knew very well. All through the graduation day, each time she looked at Jude, there was a ghost image beside her. When Jude walked across to fetch her scroll and stand by the Princess, and when they all stood together for their photo, there was another person there.

Christine looked at the pictures afterwards, searching out this extra presence. Jess could have been there with all of us, with a degree of her own. She could have the life our Jude's got.

She wanted them to talk about Jess. She wanted to bring her up all the way through that day. She wanted them to wonder what she was doing. But she realised that no one mentioned Jess for her sake, for fear of upsetting her.

Christine stopped herself bursting out with the things she wanted to say and felt the others follow her lead.

Jess had never been as bright as Jude. She'd never have gone to college anyway. Their lives would have been quite different, whatever happened.

*

Now, in August, Jude was bigger than ever and Sam still hadn't managed to arrange their mortgage. Jude was growing lethargic and teary, stuck around the house all day. She would ask Christine different things about being pregnant and bringing up bairns, but Christine could hardly remember anymore.

Christine was going out to work at the bakery and coming back to find Jude sat on the settee. She hadn't moved all day. She said her brains were rotting away.

'You've got a first class honours degree!' Christine laughed, unpacking the out-of-date bread, buns and pastries she liked to bring home. Jess had a craving for sausage rolls. 'Your brains can't rot. And if they do, it doesn't matter. You've got that piece of paper you can wave at people.'

She stood between Jude and the telly. 'Have you been watching talk shows all day?'

'Yes,' Jude muttered.

Christine was starting to wish they hadn't gone over to Cable. But she liked the talk shows as well; the American ones where they bleeped out the swearing and people had a real go at each other. She and Jude laughed when the fat black women tore off their shoes to chuck across the stage at each other. The English ones were more sedate. They had real discussions. It wasn't just a punch-up. Christine was glad her daughter still liked down-to-earth things like that.

She made a pot of tea and fetched the bag of sausage rolls through. Together they watched Nancy! live from Norwich. Today it was about grown men who liked to dress up as babies and have their nappies changed.

'Oh, that's sick, that,' Jude said.

'Hey, imagine your grandad!'

They both laughed.

'He might be into that, for all you know,' said Jude. 'When he goes down to the outhouse. He might be sat there in a nappy and a pink little dress with his dummy in.'

'Ugh. Don't.' Christine looked at Jude. 'If this is making you feel queasy, we could turn over. Jerry's on Living, soon.'

'No, it's all right.'

Christine was worried Jude would start imagining she was pregnant with a horrible old man inside her.

They watched until the end, and then Nancy was facing the camera and asking people to phone in if they wanted to take part in a fortnight's time. The theme of that show was going to be 'The Real Victims of Violent Crime'; looking at the families of murderers and showing how they were affected. Jude felt her mam stiffen on the settee.

The adverts came on.

'That would be interesting, that,' Christine said. She poured them some more tea. 'They get real psychologists on and everything to explain to you. Counselling and stuff. The people who go on there get it all for free.'

'Do you want counselling?'

'Course not.'

'And on the telly! It would be awful, mam.'

Christine said thoughtfully, 'Lily Woods gets on the telly sometimes.' She started picking bobbles off her cream jumper. 'It wouldn't hurt anyone, would it? And people should know, anyway. It's right. The real victims of violent crime are the families who have to live with it. All that shame. What was it like round here, after all that? The papers and everything.'

Jude looked at her mother. So she'd been thinking about Jess all this time. Even now, Jess hadn't gone away. Even though her mother never mentioned her, even though everyone steered clear of the topic, it was still pretty close to the surface. Jude had thought they'd all moved on. Apparently not. Her mother was looking shifty.

'You don't want it all dragging up,' Jude said, flicking flakes of pastry.

'No . . . but we could be a good example, love, couldn't we? How, against the odds, you've made something of yourself. A first class honours degree in psychology and a baby on the way. You should tell them! We should be proud.'

Jude stared at her mam. She was really serious. She was trying to make it all into something heroic. Jude couldn't believe it.

'Anyway,' Christine said, 'it would be a trip out, wouldn't it? I'm worried about you. You're getting house-bound.'

*

Now Christine was sitting in her olive dress suit in the hotel foyer, drinking her vodka and waiting for Jude. A taxi was going to take them to the studio. She needed a bit of courage for talking on the telly, though that Nancy always seemed nice enough. She made people comfortable and got them to tell all sorts of things.

Christine couldn't think of a single thing she might say to her. If Nancy came up to her with a microphone, Christine would be stuck there, dumb.

How could I tell the whole story of my life in only a few minutes? That's what people do, though.

They talk about their troubles as if it's all they think about. They can account for all the rotten stuff in their lives. Would I even know where to start? I'd sound peculiar. I'd sound like I came from a family that kept itself to itself and somehow thought it was better than everyone else. But everything bad that could possibly happen still happened to us. How do I explain that? Shouldn't I be too ashamed?

I should be ashamed that my daughter could do what she did. I should be ashamed of even talking about it.

'You're making it into something heroic,' Jude had said. 'Like we're all heroes for coming through what Jess did.'

'We are,' Christine said. 'We kept together as a family. We faced it out.'

'Without Jess,' Jude said. 'After that Jess didn't count, did she? We cut her out.'

Christine wondered how much a sister might miss her twin. After everything Jess had done, maybe it hurt Jude in particular, to be separated. Could that be worse than it was for a mother?

She stroked her daughter's hair as they talked like this, on the train through the flat fields to Norwich. God knows how much the whole thing had hurt Jude.

Christine's remaining daughter had been the one who'd had to prove her own innocence. For a while, at the start, there'd been suspicions both twins had contributed to the death of the boy. For a while, Christine might have lost both of her girls. But Jess . . . Jess had asserted, finding her tongue at last, that Jude had stood by, frozen, terrified, as Jess did the deed.

'I'm glad I've still got you,' Christine said, brushing Jude's cheek with her knuckle. The train rattled on and she realised her daughter had dropped off to sleep. 'I'm glad Jess had the sense in the end. She never dragged you down with her.'

Because she might have. She could have said anything while she was on that stand. She could have made Christine lose two daughters. The thought was unbearable. At least I have one left. At least she's here with me.

And that's what I'll tell them on this show, she thought. That's what I'll tell Nancy. At least I have one daughter left. One who never did an evil thing in her life. And here she is pregnant herself, looking healthy and resplendant. Ready to find out what it's like to be a mother.

How hard it is. How you can't explain it.

She thought about the talk shows she had seen and the people she had laughed at and now she felt a new respect for them. At least they had been able to cram their lives into a couple of sentences and made you understand.

Jude came down in the lift and tottered across the sheer floor of the foyer. She was in a short patterned dress but she looked like she'd been sick.

'Do you not want to go on?' Christine asked hopefully as her daughter sagged into a chair.

'No, it's all right. Just nerves, I think.'

'You want some colour in your cheeks before you go on there. You look like a ghost. Do you think they'll do all our make-up for us?'

'I don't know.'

They had left Dan instructions to video their show. He'd already said he wouldn't watch them. The past should stay buried, he said. He couldn't see why they'd want to go on there at all. 'Jude needs lifting out of herself,' Christine told him.

So I'm doing it all for Jude's sake, am I? She knew that wasn't true.

She was looking for a way to make her own shame public. She could imagine Nancy, tenderly telling her, at the end of the show, that shame and rage and doing nothing were all the natural responses. Surely any mother would react like that.

'I can't see how you help Jude by telling strangers all your business,' Dan said.

'I want to get things out in the open,' Christine said.

But the thought of that had started to terrify her again.

Lily Woods hadn't been impressed, either. They met in the street and Christine couldn't avoid a conversation. She'd thought Lily would be pleased Christine was at last doing something. At least she was still thinking about Jess. Lily shook her head sadly. 'These shows trivialise people.'

'You go on the telly!' Christine had expected Lily to be more supportive.

'But I don't trivialise people, do I? I take them very seriously. To me, there's nothing more important than what passes between people. If I think I'm hearing something too personal, I don't broadcast it. Not in church, nor on the telly. I tell them we need to have a private sitting. I don't go airing people's secrets.'

Christine had tutted. 'Well. Me and Jude both want to go on. It's about time people heard our side of the story.'

'You should have gone to see her,' Lily said. 'Years ago. You should have visited her, Christine. You know what I think. But you made your choice. Now you're demeaning Jess, yourself, everyone, by doing this.' Lily started walking away. 'Oh, I'm just a silly old woman, I know. But I wouldn't do what you've done, Christine Fletcher.'

Lily was just sanctimonious enough as she said this for Christine to safely disregard everything else she'd said.

And it made her more determined to air her side of the tale.

*

There was a queue outside the studios and the woman who came out with a clipboard and mobile phone to meet their taxi said that was the audience. It seemed to be all older women, lining up in the afternoon sunshine with their shopping bags.

The girl, who said her name was Melissa and that she would be looking after them, explained that this was their special day. If they wanted anything particular they had to shout up. They needed looking after. Especially Jude, in her condition. They were the ones who made the show. Without them, Nancy! was nothing.

The building was cool inside and crammed with exotic plants in pots. A sign by the reception desk spelled out: 'Reception on Second Floor for Nancy Victims of Violent Crime.'

Jude and her mother felt like stars, getting led straight past the receptionist, who nodded like she knew them.

As they took the lift, Christine was saying, 'You should have gone into TV, Jude. It looks like a good job. Lovely surroundings.' She glanced at Melissa who, flustered, was scribbling something on her clipboard. 'What kind of qualifications do you need to work here?'

Melissa looked up, grinning. 'Oh, you just need to be absolutely mental!'

Christine glared at her and Melissa turned red.

She left them in a bare-looking room that had a table of green bottles of water set out. There was a bowl of fruit and a sign saying that they weren't allowed to smoke. Christine looked at a TV in the corner, and it was showing the lit up studio with its empty chairs, ready for them.

'How long before we go on?' Jude asked.

'Two hours and twenty minutes to studio!' Melissa smiled.

*

Researchers had been phoning them for a fortnight. They needed to prepare all aspects of the story for Nancy's cue cards and there was always something else they needed to know. In the days leading up to the show Christine had become quite used to these short, rather personal phone calls from well-spoken research assistants. The phone would go at different times of the day and she would be asked where the children had gone to school, the year in which her husband had died, their marital status at the time and what had become of her mother. Christine would have expected to resent such questions, but instead she found them reassuring. Someone out there was taking a proper interest in the past.

Once, Dan had picked up the phone and his face clouded over as the girl on the other end started to ask him about his accident and his subsequent coma. 'Oh, now that I've got a hold of you, Mr Fletcher, perhaps you could tell me a little about the impact of your mishap and your . . .' Dan had slammed down the phone and stormed through the house to shout at Christine.

Christine was oblivious to his anger. She knew she was doing the right thing. And, anyway, talk shows were ten a penny. They were important, but they burned through ten, twenty stories a week, didn't they? Hers would be absorbed into a much larger body of tribulations and she was obscurely glad.

As they sat in the guest room, opening more bottles of fizzy water, a thought struck her.

'What if it turned out to be one of those reunion shows?'

'What?'

'And suddenly they brought on your Nanna?'

'It's not This Is Your Life, mam.'

Christine rolled her eyes. 'This Is Your Life is really scraping the bottom of the barrel these days. I wouldn't be surprised if they did want to have me on it.'

'There aren't enough famous people left,' Jude said.

Christine couldn't agree. 'I think there's more famous people now. People are famous for more different things.'

Jude pulled a face. 'Maybe.' She was hoping the bubbly water wouldn't give her hiccups. She said, 'It would be worse if they brought our Jess on.'

Christine coloured and eyed her daughter. Neither of them had said Jess's name since they'd got here. It was a kind of agreement between them. Suddenly their reasons for being here seemed much more real.

She went back to watching the activity on the TV monitor. It felt like a dream, the idea that they'd soon be walking into that screen.

Christine could imagine Jess watching them on telly, wherever she was. That could be possible. And the family of the disabled boy she'd killed. They were still about, weren't they? They could be watching too. Christine could feel panic building up in her.

'Jess will be out soon,' Jude said.

Christine felt her heart thudding.

'How do you know that?'

'Stands to reason. She said there were only a couple of years left . . .' Jude took a deep breath and went on. 'You know, Nancy is bound to go into the whole thing. She'll ask you about disowning her. You do know she'll ask you about that . . .'

Jude was taunting her. That's what it felt like. Christine wanted to tell her to stop. Dad, Lily Woods, anyone else, she could understand them taunting her. But not Jude. Jude was the one she was proud of. It had all been for Jude's sake. Jude growing up safely. Jude having a normal life.

'Can you really talk about abandoning Jess?'

Christine swallowed hard. 'I'm ready to talk about that.'

'There'll be people there on that stage who haven't disowned their kids for what they did. Ones who stood by them. Who forgave them. You might get into a fight with them.'

'I'm prepared to fight.'

What was Jude doing? Why's she talking to me like this? Why start now?

'They might say it was wrong, whatever your kids do . . . to disown them . . .'

Christine shook her head. She wanted this to stop.

'Jude, you're just going on because of your hormones. You listen to me. If your kid does something unspeakable . . . Well, it's not that easy to just say, never mind, I'm still your mother and I forgive you. It was murder, Jude! It was cold-blooded, outright murder!'

Jude swigged the water. 'She was disturbed . . .'

'And that wasn't my fault, either. I know people try to pin it on me. But I brought you up the same, didn't I? The two of you had everything. I've tried to compensate. Now, why should you both turn out to be so different? You've not gone round killing people. That thing about, 'Oh, she was just disturbed' doesn't hold any water with me. Not any more.'

Christine fell silent. Jude had never heard her mother say so much about the business before. Her mother had two spots of pink high on her cheeks. She was powering herself up for the TV show.

You're really fucked up, Jude found herself thinking. Cognitive dissonance or something. You're determined to come out of this smelling of roses. You're after someone forgiving you, mother. That's not going to happen.

I wish we hadn't decided to come on now, Jude thought. What were we thinking of?

On the screen there was a man in a headset, clutching a bundle of papers. He was getting the audience, who were sitting ready in their seats, to heckle and whoop. They were practising what they were going to shout.

'Mam,' she said. 'When you're on there . . . Don't say so much about us being twins.'

'How do you mean?'

'I'm your daughter. I'm there to support you, as you tell the whole story and answer Nancy's questions. But I don't want dragging in all the time, in comparison. It does me no good to be compared all the time . . . with her.'

'But I'm proud of you, Jude! That's why I do it. You're the success story. You should be proud as well.'

'I just hate being dragged in with her all the time. With Jess.'

'She's still your sister. Whatever's gone on, you two will be linked until you both die.'

Jude sat up. 'That's a horrible thing to say!'

'It's true, love.'

'You're the one saying we should forget her . . . and disown her.'

Christine was confused. 'I don't know what I'm saying anymore.'

'Look, mam. Let's calm down. We can't go on there like this. We have to have our story straight.'

'Straight? You make it sound like we're lying.'

'I mean simple. You've seen these things. You have to be sure of what you feel. You can't go on all muddled. People won't understand. When a row blows up, you'll be lost . . .'

'Jude . . .'

'You can't afford to have mixed feelings, mam. You go on there, and you're on as the woman whose daughter killed a crippled kid. And you've disowned your daughter. End of story. And I'm just there for your moral support.'

Melissa returned, poking her head round the door and saying it would be time to go to make-up soon. They wouldn't want to go on looking washed out. When she vanished again, Christine fished out her compact and examined her face.

'It sounds to me like you're the one with mixed feelings, our Jude.'

'I'm bound to have, aren't I? I was the one there.'

Christine put her mirror away and zipped up her handbag. 'Yes.'

'Fuck it,' Jude said. 'I don't care what they say. I'm going to smoke.'

Christine watched her light up. 'What did you mean, about Jess getting out soon?'

'She will, won't she? She'll get, you know, put back in the community.'

'You said she'd said she only had a couple more years left.'

Jude took the cigarette out of her mouth. 'She did.'

'When, Jude?'

'I never told you at the time. You were ill. You were coming off the pills, the last time.'

They'll talk about that, too, Christine thought. How I was ill. How I wasn't there to see to them. I was a bad mother.

She couldn't believe what Jude was saying.

'You went to see her?'

'She came to see me.'

Jude told her mother the story of Jess's brief bid for freedom.

She told her how she'd got in touch with the authorities. How they'd never had a chance to talk. How Jess looked like someone completely different; not like anyone related to them at all. Her experience had made her into someone else entirely.

Her mother cried through the telling.

'You shopped her?'

'What was I supposed to do? What would you do?'

Christine stared.

'You could see she wasn't right, mam. She looked unhinged. She looked like a mad girl. With this loony friend of hers in tow . . .'

'You saw her more than two years ago and you never said! I can't believe that.'

'What, you think I'm making it up?'

'Did she say anything about me?'

'No.'

'She must have.'

'Why?'

'We're still her family.'

'I think she's disowned you like you disowned her. You never went to see her. Neither of us did. There was only Lily Woods.'

'I sent her parcels! A couple of times I . . . Lily Woods went to see her?'

'Apparently.'

*That was why. That was why Lily looked sanctimo-
nious. That's why she always had a go at Christine.*

'That bloody woman.'

'I thought she was your pal.'

'Give me a ciggy, Jude.' Christine lit up. 'When she gets
out, did she say if she'll come and see me? Does she want
to see me?'

'She never said.'

Christine's other daughter seemed much realer to her
now. She was out there, living her own life. She had talked
with Jude and with Lily. She wasn't dead to her, or dead to
the world, after all.

Maybe it would be all right. Maybe they could sort it
out.

Christine forced herself to think that maybe, just
maybe, making this show this afternoon could be a good
thing. It could only bring Jess closer. It could be all the
provocation Jess needed to come back to her. Maybe the
long gap between them could be sorted out. Jess would
come back into her life.

Christine didn't know whether to feel scared or not.

'I think . . .' said Jude, 'she just wants to make a new
life for herself. That was the impression I got. They'll give
her a new name. A new past. She'll start up again in a
different town. They'll keep checks on her to make sure
she stays in line. She'll probably be on medication.'

Like a criminal. Like no one who had anything to do
with her family.

'Yes,' said Christine. 'You're probably right.'

'If I was her,' Jude said, 'all I'd want right now would
be a quiet life.'

How could Jude be so sure?

Jess could cause them trouble. Christine saw it now.
Jess could stir up everything.

'What if it's not? What if she doesn't want a quiet life,
Jude?' Christine asked. 'That's all we want as well, isn't it?
Like anyone normal wants to live a quiet life. But what if
Jess decides that's not what she wants? What then, Jude?'

Jude didn't get a chance to reply. Melissa had returned to take them to make-up. There was just enough time left to fix them up and then the studio would be ready.

16
The Christmas Guest

By the time Jess found who she was looking for it was Christmas time. But Jess was diligent and dogged. She got on the bus and went straight to the town where the woman lived. Seven hours on the coach to a town she'd never been to before. She was frozen and the back of the bus smelled of sick. At the coach station she asked for directions. The place was easy to find.

The woman was living in a street of old houses. The further back from the main road they were, the older the houses got. And the posher they looked inside, when they were lit up. And the people there were so confident they left their curtains open so anyone walking by could see right in their windows.

They were the kind of people who painted their living rooms bright, striking colours and Jess would never dare. When she looked into the bay window of the one particular house, the front room there was scarlet.

The air outside was musty because of the hedgerows, which looked so green and clean but smelled musty. Jess remembered their house in Brunswick Avenue in spring, with the heavy pink and white clumps of magnolia.

Jess wondered how much that old house of theirs would be worth now. Was it like here? Had professional, clever people moved in to gentrify the old place? The kind of people with scarlet living rooms and big, funny paintings over their mantelpiece. All along Festive Row Jess had been looking in windows. Mystifying paintings of all colours on show. And books crammed on shelves around their living rooms. And their Christmas trees perched right out in their bay windows, lavish but tasteful, like sentries. All except this one; this particular house, where the woman Jess had come to see didn't have any

Christmas decorations up at all. Jess walked up and down a few times. The street took a good ten minutes to get up and down, walking slow like she did.

It was Christmas Eve and she thought maybe the woman inside might be traditional and start decking out the halls and stringing up the tinsel later on. Just at the right moment. She knew that the woman – Katherine – lived alone and maybe she didn't have the heart to go putting that lot out. Jess wouldn't, if it was just her.

She would lose track of months going by. Her timing was erratic. Her periods were all over the place and so she couldn't even tell by them.

Katherine, she supposed, would know all about the time of year by her work. She imagined that she would have to know exactly where she was in order to do a job like hers. No good being forgetful or vague. And didn't the way a university works follow the same way as a school? So they started in the autumn and finished in the summer? Wasn't that what they did? By Christmas then, Katherine would be halfway through her short year's work and Jess bet that tonight she would be indoors with her feet up, having a well-earned rest.

Katherine was a clever woman. Jess didn't suppose she was watching quiz shows and daft Christmas specials. She wouldn't be watching the big Christmas Eve movie. She'd be sitting with an old book. She'd have a radio station on, the kind with hardly any gaps between the pieces of music. It would be some big orchestra playing hymns for her tonight.

Did Katherine ever panic? Maybe sometimes she lost track of time. Did she sometimes find herself thinking just the wrong thing, standing in the wrong place? What did she do when it all went wrong?

Katherine. One of the clever, careful people. She could afford to do things and live quietly. Her whole house, though bright, was quiet tonight. All Jess could hear – not very Christmassy – was Nina Simone coming softly out of one of the houses at her back.

She had heard somewhere that Nina Simone was six feet tall and strapping. Jess was almost six feet tall.

*

Now she could see Katherine in the flesh. Jess was passing by again and the door came open with a clatter and when Katherine shut it she was leaving all the lights on in her house. Burning up money. Jess knew there was no one else in there to get the benefit. Maybe Katherine could afford it. Maybe she left her house lit to fool burglars, to bamboozle the Christmas thief. And maybe she wasn't going far. She wasn't wearing a coat.

Whenever Jess's family had gone out anywhere mam would make the twins go right round the house and check that everything was switched off. All the lights, the plugs on the telly, the cooker, the kettle. She couldn't bear the thought of things left switched on. In Fine Fare, pushing the trolley down the aisle, she'd get a sudden panic and clutch Jess or Jude. She'd say she was convinced the grill was still on, burning bright orange. And eventually the kitchen would take light. They would go home to see their house burning down. Or already it would be a black hole in the ground. And they would burn down all the houses in the Avenue and it would be their fault. Every time mam took a panic they would have to go straight back home to check.

Katherine didn't seem to check anything. One of her upstairs windows was even open, letting her heat stream into the sky. It was amazing.

When she moved away from her door and came down the short garden path Jess could see her by the street light. Of course she looked a little older than the picture on the back of her book. If you have your picture in books, Jess thought, you're going to choose the best ones and keep yourself looking younger. In the picture she had seen, Katherine had a perm and her hair was brown and she was smiling in an intelligent way. Not a gawky, snapshot smiling, but a smile like, I know something really important. Here's your chance to share it.

Tonight her hair was grey and straight. She had it in a neat bob and that only made her look more clever. As she came down her path and onto Festive Row it swayed. Her mouth was set in a small, worried line. No smiles tonight, not even for Christmas Eve. Was it just another night to her because she lived alone? It wasn't just another night to Jess.

Katherine was in a long, dark skirt, hard shoes and a blouse of richest blue silk. Jess couldn't see her hands properly enough to tell what rings she wore. She was clutching a handbag.

She must be popping down the shops on the main road. Last-minute things she needed for Christmas Day. So late in the day, Katherine. And everyone else planning their holiday so far in advance. Even Jess had planned her holiday. And here was Katherine popping out for bread and milk. Sometimes, it seemed to Jess, clever people didn't live in the same world as everyone else. They were looking at other things. But they still had to come down to Earth at times, otherwise they would starve.

Katherine needed milk and sugar in her tea. She needed bread in the morning. She still had to eat. Jess stopped herself laughing. She still needed toilet paper to wipe her bum. She was in the world with everyone else after all. And it was when those people came back down to be ordinary that ordinary people like Jess could talk to them.

Yes. She was heading towards the parade of shops.

*

It was a bakery of sorts. There was a little queue and Katherine took her place oh-so patiently. The smells were fabulous. Jess could smell cheeses and fresh bread and cooked meats and herby smells. The man at the glass counter was noisy and polite. He talked like he ought to be on the telly. He had a Billy Goat Gruff beard and was asking a woman, a smart-looking woman, what kind of cake her young son might want. Her son, like her, was blonde and he was shy, looking at the glass case of cakes. It looked to Jess like the cakes there cost two pounds a piece. It was a shop, obviously, for a certain sort of person.

The blonde mother was talking as loud as the baker. Like she was competing with him. She had very bright lipstick on and she was excitable. In every sentence she called her son 'darling'. You could see how embarrassed he was. 'But do they have nuts in?' she asked the baker. 'Charlie can't have nuts, can you, darling?'

'How about a vanilla slice, then?' said the baker, rattling the silver trayful of squashy oblongs. 'Now, they are really delicious. Full of the best best fresh cream.'

'Darling?' the mother asked Charlie.

Surly Charlie shook his head quickly, still not looking at her. Charlie wants a fat lip, Jess thought.

Now she was right behind Katherine in the queue. She could see their reflections in the mirrors behind the baker. Look at my familiar pudding face behind Katherine's famous one, she thought; Katherine's face from a thousand shiny hardbacks. There's our faces together amongst the loaves of knobbly bread. How we will laugh, Katherine, when we know each other so much better, to think that we stood side by side in this mirror, framed in purple tinsel. And at that time you never realised I was there, and you didn't even know of my existence.

Katherine was impatient now. Jess could hear her tapping her heavy shoe. She could even feel the vibrations on the lino. Did she think, like Jess did, that darling Charlie needed a clip around the ear?

'Have a vanilla slice,' urged the baker.

'You will love it, darling.'

'Tell you what. It's Christmas almost – have two of my perfect, sticky slices. Two, mind you, for the price of one.' The baker beamed and spread his hands.

'See, darling! You can't miss this chance!'

And so Charlie got his cakes and the baker got paid and the two adults chimed in with their Merry Merry Christmases. Then it was Katherine's turn to be served.

'I wasn't sure,' she said. She began in such a hesitant way. The baker leaned in to catch hold of her dry voice. 'I wasn't sure if your café was still open tonight. What with the holiday and all.'

She nodded towards the back of the shop, where empty tables sat ready with bowls of brown sugar and green folded napkins.

The baker shook his head briskly. 'Of course, of course. It is always open till midnight. We are serving coffee every night, no matter what. Sit yourself down! Go!'

She relaxed into a smile. 'I just had to come out. Have some coffee out. I was thinking, I'm going to be stuck indoors all through Christmas, and . . .'

He stopped her with a wave of his hand. 'I know, I know. Stay and enjoy our hospitality here.'

'I'd like a cafetière of Mocha Java, then, please.'

'It's done. Go and sit where you are happiest.'

Jess watched her turn and blink and really consider where she was going to sit.

Jess was the last in the queue. The baker looked at her expectantly. She stared at the flour powdered on his green pinny. He was wearing a wonderful thick cotton shirt, all faded and blue. The sleeves were rolled right up to his brown biceps. 'Can I help?'

For that moment she was stuck. 'Can I have what she's having?' She nodded towards Katherine. It felt like she was taking her name in vain. But everyone was a little less polite these days. No one bats an eye.

'Of course,' said the baker and turned to get on with it. He didn't put on much charm for me, Jess thought. It must be this shabby old anorak. But it's warm.

How close can I sit next to you, Katherine?

It was such a small café. Just a few tables wedged in. One of those gas heaters on wheels keeping the place stuffy. To Jess it seemed they gave off fumes that smelled like salt and vinegar crisps. If you sat by them too long you could get drowsy. She got tunnel vision when she got hot. So she tried not to sit too close to the gas and its purple, orange, blue grille of heat. She sat herself at the table next to Katherine's. She sat herself across from her. They were both waiting for their Mocha Java. It sounded nice.

*

The baker man brought their cups and coffee pots on a single tray and he said, 'Enjoy, ladies!'

As if they were sitting together and knew each other.

Katherine gave him a smile and then, for a second, to Jess. Then she looked down, paying attention to taking her cup and saucer off his tray. By the time Jess had hers Katherine was already back inside her book, a slim red paperback with no picture on the cover. The baker ambled off to his counter.

Jess looked at the pictures on the wall behind Katherine's head and, when she was sure she couldn't tell, she watched her read. It was marvellous how fast her eyes flicked backwards and forwards across the page. But she didn't turn the pages very often. It was as if she was reading the same sentences again and again. Was she just pretending to read? Maybe she knew Jess was watching and she was waiting for an opportunity to look up and catch her.

Jess could bide her time. She dropped rough cubes of brown sugar into her empty cup. Four of them, she thought, and I'll watch them melt when I pour in the hot coffee. But I have to let the coffee brew and I don't know how long. She supposed then she had to push that plunger thing down. Typical her, she'd probably plunge it too hard, or not hard enough, and spray the whole room with scalding hot coffee.

The pictures behind Katherine's head were real pictures too. Not copies but things that someone had really painted and touched with their own hands. One was of a garden. Splashy red flowers in stone urns. It was hard to tell what kind of flowers they were. Maybe it wasn't a very good painting, but the price ticket in the corner of the frame said three hundred and seventy-five pounds. The other picture behind Katherine, to the left of her fine grey bob, was of a woman reading, curled up on a yellow sofa. Unlike Katherine, she wasn't caught up in the story. She was thinking about something else. Her picture cost four hundred and twenty-five pounds. Fancy buying a picture of a stranger. This strange woman with a sidelong glance on your wall. And how odd for that woman it must be, thinking of herself being sold like that. It wasn't as if she was that attractive, either, going by this picture.

That was when Katherine put down her book. She had reached the end of her page and decided that her Mocha Java had stood long enough. Then she put one palm on top of the plunger and the other palm down on her hand and she braced herself. She pushed and the wheel thing inside squashed a small way down. Thick coffee gushed up inside and Jess watched the gritty clouds swilling about underneath. Katherine looked at Jess.

'I hate doing this. It's very strong, this one.'

Those were the first words she said to Jess. Jess coughed and smiled.

'I've never done it before.'

Katherine nodded and pushed some more, suddenly the expert. Then her coffee was ready, looking clear and brown and hot. A little trickle of steam curled from the spout.

'What you said you were having sounded so nice, I thought I would try it too.'

Katherine smiled again, but it was the sort of smile when you don't want to talk anymore. She poured her coffee and Jess had a go at hers, putting her palms on the knob of the plunger just like Katherine had. Katherine watched her do all of this and nodded encouragingly when she poured her cup. It steamed and it was frothy.

Katherine told her, 'I've got one of these and coffee in the house. But you can stay in by yourself too much, I think. I'm paying double here, what it would cost me to drink at home.'

'Like pubs,' Jess said. 'But that doesn't stop people going to them.'

Katherine took the daintiest sip of coffee.

'People like the company of pubs and cafés and things,' Jess said. 'It's important. Otherwise we'd all be sitting indoors by ourselves.' She tried out her own coffee. Not as hot as she'd expected. It was very bitter. 'Especially this time of year.'

She wished she hadn't said that. That was the kind of thing just anyone said. People in shops, at bus stops. Things were better or worse than they usually were, all because it was 'this time of year'. It was a boring thing to say. Everyone knew it was Christmas. And she wanted to be extraordinary for Katherine. She wanted to say good things to her.

'Is that a good book?'

Katherine closed it again and moved it from hand to hand, as if weighing it up. 'Oh, this? I'm rather embarrassed being found reading this.'

'What is it?'

She showed Jess the pictureless red cover. Gold letters said: 'Pieces of Belinda. By Timon.'

'I haven't heard of it.'

Katherine looked surprised. 'I thought everyone was reading this. Isn't it meant to be a bit of a scandal? That's why I'm abashed to be found with it.'

'What's it about?'

Was that just a hint of a look about Katherine that said she wished she hadn't started this? But she explained, 'It's meant to be a true story. The author is a young black man who had an affair with a much older woman from Edinburgh. It's a kind of love story and some of the writing is a little bit . . . ripe.'

'It's a dirty book?' Jess gave a little laugh, which came out gruff.

'Each chapter is named after a different part of Belinda's body. And then he tells you all about it.'

'The poor woman,' Jess said. 'I bet she's ashamed.'

'She's meant to have vanished in real life. Or, from real life, as it were. She was a UFO enthusiast and they said in the news that she was abducted from Concorde in mid-air and that was why this Timon character wrote the book about her.'

'I don't think much of aliens.'

'Me neither,' Katherine said. 'We have enough problems down here on Earth, without looking further afield.'

They paused then and it looked as if Katherine wanted to get back into her book.

'I might read it,' Jess said. 'Where did you get it?'

'Oh, you can get this in all the shops. It's quite vulgar and you can buy it anywhere.'

'I suppose you read a lot of books.'

That was chancing it, she realised. And Katherine's expression was asking her: What do you know about me?

'You seem like a clever type of woman. Always reading.' Jess nodded at the picture to Katherine's left, of the woman with her book. 'Her type.'

Katherine looked at it and came out with a small, forced laugh. 'I don't know about clever. But yes, I am stuck into books most of the time.'

'I thought. You make it look like a natural thing to do. You brought a book with you, just popping out for a cup of coffee.'

'I suppose,' she said, and stopped. She found her page and opened the book wide, making sure that she cracked its paper spine. She didn't seem to look after her books very well.

'Are you a teacher, then?' Jess asked.

'A lecturer. At the university.'

'Lovely.' Jess shook her head. 'So you spend all your time with books.'

'Except sometimes,' Katherine said, 'I have to see horrible students, too.'

They both laughed.

'And will you be teaching them to read that mucky book?'

'This?' she frowned. 'Perhaps. I like to keep up with what's going on. It's all muck and filth these days, isn't it?'

'Isn't it just?'

Another pause and Katherine said, 'I'll get back into it, anyway.'

Jess shrugged and smiled and sipped her cooling coffee, looking at the pictures behind Katherine.

As the minutes passed she was getting almost drowsy with the gas heater.

She even had those flashes of dreams she sometimes got before falling asleep. But she wasn't going to sleep yet, and the dreams were still there, unspooling all the time. It made her think her dreams went on regardless, even when she wasn't asleep to see them.

She got a picture of Grandad Fletcher. Best Grandad in the world. On Christmas Day, pulling a purple cracker with Judith. A party hat crumpled in his frizzy white hair. She didn't even know if he was still alive. Hullo again, Grandad, love.

She shook herself clear again. Her head was like a snowstorm paperweight.

Katherine noted her sudden movement as she was finishing the dregs of her coffee. The chewy grit in the bottom of her cup. That was the best bit.

Katherine picked up her bag and her scandalous red paperback and then, suddenly, she was leaving.

'I'll be saying Merry Christmas, then,' she told Jess.

*

And now the problem, Katherine.

What to do?

Don't fret, Katherine. I'll figure something out.

Not that it was Katherine's problem. She was indoors now and back home for Christmas. She needn't come out

271

until the Festive Season was all over and done with. She had met Jess now and Jess was just the big woman in the shabby tatty anorak she had talked to in the café. It was only a few minutes' chat, about nothing in particular. Maybe Katherine had forgotten about Jess already, as she shut her door behind her and went off down her bright hallway and paused in the doorways, careful, checking that she was still alone in her house. Or maybe she was still thinking about Jess, thinking she sounded like a simple woman with all her questions. Jess was asking her naive questions and showing her ignorance and now Katherine felt sorry for her. Or scornful. She was having a little chuckle at Jess's expense – Who was that batty, scruffy woman? – as Katherine started to pour herself a small, seasonal dry sherry. At any rate, it isn't Katherine's problem.

It was Jess's problem. And now she had to think of something.

She had let her go.

Up Festive Row again. Jess was coming up Katherine's dowdy leafy avenue one more time. Stiller and quieter on the Christmas street again.

She came level with Katherine's house, number thirty-six and – Joy! Bliss! What fantastic luck!

From the lock of the shut door hung Katherine's jangle of keys. They sparkled miraculously in the street's sodium light. You silly, silly cow, Katherine. A dizzy cow, in a world of her own and there was Jess, thinking she was careful with all her cleverness. She really hadn't a clue.

So now Katherine would just have to be told. Someone would have to do the good deed and trog up the garden path and ring Katherine's bell and clatter her letter box and let her know just what a dozy twat she'd gone and been.

So Jess thanked her lucky stars and Katherine should have thanked hers, too. Jess, because she had an excuse now and Katherine, because Jess was saving her bacon. Imagine who, if not for Jess, could have been in possession of all Katherine's keys.

Jess was up the path in a flash.

She was reaching up and clutching the jangle of keys.

She was drawing them out and holding her breath, listening to the rasp of the tiny teeth as the Yale came free.

And boldly she gave the bell an unashamed dring.

She could see her now: sherry glass up to her mouth. Waiting for the tang of her favourite tipple. And then the doorbell goes and gets her right in the spine. She would jolt and, perhaps – did Jess hear right? – Katherine curses.

Here comes Katherine's silhouette, pebbled in the glass of the door.

The door creeps open. She's not so cautious that she has a pensioner chain to keep the door only a fraction open. The door comes wide open and Katherine looks at Jess in surprise. And Jess is pleased Katherine knows her immediately. Jess grinned.

Katherine looked startled, having Pudding-face grin at her. Jess held out the bundle of keys.

Katherine reached for them, frowning heavily. 'How did..?'

'Well, I was passing by. I saw someone had left these precious things stuck in their lock. Silly thing to do.'

Katherine clutched them to herself. She didn't quite snatch them off Jess, but she almost did. 'Jesus. Thank you. Thank you very much. I'm so stupid.'

Jess shrugged. 'It's a coincidence, isn't it? That it was your house. Lucky I was coming by. Lucky I took the trouble.'

'I'm very grateful,' Katherine said. 'Someone could have just taken these, and then I'd be stuck.'

'You'd be buggered.'

'Indeed.'

'Lucky you've got good neighbours.'

Katherine gave herself away a bit there. She couldn't keep the surprise out of her voice as she asked Jess, 'You live around here?'

'Not really. I live across town.'

'Oh.'

'I don't know what I'm doing this far out tonight. He's chucked me out. Well, I walked out. I'll let him stew. It's always the same when he lashes out like that.'

'What?' Katherine looked confused. She wasn't expecting Jess to babble at her like that, all of a sudden.

And then the master stroke. The tears that had been busy balancing on those deep-set, unreadable eyes started to creep and glimmer on Jess's pudding cheeks.

'Look,' Katherine said. 'It's freezing. Come in. Have a drink. It's the least I can do after . . .'

Jess smiled sadly. 'After I saved your bacon.'

'Exactly. Come in . . .'

'Sheila. I'm She.'

Jess was stepping inside now.

'You're who?'

'People call me She.'

Katherine closed the door behind Jess, and, under the pretence of taking a deep, shuddering breath, Jess inhaled the smokey, musty, flowery scent of the hallway.

'My name is Katherine. Come through to the kitchen, She.'

*

They passed through two, three different coloured rooms before they came to the kitchen. Katherine moved so quickly and surely through her own house and Jess wanted to keep up, so she didn't have time to inspect each of these rooms as she would have liked to. The first place she really saw was the kitchen. And it seemed to be the heart of the house. Funny. Whenever Jess invented a house for herself, the room she spent the most time on was always the kitchen. It was where all of life would go on. It was where her transistor radio would play twenty-four hours a day and the washing machine would never stop its busy sloshing. Everyone who would go through the house would do it via Jess's kitchen. Mind, it wouldn't be as lah-de-dah as Katherine's. Katherine had every-thing.

Katherine was all flushed and busy now. Was Jess mistaken, or was that a giddy, excitable look about her? She was opening kitchen cupboards (bright blue!) and pulling out tall glass tumblers. She was yanking a bottle of wine off a full rack. Red wine in a green bottle, Jess thought, looks purple and black inside. 'Let's have a drink to celebrate.'

'Celebrate?'

Katherine waggled the keys at Jess and tossed them on the bench. 'Good neighbours.'

Katherine was much more contented in her kitchen. Jess could see how confident she really was.

It was all mod cons. Jess didn't know what half the things were. There was a smell not unlike that in the bakers.

The pine kitchen table looked like an old butcher's block, scarred and none too clean. Heaps of books, old and new, weighed down handwritten and typed-up pages and reams of recent newspapers. There were pens and used ashtrays and those funny yellow notes everywhere. Those stick-it notes people remind themselves with.

'You were working,' Jess said.

Katherine shrugged. 'A little bit. Do you mind wine in a tumbler? Saves time, I always think.' Jess watched the wine sluice and gush into the glass. The noise of it made her bladder twinge. Katherine said, 'I like to write a little every day. I have to keep my practice going. It's like piano practice, or swimming. You have to keep limber.'

Jess took her glass and held it up to the soft shaded light. 'You're quite gabby, really. Like me.'

'Maybe I've decided you're an all right person,' Katherine said. 'Saving my bacon.'

Jess wondered if Katherine was already drunk.

'A toast.'

'What to?' Jess asked, staring past Katherine, amazed that she didn't have curtains or blinds on her kitchen windows. Just these stark black squares staring in.

'To the baby Jesus,' Katherine chuckled and knocked the wine back. Jess followed. 'She, did you say?'

'Mm?' Now Jess was looking at wicker baskets hanging by the back door. They were full of pinkish-coloured pot-pourri. It didn't smell very strong to her.

'You said I have to call you She.'

'Yeah.' Jess poked about in the pot-pourri because she thought she saw something in there. Small and green and yellow. Tiny, with sharp bits.

Katherine gave that laugh of hers. '"She Who Must Be Obeyed".'

Jess pulled out the strange object. It was like something out of a cracker.

'That's out of a novel by Rider Haggard. I'm not trying to be funny.'

'What's this?' Jess was holding the thing in her palm and, as she asked, she already knew what it was.

'A humming bird,' Katherine told her.

'Real?'

'Dried out. Beautiful, isn't it?'

Jess couldn't believe she was touching the thing. 'No.' She dropped it back.

Now Katherine was pulling out stools for them, either side of the wide and messy table. She cleared a space. Jess liked the way the ceiling light cast a particular, gentle circle of yellow onto the middle. So she sat down with Katherine.

'Tell me about where you live,' Katherine said. 'When you were out there, you didn't sound too happy. Has something happened?'

'I was babbling and gabbling . . .'

'No, you definitely said that there was trouble at home. Have you got kids there?'

'Not any more.'

'A husband?'

'Of course.'

'And it's your husband who lashes out?'

'I never said he lashes out.'

'Yes, you did, She.'

Jess looked at the pin board to one side. Lots of postcards, stuck up higgledy-piggledy. There weren't any photos. 'He's having one of his funny do's tonight.' Jess drank then, suddenly draining her tumbler like she was thirsty. Katherine's was empty too, and she did the honours.

'We can talk about it, if you want.'

Soon it would be time to open another bottle.

Katherine was being – Jess had to admit – everything she thought she would be.

She was understanding.

*

Jess woke in the dark and her heart was beating loud and fast because it was so dark and she didn't know where she was. She thought it might be beating fast, also, because it was Christmas Day and she had always loved waking up on Christmas Day. Then she realised it was beating fast because of all they had drunk last night. She still felt drunk.

She was on the settee, her knees bent up and her feet wedged up to the arm rest. Katherine had been kind enough to pull a duvet over her. It was sweltering hot. Jess was still in all her clothes. Katherine hadn't thought to undress her.

She could see a digital clock blinking and it was six twenty-seven.

When she stood up and shrugged off the duvet she found that she was even drunker than she'd thought. Her feet were heavy on the hollow, bare wooden floor. I'm such a lummox, she thought. That's what the PE teachers used to call her, at school and in the Home.

Mustn't wake Katherine, upstairs in her boudoir. Mustn't wake Katherine with all this stumbling about. But Jess wanted to look out of the front window. She prised apart the velvet curtains. Couldn't even see what colour they were. And it was still lights out on Festive Row. Pitch dark with the yellow street lights glaring. The street lights were the same colour, no matter what night it was. She liked it when she would first notice them coming on and they were powering up and their colour was pinkish orange, before they turned bright.

When she craned a little she could see lights in bay windows a few doors down. They must have kiddies; they must all be up especially early and the front room must be filled with the noises of ripping and shredding of gift wrap.

She went back to the settee and decided to sleep off the drink for half an hour or so.

*

Funny thing, drink. And funnier still that it never had the effect on Jess like it was supposed to.

Oh, she had watched the talk shows, the chat shows, the cough-up-your-whole-life and tell-all shows. She had seen them on daytime TV. The message of those shows was basic and easy to get and the message was that whatever comes round comes back around. That's to say, whatever happened to your parents was sooner or later going to happen to you.

One still afternoon in the Home Jess learned a lovely new word. She learned a lovely new word one afternoon when she couldn't be arsed to move off the settee in the television room and kept on watching talk shows. She learned the word 'predisposition'.

It explained everything about life. If you were like this, and you had this thing wrong with you, well, it was because this other thing happened to you when you were little. Or it happened to your mother or your father. Or you had a need somewhere deep inside yourself and the things inside that made you. All in all, this word 'predisposition' meant that you weren't guilty.

So ease up, lighten up and never mind.

Whatever you get up to, you'll be able to make it okay. It isn't none of it really your fault.

Watching the telly that afternoon she was cheered. Blinds pulled against the sun, sitting in her own blue swirls of smoke. She was cheered up.

But she should have been an alkie. Booze never worked on her like it worked on mam or Grandad. She liked a drink and everything. It was different for them. Growing up she knew of booze and pills as the things that could make you over into a different way of being you. Either bigger or smaller it made you and you didn't have to be the same. It never worked on Jess like that.

It made her throat swell up like a bullfrog. Like when they do mating calls and puff themselves up. It pushed her heart up into her throat and she could feel the beating all along the inside bones of her head. Sooner or later, enough booze, and it made her feel like her head would explode. Maybe it poisoned her. She could feel it in every vein. She could never ride with it. She could never let herself get swept away.

Did she always want to be in control?

She never thought that was the way she was.

A lummox. Maybe.

Why did people go on talk shows anyway? If that was giving up control and going with the flow and letting go, then you could forget it. Why would you want to tell all to millions? No. Jess liked having her secrets.

Find one person who you can make want to listen. Then you can start to tell things. That's what she thought.

*

Your face is looking right into mine.

Look at you, first thing in the morning and already you have combed your hair. It sheens.

You are in a white kind of satiny dressing gown. Your arms are folded under your breasts. Your breasts are bigger than I thought. A nice shape. You're a handsome woman, Katherine.

I would say that you are in your prime.

As Jess looked up and woke up properly she saw that Katherine had put some lamps on and they were soft. An apricot glow. Artistic lighting in the sitting room, of course. Lighting meant to be gentle, but that morning it felt harsh on Jess. Her chin was cool under Katherine's breath and she realised she must have drooled and slobbered during her lie in.

'Good morning,' Katherine said, smiling oddly. 'Good Christmas Morning.' And Jess gave her chin a sly wipe on Katherine's spare duvet.

'I'm sorry,' Jess said. 'I didn't mean to pass out on you.'

'No one ever means to pass out.' Now Katherine was stepping away. 'We put away a lot of wine.'

'But I'm still here on Christmas morning.' Jess struggled to get up, sounding miserable. 'I shouldn't be here. Spoiling your Christmas.'

'Oh, hush.' Katherine seemed almost cross. 'You're my guest, we decided. If you can remember. And besides, it didn't sound as if you could go home last night.'

'Didn't it? What did I say?'

Jess had to follow Katherine through to the kitchen to keep this conversation going. She was almost pleased to see that Katherine's slippers were quite old and shabby. Otherwise she was just too perfect. From seeing the worn holes in those slippers Jess got the same pleasure she would if she saw dirt in the corners of Katherine's cupboards or eggs left to rot in her fridge.

By daylight the kitchen looked different. Jess could see the garden, the grass all silver with morning frost. There was a statue in the middle, a woman in no clothes. She's got chunky hips, Jess thought. An old-fashioned type of woman.

Katherine was putting the coffee on. The coffee pot was exactly the same as the ones they had in the café.

'What was I telling you last night?' Jess asked, sitting down heavily at the table. God, she felt grimy and crumpled. When Katherine sat down opposite she looked pristine. No make-up on, pale skin gleaming with health and expensive moisturiser.

'Wait,' she said, winking as she pushed that coffee plunger down with both palms. An expert. 'You mean you don't remember how we talked last night?'

Jess shook her head. 'Hardly anything. Wine always has that effect on me. Was I gabbing away about my silly problems?'

'They don't sound silly to me.'

Katherine told her off as the room filled up with the flat, bitter, smokey smell of the coffee. And Jess had her hooked now.

'You and your husband have got some problems. That was the gist of it. And you couldn't go back last night.'

'I don't reckon I could,' she shrugged. Katherine had beautiful white china coffee cups. In them the coffee looked black. 'He's not usually violent. He's not like Tony used to be.'

'Tony was your first husband.'

'Did I tell you about him as well?'

'A little.'

'Well, Barry isn't like what Tony used to be. But to him it's like he lives in Tony's shadow. He never even met the bloke, but it's like he has to prove that he's as much of a man to me as Tony was.'

'And where's Tony now?'

'He's dead.'

'Oh. You never told me that last night.'

'It's not a nice story. He hung himself.'

Katherine's face creased. She was really listening. 'You never found him, did you?'

'Oh, no. Thank God. He didn't do it at home. No way he would have done it at home. Not where I or one of the kids would have found him. He protected us. That's what people never understood. He did it that way to protect us. Above all, Tony was a family man. No. He hung himself in prison.'

'You never talked about him much last night. It was mostly about Barry.'

'God, Katherine. Honestly, it's like you had me hypnotised or something. I don't remember anything.'

'You obviously needed to talk it all out. And have a good cry. Will you go back to Barry today?'

'He's a good bloke. He doesn't stay mad for long. But I reckon he'll have done what he said he was going to. Piss off back to Scotland for Christmas. Come back after their precious bloody Hogmanay. That's Barry.'

Jess was stirring her coffee round and round. She hadn't told her hand to stop yet.

I'm telling her lie upon lie, she thought. I've made up a whole life for myself. Wonderful.

'It's my own fault, Katherine. I'm sorry about swearing.'

Katherine had reached a decision. The way she set her cup down, with a resounding click, meant that she had decided to take Jess in hand. 'I'm going to do my Good Samaritan bit. You're staying with me for the day. I'm cooking Christmas lunch and you're having it here with me.'

Jess looked at her steadily. 'I don't need your charity.'

A yelp of laughter. 'Charity? She . . . if anything, it's your charity to me. If you stay here today, you'll be saving me from myself. I would only sit and get maudlin and drink too much alone and that would be my Christmas.'

'If you're sure.'

'I am.'

'I feel such a scrounger.'

'Rubbish. Now, go up and use the bathroom. Make yourself at home. Can we agree that you're my guest and no more qualms?'

'All right.'

'Good girl. I'll start peeling carrots and potatoes and things. And I'll break open a bottle of wine, ready for you to come down. Hair of the Christmas dog. What the hell. We can afford to be decadent today.'

And Katherine sent Jess upstairs.

*

Upstairs there were more rooms than Katherine would ever need. Jess thought she should have some people staying round there and she could make them pay. She could be quids in. Those students she taught; they could be staying in these rooms with the untouched perfect beds. The bedside lamps couldn't have been used in ages. It was a far better place than where Jude had lived as a student. Jess couldn't believe Katherine lived in such abundance.

She found her study. So many books. Everything shoved in, just so. Dizzying to think that Katherine had all of this inside her head and yet she still had the time to talk to Jess about her life. That made Jess feel already famous, in a way.

At last, the bathroom. The shower was encased in a square of glass that looked like crystal. The carpet was fluffy. It was a film star bathroom with row upon row of bottles and jars. All kinds of ointments. All of the things that went into making Katherine what she was. This room saw Katherine naked every day. These were the things Jess was thinking as she locked the door, picked a towel off a whole fluffy heap of folded cream towels and pushed her aching face into the fabric.

When she started to take all her clothes off she felt that she was truly a guest. It was when you felt safe to take off every stitch that you became a proper guest.

*

She was wearing a dressing gown that belonged to Katherine. So rich and thick and woolly. If she had known this was going to work, she'd have brought a change of clothes. Still, here she was on Christmas Day, all clean as a new pin, wearing a scarlet dressing gown. The arms were a bit short for her. She even felt a bit too warm with all this central heating on. It wasn't what she was used to.

'I love your study. I always wanted a room like that. It's just what I thought a person like you would have.'

Katherine had her head in the oven as Jess came into the room. Already Jess could hear the hissing and spitting of oil in the roasting pan. Katherine had a bottle of oil of the deepest green. There was what looked like a little tree inside, with berries still on. Was it special oil for Christmas turkeys? Katherine banged the oven door closed and brushed off her hands as she stood. Pans were bubbling on top of the immaculate hob.

'It's a state up there at the moment,' she said. 'I haven't had a proper tidy up since the start of the semester.'

'What's a semester?'

'Oh, that. It's just what we call a term. Like in school. I mean since September. It's chaos in there. Papers, books, all my notes. I can't find a thing.'

'You should get someone in to organise you.'

'I couldn't let anyone else touch my papers. I'm superstitious. Let me pour this wine. It's just Chardonnay from Waitrose.'

The wine looked green, too. Pale green. 'I didn't think you'd be superstitious. I only thought stupid people were like that. People like me.'

'I'm very superstitious. When I sit down to write, everything has to be laid out just so. Before I can set down a single word, I have to be sitting the right way, with the correct pen and all my pencils set out. It's a bit like being crazy.'

'No, it's not.'

'If I'm on the computer, it's worse, because I'm always terrified I shall do something wrong. I go through all the rigmarole, you know . . . finding the right disk, waiting for everything to load in, clicking on the relevant files with the mouse. Hoping fervently that everything is saved where I left it.'

Jess nodded. 'Everything is saved where you left it.'

'Honestly, it's like praying to some pagan god before you can approach and make your tribute.' Katherine chuckled, pleased with this comparison. 'Do you use a computer?'

'Me?' Jess asked. 'What would I use a computer for?'

'Very wise,' Katherine said hurriedly. 'If it wasn't for work, I wouldn't touch one at all. I'd write everything in pen and ink.'

'But the books you write aren't, like, made up ones, are they?'

'Mm?'

'I mean, they aren't fiction . . . books. They aren't novels like writers . . . write.'

'Oh, no. My books are dry as dust. Dusty boring stodgy academic old things. Usually about horrible head-cases with dreadful lives. No one reads them.' Katherine shrugged and gave that careless laugh again.

'I didn't mean to be rude,' Jess said.

'I know. I'm too touchy. You see, what I write is just meant for other experts in my own field. It's a very narrow field, when you look at it. Tiny. Full of other people who are terribly interested in horrible head-cases.'

Jess said, 'I think you're quite famous.'

'Do you?'

Jess took a breath. She decided to say it. 'I've seen your book.'

'You have?' Katherine's eyes opened wide. 'Sorry, I really didn't mean that to sound patronising. But where have you seen my books?'

Jess took the pale green bottle and she refilled their glasses. She watched the wine wash up the sides. 'I saw that book in a library. That book about the children murdering other children.'

'The Child Killers? You read that?'

'A little bit. It was quite hard going. I think I was getting the gist.'

Jess thought Katherine looked impressed. And just a bit pleased with herself.

'Well. The message is getting out there.'

'Out there?'

'I mean, into the real world.'

'And is that where I live, Katherine?'

'Definitely, She.'

'Or did you just mean that your word was getting out among stupid people?'

A frown! Jess thought. Oh, a frown!

'No, that isn't what I meant.'

'Ordinary people.'

'I hate that word 'ordinary',' Katherine said.

'I find it comforting, sometimes.' Jess drained her glass again. 'Anyhow, I recognised you suddenly last night, when we were talking. I thought I knew you. Then, upstairs, when I saw all your books and papers, it clicked. I knew who you were. The Child Killers woman.'

Katherine smiled a hard, bright smile. 'I'm so pleased. I'll get back on with dinner.'

*

Christmas Dinner was a bit of a failure. Jess watched as Katherine got cross and ashamed of herself when she made a hash of the gravy; pouring hot water into the roasting pan, stirring in flour and all she got was a greasy, colourless mess of liquids. Jess smiled to herself because Katherine threw an impatient strop and clattered down her stirring spoon.

Jess breathed in the fumes of the turkey, which Katherine set before her, expertly trussed and showing its thighs and its stuffing-clogged hole to the ceiling. Jess carved. She took command. She told Katherine to leave the gravy and fetch her glass and come and sit down as she sawed through the delicate sinews and she told Katherine that the turkey was so well cooked it was still moist enough to eat without gravy. When Katherine brought the parsnips and potatoes they were too well done. The parsnips were tipped with black. The discs of carrot were hard. The two of them made do with great dollops of bread sauce and cranberry; too sticky and sweet. Katherine's mood was despondent now. She thought she had failed.

'Fancy inviting you to stay and eat this horrible stuff,' she said. Her words slurred slightly.

'I've had worse. This is okay. I used to have to help out in the Home with Christmas Dinner. We had to cook for sixty. And it was never right. Something would always get fucked up.'

Katherine was picking at her shreds of turkey, too absorbed to ask what Jess meant by 'the Home'. She burst open a roast potato and squashed out the mushy white. 'You must miss all of that company. Now that it's just you and . . . Barry, was it?'

'Do I?' Jess had to think for a second, recalling the name of her pretend-groom. 'You can give too much of your life away to other people, I think. I did my bit. Now I'd settle for a bit of peace. I'd settle for a life more like the one you've got, Katherine.'

Such a wry smile. As if Katherine knew better than Jess. 'I rather like the sound of the busy home you lived in. It sounds like a communal house.'

'I suppose it was.'

Katherine sat back, abandoning her meal. 'I'm sorry, She. We shouldn't be raking over the past like this. You don't want to upset yourself.'

Katherine took away the plates.

How did she know? How did she know that Jess didn't want to upset herself?

*

When Jess wanted to she could really work herself up.

She would stop everything; the room that she was standing in, the traffic outside. She would stop everything she was doing because it wasn't that important. She wasn't the kind of woman who, whatever she was doing couldn't be done the next day or the day after. She could stop dead and she could even slow her breathing down to almost nothing. She could make her own heart-beat come down to a near standstill.

Then, when she was like this, she would try to keep her mind empty. She cleared it all out. And of course she couldn't. She couldn't go completely blank. That was when she would work herself up. She let the things start to come back in. All the ideas and the pictures came back into that stopped moment. She never knew she knew so much until she stopped herself like that.

That was how she worked herself up. She upset herself into a lather and a sweat and Katherine, Katherine, do you know something else?

She enjoyed it.

*

They repaired to the living room. Katherine's word; repair.

Now they had another bottle of wine and Katherine was the gracious lady of the house. She was a touch more careless and her words slurred happily. Jess was amazed at how fast she got drunk.

Jess followed her. She was still in the red dressing gown. She felt sexy, going about all day in the thick, rich dressing gown.

By the time Jess caught up, Katherine was putting on a record. Old-fashioned, like jazz. Frank Sinatra. He was playing loud. Katherine held up the sleeve and pointed at the painting. Frank thumbing over his shoulder at blue skies. 'Come Fly With Me'. Katherine said, 'Don't you love Frank?'

Jess was an Elvis fan, but she didn't tell Katherine that yet. She didn't think Katherine would have anything by the king. She thought Katherine would be mostly classical stuff.

Katherine was doing a little shuffling dance on the rug in front of her mantelpiece.

'He makes me want to wear a trilby hat and a raincoat and a suit and hang about in the street! Smoking cigarettes and watching the world go by!'

Jess was surprised by this. She'd thought they'd be onto opera by now.

'Here,' Katherine said, as Frank went into another verse about being starry-eyed and getting up there. Katherine plucked the glasses off the mantel and poured wine, this time red. She sloshed a drop or two onto her satiny gown and swore. They toasted each other, Frank, and the baby Jesus. Then she made them both dance, clutching at Jess's sleeves. They were both in their dressing gowns, like real sluts at this time in the day, dancing on the living-room rugs. Not dancing properly, Jess thought; just kind of swinging about.

Frank slowed down. Katherine let go and sighed heavily. It was like a put-on sigh and she seemed embarrassed by her sudden little show. She took a big glug of wine.

Jess thought: I want to kiss you.

Katherine put down her glass. 'We should have presents now. That's what ordinary people do at this point. We should have presents wrapped up for each other!'

*

Naptime, Katherine. You've passed out, sweetheart.

Katherine was a lightweight, Jess decided, and she couldn't handle her booze. She was lying on the settee still warm from the night Jess spent on it. The little nest Katherine made her was still intact and rumpled and Katherine lay like Snow White in the mess.

What was Jess to do in the meantime? All alone on Christmas Day? She played Frank Sinatra again, quieter, but, even so, his smokey voice drawled loud through the house. Come Fly With Me, Katherine, Come Fly, Let's Fly Away . . .

And fuck me if it isn't snowing.

Jess drew open the heavy curtains and there it was, rushing and dwindling down.

She was free in Katherine's house. She could do anything.

She popped a video in. Mommie Dearest. Seen it. But if she left it playing while she went for a hunt upstairs and

Katherine woke, she would think Jess was behaving herself and watching a film.

Upstairs we go.

Jess wanted to be in the study.

Her bare feet on the deep pile of the carpet. There was an electric charge on the air. It was like walking into Katherine's whole mind.

Katherine's books and papers were open on the table, open to Jess's fingers. She walked her fingers on the pages.

These were Katherine's notes. Maybe they were the most recent things she had written down. This jagged, thoughtful writing.

being made to recognise
but it's agency
for a monster it is agency
Narcissus in the pool
her own Milton and Shelley's Milton
is there ever a fall?
a liberating sense of self that can be – has the capacity -
for being a monster

It was all scribbled notes. Was this the kind of scrambled garbage that went on in Katherine's head? That oh-so refined head of hers? She was worse than Jess! Jess's thoughts kept flitting everywhere. She thought she was bad. Katherine was worse.

A scattering of opened books. It would take Jess the rest of her life to read them. She wondered how fast Katherine could read. One of those special skills she had that Jess never would. And those were skills, Jess thought, that she could really do with.

Katherine was a naughty thing. A bottle of gin in the study. And tumblers with not a speck of dust in them.

Jess poured a glassful and then she turned to the ancient typewriter on the desk. A sheet of paper was already rolled into it. Jess hit the keys carefully, one by one. She tried out her title, just to see what it looked like in neat print.

17
The National Outpouring of Grief

By the New Year, Lily Woods and Christine had their double act down pat.

They had expected, this many months down the line, for people to have lost interest in what they were doing, but that didn't seem to be the case at all. Every Sunday they were going off to other towns to stand in venues in front of audiences and go into their trance. They were doing so well they could afford to go by train now, first class. Lily Woods could kiss the National Express coaches goodbye.

'Mind,' she said on the way to Manchester for their first booking of the New Year, 'First class isn't as special as I thought. All they've got is a few curtains and doilies out.'

Christine wondered if that was how people always felt when they made it. The anticipation was the exciting thing; the actual arriving turned out to be a let-down. In her case there had been no anticipation at all. She was in demand all of a sudden, unasked for.

It was all Lily Woods' fault. Lily had branched out and claimed she needed Christine to help her. Christine got half of what Lily made, from TV, personal appearances and churches; everything. All Christine had to do was sit there all dolled up and let Lily and the audience channel their thoughts through her.

The experience made Christine feel sickly sometimes. There was something palpable on the air. Real vibrations. She now thoroughly believed in the world of spirit and that, every time Lily started up their act, it really felt like something unearthly was going on.

You needed to start believing something, Lily told Christine, when they started talking to each other again.

And this is it. I'm glad you've found some measure of faith. That's what will get you through in the end.

And Lily was quietly delighted that it was her beliefs that Christine had come to share. Christine had been made to realise her life wasn't already over. Not yet. Even with all the sadness and disappointments, there was still good that Christine could do. She had tragedy in her life, sure enough. But some folk were worse off. Those were the people Lily and Christine went out to see.

Christine looked at her elderly friend, who, quite at home in first class, was fanning herself with the drinks list. 'It's a bit close in here,' she said. Lily looked quite red in the face. She always got herself excited on the days they did an appearance.

'I wonder what she'll say today,' she whispered at Christine.

It was, in its way, a thrilling thing they were doing. A wonderful gift they shared between them. Every time they did it again they would discover something new. It was something, to their knowledge, that no one else in the country, even in the world, was doing.

Some of the papers had denounced them as fakers, as charlatans. Lily had been called sick in the head. But they were booked solidly for months.

Christine looked up at her outfit, in its travelling case on the rack above. She'd be able to afford new outfits soon. She had to dress well on these jobs. She had given up working at the bakery and didn't miss it half as much as she expected.

'We should record everything she says,' Christine said. 'We're daft not to, really. Relying on our memory.'

'That's a good idea,' Lily smiled. She smiled tenderly at her neighbour. A motherly smile. Lily was delighted at the amount of time she and Christine had come to spend together, ever since last September. She had developed what she liked to think of as a proper maternal bond with the girl.

There was a third person in the equation, of course. Someone Lily had never expected to get to know. But now Diana seemed as much a part of their lives as anyone she had ever known. She knew the sound of her voice, the drift of her thoughts, the excitable lull just before she started to speak again; describing and explaining what had been happening to her. Lily's life felt very full, recently, with the experiences of these women.

The first glimmerings of this new life had made themselves apparent last September, during the last coach trip Lily had ever made with the National Express. She and Christine had booked their tickets together; both moved by an impulsive, unspoken need to take themselves off to London, like so many others were doing. They had watched the endless queues leading up to Kensington Palace on the evening news and both realised that they wanted to be there.

'You're bloody mad,' Dan had said. 'What's the point? I can see the point of sending money to the charities . . . but queueing all day like that . . .' He shook his head. 'Them people there are just going for a day out. They want to get themselves on the telly.'

'We've both been on the telly already,' said Lily primly. 'We want to go for our own reasons.'

Dan thought it was women going on daft. He was still embarrassed by his own reaction to Diana's death. In the Fletchers' house he had been the first to hear the news, sitting up in bed with his earphones on because of the tinnitus. He had listened to the early reports with his mouth opening, leaving his headset on when he went for a leak in the middle of the night.

Christine found him stumbling in the dark with tears down his face. She switched on the light and was shocked. Her dad looked terrible, in his pyjamas, clutching the banister and moaning.

He had turned to look at his daughter; her hair mussed and shining gold, her nightie buttoned up to the neck. He dragged off his earphones and grabbed her. 'It could have been you! It could have been you.'

She managed to calm him and they had gone down to the kitchen, the heavily pregnant Jude joining them, bleary-eyed and bad-tempered, to watch the early morning bulletins coming in. Every now and then Dan would steal a glimpse away from the portable telly to look at his daughter, who seemed shaken and white. He kept thinking that, had Prince Charles met his daughter instead of Diana in 1980, that could have been her in that underpass in Paris tonight.

All Christine could say about the business was, 'I'll never be a lookalike now.'

Dan had cried all night, embarrassing himself in front of Christine and his granddaughter. They put him to bed for much of Sunday and by the time he was up and about again, he tried to play his reaction down.

He came downstairs and tried to act like nothing had happened. He seemed almost sanguine about the tragedy. He even complained that the media was going mad about it.

Christine looked at him and thought: That's how you shrug people off. You're upset at first, but then suddenly, overnight, you've forgotten them. That's what you did with mam, and our Jess. So of course you can do it with Diana. How do you manage it?

She knew he wasn't really a heartless old man.

By then Jude and Christine were hooked on every report they could get. And Dan had jeered about Christine and Lily's planned two-day trip to London. They were going to sleep on the coach all the way down and all the way back. They were going to queue for hours with their floral tributes (which would wilt in their arms all day) and sign the book of condolence.

'Who do you think is going to read that?' he snapped. 'Do you think someone is going to sit down and read a million strangers' names?'

Although Lily and Christine weren't to be deterred Dan wouldn't let Jude go. He made a scene when Jude suggested it. She'd lose the baby, he said, sitting cramped up on a coach with all those daft mares. Jude could see the sense of that and promised to video all the news programmes, just in case her mam and Aunt Lily came on the telly.

'Dad doesn't understand,' Christine said in the night on the coach. 'He doesn't understand how you have to do these things in person.'

'He doesn't have a compassionate bone in his body,' Lily said.

'That's a bit harsh, Lily.'

'Maybe. But what about his wife, eh? He didn't go running after her, did he? We did. We found her.'

'Dad's deep,' Christine said. 'You can never tell what he really feels.'

'He keeps it locked inside. That's why he flares up like he does.'

Christine sighed and got out their pillows to help them sleep on the hard coach seats. They had talked to one or two of their fellow-mourners but they didn't seem very chatty.

*

It was halfway through the night, somewhere in the Midlands, that Christine woke up to find Lily staring into her face.

'Lily? Sit down straight. What are you playing at?'

'It is like an airport,' she said, in a flat tone.

'Lily?'

'They always said I went on too many holidays.'

Her words were ringing out in the coach. Others were taking notice.

'I did see an awful lot of airports. I wonder if, amongst all the people you've contacted before, any of them have ever told you . . . ? Heaven is like the VIP lounge in an airport. Even down to the carpet. I'm in the Departures lounge.'

Christine shook herself awake. She had seen Lily like this before. Someone was coming through.

'Lily . . . Snap out of it!'

The woman in the seat behind looked shocked. She was nudging her neighbour. Across the gangway faces were staring, open-mouthed.

'I had to make contact. I had to come through. I had met a few people in your line of work. But you were the right one, Lily. You would understand. And your friend, Christine . . .

'She'll have her part to play, too. To make sure my work goes on . . .'

'What are you talking about, Lily?'

Christine could hear the fellow-mourners whispering. She could feel their attention on them.

'People are in shock. People are devastated. I never knew it would have an effect like this. I am as flabber-gasted as anyone.'

Christine fell silent. Lily was clutching hold of her arms.

'The people need comforting. They need telling that I'm all right. That everything after . . . whatever happens on Earth . . . is really all right.'

There was a loud, broken sob from the woman in the seat behind them.

'There is nothing to be afraid of. I have chosen you both to do this work for me. And I will come to you both when you ask me.'

Lily blinked then and slumped back into her seat. She waited for her eyes to focus on Christine's astonished, familiar face.

The coach passengers were stirring. Some were lifting themselves out of their seats and moving towards Lily. More of them were crying now.

'Lily . . .' Christine hissed. 'What have you done?'

*

Having arrived in London, they went about the business of queueing with their flowers and luggage, with the same stunned, entranced expressions as everyone else.

What Christine would remember most was the smell of the flowers. Heavy and sweet.

When it came their time to sign the heavy, creamy pages of the book of condolence, they did it with trembling fingers, the same as everyone else. But to them the gesture, the need to impress their message and their hope of getting it through, seemed almost redundant.

On the way back north on the coach Lily had, plainly and determinedly, outlined her plan to Christine. She explained to Christine the vital role she herself would have to play.

Christine balked at first and started to refuse. Yet she couldn't. She knew in her heart it was the right thing to do. She had seen Lily Woods in her trance. She believed in every word she said. How could she say no? Already, before they arrived home, unwashed and beleaguered, she was planning the kinds of outfits she would have to wear. Nothing too ostentatious, of course.

*

Their act had become so routine that they would barely have to think about it until they arrived in Manchester. It felt like they were on the way to meeting an old and mutual friend. Their first engagement of the year was in a spiritualist church. It wasn't one of their more lucrative do's. It was one that they did 'for the sake of others'.

'I don't like leaving Jude and the baby with dad,' Christine said suddenly.

'He's been all right,' Lily said. 'He hasn't shouted at anyone in ages. And he dotes on the bairn.'

'A little boy in the family at last.' Christine smiled. 'Oh, I know. I should just be grateful.'

'It's not many people,' Lily said, 'who have four generations under one roof. You should be glad. It's like old-fashioned times, when family meant something.' A thought struck her. 'It's like the Royal Family, actually.'

Christine looked at her. 'That Sam was a bloody waste of time. Another useless fella.'

'Give the lad a chance. He'll get them a house.'

'He's taking his time. He's missing Brad growing up and everything.'

'The bairn's only a few weeks old, Christine!'

'It's still not right. Dad shouldn't be changing nappies at his time of life. I'm scared he'll have one of his turns.'

Lily sighed. How many years of this family's problems had she heard about?

'I never got post-natal depression, did I?' Christine asked. 'I didn't get a chance. I didn't have time for it.'

'Jude's always got to be different. She'll come round. She'll be okay.'

Christine rolled her eyes. 'Oh? And who's telling you that? Diana, I suppose.'

Lily coloured and stared out of the windows at the rolling moors. 'Michael, actually. He was telling me last night.'

'Michael?' Christine's eyes went narrow. 'What's he still poking his nose in for?'

'He's very pleased to be a grandad.'

'Huh.'

'He would have been a grandad. He'd have been an ideal one, if he was here.'

'Well, he's not.'

Lily bridled. Christine was in a foul mood today. 'Actually, Michael wasn't very happy about you and your Jude going on the Nancy! show to tell the world all about everything.'

'What's it got to do with him?'

Lily ignored that. 'He said, if Jess had seen it, she'd have been upset. You disowning her on the telly like that.'

Christine scowled. She wished she hadn't gone on, either. She hadn't thought much of the way Nancy asked her questions. She'd had to keep looking at her cue cards. Nancy gave the impression of not giving a flying fuck about her guests.

But that was ages ago now. Everything had changed again. Life was better. They had baby Brad now, and Christine had a new career. But Lily was still going on.

'He says Jess is out now. She's out in the world again.'
Christine blinked.

'He knows where she is?'

'He's keeping tabs on her. He's her guardian angel.'

'What's he want to do that for? She doesn't deserve it.'

'Ah, now, Christine. It's no use being bitter.'

'Isn't it?' Christine rounded on her. 'Jess let the family down. Most things you can forgive. Everyone has their moments. What Jess did, Lily . . . that was beyond everything else.'

The two women stared at the olive-coloured fields sliding by.

Christine asked, 'Did he say anything else? Nothing for me?'

'He comes to me much less these days, you know. I think he's made his peace at last. He's much further away. Starting a new life of his own.'

'Well,' said Christine quietly. 'Good.'

'He wanted to tell you, though . . .' Here Lily licked her lips, her tongue darting out nervously. 'He wants you to know that justice was done.'

'What?'

'Any confusion you might have had over the girls . . . and any lingering doubt you might have had in your mind . . . is unfounded. Jude was completely blameless. Jess was the one who killed that boy. Plain and simple. Jess was the guilty one, the disturbed one, and justice was done. Now she's done her penance and she's out in the world, trying to start again and her father is keeping watch over her. You can put all doubts about Jude out of your mind.'

Lily settled back in her padded seat and closed her eyes, as if a great weight was off her back.

Christine was shaking her head. 'But I never thought that, Lily. I never, ever had any doubts in my mind.'

'Well,' said Lily, opening her eyes. 'That's all right then, isn't it?'

18
User Friendly

You base your life on other people.

When they pop you back into the Community, what else are you to do?

They give you little classes and they draw up lists on blackboards, white boards, flip charts and printed sheets with pictures to click into your files.

These are the things that make you up a life.

This is lifestyle.

*

For her pin number, the first time she used a cashpoint, taking money out of her new account, she used the date of her birth. 1975.

As she tapped it in, knowing she'd remember that, she heard the voice of her personal tutor in the back of her head, saying: That seems practical now, but it's an easy pin for someone to find out. They could use that and have all your money off you. Try a different one, a random one.

Crisp packets swirling round her feet and no one queueing behind her. Jess decided to keep her birthday year. She had less than fifty quid in the account. And besides, 1975 was the only thing about her that hadn't been changed.

*

It reminded Jess of Personal Development Studies at school, the classes they gave to kids who weren't bright enough to take one more foreign language or computers.

Jess had been at school long enough to pick up a few of those valuable lifestyle lessons given by teachers who taught from glossy brochures.

She could still see Peg now, licking her finger and flipping the pages at the front of the class, breathing heavily, saying; 'This will prepare you for when you have to enter the World . . . of Work.'

It was all about the right way to orient yourself in the adult world.

They learned a smattering of everything. They learned practical things.

When she told everyone about her classes at home (Jude was doing Computers and got no Personal Development at all) Jess had found herself flummoxed trying to explain.

Two highlights had been Peg reading out from the brochure; telling the dumbos of class 1G the proper way in which to boil an egg and the proper way in which to wipe their bottoms.

Jess, laughing, told her family what she had learned today over the table at tea.

Grandad Fletcher went mad. He paid taxes to have teachers teach kids of 12, 13, 14 how to wipe their own arses properly?

If they didn't know now they never would.

Oh, he was scandalised. He quivered and jerked with rage.

Jess explained that it was all very biological and medical. How you must do it from front to back for fear of spreading germs in the wrong direction.

Her elaboration failed to butter her Grandad up and he sent her from the kitchen up to her bedroom and mam and Jude had laughed and laughed.

Happy days.

*

The classes leading up to getting out, the lessons in how to reintegrate yourself into Society At Large, they were much the same.

They took into account how the world had moved on.

They took into account how to visit the bank, the post office, the international airport.

The time that these young people had spent in the Home had to be made up for. In a way they were Time Travellers, needing to be briefed.

Things had moved on and had, in some ways, become easier.

Many things – so many things – had become user-friendly.

Jess and everyone else let out that year were about to become users.

For the first time, properly, in her life, Jess became an adult user.

*

You had to pay for the water you used? And what was Council Tax for?

She got a white slip from the Council saying she could vote. In the Local Elections fellas in suits came to her door and she always let them in. Let them convince her.

She would tell them, over a cup of tea, 'Well, you've got me convinced. You've got me hooked.'

She never voted, though. It looked complicated and what if she did the wrong thing?

She let in Mormons and Jehovah's witnesses. She took their magazines full of drawings of what the Kingdom of Heaven would be like. It looked nice. She pored over the magazines with the American men in grey suits and backpacks on their backs. The ones that always came round the doors in pairs in case they got someone strange.

Jess let them think they had convinced her.

She wouldn't buy a TV licence. She only watched daytime telly, when they had talk shows and lifestyle shows on. If any kind of van pulled up in her new street, she closed the curtains and switched the telly off. Any kind of van could have detectors in the back and they might find her. They could tell what channel you were watching. They could even see inside your house, probably.

*

Jess realised on coming out that people – even if they didn't have a Personal Development file full of worksheets and fact sheets – still based their lives on what other people did.

When she had a place of her own – a council flat by the sea in Norfolk – she wanted azaleas in her small square of garden. White and yellow rare azaleas which, when they burst open, looked like fried eggs. She wanted something as exotic as Chilean potato blossom on her bushes, twisting up the mildew-green fence.

She wanted them because Katherine Marshall had them.

She wanted the things that Katherine had in her house.

A cafetière, real paintings by artists no one knew, a whole wall of books with spines cracked, Frank Sinatra records and triple-lined curtains of shot Venetian silk.

Jess wanted her own place to be as close-fitting, as delectable, as user-friendly as that.

*

Chilean potato blossom was purple and yellow.

The touchiest of lilacs, the richest of creams.

She wanted those colours to froth in her garden and to sit nicely in vases on her kitchen table.

I want swags on my curtains!

I want daydo rails!

I want to sponge my own patterns on my own four walls!

I want to rag roll and put stencils on my own furniture!

I want to box in any unwanted feature in my rooms with MDF wood and paint it and stencil it and have a Show Home!

*

That year she entered thick and fast into correspondence with Katherine. She told her how she had moved in. She told her about the objects she had accrued.

There were all these cheap shops. Even shops where everything inside cost less than a pound. There was a shop where she bought pots for plants, a tea pot, a gravy boat, plates, cutlery, underwear, records with everyone's Greatest Hits on.

The quality wasn't as good maybe. Makeshift, but it would do. She had a picture with a teddy on and one with kittens. One telling guests to her house, 'If you sprinkle when you tinkle, be a sweetie, wipe the seatie.' And she got a posher phone, from a more expensive shop. An old-fashioned looking phone and, when you pressed them, the numbers lit up.

*

In her letters Katherine voiced qualms about actually writing again.

Jess could tell she was nervous.

Katherine wanted to do justice, but was she good enough?

Jess read her letters and knew, even though she twisted and prevaricated, Katherine was hooked.

Katherine couldn't abide deadlines. Her head went into a whirl once someone was expecting a book from her. Now Jess would be expecting one too.

An injustice had been done. Katherine said she would have to swallow her fear and her pride and write her revisionist book.

Jess loved that word 'revisionist'.

'If I can drum up enough juices to write the damn thing – then I shall, Jess.'

Good, Jess thought, holding the thick notepaper and sniffing it for perfume. Hint of cigarillo smoke on it.

'I can't call you She. Sheila's a made up name. Can I just call you Jess? That's who you'll be in the book.'

Jess shrugged. Only in private call me that. When you interview me and talk to me for the book. Outside I have to be Sheila forever now.

She liked being She. The cat's mother.

'I still think of you as you were at 12, 13, 14 and when we talked then and how I never saw through – how could I never see through? – all those lies you told everyone.'

*

I told lies to everyone, Jess thought.

It was true.

But I didn't do it for my sake. That was something else I didn't know. It was something else I was too thick to know. They should have told me, back in Personal Development studies, what the point of lying is.

It's to make things come out the way you want them.

It's to make the world work for you.

The point of lying isn't to do things for the sake of other people.

It isn't to ruin your own life.

But I lied and I knew what I was doing. I lied and I took it all on the chin.

I knew Jude was better than me. I knew that, given the chances, she'd be better at living our life.

So I told some whoppers.

And she let me. They all let me.

She didn't deserve a sister like me.

*

Jess went out and bought herself a food mixer in Argos, where she took a liking to the man who worked on the conveyor belt and presented the heavy food-mixer box to her.

'Feels more like a cement mixer,' he grinned and Jess was looking at his meaty forearms and his shirt sleeves rolled up. He was called Tom.

*

I want to blend up Lazy Garlic and Ginger. I want to crush scents into one fantastic paste. I could make curries with the orange, yellow, scarlet spices I bought in jars on a rack.

Crushing all the raw spices and colours into one, like poster paints on my almost scratchless new chopping board.

Now that I have my own environment, I can, if I want, make inedible foods! Curries so hot you have to go running to the cold water tap!

I could make unsightly rooms with colours that clash and jar!

And the people who come here, should I care to invite them, will have to eat my food and will have to look at these colourful, stencilled walls. And if I chose to dress myself in bin bags then I could do that as well.

When Tom from Argos came round she cooked him a curry in her new wok, using the page from her file about curries. He was impressed. He asked her about her life, and Jess told him carefully, getting every detail just right.

He ate her curry even though she realised, as she tasted her own, that the mince wasn't cooked quite through. Tom ate up every last bit though, and said that he didn't think it was too hot at all.

*

Jess had a man. He was like a big toy to her. A great ape or dog. Something she had never expected to have.

He was older than her father was at the age he died. She remembered the soft bristles on her cheek when her dad kissed her. It was the same with Tom when he kissed her a careful hello.

Nothing had ever come from Cilla. Cilla had been absorbed back into a life somwhere. She'd been let out before Jess was, probably back to the Wirral. Her life would have sealed back around her.

Sometimes Jess thought she might go to Liverpool to look for Cilla. But what could she do when she got there? Knock on every door she came to? Walk around the streets until she saw those familiar girlish bunches waggling on someone's head? Listen for the slap of those flip-flops on paving stones?

Best start all over again, Jess thought. Relegate Cilla to that part of her life she'd stayed indoors. These people went into compartments, like her family before the Home. There was no chance of Jess going to look them up, either. The only way was to get in with new people. That was the way things went.

Katherine Marshall said you should look back. She was very into dredging everything up. In her line of work that was natural, except it wasn't her own past that she was trawling and salvaging. That made it different and easier. Katherine poked through the canal bottoms of other people's lives, but she always stood on the bank wearing neat white gloves and she never got her feet shitty.

You have to work to bury old ghosts and shut old doors and windows – or words to that effect – was what Katherine told her. You must go to see your sister and your mother and you must deal with these issues.

Issues, like magazines coming out every week, smelling of glossy paper and coloured inks.

Issues like matter and oily blood from cuts and scabs.

Jess told Katherine that she never did the murder.

Katherine was the first person Jess told the truth to.

She had harboured the secret for years. She had kept it tethered and docked. She expected the telling of it to be her great, eventual revenge. And did she imagine the world would believe her? Would the world applaud her reckless virtue in saving her sister's bacon and good name?

This was Jess revisiting her issues, the ones she'd kept pressed close to her body all this time. They were like wads of secret papers inside her clothes, padding her out.

But she had a good new name. She didn't want it spoiling. Maybe telling the truth was tempting fate. She should use her new name to start anew, like they said in the classes she'd taken.

She should mark the box X for no publicity.

Especially now that she was seeing a lot of a man in Cromer. Here she would live quietly by the sea. They would have a council flat and a dog and maybe they could get a beach hut for the summer.

*

Living by the sea came natural to her.

This town seemed ideal. Every evening when she knew the tide was coming in she would go for a long walk, long past the point were the prom ran out. She would walk along the heavy grey sand, as close to the incoming tide as she dared.

She picked up rocks and stones, saltwashed and smooth, though she knew she shouldn't. She put them in her garden and made a display of them inside her house, in the chimney piece, arranging them with thick yellow candles, like she'd seen on one of the lifestyle shows.

Once or twice she thought about her mother. If the book ever came out and Christine read it and realised what Jess had gone through, they might wind up in the position of seeing each other again. That could happen. Jess could show and explain her new life to her mam.

No. It was too late. She couldn't imagine what her mam was like now.

The woman who had sent her cast-off bras for a couple of years, but never visited her.

It was too late for that.

Long walks on the beach. Fixing up her home. Practical things.

When Jess started to let Tom come with her on her evening walks and he saw her popping sea rocks into her bag, he said, 'If there was a coast guard, you could be had up for doing that.'

Tom was a mine of information. She could do anything, mention any topic and out would come some nugget of gold, in his quiet Norfolk accent.

'What if everyone came and took rocks off the beach, eh?'

Jess looked up and down the long stretch of coast.

'It would be empty,' he said. 'The rocks hold back the sea. They are its only obstacle to crashing in and drowning all the land. If everyone came and did what you did, we'd all be swept out to sea.'

She thought about it and considered tossing her stones back down on the sand. No, bugger it. They were the only ones here on the beach tonight.

Tom made her listen to the waves as they came in thicker, faster and closer. They stared further out to sea, at the muggy grey of the horizon, to see the swells coming and guessing how long before a really huge wave would come to sweep over their feet. There was a sound, if you listened really close, a delicate sound underneath all the crashing of water and it was just like the ripping of silk.

'What is it?'

'That's the rocks, being carried along in the surge of water, flying along, even the heaviest rocks, racing up to the shore. The noise you hear is them being tossed through the water, bashing against each other and plopping down into new places in the sand.'

'Oh,' said Jess. To her it still sounded like the tearing of silk. The whole sea that pushed up to the door of her new flat was shot Venetian silk, triple-lined and she loved to come in the evening to hear its edges rip and fray apart.

*

Tom was a gentle man with her, a quiet man. He seemed to know, without her saying anything, that she hadn't had a man before and he didn't ask why.

They had fish and chips in a place by the prom. They were the best she'd ever tasted, though the waitress was a bit tight with the sachets of ketchup.

'Remember those sauce bottles in the shape of tomatoes?' he asked.

She told him about going to the Sixties Cafe when she was little and how they'd had those squeezy bottles there. She said about meeting her Grandma and how she'd never seen her before.

'Your granny moved away?' he asked.

She nodded.

'And your dad died as well?'

'Yes.'

'It must have been hard on your mam.'

Tom had bought her a toy double-decker bus from a stall by the sea. It was plastic and scarlet and had a sticker on its side saying, 'Buy British Toys.' It seemed like an odd kind of present to her, though she didn't say so. It sat on the table between them as they finished up the bread and butter.

Tom said he hadn't really had a girlfriend before, because he'd been living with his old mam. When she died he'd thought that was the end for him and company.

'Was your mam nice?' Jess asked.

He looked at her like he'd never really thought about it before. 'She always used to fall out with her friends,' he said. 'She'd cause rows at bingo if anyone took her usual chair.'

Jess laughed. 'Did you used to go to bingo with her?'

'They have these big cash prizes. You should go. I'll get a members' form. We won once and went to Disneyland on the proceeds. That was her last trip.'

Jess looked at him, trying to imagine this grown man, this great big toy of a man, enjoying himself in Disneyland.

Lily Woods had once told the twins, 'When I get a load of money and you two start behaving yourselves, then I'll take you to Disneyland. Would you like that, girls?'

Jess wondered if Jude had ever got to go. She should have asked her that time she saw her, in Liverpool. It would be interesting to know. All the things Jude had got that Jess never had. She would never know now.

*

They walked through the quiet streets of the town, looking in the dark windows of hat shops and junk shops. They laughed at a pair of tall china Siamese cats and said it would be fun to put them in your living room and pretend that you really liked them, that you thought they were stylish.

'It's funny, the kind of things that people used to like,' Tom said. He rubbed his chin thoughtfully.

Then he took them into a pub that faced right on the sea. It was dark and smokey inside and they sat in the middle, opening their packets of crisps and laying them in the middle of the table so they could share each others' flavours.

'Will you be my girlfriend then, She?'

The easy day had made her lazy and, for a second there, she had almost forgotten her new name.

'Your girlfriend,' she laughed and looked and saw that his eyes were serious. 'Tom, you've been really nice to me and that.'

He sighed, going back to his pint. 'Mam always said no woman would ever want me. Said I wasn't the type to go knocking around with girls. I don't know why, I just believed her. She was a woman, so she would know.' He swallowed. 'She must have been right.'

'No, Tom. It's me.'

Jess thought about Tom working in Argos. He was one of the ones who brought the boxes in from the store room, sliding them in on conveyor belts. He took your ticket at the counter and went to match it to your chosen box. He took great care that nothing got damaged. Jess had watched him working.

'You don't know anything about me, Tom,' she said.

'You're a bit of a mystery,' he admitted. 'But what do I need to know? I know you're from the North and you had a bit of bother with your family and all. But you like me, or you wouldn't let me come along on your walks or make curries for me. We rub along fine, don't we?'

'Yes,' she said. 'We do.'

'Well?' Hope was coming up in him again.

'What if I'd done something really bad?' she asked. 'Or if everyone thought I'd done something really bad? What if everyone believed it so much that it might as well be true?'

Tom looked shocked. 'Well, that would be wrong. And if you said it was wrong, then I'd believe you, She. And I'd tell anyone, No, I believe her, because . . .'

'It doesn't work like that.'

'But what could you have done, someone like you?'

'Don't get me started on this, Tom,' she warned. 'I don't want to tell you. Let's just be friends and have a nice time . . .'

Tom shrugged and agreed, but he still looked troubled. He still looked hopeful.

*

In the morning's post there was another letter from Katherine.

Jess recognised her tidy print and the postmark and her expensive stationery.

She made herself a pot of tea and wouldn't open the letter until she was sitting ready at the kitchen table in her dressing gown. Letters were to be savoured.

Dear Jess,

Just a quick note to appraise you of 'developments' so far. I'm keeping it all very quiet. We don't want anything leaking out until we're quite sure this is a project that will actually happen. I'm sorry for the 'businesslike' tone of this letter, but this is important and we have to be sure.

I have talked with my agent and she is extremely excited about this book. She says we will have them fighting over this story. Newspapers will want to serialise it and have what I believe is called an 'exclusive'.

What you must realise – and this is terribly important – is that, if you agree to this deal, then I will try to keep your current identity and whereabouts secret. But I cannot ensure that. I cannot give any guarantee that a newspaper won't try to find you, to bypass the book and go straight, as it were, to the 'horse's mouth'.

Now you have to be sure. I know how hard you have worked at putting a new life together for yourself. You must weigh it all up. If you really believe (as I do) that this book needs to be written and the record setting straight, then I will be only too happy to go ahead. A great injustice has been done. You were a confused and vulnerable child. They let you take the blame. It is a story I very much want to write. On the other hand, you must be aware of the risks involved.

I am going to be away this weekend at a conference on Female Circumcision but I'll be back for teaching next Tuesday. Please ring me at home about this.

your friend,

Katherine (Marshall.)

19
Out of Mercy

Sam's mother didn't mind looking after the baby. She didn't mind being asked at all.

So long as people were up front about what they wanted and what they needed from her, there was no problem. If there was one thing that her daughter-in-law did right it was telling things straight down the line and asking when she needed a hand. She was better than Sam at things like that. Sam would always get flustered and start stammering. He needed a wife to keep him in check.

Maybe Jude was a bit too up front. Maybe she was a bit selfish in the end. But at least she made herself clear.

Sam's mother was a forthright woman. That's how she would put it herself. She had raised seven children of her own and now did voluntary work in a hospice. She was used to disasters and emergencies of all kinds.

When Sam phoned his mother and explained the situation with Jude and the baby, she was only too pleased to come and muck in and help out.

Dorothy got on the train at Carlisle and was in Newcastle by tea time. She brought enough luggage for a month.

At first she had quite taken to her daughter-in-law. Not exactly the type she had expected Sam to marry, and disappointed there had been no wedding. But Brad was a beautiful child, with a real look of Sam and Sam's father about him. She loved their house on the new development outside of Newcastle, too, with its large hallway and generous living room and the guest bedroom which, she knew, had been decorated all to her own taste, for when she came to visit.

She knew that Jude's mother, the famous Christine, didn't visit as much as she should. Dorothy didn't think much of Christine or her dubious occupation. 'It is all a joke, isn't it, Sam?' she had asked hopefully. 'She doesn't really go round impersonating members of the Royal Family?'

Sam had assured her it was all true. He thought it was hilarious that he had Princess Diana for a mother-in-law.

Dorothy had learned to try hard to not believe that the Fletchers were trouble.

At the christening there had been that strange old woman, some kind of aunt to the family, Dorothy believed. In the pleasant old village church, Lily had pushed herself right up to the front (to the font, in fact) as if she was important, and kept saying that Brad would have a great future.

Lily had even cornered Dorothy at the reception and told her horrible things, grotesque things, with a gleam in her drunken eye, all about the afterlife. She told her that Dorothy's mother's name had been Alice and that Alice was having a whale of a time in heaven; this world's tribulations and her replacement hips all behind her now.

Well. Christine could have told Lily Dorothy's mother's name. Lily was clearly a fraud.

At Newcastle station Dorothy scooted across the white marble-effect floor and into a taxi. It would be expensive, all the way out to Sam and Jude's house, but Sam had said don't be late. Jude was cooking a light supper and he would try to be back early from the office and then Jude would have to leave.

It was all a little dramatic.

The way Dorothy thought about it: if Jude had nothing to hide, then she needn't go dashing off to be with her family, such as it was.

That's what she was doing though. She wanted to race off to be with them.

It all sounded highly suspicious.

Jude was making herself look like she had something to hide.

Dorothy glanced out at the strings of lights across Tyneside.

It was the most grotesque story she had ever heard.

She never bought those kind of newspapers herself and it was Eunice, one of her daughters, who brought the tabloid into her house. There was her son, his arm around his wife and even Brad, in the photo in the lead story. They were, the tag-line shrieked, staunchly defending themselves against outrageous claims made by Jude's long-lost sister. Or rather, Jude was defending herself against outrageous claims.

Sam looked rather handsome in the picture, she thought. People would surely realise it wasn't his side of the family to blame for the fuss.

'But will it go to court?' Dorothy asked her son on the phone.

'It could well do,' he said and his mother thought, why is he lowering his voice on his own phone? Oh Sam, whatever have you got yourself into?

'You don't want your name dragging through the courts,' Dorothy said firmly. 'Isn't it bad enough that it's in all the newspapers?'

'Jude has got to defend herself,' Sam told her. 'I think she's been marvellous . . . and brave.'

'Hm,' said his mother. 'I can't pretend to understand any of it at all.'

'It's quite simple. It's like it says in the press,' he said. 'Her sister is coming out with this book and she's making up a pack of lies about Jude.'

Dorothy's voice was fierce. 'You never said before that her family was mixed up in . . . this kind of business.'

'Because of something her sister did, Jude should spoil her life?'

'Hm,' said Dorothy again. At the other end of the phone, Sam knew that she would be fiddling with her cameo brooch. It was one of her habits. 'What I can't see,' she went on, 'is how this Jessica person might think she would get away with it. All this attention. And how did she manage to make Katherine Marshall believe her? I believe the woman's quite respected . . .'

'What are you saying, mum?'

'Have you thought – and I am only saying this because I am your mother and what no one else can say to you, I can – haven't you thought that there might be just a grain of truth in these . . . allegations?'

Almost before she had that last word out the line broke off with a click and a buzz. Dorothy almost dropped her receiver in shock.

Sam had never put the phone down on his mother before.

*

She arrived at their house in the pitch dark, stepping gingerly into a road still thick with mud and sand from tractors. Sam's house was one of the very first to be finished on this rather exclusive estate.

She paid her taxi and stared at the lit windows of the house and the two cars on the drive. Jude's Fiesta was crammed with luggage. She hadn't even bothered to say how long she would be at her mother's. Typical of her.

Sam met her on the doorstep with the baby in his arms. Brad was in a pair of orange dungarees and his arms went straight round granny's neck for her to hold him.

'Let her get in the door,' Sam grinned. 'Jude's just finishing up supper.'

Hm, Dorothy thought. He's giving the child over in order to deflect me. He doesn't want any difficult questions.

Jude came into the hallway, rubbing her hands on a tea towel.

Lady Macbeth, Dorothy thought.

'Soon be ready,' Jude said brightly. 'Hotpot.'

'Come and have a drink in the living room,' Sam said. 'We've stocked up with your gin and . . .' He was grabbing at his mother's elbow.

'How is your grandfather?' Dorothy asked Jude as she was bundled away.

You could see the strain on the girl's face. For a second Dorothy almost felt for her.

'Oh, he's not too well. It's all down one side. Mam says he'll probably have to go . . . you know . . . into the Home. But she doesn't want him to.'

'It must be very hard,' Dorothy said. 'Strokes are terrible things.'

'Poor old bloke,' said Sam and they stood there awkwardly.

Dorothy remembered him as a rather coarse old man. At the christening he had made a fuss over something and nothing – who got to sit in the front pews – and raised his voice in the Norman church. 'Do they think,' she asked, 'that it has anything to do with all the recent . . . publicity?'

Jude coloured at that.

Sam took his mother's arm more firmly and steered her into the living room.

Jude said, 'I'll start dishing out,' and disappeared into her kitchen.

Dishing out, Dorothy thought, carrying the baby. It took her appetite right away.

In the living room Sam installed his mother in the high-backed Laura Ashley chair, their one good piece of furniture so far. As he poured her a welcome drink, he was explaining how Jude herself had chosen the tartan fabric for that chair and the shop had been so impressed with the effect and her taste that they'd had another covered the same and put it in their window display.

Dorothy had heard the tale before. She was thinking: if that girl has my family's name dragged through the courts, and if that book that Katherine Marshall is writing is full of terrible things that will put my family to shame, I'll never forgive her. I'll have to work on Sam. He won't want to stay involved with the likes of that.

*

For all her misgivings, Dorothy had to admit that dinner was rather good. At least Jude could cook. And she had used the casserole dish that Dorothy had bought them on her last visit. She had been shocked by their cheap crockery.

She speared a baby onion, one she'd been saving till last, and glanced at Sam, who was feeding Brad in his high chair. Jude looked frazzled and distracted all through dinner, picking at her plate and not giving her son a moment's thought.

Jude looked to Dorothy like a person with a lot on her mind. Not just her grandfather's stroke. Something else. She looked like a woman with something on her conscience.

Dorothy spoke up, emboldened by gin. 'I don't understand why your sister and this Katherine person would want to talk to the newspapers.'

Jude looked up with her mouth open. As if she thought Dorothy was speaking out of turn, as if she had said something in bad taste.

Well, thought Dorothy, and soldiered on. 'I mean, according to the scurrilous pieces I've read, the affair has rebounded badly on your sister. The press are at her door and her so-called new identity has been splashed all over the place. Now, why should she want to do that to herself?'

Jude stared at her plate.

'It's true,' Sam said. 'That man she was thinking of marrying – the papers said he was a bit backward – actually thumped a photographer who was chasing them. He was taken into custody himself.' Sam shook his head.

'So talking to the newspapers wasn't very clever, was it?' Dorothy said.

Jude put her fork down with a clatter. 'Jess didn't,' she snapped. 'She wanted to be in the papers less than we did. They got hold of some old friend of hers, from when she was locked up.'

Dorothy clucked her tongue as Jude said 'locked up'.

'This girl called Cilla,' Jude went on. 'She was a bit backward too, by the sounds of it. She told them all sorts and they didn't have to do much investigating to find her.'

'Shit,' said Sam, and his mother shot him a glance.

'Jess didn't want to be in the papers at all,' Jude said, collecting up their plates.

'Why do you sound like you're defending her?' Dorothy asked.

'What?' Jude's voice came out angrier than she meant it to.

'Well. It's you she's lying about. You're the one who . . .'

'She's my sister,' Jude said.

'Some sister,' Dorothy shook her head.

Jude snapped at Sam, 'Can't you get her to shut her mouth?'

'Jude!' he said and the baby started to cry.

Dorothy sat back in her chair. The dining-room set was her old one. It was almost like being in her own house. The thought made her brave.

'I don't think you should be seen to defend her,' she told Jude. 'She might be your sister but she's still a murderess. You know that better than anyone. You were there, for goodness' sake, when she killed that poor boy. I think you should think very carefully about defending any of her actions. To the outside world, it will look very bad.'

Jude stared at her and very carefully put the lid back on the casserole dish. Then, taking it in both hands, she dropped it on the dining-room floor, where it smashed, bleeding gravy and chunks of vegetable on the bare wooden boards.

Then she whirled out of the room.

*

Ever since that night at college, when Jess had appeared out of nowhere and into their lives and talked so strangely in Jude's bedroom, Sam had been careful with the whole topic.

Best leave well alone.

He knew well enough how Jude could flare up. He knew she had been right to phone up the police and tell them Jess had escaped. He took her word for it that Jess was unstable and could cause them great harm.

Sam kept quiet but he had pondered over the whole thing.

It had taken him a while to throw in his lot with Jude.

But she'd been pregnant. There was really no choice.

Now Jess was out in the world, that nagging worry of his was worse than ever. But he knew better than to talk it through with Jude. They had a son, a tiny son, and he was their first concern.

Anything Jude could suggest she could do to make the situation better sounded good enough to Sam. So he acquiesced to her going down to see her family like this. No one knew better than Jude how to deal with this new development.

But it scared him. He would never admit it to his mother, even though she was here now, and full of reassuring common sense; he would never tell her of his real fears.

When he had bought the papers that printed Jess's story his blood had turned cold. His first reaction was to take their son away. Far away from Jude. Just the possibility that what Jess was saying was true, was enough to set him off.

Because he'd always, at the back of his mind, remembered how aggrieved Jess had looked that night he'd seen her. She'd looked like someone who'd been wronged. Time and again he'd put the thought out of his mind and concentrated on loving Jude, looking forward to their baby and their life together.

Then the papers came.

And he asked Jude, out loud, in the middle of the night; the most honest question he could imagine. One that had plagued him.

'Is there any truth in it?'

'What?' Her voice was dry in the dark. She always parched up in the night and had a glass of lemonade by her bed, which went slowly flat through the night.

'In the stories. In what she says?'

He felt her bristle and tense. He could hear her powering up to yell at him. He knew the signs. He knew by now how hard she was. How fierce. He knew he was right on the raw spot he had instinctively kept away from. And in that moment he realised he'd never have hooked up with her and got them this house if she hadn't found herself pregnant in their third year of college.

It was a night for facing the truth.

He was feeling parched, too. 'In the papers Jess says it was you who did it. She says that yes, she kicked the boy and kicked him until he stopped moving. But only because you told her to. And all the while you were sitting on him, holding him down. She says it was you who pushed his face down, ripped the wires out of his head. You held his face down until his lungs were full of water and mud.'

He stared at the dark ceiling.

Why am I doing this now? he wondered.

When Jude spoke her voice was softer than he expected.

'No. I stood back, Sam. You have to believe me. The worst thing I did was not stopping her. She kicked him and kicked him. She kicked him in the balls again and again so he couldn't rape her, like he'd threatened, and give her babies. She had this terror of those boys making her pregnant. She was obsessed with the idea they were going to. Then, when he was rolling around in pain, she fell on him. She was a big girl. She forced his face into the mud.'

They were quiet. He heard the pillow rustle as she turned to face him.

She said, 'You know I couldn't stand it if you didn't believe me.'

He waited a moment too long. 'I do, Jude.'

'I need you to believe me, Sam.'

'I do. It's just . . .'

'What?' Now her voice was harder.

'It's just . . . back then, she took the blame. But she was just a kid. Now she's not a kid. This is an adult's story we're getting in the papers and in this book. Someone exactly the same age as you. For the first time, it's your word against hers.'

Jude stiffened again. She turned away. 'It's not equal. She's been put away. Who is she? What rights has she got? She's no one.'

'She's your sister,' Sam said, touching Jude's bare shoulder, forcing her to face him. 'As far as the world's concerned, it's your word against hers.'

She lay flat and silent and wouldn't look at him.

Sam held his breath.

Jude got up out of the bed. She pulled on her robe. 'Brad needs feeding,' she said.

'No, he doesn't . . .'

'Yes he does.'

She turned, and bending quickly over the cot, picked up the baby and left the room.

That night she slept downstairs with the baby in her arms.

They didn't talk about the business again, until his mother turned up.

*

Jude kissed the baby and her husband goodbye and said she would phone when she got there. It would take two or three hours, depending on the traffic. She didn't say another word to her mother-in-law.

Dorothy sat on the tartan chair in the living room with her knitting out, watching a quiz show with the toddler playing at her feet.

Jude took a look at her son and thought about picking him up again. But it would disturb him. It would alert him to the fact she was leaving.

She left her house in tears, feeling like she was leaving it for the last time.

That would be how her Grandad would feel, she knew, when they took him off to the Home. It would be true, too.

Sam kissed her again by the car. He looked into her face, scrutinising her.

He's too needy, she thought. He looks to me for strength. He always has. I should never have got together with him.

She hissed out her breath and felt the weight of his palms on her hips. She didn't know when she was coming back home, to him and Brad.

'You don't have to go there by yourself,' he said.

'I do.'

'We could come with you.'

'It's family business, Sam. I've dragged you in enough.'

He gave a snort. 'You mean you can't depend on me.'

She opened the car door. 'What?'

'That's why we've not talked about it. Because you don't think you can depend on my support. Ever since . . .' He looked away. In the light from the house she watched his eyelashes. They were white. She loved that. He said, 'Ever since I actually asked you, that night. I asked you if it was true, what Jess was saying. It was as if, for a second, I doubted you. But it wasn't like that. Believe me. Now you can't depend on me.'

Jude weighed her car keys in one hand. 'No . . . I can see why you would have to ask that, Sam. I could see why you would have to be sure.'

'Good.'

'I don't blame you for that.'

'I just had to ask. So I can stand by you. You know that.'

She nodded. 'The thing is, I've never thought I could look to you for any kind of support. Really. You're useless. Completely bloody useless.'

His hands fell away from her sides.

'I just have to look at you when your mother's around. You can't even stand up to her. That old bitch. How can you let her talk to me like that? And then you say you'll stand by me?' Jude laughed bitterly and clambered into the driver's seat. 'If that's what your support is like, then I'm better off without it, frankly.'

He couldn't think what to say. He couldn't believe she was even talking like this to him.

He stood away from the car as she started it up and watched it as she pulled away, not even looking back at him once. Sam watched as the car hauled out of the drive and away.

*

Jude drove south on the A1, playing George Michael. The rain slashed down and suddenly she felt quite alone and set apart between the two sides of her family.

For days now she had been fighting down the panic. All the thoughts she had managed, with some success, to keep at the back of her mind, for so long, had come creeping back.

She could answer Sam's questions. She could keep her voice level. She could make him believe what he wanted to believe.

Everything she had kept back all this time, she was still managing it now. Even now, even with Jess splashing everything over the papers.

I answered Sam well. I made it seem real. There's no reason why he, or anyone else, should doubt my version of things.

She drove on.

Jude had always known she could depend on Jess. She'd always known Jess would stay true to her word. It was something deeper than a pact, it was even deeper than being sisters. They were almost the same person, their mother had always told them. They had never needed to explain anything to each other.

Jess had decided, in her quiet, determined, Jesslike way, to go the way she had in life. She had made herself the guilty one so that Jude could have an ordinary life.

And Jude had known that. Even separated, for the first time in their lives; one at home, one in custody, they had both sensed what the other was thinking. That's how Jude had seen it.

Jess had made the choice to take the blame. To sacrifice her own freedom.

It hadn't been a child's decision. They couldn't claim it was. It was the most adult thing either of them had ever done. Lying awake that first night, miles away from her twin, Jude had sensed and guessed the enormity of what Jess had done.

She did it for me. She took that choice for me and said I stood by while she killed him and that I ran away and that I had nothing to do with it.

Jess always knew I was the better equipped of the two of us. I stood the best chance of having a normal life, a successful life. Jess was too frightened. She was always too scared. By admitting the guilt she was exempting herself. She would never have to face the problems of an ordinary life. She was too scared of what she'd seen already.

She wanted to be locked up.

She did it for me. So I could have the life I have now.

But now she's doing this. She's jeopardising everything. Everything I've made for myself.

Everything she's given me.

She did it for me, Jude told herself yet again. She's got no right to take it all from me.

Mam once said we were two halves of the same person. Just by keeping her gob shut and not blaming me, Jess got the roughest deal. And I got my life.

Jude could never feel as grateful as she wanted to.

And I did want to feel grateful to her. Sometimes I thought of her in a cell. Thinking herself a murderer. I did think about that. But it never rang true. After she went Jess never seemed like a real person to me.

Is that my fault?

When she turned up, that one time, in college, she never even looked like herself. Dishevelled, a bit mad, her hair all wild. She looked like a bad impersonation of us.

I could never make her suffering real enough. I couldn't imagine it. It's not really suffering anyway. She had nothing to get at her conscience. Not really.

Jess was safe on all fronts.

She had no right to turn back on her decision.

She can't spoil my life now.

It wouldn't be fair.

If you make that kind of decision, on behalf of others, you have to stick by it. Especially if the other person is your twin.

Jude drove south through the dark and she could almost feel Jess's stubborn silence, like a buzzing in her head. We had a bond all those years. It was like we knew what each other was planning, like we could anticipate each and every move. When she took on the blame for Arthur's death I knew what she was thinking and I knew it was because she wanted to opt out of everything. She knew she wasn't brave enough to live a normal life. The bond between us, even separate as we were, let me know what she was thinking.

But I let her suffer. I know she suffered and all because of me.

I let other people come between us.

It takes other people to ruin a bond like that. Meddlers like this girl, this prison friend of hers, in the papers, or the woman writing that book. Those are the people who spoil things. Why couldn't they just leave it alone? We were all sorted out. All of us.

Jude realised she could just stop now, lost between the two poles of her life and disappear. They could say someone had killed her in road-rage, or they could say she was abducted by spacemen. But she would never have to see any of them again.

That was shite, though. She had to see her mam and her Grandad. She had to go home.

And she had to play her part. The part that she had decided on when they were twelve, coming on thirteen. That of the innocent sister. The one who had been standing by, watching in awestruck terror as murder was committed. The one who had the right to act wronged should anyone ever say otherwise.

Home. She had to get home.

Jude put her foot on the accelerator. She had to get back to Brunswick Avenue. And once she was there she had to take charge. Once she was there it was she who had to allay all their fears.

She had to get back for Christine.

*

Christine sat waiting for Jude to turn up, jumping anxiously each time she heard a car in the Avenue. Lily had offered to sit with her, but she said no. Even in the state he was in, Dan still got het up when he knew Lily was in his house.

He lay upstairs, trapped under two duvets. He could hardly even sit up by himself. Every hour Christine would go up and check on him and she hated it every time. The doctor was coming in the morning. Soon they would have to decide about him. They couldn't put it off much longer. Christine couldn't deal with him on her own, nor could she deal with the deciding on her own. She needed Jude to help her decide what to do for the best.

It was incredible for Christine to hang on waiting for her daughter like this. To think: things will be better when Jude gets here. When had she come to depend on her daughter like that? On anyone, come to that.

Jude was strong, Christine knew that much. How she'd coped with all the newspapers and everything recently, Christine just didn't know.

Jude had nothing to be ashamed of. That was how she could be so strong and sure. That must be it.

Christine was grateful for that.

Imagine having nothing to be ashamed of.

Christine felt hapless and useless. Tonight she'd had to change her dad's pyjamas as he lay there in bed. She'd done it wrong and the shit had gone everywhere, all over the sheets and up his back and it stank. She'd turned him over so she wouldn't see his tiny old prick and he'd cried and that had started her off.

She remembered how strong he had been. Her quiet dad, sitting in the outhouse with her and giving her a sip of illicit brandy. Christine even found herself missing him bursting in and losing his temper and really going mad. She'd give anything to have him come thundering in now and yelling the odds at her. 'WHAT are you DOING you silly young BITCH, snivelling and drinking ALL that WHISKY?'

The doorbell went and made her jump.

She hadn't heard a car pull up.

Woozily she stood and tottered as the bell went again. It would wake dad up.

Christine hurried into the dark hall.

But Jude had her own key. She wouldn't ring the bell, would she?

Christine squinted into the spyhole and there was a strange woman there, a little older than herself. She opened the door.

'Mrs Fletcher?' The women looked haggard and drawn. She was in an anorak with stretched housepants underneath. She looked like she'd come dashing out of her house on an impulse. Her voice was thick and lisping. Christine blinked and saw that she had two clunky, old-fashioned hearing aids coming out of the sides of her head. 'Are you Christine Fletcher?'

'Yes,' said Christine.

'Can I come in?'

Christine swallowed. 'It's late, really, and . . .'

'I think,' the woman clutched her handbag in front of her bosom. 'I think you should let me in.'

*

Christine knew before the woman sat down and introduced herself that she was Arthur's mother. There was
even a resemblance.

For years Christine never had a mental picture of the
boy Jess had killed. It was only with the recent stuff in the
press that the school pictures had been printed again and
Christine could look at them and think: that was the boy
who started all this. That belligerent, defensive look to
him. His badly knotted school tie.

Back then, at the time of the killing, Christine hadn't
been able to look at the papers. All she knew at first – in
the fog of her panic and despair – was what Jude kept
repeating: 'Our Jess killed a big boy. She held him down
till his lungs were full of black mud. He was a much bigger
boy than her.'

'He was a daft lad,' Jude had said. 'A boy with no ears.
You couldn't hear what he was saying. He said awful
things, though. He threatened her. He said he would . . .
he said he was going to fuck her, and give her his babies.
She taunted him. She taunted all of them, mam. He had
these wires coming out of the holes in his head. He was
cruel and bitter, the way he talked.'

Christine hated it when Jude had talked her through
the story. She rocked her remaining daughter as she said
all of this and wished and wished Jude would shut up.

'He scared Jess badly. That's why she did what she did.
He was evil. There was something horrible about him.
He'd of done it as well. He was after her.'

When Christine saw Arthur's picture she remembered
Jude saying things and she thought, but he looks like a
child. He looks fifteen. She looked at the thick wires
coming out of the holes in his head in the old school photo
and she'd cried. Now it was real to her.

The woman's name was Maxine. Arthur had been her
only child. He'd been stone deaf from birth. Her
husband couldn't bear living in a house where no one
could hear him, so he'd cleared off. Arthur had been all
Maxine had in the world. She knew he was a bad lad in

lots of ways, but who wouldn't be? Life had been cruel to him.

Maxine talked, her words sometimes running into each other and making her difficult to understand. Christine listened to her.

'He was a bully,' Maxine said. 'I knew that and that's what they said afterwards. He got in with a bad lot of lads. But he didn't deserve to die for that, did he?'

He was going to fuck her, Jude had said. He'd told her he'd get her alone and that would be it. He knew just what to do. For some reason he'd fixed his sights on our Jess.

'No,' said Christine.

'All the other lads from that class went and got on all right. I see them in town. Some of them with wives and kids in buggies. They can't even say hello to me, let alone stop and talk and they know who I am. Everyone is ashamed, Mrs Fletcher. Look – even you're ashamed, talking to me. What have I ever done, or what did Arthur do, to make everyone too ashamed to talk to me?'

'I don't know.'

Jude had told Christine all of this at the time of Jess being put away. Through the telling Christine had burned with shame. How had sex become something terrifying for her girls? How had she brought up girls who could be terrorised like this?

I was so free. I was so free and easy.

She wanted to tell her girls: do you know where you came from? It wasn't your dad. You think that, you mourn him, you call him your dad.

But you come from the boy in the Reptile House. The skinny savage boy who fucked me in his office. I felt no terror. I courted it. I courted the danger and loved it.

What happened to you? How did I make you so scared?

How could you become so scared you end up doing something like this?

At the time Jess was put away, Jude had told her how the boy with no ears had terrorised them. But never since. Jude hadn't talked about it much in the years since.

Maxine was going on.

'They said at the time he was bullying your girls. Well, he was bullying Jess. And that he pushed her into doing what she did. I've thought about this a lot. Arthur had his father's temper. He had that naturally and it wasn't all down to his defects and the way people picked on him. I know he must have picked on your daughter. He could be cruel as well. I couldn't control him, Mrs Fletcher.'

'Christine. My name is Christine.'

'I know.' Maxine's eyes flashed. 'I've read it in the papers.'

Christine was thinking, our Jude is going to come back and find me with her. She licked her lips. 'What do you want me to do?'

Maxine looked surprised. 'No one can make it better.'

'No.'

'But they can try to.'

'What can I do?'

'All this stuff in the papers again. It's doing my head in. All of this coming back.' She stared at her hands on the table. 'I read what happened to your dad. I'm sorry about that. All of us could have done without this coming back.'

Christine got up to put the kettle on, to give them a pause.

'I don't want your tea,' Maxine said. She made it sound as if it would poison her. 'What I want to know is this. Could there be any truth to what your Jess is saying in the papers? Could it be true?'

Christine was trapped by the sink. Maxine was twisted round on her chair. Christine felt her lips move without any sound coming out.

'What?' Maxine shouted, reaching up to the side of her head.

'I said . . . No. No, it's not true. It's all lies in the paper. It's all lies.'

'How do you know?'

I just do, Christine wanted to say.

'How do you know, Mrs Fletcher?'

Jude told me what happened. I got the full, unbearable story before anyone did. I know exactly what happened that day. It's almost as if I was there.

So I know the truth and everything you've read is false. Jess is lying.

But she couldn't say anything to Maxine.

'Mrs Fletcher?'

It was like being hit again and again. It felt like Maxine's questions would go on forever. Yet she wasn't saying anything that Christine hadn't thought for herself.

Even before the papers, even before Jess had come back into the world, Christine had allowed herself to wonder. She found herself wondering, torturing herself over Jude.

Now this woman wanted a way to find out for sure. This woman deserved to know. She deserved proof of some kind.

'Lily Woods,' Christine said suddenly. 'Lily Woods told me that it was Jess to blame . . . for your son.'

'Lily Woods,' said Maxine. 'I know her. I've seen her do her talking to the dead. She never got Arthur for me. Is she right? Does she know for sure that Jess killed my son, and not the other one?'

'I believe what Lily says.'

Maxine gave her a ghastly smile. 'You do look just like Princess Diana. Even when you're not made up, like now.'

Christine said, 'Lily talked with the spirit world. She found out for sure. She said Jude was innocent. I know what Jess is saying to the papers is untrue.'

'The thing is,' said Maxine. 'if it was true – and this is what I can't help going over in my mind – the wrong person was put away. Your Jude got away with murder. And she's been having a fine time, hasn't she? New baby, new house. Husband in computers.'

Christine said harshly, 'Jude wasn't to blame.'

They looked steadily at each other.

'If she was,' Maxine said, 'then I couldn't rest easy. I'd go to my grave, my own grave, knowing that the wrong girl was punished. And the other one was scott free, laughing about my Arthur being dead.'

'No one is laughing about that.'

'But you see my point, don't you?'

Christine nodded. 'Yes.' She was putting herself in the other woman's position. 'Of course you'd have to know.'

'Well,' said Maxine, standing up, satisfied. 'That's all right then.'

Christine thought for a second, she's going to leave! She's getting up and leaving! And she was ashamed at her own delight.

'Come on, then,' Maxine said.

'What?'

The woman looked impatient. 'We can find out, can't we? You can give me proof.' She was buttoning her woollen coat back up. 'You can fetch Lily Woods round here. She can do her business and tell me to my face what the truth is. We can go and get her now.'

'It's late . . .' said Christine, flustered.

'You're telling me it's late,' Maxine said. 'Ten years too late.'

*

As they left, Christine cast an anxious glance up the stairway, but she couldn't hear anything from her dad's room.

They crossed the street and knocked at Lily's house.

'She might be away on a trip,' Christine said.

'I doubt it. You're still here. She doesn't do her appearances without her real-life Princess Diana with her.'

The way she talked made Christine shiver.

Lily stood in the doorway looking confused.

As Christine explained hurriedly, stammering, Lily looked at Maxine and the colour drained out of her face.

'Will you do it, Lily?' Christine was pleading with her. 'Will you do it for me?'

Lily clutched the doorframe. 'I've got the oven on.'

334

'Switch it off,' Christine said. 'We'll wait.'

Lily dashed back into her house, her head spinning.

'We have to go and do it at Christine's house,' Maxine shouted down the hall to her. 'We can't leave her poor old dad on his own.'

Lily came out with them, locking her door and shrugging on her coat, not even realising that she'd left her slippers on.

*

They switched on the standard lamp in the living room and sat Maxine down, and Lily said she had to splash some water on her face before she could begin.

Maxine nodded her assent and said to Christine, 'I'd like you to be here, too. I want you to hear this as well . . .'

Christine nodded.

She followed Lily to the kitchen and watched her run the tap till it was icey.

'Lily?'

Lily was rubbing her bleary eyes with water.

'Lily?'

'What's she come here for?' Lily moaned. 'What can we do to help her?'

'Who else has she got, Lily?'

Lily closed her eyes.

'And this is what you do all the time, isn't it? Passing on messages and reassuring . . .'

'I can't do it at will!' Lily snapped.

Her whole body was rigid with tension.

'But you can, Lily,' said Christine. 'You've done it before.'

Lily sighed and shook her head and drank a glass of water down straight.

'Lily?' Christine asked, but Lily wouldn't be drawn. She turned and marched into the living room, where Maxine was ready for her private sitting.

*

'Arthur has grown into a fine man. I can see him right now. He has made himself apparent, so I can see. He is standing beside you, Maxine. Can you feel his presence?'

Her eyes wide, Maxine stared to her left and her right.

'He is standing on your left, by the standard lamp. He's six feet four and he's got fine wide shoulders and all this wonderful curly hair.'

'He always had his curls,' said Maxine. 'Ever since he was born.'

Lily nodded and closed her eyes again.

Christine watched her nod dreamily, that strange smile playing on her face. Christine was used to Lily going off into her states. But there was something different tonight.

'He's married!' Lily burst out happily. Her feet did a little involuntary kick, as if in pleasure. 'He's married a lovely girl and they've got two kiddies. Two girls.'

Christine thought, her skirt's ridden up. You can almost see her pants. She really must be in a trance, for her to sit like that. You wouldn't sit in that state if it wasn't genuine, would you?

Maxine looked shocked. She swallowed. 'The kiddies . . . do they have their hearing?'

Lily took a deep breath and smiled. 'Maxine, there is no deafness in heaven. No sickness, nothing like that.'

'And Arthur..?'

'Move your curls, Arthur, love. Ah. He's got his ears. He can hear everything fine. He loves it there. And he says . . . he can hear all your prayers, Maxine.'

Maxine allowed herself a small smile at this.

'What are his daughters called?'

Lily's eyes flickered. 'Alison and Patricia.'

'I can't believe this!'

'It's all true, Maxine. He's telling me.'

'It's wonderful!'

Suddenly Christine felt very distant from the scene. She was seeing Lily going about her work as if for the first time.

'Lily,' said Maxine.

'You can talk to Arthur directly,' Lily said.

'Arthur, I must ask you . . .' She hesitated. 'Arthur, it's your mam. I know this will be painful for you – but you must understand how I need to know. You are resting in peace, but I need to, too . . . when my time comes . . .'

'Ask him,' Lily coaxed her gently. 'Go on.'

'Arthur, I need you to tell me who . . . is responsible for your . . . passing over. I need to know if it was really Jessica or . . .'

Lily's voice took on another, deeper timbre. It made Christine jump. Lily's voice took on the same lisp, the same indistinct quality of Maxine's voice.

'Mam . . . I love you. And I'll tell you the truth. It was right that she was put away. Everything she's saying in the papers is false. You can rest easy, mam. Jessica was responsible. Jude went running for help because the other girl, the wicked one, had gone crazy. It was Jessica who killed me.'

Maxine burst into tears and looked away.

'I have to go, mam. I love you. My girls love you too . . . and when you pass over, we will be waiting here for you . . .'

Lily sank back into her chair.

Christine watched her regather her strength and watched Maxine cry her heart out in the armchair.

Next thing, they were standing in the hall.

Maxine was touching Christine's face. 'You understand, love, don't you? I had to know.' Christine was nodding. 'It's a very evil thing that has happened to all of us. We all needed to know. I had to come . . . to find out . . . and hear for myself.'

'Yes,' said Christine. 'I know.'

'I'm going,' said Maxine. 'You don't know what this means to me. To be told . . . all that . . . and that in heaven there's no such thing as being deaf.' With that she was gone, the front door slamming loudly behind her.

'Christine?'

Her dad's voice came, tremulous, down the stairs to her.

'Yes, dad?'

She went running up, breathing raggedly, and he only wanted some more of his orange squash pouring.

'Who was that at the door? Was it Jude?'

'Not yet, dad.'

'Tell me when.'

'I will, dad.'

Christine thudded back down the stairs feeling numb.

She went to see if Lily had pulled herself back together.

'That was all right, wasn't it?' Lily asked.

'What I can't get over,' said Christine, 'is that, really, the poor woman's no better off. Her lad's still dead, isn't he? She went off like . . . you'd brought him back to life.'

'Well, I did, didn't I? She heard his voice.'

Christine nodded slowly.

Like we hear Diana's voice, she thought.

Like I heard Michael's voice.

And all because of you, Lily Woods.

Lily was smirking to herself, at her own success.

Suddenly Christine wanted to knock that smile off her face.

'It's all lies, isn't it, Lily?'

Lily looked at her sharply.

Christine was on her feet. 'It's all fucking lies! All of it!'

'Christine . . .'

'I've been fucking stupid! You had me believing all sorts . . . all sorts of shite!'

'Christine . . .' Lily swallowed painfully. 'I do have a gift . . . I . . .'

Christine was gabbling away to herself. 'I've had my doubts now and then, about Diana and some of the crap you were coming out with to do with her . . . . I mean, I just thought it was a laugh and it was bringing in a few extra bob. But . . .'

Lily was backing away from her, into the hall. 'Christine . . . don't do this . . .'

'But I saw you tell that woman tonight that you could see her son and he had his ears back! I could see you were making it all up! Just like when you do Diana. It's all a load of shite! Then it clicked – you lied about Michael as well. To me! And you lied about Jess and Jude and . . . !' Christine grabbed Lily by her coat. 'You've just gone round telling people what they want to hear! You stupid old bitch. You've fucked us up good and proper, haven't you?'

Lily shrieked as Christine hauled her down the passage to the front door. 'I want you to get out and . . .'

Lily burst, 'What about your mother? What about Margaret?'

'What about her?'

'I found her, didn't I? I couldn't have . . . lied about that. We found her because Michael told me!'

Christine shook her head. 'I don't know what to believe. I don't believe anything. It's all a fucking mess.'

She seized open the door, pushed Lily with the flat of her hand and the old woman sprawled onto the gravel of the driveway.

Christine slammed the front door shut.

*

Lily brushed off her knees and gasped as she stood up. The Avenue was silent. Her tights were ripped.

If Christine didn't believe her anymore, then no one would.

Lily depended on Christine being with her now.

Lily herself hardly knew what to believe anymore.

The voices still came, but she couldn't always be sure. There were so many of them. Some of them talked too loud, some talked too quietly. It became confusing. Lily was too old.

The people who you sat with were always wanting and needing to know. Like everything depended on just the right answer. Usually Lily was all right. If she wasn't sure, if it *was* too confusing, she could make it a little vague. Put on a few vague embellishments. That was all it took. But when she *was* tested . . . when someone asked for a plain yes or no . . . that *was* different.

I should never let myself be put in that position.

Again and again she had let that happen, though. Faced with giving a yes or no. That position forced her to make something up. Making things up was wicked. That was the truth she had hidden from herself. Lily Woods, whose father had beaten her senseless as a child for making things up. She'd made up wicked things and said that the ghosts had told her. Her father beat her till she bled; a wicked child her age, knowing bad things older than her years.

You can't give up making things up, or hearing things, or knowing the secrets that other people don't. It wasn't Lily's fault. It was her nature.

As it was to tell people what they wanted, what they needed to hear.

Was that wicked?

She hurried away from the Fletchers' house.

As she unlocked her own door she turned to see a car pull up on the Avenue and watched it turn into the Fletchers' drive. Jude's car. Jude was home.

Lily darted into her house.

*

There's my daughter.

She's let her hair grow since she had the baby. She's got her figure back nicely. She's in a smart dress from Marks and Spencer's. Her lips are pursed because she's found me drunk in my own kitchen with tears down my face.

Jude made her mother strong black coffee and sat down with her.

I know all my daughter's secrets. Any mother does. Jude herself will realise this when Brad grows up. She will know everything, every thought that goes through his head. It's how things are. Your own kids can't lie to you, not really.

I watch her drink her coffee and I wonder if she thinks she can lie to me. I wonder how much I know really.

I never set much store by Lily's looking into the spirit world. I'd never have depended on that for truth. But I have believed what Jude has told me, all these years. So far I've let it go unquestioned.

But she's the daughter closest to me. The one who is most like me. She always was. Jude's mind has always been an open book to me. Never any need to cross-question her.

Christine prided herself on this, and, as they quietly sipped their coffee, reminded herself gratefully that Jude wasn't a monster and wasn't a liar. She reminded herself how much she was like her mother.

Like, for instance, Christine knew that Jude thought she was pregnant again. She had given that much away on the phone last week. Sam didn't know yet. It was an accident. Jude didn't think he'd be pleased. Something about world population. But Christine had been delighted and promised to keep mum. She'd carried her daughter's secret with her carefully, as carefully as Jude, now that she could see her in the flesh, was carrying herself. Then all this business in the papers had flared up and Christine's pleasure had been spoiled.

'Brad's all right, isn't he?' Christine said at last, mastering her voice.

'Course he is.'

'And Dorothy is there? She got there all right?'

'Yes.' Jude tutted and sat down. 'That old witch.'

'It's good of her to help out . . . While you're here.'

'She's a fucking nightmare.'

'You'll be tired. Driving all this way.'

'It isn't far.'

'It's far in your condition . . .'

Jude glared at her, as if someone else was there to hear the secret.

'The doctor's coming in the morning,' said Christine. 'About your Grandad.'

'Good. He's okay, isn't he? He hasn't got any worse?'

Christine shook her head.

'Good. I'll unload the car and turn in, I think.'

'Don't you want to phone Sam?'

Jude drained her cup. 'Not really. I'll only hear her in the background, bitching on about me.' She straightened up. 'I'll fetch those bags in.'

'Jude . . .' Christine began.

'What?'

'You didn't have any bother with Sam, did you? I mean, with the stuff in the papers. He never . . .'

'Believed it?' Jude smiled. 'Not really.'

'You've got a good man there, you know.'

'What, because he stands by me?' Jude snorted. 'Because he believes what I say?'

'Because he knows you and trusts you.'

'More fool him,' said Jude.

'You sound so hard, Jude. You never used to sound like that.'

'I always did, mam. This is how I always sounded. Jess was the soft-hearted one.'

Christine nodded, as if remembering. 'Yes. She was.'

Jude got up and leaned against the doorframe. She watched her mother as she said, 'Which makes it all the more incredible, I suppose, that she could suddenly flip like that. Do what she did.'

'It does.' Christine's throat was dry.

'Will you get in touch with her?' Jude asked. 'Will you talk to her?'

Christine shook her head. 'I don't know. I don't think I can.'

'She knows you'll never forgive her. She said in the papers she doesn't believe that.'

Christine winced. 'I read what she said, Jude. I know. She says she wants me to hear the real story. Then I'll know there's nothing to forgive.' Christine looked down again. 'That's what she says.'

'Nothing to forgive.' Jude sighed. 'Who does she think she is?'

Jude's tone was steady. She didn't waver at all. She watched her mother staring down into her coffee cup and marvelled at her own steadiness. She'd never thought she could carry this off. Not like this. Everything, it seemed, had got as bad as it could get. Jess had made her accusations, as strongly as she could, the way Jude had always feared she would. And here was Christine questioning her, albeit gently, obliquely, testing out her resolve and her version of things.

And still Jude could hold her own. She could brush it all off. Assert her innocence. It was easy.

She watched her mother tremble. And look up at her again.

'Tell me again, Jude. Just tell me.'

Jude licked her lips. 'Tell you what, mam?'

'Tell me it wasn't you.'

Jude felt her heart leap inside her chest. This was the killing blow. This would surely be the last time her mother would ask her.

She looked at her mother and the way she was trembling and Jude felt nothing but disgust.

'If I tell you again that I was innocent, that'll make it okay, won't it?' Jude said. 'It'll make you think you made all the right choices. You won't have to feel as guilty about fucking everything up. Is that what you want? Just to feel a bit better about the whole situation? That's just selfish, mam.'

Jude turned to walk down the hallway.

'Jude!' her mother shouted after her. 'Just tell me!'

Jude rounded on her savagely. 'If you can't believe what I've told you all these years, then you can fuck off. Of course I told you the truth. Of course I fucking did.'

She turned on her heel and slammed out of the house to fetch her bags.

Christine sat at the table and sobbed.

I've really upset her. I showed how much I doubted her. All these years and I never showed anyone that. How could I do that to her tonight?

She wanted to run after her daughter and tell her. She wanted to hold her. But Jude would never let her. She would shrug her off, push her away.

The family's been ruined, Christine thought. That's it for us. We'll never be together now.

We did this ourselves. Nothing to do with the papers.

We could have done this to ourselves at any time.

I never trusted her enough. She sees that now.

Christine listened to Jude out on the driveway and it made her think of Michael, packing and unpacking his hatchback when he used to go on his courses. Jude was competent, just like he'd been. She listened to her daughter lumber back indoors and carry her bags up the stairs.

I should help her with those, Christine thought, standing up in the kitchen. If she really is pregnant, she shouldn't be lugging all those bags.

But Jude would never want her mother's help again, she was sure of it.

I've driven another one away. I've lost another daughter tonight.

Christine stood there, thinking. What had made her ask Jude like that? What had possessed her to do it?

Her thoughts were jumbled because of the drink or two she'd had, but suddenly she knew it was all down to Lily. She thought it out. If Lily had lied about Michael contacting her, then they didn't know for sure that Jess was wrong. All that stuff in the papers – the columns of print that Christine could barely read – all that could be true. Jude could be a murderer. That had been how her thoughts had gone.

Why hadn't Jess said anything sooner? Why would a girl take all the blame for her sister? Surely no one would do that. Christine couldn't imagine it. She wouldn't do that. Neither would Jude. So it couldn't be possible.

Jude was in the right. Christine had wronged her.

It was all down to Christine again.

Whichever way it worked out, one way or another, one of her daughters had done something bad. At some level that was Christine's fault. It was Jess, it had to be Jess, but Christine was still to blame for bringing up someone who could murder a kid.

She'd courted disaster. She'd brought the badness into their lives somehow. She'd been to blame for her mother leaving. She'd fucked in the Reptile House, thought only of her own pleasure. That was at the heart of this. She'd brought the badness into their lives just by her own selfishness.

It was irrelevant who killed the kid. Christine might as well have done it herself.

Everything was ruined.

Just a week ago she'd thought they were all settled. Things had seemed better than they'd been for years.

She'd thought they'd all moved on. She'd thought things were better now.

She could hear Jude's footsteps in the girls' bedroom right above the kitchen. Her Judith, her Jessica. Her girls.

Christine was a grandmother. Maybe twice over already.

And already she had disowned Jess.

If Jude had been the one who was put away back then, Christine wouldn't have a grandchild. Brad wouldn't exist.

Surely the life of that child was worth keeping quiet for? Any number of white lies?

Christine didn't know any more. She wanted to believe it was worth it. They had Brad and they had another baby on the way. There was a book coming out and it was her other daughter's side of the story and Christine could either read it or she could not.

Just so long as she never saw Jess again, she wouldn't have to decide. The decision was already made.

She believed Jude. She had to and she had to make peace with Jude. She wanted to see her grandchildren. She wanted that more than anything.

It *was* like she told her mother when she saw her again. You shouldn't go raking over the past. That's how you got trapped in it. You should make your decisions and then you can deal with the consequences. But don't dwell. That's not how people live today.

She wished she had Michael to talk to.

But she hadn't had him for years. And he had lied to her as well. The only person she'd really had was her dad. Even as he was, he'd never lied to her. And it was him she was putting in a Home.

My life would have been different if I hadn't had to look after him. I've been stuck between him and my girls all my life.

Christine looked around at the empty kitchen.

They've surrounded me and kept me here all this time. I've had to explain and apologise and forgive again and again, all because of them.

But every decision and every big moment in my life . . . they've all happened to me when I was on my own.

The thought shocked her deeply.

All my life, she thought, *when it really mattered, they've left me on my own.*

I'm so fucking lonely.

*

'It's me, Grandad. Jude.'

She stood in the doorway, looking at the dark shape on the bed.

'I've kept awake for you,' he said. His words were slurring worse than usual. 'I wanted to see you tonight.'

She came to sit by him, in the chair Christine had pulled up beside his head.

'Is your mother in bed?'

'She's downstairs. Drunk. She's not making much sense.'

'She's like her mother,' Dan said. 'She could never face trouble, either. Margaret.' He said the name like he was trying it out on his tongue again. 'She always went hysterical.'

Jude was uncomfortable. 'The doctor's coming in the morning.'

'They're going to put me away,' he said. His eyes slid to look at Jude. 'You're going to put me away. Your mother's got you here so you can both gang up and convince me.'

'That's not true, Grandad.'

He snorted. 'You can't lie to me, Judith Fletcher. You never could. You were always the one I could see right through. You're the one who's most like me.'

'We'll see what the doctor says in the morning,' said Jude stiffly, starting to get up.

'These things in the paper, that they're saying about you . . .'

'Don't read that stuff. It's just Jess. She was always cracked.'

'No, she wasn't, Jude. It would be only too easy, to dismiss her, if she was.'

'Don't think about it now.'

Jude leaned over him to kiss him goodnight. As she brought her ear up close to his face, he whispered thickly: 'You've been lying your whole fucking life, you whore.'

Jude jumped back.

She stared at him.

He had hold of her wrist in both his hands.

'What did you say?'

'I SAID you're a lying fucking WHORE. You killed that LAD. And like a selfish CUNT you let JESS go to prison FOR you.'

His fingernails were digging into the soft flesh of her arm. She dragged it off him and he scratched down hard.

'I know the truth of you, Jude,' he spat. 'I always did.'

'You don't know anything.' Her heart was beating up inside her throat.

'If you put me away I'll tell them. I'll tell them what you ARE. How you came back that day you killed that BOY and we buried your clothes in the garden. How you cried for

TWO whole days when they took Jess AWAY and I knew WHY. I knew why you cried like that.'

She paused a moment, looking down at him. 'Goodnight, Grandad.'

'I'll talk to your mother. I should have told her years ago.'

'And she'd believe you?'

He glared at her. 'You've wrapped us all around your little finger. Why? Why were you the most important one? Why should you get away with it?'

She shrugged. 'Don't tell mam anything. You'll only be wasting your breath, Grandad. She's made her choices. We've all made our choices. Now we move on.' She headed for the door. Then she felt a surge of anger and it came spilling out. 'You're the one who keeps dragging us back. You're the one who's made us miserable all this time. Mam would have found another fella if it wasn't for you. She might have been happy. She wouldn't be that drunken mess downstairs if it wasn't for you.'

'I'll be gone soon anyway,' he sniffed. His eyes were red and swollen. 'You'll put me away.' He stared at her and shook his head. 'I hope you can live with yourself. I don't see how you can.'

Jude took one last look at him before closing the door. 'I'm going to try.'

*

20
Better

Tom wasn't himself with her.

He said he could deal with whatever had gone on in the past. He loved her. He could forgive anything that she could tell him.

Yet Jess knew he wasn't a very worldly man. His mother had kept him indoors and shielded him from the worst of the world.

Nowadays he didn't even know what to call her.

He had fallen for a woman called She. When the newspaper men came chasing after her, knocking at her door, trampling down the flowerbeds, coming up to her on the beach, they had called her Jessica. Tom had attacked a photographer for her sake, bellowing as they wrestled on the pebble beach, defending a woman whose name he didn't even know.

He and the photographer had covered themselves in bruises and cuts. He clawed the film out of the flashy camera and hurled it into the sea. As it flew it unwound and spiralled, glittering, into the waves. He'd had to go to the police station for that.

That night Jess phoned Katherine Marshall and, trying not to let her voice break down, told her she would have to stop all of this. Jess didn't want the book to be finished, or for it to come out. Already Jess was hurting people again.

Katherine tried to talk her out of it. The process had already started. People had to know the truth now.

Katherine hadn't known there would be this level of interest. She hadn't reckoned on this much bother. How did she know the journalists would get hold of Cilla from the Wirral and that Cilla would happily tell all she knew?

The charges against Tom were dropped. The police said to him that if he had any sense, he wouldn't involve himself with a woman like that.

Jess was reading the papers, looking at the things they said about her, looking at the bits where they said that Tom was simple-minded.

It's all my fault, she thought.

She was so selfish, getting all this attention, just to say that she was innocent. And now others were getting hurt on her account.

Tom was out of his depth.

'I believe you, She,' he said. 'I believe you if you say you didn't kill that boy.' Then he grabbed her in a rough hug. 'You were only a kid,' he sobbed. 'What did you know? It's so cruel.'

Katherine phoned several times that day.

'The book is finished, nearly. It's your story. I've done it for you. Everyone wants it to come out.'

Katherine went on talking in her ear and Jess looked across the room at Tom, who was reading the papers.

I wanted Katherine to write that book so much. That Christmas I baited and bearded her in her den. I goaded her to use her expertise. I wanted her to write a proper book that would tell the truth. Just to see if that was possible.

I wanted that with all my heart.

That's what I wanted then.

'If it comes out, Katherine,' Jess said. 'What if more people get hurt? What if it gets worse?'

'It won't,' Katherine said. 'I promise.'

Jess put down the phone. All Katherine's thinking about is the work she put into writing the thing. What's her promise worth? She's just proud of herself.

She's only thinking about that.

*

Tom had taken to sleeping on the settee.

Last night Jess looked at him lying there and he looked like a great big guard dog, the rug pulled over him. Her heart went out to him and she touched his shoulder. She asked him to come to bed.

He looked scared stiff but he followed her into the room. They undressed with their backs to each other, lay down and she turned out the light.

They tried to make love.

'I'm not very used to this.'

'Me neither.'

'Are you enjoying it?'

'Yes. Are you?'

'I'm not sure. Is it uncomfortable?'

'A bit.'

'Oh. What are we like?'

She could feel him, laughing gently. 'I don't know. What are we like?'

'Useless, Tom. That's what we are.'

'Do you think we'll get any better?'

They stopped after a while and Tom fell asleep and Jess stared up at the ceiling, thinking that one over for hours.